"For the better part of the past two decades, James Blaylock has been documenting with quiet and uncommon eloquence the existence of a California that lies just around the corner of the eye ... The vividly drawn stories that make up *Thirteen Phantasms* form a marvelous introduction to the elusive portion of the Golden State and to the mind of one of the most significant fantasy writers of our time."

—Lucius Shepard

"This collection stands on the ill-defined border between fantasy, magic realism, and mainstream fiction, but it should definitely stand on the shelf of any reader interested in the literary end of the genre ... Blaylock's genius as a story-teller perhaps shines best in compact stories about the strangeness in the lives of otherwise very real people."

—*Tangent*

"I can't recall enjoying a recent collection more than I savored James Blaylock's *Thirteen Phantasms* ... Blaylock proves that whimsical surfaces can hide the steeliest armatures ... Blaylock's topflight novels have earned him recognition as one of the country's finest fantasists. But his short fiction is less well-known, and this career retrospective is the perfect opportunity to become acquainted with Blaylock and his troupe of earnest eccentrics."

—Paul Di Filippo, *Asimov's Science Fiction Magazine*

D09973939

continued . . .

"[James Blaylock's] stories stride confidently through the narrow no-man's-land that lies between mainstream literature and genre fiction, edgy narratives with quirky details that illuminate not only the hearts of his characters, but all the strange and wonderful things that lie at the periphery of our vision."
—Charles de Lint

"*Thirteen Phantasms and Other Stories* is a career writ small—a collection of fantasies filled with the odd, the unusual, and the wonderful, all of which express a faith in the human spirit and in the glory to be found in our day-to-day lives."
—Jonathan Strahan, *Locus*

"Highly recommended as a change of pace from whatever you might be reading."
—*Science Fiction Chronicle*

"*Thirteen Phantasms* represents the cream of over twenty years' worth of [Blaylock's] oeuvre. Blaylock's worlds seem so real because he is able to combine realistic detail with subtly drawn fantasy."
—*Interzone*

"[*Thirteen Phantasms*] demonstrates the author's superlative gift for transforming the autobiographical and the mundane into numinous and wondrous fictions . . . the author's fully dimensional, eccentric characters inhabit narratives in which intricate, quotidian details and objects become filled with a magic and weirdness inextricably connected to the people who interact with them."
—*Rambles*

"An extraordinary gathering of stories that reveals the enormous range that can be found in specific regional settings, exemplifies the magic that can be discovered in the large writ small—how a universe of wonder can be found just around the corner of our everyday world. Edgy yarns situated on that slipstream gap between mainstream literature and genre fiction, the contents of *Thirteen Phantasms* illuminates the strange and the magical that awaits on the boundaries of our vision for those readers willing to travel where Blaylock's brilliant, poetic prose will take them."   —*The Blue Iris Journal*

"James Blaylock hasn't let the world speed by. He looks at every detail, every nuance, and finds the marvelous in the mundane, the extra in the ordinary . . . [This] is as good a read as it gets. Blaylock's short stories are pure literature, and filled with enough odd twists and turns to keep you turning the pages . . . It's a classic in every sense of the word, and belongs on your bookshelf, sandwiched between works by W. W. Jacobs and Ernest Hemingway."   —*Green Man Review*

"Very highly recommended . . . near perfection . . . this is the greatest short story collection I have ever read . . . Blaylock's musings are far richer in texture, deeper in spirit, and, YES, [more] demanding of the readers' attentions than the average drivel on the market today. There is no skimming a Blaylock story . . . a great compilation."   —*Under the Covers*

"Blaylock is one of the quirkiest and most original writers around . . . The stories in this collection were published over a period of twenty-five years, and you can see the progression of Blaylock's talent . . . all [the stories] bear the unmistakable mark of Blaylock's genius for fantasy, and his belief that all the little details in our everyday lives can sometimes add up to more than the sum of their parts."

—*Books Under Review*

13
Phantasms

and other stories

JAMES P. BLAYLOCK

ACE BOOKS, NEW YORK

THE BERKLEY PUBLISHING GROUP
Published by the Penguin Group
Penguin Group (USA) Inc.
375 Hudson Street, New York, New York 10014, USA

Penguin Group (Canada), 10 Alcorn Avenue, Toronto, Ontario, M4V 3B2, Canada
(a division of Pearson Penguin Canada Inc.)
Penguin Books Ltd., 80 Strand, London WC2R 0RL, England
Penguin Group Ireland, 25 St. Stephen's Green, Dublin 2, Ireland (a division of Penguin Books Ltd.)
Penguin Group (Australia), 250 Camberwell Road, Camberwell, Victoria 3124, Australia
(a division of Pearson Australia Group Pty. Ltd.)
Penguin Books India Pvt. Ltd., 11 Community Centre, Panchsheel Park, New Delhi—110 017, India
Penguin Books (NZ), Cnr. Airborne and Rosedale Roads, Albany, Auckland 1310, New Zealand
(a division of Pearson New Zealand Ltd.)
Penguin Books (South Africa) (Pty.) Ltd., 24 Sturdee Avenue, Rosebank, Johannesburg 2196,
South Africa

Penguin Books Ltd., Registered Offices: 80 Strand, London WC2R 0RL, England

This is a work of fiction. Names, characters, places, and incidents either are the product of the author's imagination or are used fictitiously, and any resemblance to actual persons, living or dead, business establishments, events, or locales is entirely coincidental.

THIRTEEN PHANTASMS AND OTHER STORIES

An Ace Book / published by arrangement with the author

PRINTING HISTORY
Edgewood Press edition / 2000
Ace trade paperback edition / April 2003
Ace mass market edition / February 2005

Copyright © 2000 by James P. Blaylock.
For a complete listing of individual copyrights, please see page 289.
Cover art by Greg Spalenka.
Cover design by Rita Frangie.

ISBN 0-441-01257-4

ACE
Ace Books are published by The Berkley Publishing Group,
a division of Penguin Group (USA) Inc.,
375 Hudson Street, New York, New York 10014.
ACE and the "A" design are trademarks belonging to Penguin Group (USA) Inc.

PRINTED IN THE UNITED STATES OF AMERICA

10 9 8 7 6 5 4 3 2 1

Contents

Five Hundred Dollars

B ack around 1960 my family started spending long week-
ends up in Morro Bay, just north of San Luis Obispo. At
the time there was a small downtown and a long row of
shops and seafood restaurants along the foggy waterfront,
with a couple of fishing piers with boats docked. You could
catch sculpin and cabezon and perch off the pier and buy
saltwater taffy at the bait shop and doughnuts and coffee
across the Embarcadero. There was an aquarium down the
bay a quarter of a mile, with big rusting tanks floating with
kelp and dripping water and with the mandatory octopus and
moray eels and half a dozen varieties of coastal fish that always included a toothy sheepshead.

One Saturday evening I was wandering along the Embarcadero down near the aquarium. I must have been about
twelve years old. I remember it was dusk and that it was
rainy. There was an antique shop down there, long since
disappeared, that sold oriental oddities, very crowded with
merchandise, very dark and attractive to a susceptible
twelve-year-old. I stepped in out of the evening and right off
the bat saw a pair of carved wooden temple dogs the size of
St. Bernards, crouching in the typical pose, with a half dozen

temple puppies, I guess you'd call them, crawling on the parent dogs' backs. I can still picture them absolutely in my mind: dim yellow and red paint, chipped and faded over the long years, the startlingly vivid expressions on the carved faces, the massive solidity and antiquity of the things. I can also remember that the pair of them cost an even five hundred dollars.

This was back in the days when you could buy a lot on the ocean for five thousand and a house for twenty-five, but even so, five hundred dollars was an easily imaginable sum, even to a twelve-year-old, and the world was suddenly full of exotic suggestion and possibility, as if a door had been opened. The dark shop full of antiques, the salt air and the rain and the lowering evening, it seems to me now, were emblematic of that moment when we plant the magic bean or put on the odd spectacles that we've bought from a dwarf in an alley or peer into the old mirror and see things moving behind us that aren't there when we turn around and look.

Of course I couldn't have foreseen it at the time, but this matter of five hundred dollars would become oddly significant over the years, and it plays in my mind now like an O. Henry story, the second chapter occurring some five years later when I had my first job at the old Collar and Leash Pet Store in Garden Grove. Half the store was devoted to aquaria, which I maintained, ordering fish and aquatic plants with a certain degree of latitude. I was devoted at the time to aquatic oddities—South American leaf fish and air-breathing African Ctenopoma and buffalo head cichlids and red-eyed puffers—fish whose shape, coloration, and languid movements mimicked dead leaves or was somehow otherworldly or bizarre. The perfect aquarium, to my mind, was a dimly lit, still-life collection of plants and driftwood and hovering fishes reminiscent of a leafy pool in a jungle river. The public's notion of an aquarium bore little resemblance to my own, and aside from routine maintenance, my particular favorite aquariums often went happily undisturbed for months or even years. (This difference between what the public wanted and what I wanted didn't end with aquaria, by the way. Reviewers have suggested that my stories are sometimes "eccentric," and I understand entirely what they mean. Stories like "The Shadow on the Doorstep" and "The Pink of Fading Neon" and "Paper Dragons" bear an atmospheric resemblance to the sort of aquaria I used to keep, and in fact strike me at this moment as being quite evidently aquarium-like, just as certain aquaria, with their wavering shadows and rising bubbles and rock caves and lurking fishes seem to suggest their own hidden mysteries.)

As for the five hundred dollars, its ghost reappeared to haunt me in the form of a bill of fare, loosely speaking, from a company called Gators of Miami, the Noah's ark of animal importers, which at the time would ship virtually any animal in the world straight into Los Angeles in a wooden crate. The Collar and Leash didn't deal in exotic pets, but the Gators catalogue was something I studied with the avidity of a connoisseur. I remember sitting among the aquaria one Friday evening, alone in the shop, browsing through the catalogue, when my eye fell upon a list of available African mammals, and I saw, with a shock of momentary elation, that for five hundred dollars I could buy a hippopotamus. All I needed beyond that was a borrowed stake-bed truck to haul the beast home from the air freight terminal.

The world, I'll say again, was a different place back then. I was making about a dollar-fifty an hour at the time, and I no more had five hundred dollars in mad money at eighteen years old than at twelve. I went round and round with it in my mind, though, imagining the creature in the back garden, eating whatever hippos ate—canned spinach, perhaps, and alfalfa. I could dig it a pool.

All of this sounds slightly cockeyed, looking back, but it still seems wonderful to me that there was a fleeting moment in my life when a hippopotamus was five hundred dollars and a phone call away. And in the years that followed, hippos loomed large in the southern California mythos. There was an article in the newspaper some time later involving an enormous ghostly hippo that had appeared on a foggy residential street in Huntington Beach, disappearing moments later, and never apparently, seen or heard from thereafter, the mystery unsolved to this day. And then of course there was the sad death of Bubbles the hippo from the wild animal park, who traveled over the hills into Laguna Canyon and occupied a weedy pond for a week until it was accidentally killed by the men sent out to rescue it. Let it have the damned pond: that was my idea of it, and I still feel that way. Put a picket fence around it and let it be. When visitors came to town you could have said to them, "There's a hippo back in the canyon." For a moment they'd think they heard you wrong, but then, slowly and certainly, something would change in them. Unless their souls were dead they'd be filled with a puzzled type of I'll-be-damned curiosity. Proust tells us that the purpose of the artist is to "draw back the veil that leaves us indifferent before the universe." A wild hippo in Laguna Canyon would do the trick. The condominiums they've built in the years since are simply an eyesore.

I think it was in the summer of 1972 that I traveled up the coast with a friend of mine, camping here and there. It was on that trip that I saw the gluer Volkswagen bus with the tide pool ornamentation that put in an appearance in my book *The Paper Grail*. The early '70s were strange times in their own way, and during the days I spent on the coast road there were cult murders in the Big Sur vicinity, and severed human heads were found perched on guardrail posts along the highway. We camped on a beach near Monterey for a couple of days, one of which we spent wandering around Cannery Row. I was looking for the ghosts of Steinbeck and Ed Ricketts, and although I didn't entirely find them, I found something nearly as good. Cannery Row wasn't yet the tourist attraction that it's become in more recent years, and the old canneries stood abandoned and boarded up, paint peeling, windows broken, the whole place "reclaimed by the weather," to borrow a phrase from Joan Didion.

There was a junk shop, though, operating at the time, still trading on the old romance. You could buy used fishing nets and glass floats and pieces of interesting nautical debris. I remember that there were South Seas imports and imported rugs smelling of damp wool and a thousand and one junk objects that didn't quite qualify as antiques but would have been exotically out of place, say, in a mere thrift store. In the back, on a wooden table, sat a wood-framed glass box, like an upended aquarium. Inside, "hermetically sealed," was the upper half of a mummy. It was mostly brown skeleton and empty eye sockets, but it still had leathery shreds of flesh and sparse hair. A faded sign claimed that it was a "Mayan Princess" and it was draped with a bit of silk and wore a pillbox hat sewn up out of carnival-colored cloth, meant, I suppose, to give it the air of royalty. The price tag was five hundred dollars, exactly.

I don't know how long I stood looking at it, but of course there was no chance of my buying it, as much as I might have liked to. This was a five-dollar-a-day trip, and by the time we were into the last couple of days of it, we were reduced to eating canned baked beans flavored with broken-open Pismo clams that we'd dug up out of the sand at low tide. I'd like to tell you that if I'd had the five hundred I would have fished it out of my wallet and taken the mummy home, but I'm not at all certain I would have. In any event, I didn't.

One last thing: a couple of years later I was up there again on the same mission—killing time on the coast—when I stopped into that same shop. It was half empty by then and was going out of business. The Mayan princess was still unsold, although the price had been reduced to two hundred and fifty dollars. They'd moved her into the window to attract passersby. Perhaps irrationally, to my mind the mummy had lost some of its luster now that it had been put on sale. It seemed to me to have become a cut-rate mummy, without the allure that it had once had, back when it was part of the larger, weather-decayed, misty and dilapidated picture that was Cannery Row in its dying years. If you go up there today (which I very much recommend, if only to get a glimpse of the chambered nautili in the aquarium) you can see how things turned out, but you'll search in vain for the mummy.

All of that was nearly thirty years ago, and in the intervening decades I've never again been offered that kind of five hundred dollar opportunity. In a shop in San Pedro I found a whale's eyeball floating in a jar of formaldehyde, but the shop keeper wouldn't sell it at any price. And now that I can afford five hundred bucks for a hippopotamus, the cost of such a creature has gone up considerably, and the city of Orange, where I live, has a statute against "barnyard animals" which I'm pretty sure they'd stretch to cover hippos.

But there's something about the three incidents that still haunts me—phantomwise, as Lewis Carroll put it—and I've come to suspect that I was never meant to own these things at all, at least not in any physical sense. It's enough, perhaps, that they make up the stuff of my stories and my dreams, as if they've been paying me solid dividends all these years.

I've always been fond of quotations, of the wonderful things that the best writers can do with words. Some day I'm going to write my favorites out on slips of paper and put them into small jars, like the bug collection I assembled for tenth-grade biology, each one labeled and categorized. One of my favorites is from Aristotle, who said, "What I tell you three times is true." That one's vast, like a cathedral, full of shadow and light. It has the ring of temptation in it, of Peter's denial of Christ, of the three-time loser, of going down for the third time, of the third time's the charm, of three strikes and three cheers and three coins in the fountain. Like ghosts and flying saucers and materializing hippos, the statement is a true thing in some odd and inobvious way, even though there's no evidence for it. You have to take it on faith.

Jim Blaylock
Orange, California
March 7, 2000

Thirteen Phantasms

There was a small window in the attic, six panes facing
the street, the wood frame unpainted and without mold-
ings. Leafy wisteria vines grew over the glass outside, filtering the sunlight and tinting it green. The attic was dim
despite the window, and the vines outside shook in the autumn wind, rustling against the clapboards of the old house
and casting leafy shadows on the age-darkened beams and
rafters. Landers set his portable telephone next to the crawl-
space hatch and shined a flashlight across the underside of
the shingles, illuminating dusty cobwebs and the skeleton
frame of the roof. The air smelled of dust and wood, and the
attic was lonesome with silence and moving shadows, a
place sheltered from time and change.

A car rolled past out on the street, and Landers heard a
train whistle in the distance. Somewhere across town, church
bells tolled the hour, and there was the faint sound of freeway noise off to the east like the drone of a perpetual-motion
engine. It was easy to imagine that the wisteria vines had
tangled themselves around the window frame for some secretive purpose of their own, obscuring the glass with leaves,
muffling the sounds of the world.

He reached down and switched the portable phone off, regretting that he'd brought it with him at all. It struck him suddenly as something incongruous, an artifact from an alien planet. For a passing moment he considered dropping it through the open hatch just to watch it slam to the floor of the kitchen hallway below.

Years ago old Mr. Cummings had set pine planks across the two-by-six ceiling joists to make a boardwalk beneath the roof beam, apparently with the idea of using the attic for storage, although it must have been a struggle to haul things up through the shoulder-width attic hatch. At the end of this boardwalk, against the north wall, lay four dust-covered cardboard cartons—full of "junk magazines," or so Mrs. Cummings herself had told Landers this morning. The cartons were tied with twine, pulled tight and knotted, all the cartons the same. The word ASTOUNDING was written on the side with a felt marker in neat, draftsmanlike letters. Landers wryly wondered what sort of things Mr. Cummings might have considered astounding, and after a moment, he decided that the man had been fortunate to find enough of it in one lifetime to fill four good-sized boxes.

Landers himself had come up empty in that regard, at least lately. For years he'd had a picture in his mind of himself whistling a cheerful out-of-key tune, walking along a country road, his hands in his pockets and with no particular destination, sunlight streaming through the trees and the limitless afternoon stretching toward the horizon. Somehow that picture had lost its focus in the past year or so, and as with an old friend separated by time and distance, he had nearly given up on seeing it again.

It had occurred to him this morning that he hadn't brewed real coffee for nearly a year now. The coffeepot sat under the counter instead of on top of it, and was something he hauled out for guests. There was a frozen brick of ground coffee in the freezer, but he never bothered with it anymore. Janet had been opposed to freezing coffee at all. Freezing it, she said, killed the aromatic oils. It was better to buy it a half pound at a time, so that it was always fresh. Lately, though, most of the magic had gone out of the morning coffee; it didn't matter how fresh it was.

The Cummingses had owned the house since it was built in 1924, and Mrs. Cummings, ninety years old now, had held on for twenty years after her husband's death, letting the place run down, and then had rented it to Landers and moved into the Palmyra Apartments beyond the Plaza. Occasionally he still got mail intended for her, and it was easier simply to take it to her than to give it back to the post office. This morning she had told him about the boxes in the attic: "Just leave them there," she'd said. Then she had shown him her husband's old slide rule, slipping it out of its leather case and working the slide. She wasn't sure why she kept it, but she had kept a couple of old smoking pipes too, and a ring-shaped cut-crystal decanter with some whiskey still in it. Mrs. Cummings didn't have any use for the pipes or the decanter any more than she had a use for the slide rule, but Landers, who had himself kept almost nothing to remind him of his own past, understood that there was something about these souvenirs, sitting alongside a couple of old photographs on a small table, that recalled better days, easier living.

The arched window of the house on Rexroth Street in Glendale looked out onto a sloping front lawn with an overgrown carob tree at the curb, shading a dusty Land Rover with what looked like prospecting tools strapped to the rear bumper. There was a Hudson Wasp in the driveway, parked behind an Austin Healey. Across the street a man in shirt-sleeves rubbed paste polish onto the fender of a Studebaker, and a woman in a sundress dug in a flower bed with a trowel, setting out pansies. A little boy rode a sort of sled on wheels up and down the sidewalk, and the sound of the solid-rubber wheels humping over cracks sounded oddly loud in the still afternoon.

Russell Latzarel turned away from the window and took a cold bottle of beer from Roycroft Squires. In a few minutes the Newtonian Society would come to order, more or less, for the second time that day. Not that it made a lot of difference. For Latzarel's money they could recess until midnight if they wanted to, and the world would spin along through space for better or worse. He and Squires were both bachelors, and so unlike married men they had until hell froze over to come to order.

"India Pale Ale," Latzarel said approvingly, looking at the label on the squat green bottle. He gulped down an inch of beer. "Elixir of the gods, eh?" He set the bottle on a coaster. Then he filled his pipe with Balkan Sobranie tobacco and tamped it down, settling into an armchair in front of the chessboard, where there was a game laid out, half played. "Who's listed as guest of honor at West Coast Con? Edward tells me they're going to get Clifford Simak and van Vogt both."

"That's not what it says here in the newsletter," Squires told him, scrutinizing a printed pamphlet. "According to this it's TBA."

"To be announced," Latzarel said, then lit his pipe and puffed hard on it for a moment, his lips making little popping sounds. "Same son of a bitch as they advertised last time." He laughed out loud and then bent over to scan the titles of the chess books in the bookcase. He wasn't sure whether Squires read the damned things or whether he kept them there to gain some sort of psychological advantage, which he generally didn't need.

It was warm for November, and the casement windows along the west wall were wide open, the muslin curtains blowing inward on the breeze. Dust motes moved in the sunshine. The Newtonian Society had been meeting here every Saturday night since the war ended, and in that couple of years it had seldom broken up before two or three in the morning. Sometimes when there was a full house, all twelve of them would talk straight through until dawn and then go out after eggs and bacon, the thirty-nine-cent breakfast special down at Velma's Copper Pot on Western, although it wasn't often that the married men could get away with that kind of nonsense. Tonight they had scheduled a critical discussion of E. E. Smith's *Children of the Lens*, but it turned out that none of them liked the story much except Hastings, whose opinion was unreliable anyway, and so the meeting had lost all its substance after the first hour, and members had drifted away, into the kitchen and the library and out to the printing shed in the backyard, leaving Latzarel and Squires alone in the living room. Later on tonight, if the weather held up, they would be driving out to the observatory in Griffith Park.

There was a shuffling on the front walk, and Latzarel looked out in time to see the postman shut the mailbox and turn away, heading up the sidewalk. Squires went out through the front door and emptied the box, then came back in sorting letters. He took a puzzled second look at an envelope. "You're a stamp man," he said to Latzarel, handing it to him. "What do you make of that?"

Landers found that he could stand upright on the catwalk, although the roof sloped at such an angle that if he moved a couple of feet to either side, he had to duck to clear the roof rafters. He walked toward the boxes, but turned after a few steps to shine the light behind him, picking out his footprints in the otherwise-undisturbed dust. Beneath that dust, if a person could only brush away the successive years, lay Mr. Cummings's own footprints, coming and going along the wooden boards.

There was something almost wrong about opening the boxes at all, whatever they contained, like prying open a man's coffin. And somehow the neatly tied string suggested that their packing hadn't been temporary, that old Mr. Cummings had put them away forever, perhaps when he knew he was at the end of things.

Astounding . . . ? Well, Landers would be the judge of that.

Taking out his pocket knife, he started to cut the string on one of the top boxes, then decided against it and untied it instead, afterward pulling back the flaps. Inside were neatly stacked magazines, dozens of issues of a magazine called *As-*

tounding Science-Fiction, apparently organized according to date. He picked one up off the top, December of 1947, and opened it carefully. It was well-preserved, the pulp paper yellowed around the outside of the pages, but not brittle. The cover painting depicted a robot with a head like an egg, holding a bent stick in his hand and looking mournfully at a wolf with a rabbit beside it, the world behind them apparently in flames. There were book ads at the back of the magazine, including one from something called the Squires Press: an edition of Clark Ashton Smith's *Thirteen Phantasms*, printed with hand-set type in three volumes on Winnebago Eggshell paper and limited to a hundred copies. "Remit one dollar in seven days," the ad said, "and one dollar monthly until six dollars is paid."

A dollar a month! This struck him as fantastic—stranger in its way, and even more wonderful, than the egg-headed robot on the front cover of the magazine. He sat down beside the boxes and leaned back against the wall so that the pages caught the sunlight through the window. He wished that he had brought along something to eat and drink instead of the worthless telephone. Settling in, he browsed through the contents page before starting in on the editorial, and then from there to the first of the several stories.

When the sunlight failed, Landers ran an extension cord into the attic and hooked up an old lamp in the rafters over the catwalk. Then he brought up a folding chair and a little smoking table to set a plate on. He would have liked something more comfortable, but there was no fitting an overstuffed chair up through the hatch. Near midnight he finished a story called "Rain Check" by Lewis Padgett, which featured a character named Tubby (apparently there had been a time when the world was happy with men named Tubby) and another character who drank highballs. . . .

He laid the book down and sat for a moment, listening to the rustling of leaves against the side of the house.

Highballs. What did people drink nowadays?—beer with

all the color and flavor filtered out of it. Maybe that made a sad and frightening kind of sense. He looked at the back cover of the magazine, where perhaps coincidentally, there was an ad for Calvert whiskey: "Just be sure your highball is made with Calvert," the ad counseled. He wondered if there was any such thing anymore, whether anywhere within a twenty-mile radius someone was mixing up a highball out of Calvert whiskey. Hell, a *hundred* miles . . .

Rod's Liquor Store down on the Plaza was open late, and he was suddenly possessed with the idea of mixing himself a highball. He took the magazine with him when he climbed down out of the attic, and before he left the house, he filled out the order blank for the *Thirteen Phantasms* and slipped it into an envelope along with a dollar bill. It seemed right to him, like the highball, or like old Mrs. Cummings keeping the slide rule.

He wrote out Squires's Glendale address, put one of the new interim G stamps on the envelope, and slid it into the mail slot for the postman to pick up tomorrow morning.

The canceled stamp depicted an American flag with the words "Old Glory" over the top. "A *G* stamp?" Latzarel said out loud. "What is that, exactly?"

Squires shook his head. "Something new?"

"*Very* damned new, I'd say. Look here." He pointed at the flag on the stamp. "I can't quite . . ." He looked over the top of his glasses, squinting hard. "I count too many stars on this flag. Take a look."

He handed the envelope back to Squires, who peered at the stamp, then dug a magnifying glass out of the drawer of the little desk in front of the window. He peered at the stamp through the glass. "Fifty," he said. "It must be a fake."

"Post office canceled it, too." Latzarel frowned and shook his head. "What kind of sense does that make? Counterfeiting stamps and getting the flag obviously wrong? A man wouldn't give himself away like that, unless he was playing some kind of game."

"Here's something else," Squires said. "Look at the edge. There's no perforations. This is apparently cut out of a solid sheet." He slit the envelope open and unfolded the letter inside. It was an order for the Smith collection, from an address in the city of Orange.

There was a dollar bill included with the order.

Landers flipped through the first volume of the *Thirteen Phantasms*, which had arrived postage-due from Glendale. There were four stories in each volume. Somehow he had expected thirteen altogether, and the first thing that came into his mind was that there was a phantasm missing. He nearly laughed out loud. But then he was sobered by the obvious impossibility of the arrival of any phantasms at all. They had come enclosed in a cardboard carton that was wrapped in brown paper and sealed with tape. He looked closely at the tape, half surprised that it wasn't yellowed with age, that the package hadn't been in transit through the ether for half a century

He sipped from his highball and reread a note that had come with the books, written out by a man named Russell Latzarel, president of a group calling itself the Newtonian Society—apparently Squires's crowd. In the note, Latzarel wondered if Landers was perpetrating a hoax.

A hoax . . . The note was dated 1947. "Who are you *really?*" it asked. "What is the meaning of the G stamp?" For a time he stared out of the window, watching the vines shift against the glass, listening to the wind under the eaves. The house settled, creaking in its joints. He looked at Latzarel's message again. "The dollar bill was a work of art," it read. On the back there was a hand-drawn map and an invitation to the next meeting of the Newtonians. He folded the map and tucked it into his coat pocket. Then he finished his highball and laughed out loud. Maybe it was the whiskey that made this seem monumentally funny. A hoax! He'd show them a hoax.

Almost at once he found something that would do. It was a plastic lapel pin the size of a fifty-cent piece, a hologram of an eyeball. It was only an eighth of an inch thick, but when he turned it in the light it seemed deep as a well. It was a good clear hologram too, the eyeball hovering in the void, utterly three-dimensional. The pin on the back had been glued on sloppily and at a screwball angle, and excess glue had run down the back of the plastic and dried. It was a technological marvel of the late twentieth century, and it was an absolute, and evident, piece of junk. He addressed an envelope, dropped the hologram inside, and slid it into the mail slot.

The trip out to Glendale took over an hour because of a traffic jam at the 605 junction and bumper-to-bumper cars on the Golden State. There was nothing apparently wrong—no accident, no freeway construction, just a million toiling automobiles stretching all the way to heaven-knew-where, to the moon. He had forgotten Latzarel's map, and he fought off a feeling of superstitious dread as the cars in front of him inched along. At Los Feliz he pulled off the freeway, cutting down the offramp at the last possible moment. There was a hamburger joint called Tommy's Little Oasis on Los Feliz, just east of San Fernando Road, that he and Janet used to hit when they were on their way north. That had been a few years back; he had nearly forgotten, but the freeway sign at Los Feliz had jogged his memory. It was a tiny Airstream trailer in the parking lot of a motel shaded by big elm trees. You went there if you wanted a hamburger. That was it. There was no menu except a sign on the wall, and even the sign was nearly pointless, since the only question was did you want cheese or not. Landers wanted cheese.

He slowed down as he passed San Fernando, looking for the motel, for the big overarching elms, recalling a rainy Saturday afternoon when they'd eaten their burgers in the car because it was raining too hard to sit under the steel umbrella at the picnic table out front. Now there was no picnic table, no Airstream trailer, no motel—nothing but a run-down industrial park. Somehow the industrial park had sprung up and fallen into disrepair in—what?—less than twenty years!

He U-turned and headed the opposite direction up San Fernando, turning right on Western. It was better not to think about it, about the pace of things, about the cheeseburgers of days gone by. . . .

Farther up Western, the houses along the street were run-down, probably rentals. There was trash in the street, broken bottles, newspapers soaked in gutter water. Suddenly he was a foreigner. He had wandered into a part of the country that was alien to him. And, unless his instincts had betrayed him, it was clearly alien to Squires Press and the Newtonian Society and men named Tubby. At one time the mix of Spanish-style and Tudor houses had been elegant. Now they needed paint and the lawns were up in weeds, and there was graffiti on fences and garage walls. Windows and doors were barred. He drove slowly, calculating addresses and thinking about turning around, getting back onto the freeway and heading south again, just fleeing home, ordering something else out of the magazines—personally autographed books by long-dead authors, "jar-proof" watches that could take a licking and go on ticking. He pictured the quiet shelter of his attic—his magazines, the makings of another highball. If ever a man needed a highball . . .

And just then he came upon the sign for Rexroth Street, so suddenly that he nearly drove right through the intersection. He braked abruptly, swinging around toward the west, and a car behind him honked its horn hard. He heard the driver shout something as the car flew past.

Landers started searching out addresses. The general tenor of the neighborhood hadn't improved at all, and he considered locking his doors. But then the idea struck him as superfluous, since he was about to park the car and get out anyway. He spotted the address on the curb, the paint faded and nearly unreadable. The house had a turreted entry hall in front, with an arched window in the wall that faced the street. A couple of the windowpanes were broken and filled with aluminum foil, and what looked like an old bed sheet was strung across as a curtain. Weeds grew up through the cracked concrete of the front walk, and there was black iron debris, apparently car parts, scattered on the lawn.

He drifted to the curb, reaching for the ignition key, but then saw, crouched next to a motorcycle up at the top of the driveway, an immense man, tattooed and bearded and dressed in black jeans and a greasy T-shirt, holding a wrench and looking down the driveway at him. Landers instantly stepped on the gas, angling away from the curb and gunning toward the corner.

He knew what he needed to know. He could go home now. Whoever this man was, living in what must have been Squires's old house, he didn't have anything to do with the *Thirteen Phantasms*. He wasn't a Newtonian. There was no conceivable chance that Squires himself was somewhere inside, working the crank of his mechanical printing press, stamping out fantastic stories on Winnebago Eggshell paper. Squires was gone; that was the truth of it. The Newtonians were gone. The *world they'd inhabited*, with its twenty-five-cent pulp magazines and egg-headed robots and Martian canals, its highballs and hand-set type and slide rules, was gone too. Probably it was all at the bottom of the tar pits, turning into puzzling fossils.

Out beyond the front window, Rexroth Street was dark and empty of anything but the wind. To the south, the Hollywood Hills were a black wall of shadow, as if there were nothing there at all, just a vacancy. The sky above the dark line of the hills was so closely scattered with bright stars in the wind-scoured night that Latzarel might have been dreaming, and the broad wash of the Milky Way spanned the heavens like a lamp-lit road. From up the hall, he could hear Cummings talking on the telephone. Cummings would be talking to his wife about now, asking permission to stay out late. Squires had phoned Rhineholdt at the observatory, and they were due up on the hill in an hour, with just time enough to stop for a late-night burger at the Copper Kettle on the way.

Latzarel took the three-dimensional picture of the eyeball out of his coat pocket and turned it under the lamp in the window, marveling again at the eyeball that hung impossibly in the miniature void, in its little nonexistent cube of frozen space. There was a sudden glow in the Western sky now—a meteor shower, hundreds of shooting stars, flaming up for a moment before vanishing beyond the darkness of the hills. Latzarel shouted for Squires and the others, and when they all ran into the room the stars were still falling, and the southern sky was like a veil of fireflies.

The totality of Landers's savings account hadn't been worth much at the coin shop. Gold standard bills weren't cheap. Probably he'd have been better off simply buying gold, but somehow the idea wasn't appealing. He wanted folding money in his wallet, just like any other pedestrian—something he could pay for lunch with, a burger and a Coke or a BLT and a slice of apple pie.

He glued the last of the foam-rubber blocks onto the inside top of the wooden crate on his living-room floor, then stood back and looked at the pile of stuff that was ready to go into the box. He'd had a thousand choices, an impossible number of choices. Everywhere he had turned in the house there was something else, some fabulous relic of the late twentieth century: throwaway wristwatches and dimmer switches, cassette tapes and portable telephones, pictorial histories and horse-race results, wallet-size calculators and pop-top cans, Ziploc baggies and Velcro fasteners, power screw guns and bubble paper, a laptop computer, software, a Styrofoam cup....

And then it had occurred to him that there was something about the tiniest articles that appealed to him even more than the obvious marvels. Just three trifling little wonders shifted backward in time, barely discernible in his coat pocket, might imply huge, baffling changes in the world: a single green-tinted contact lens, perhaps, and the battery out of a watch, and a hologram bird clipped out of a credit card. He wandered from room to room again, looking around. A felt-tipped pen? A nylon zipper? Something more subtle . . .

But of course if it were too subtle, it would be useless, wouldn't it? What was he really planning to do with these things? Try to convince a nearsighted man to shove the contact lens into his eye? Would the Newtonians pry the battery apart? To what end? What was inside? Probably black paste of some kind or a lump of dull metal—hardly worth the bother. And the hologram bird—it was like something out of a box of Cracker Jacks. Besides, the Newtonians had already gotten the eyeball, hadn't they? He couldn't do better than the eyeball.

Abruptly he abandoned his search, changing his thinking entirely. Hurrying into the study he pulled books out of the case, selecting and rejecting titles, waiting for something to appeal to him, something . . . He couldn't quite define it. He might as well take nearly any of them, or simply rip out a random copyright page. The daily papers? Better to take along a sack of rotten fruit.

He went out of the study and into the kitchen hallway where he climbed the attic ladder. Untying the last of the boxes, he sorted through the *Astounding*s, settling on March of 1956—ten years in the future, more or less, for the Newtonians. Unlike the rest of the issues, this one was beat up, as if it had been read to pieces, or carried around in someone's coat pocket. He scanned the contents page, noting happily that there was a Heinlein novel serialized in the volume, and he dug through the box again to find April of the same year in order to have all of the story—something called *Double Star*. The torn cover of the April issue showed an ermine-robed king of some kind inspecting a toy locomotive, his forehead furrowed with thought and wonder.

Satisfied at last, Landers hurried back down the ladder and into the living room again. To hell with the trash on the floor, the bubble paper and the screw gun. He would leave all the Buck Rogers litter right here in a pile. Packing that kind of thing into the box was like loading up the Trojan Horse, wasn't it? It was a betrayal. And for what? Show-off value?

Wealth? Fame? It was all beside the point; he saw that clearly now. It was very nearly the antithesis of the point.

He slid the *Astounding*s into a niche inside the box along with the *Thirteen Phantasms*, an army-surplus flashlight, a wooden-handled screwdriver, and his sandwiches and bot-tled water. Then he picked up the portable telephone and made two calls, one to his next-door neighbor and one to Federal Express. His neighbor would unlock the door for the post office, who would haul the crate away on a handcart and truck it to Glendale.

The thought clobbered him suddenly. By what route? he wondered. Along what arcane boulevards would he travel?

He imagined the crate being opened by the man he had seen working on the motorcycle in the neglected driveway. What would Landers do? Threaten the man with the screw-driver? Offer him the antique money? Scramble out of the crate and simply walk away down the street without a back-ward glance, forever changing the man's understanding of hu-man behavior?

He stopped his mind from running and climbed into the crate, pulling the lid on after him. Carefully and deliberately, he started to set the screws—his last task before lunch. It was silent in the box, and he sat listening for one last moment in the darkness, the attic sitting empty above him, still sheltered by its vines and wooden shingles. He imagined the world re-volving, out beyond the walls of the old house, imagined the noise and movement, and he thought briefly of Mrs. Cum-mings across town, arranging and rearranging a leather-encased slide rule and a couple of old smoking pipes and photographs.

The Saturday meeting of the Newtonian society had come to order right on time. Phillip Mays, the lepidopterist, was home from the Amazon with a collection of insects that in-cluded an immense dragonfly commonly thought to have died out in the Carboniferous period. Squires's living-room floor was covered with display boxes and jars, and the room smelled of camphor and pipe smoke. There was the patter of soft rain through the open casements, but the weather was warm and easy despite the rain, and in the dim distance, out over the hills, there was the low rumble of thunder.

The doorbell rang, and Squires, expecting another Newtonian, opened the heavy front door in the turreted entry hall. A large wooden crate sat on the porch, sheltered by the awning, and a post-office truck motored away north toward Kenneth Road, disappearing beyond a mist of rain. Latzarel looked over Squires's shoulder at the heavy crate, trying to figure out what was wrong with it, what was odd about it. Something . . .

"I'll be damned," he said. "The top's screwed on from the inside."

"I'll get a pry bar," Hastings said from behind him.

Latzarel heard a sound then, and he put his ear to the side of the box. There was the click of a screwdriver on metal, the squeak of the screw turning. "Don't bother with the pry bar," Latzarel said, winking at Squires, and he lit a match and held it to his pipe, cupping his hand over the bowl to keep the raindrops from putting it out.

Red Planet

I'm going on a bus. By God! On a bus. Out of Dubuque on the midnight line and Greyhounding through the midwest firefly night. Sleeping in the recliner at sixty miles an hour across moon-brightened plains. Stop off in Memphis. Lunch in New Orleans. Breakfast here, dinner there. By God, around the country on a bus. Around the *world* on that sucker!

Monty, grinning ear to ear, bag in hand, strides into the mouth of a red brick depot. He removes a crumpled hat, looks left, looks right, and smacks suitcase first into the tail end of an old grey lady in a red suit, pink hat, and lace veil, knocking baggage askew and the old lady onto dimpled knees, gasping and shaking.

"I really am sorry ma'am, I . . ."

"Beast!" she screams. "Beast!"

"Pardon me ma'am, you see . . ."

My God. Old lady's setting in to pound me now with that there little bag on a string. Probably filled with rocks or dimes or something. Best set things to right. Make another effort to beg her pardon.

Monty, hat in hand, opens his mouth, when a third voice pipes in. "Leave the lady be, young man."

Yes sir, will do sir, count on me sir. Lady can be and I'll leave. Got to catch a bus. So sorry. Monty, backing off toward the ticket window, leaving the grey lady in a huff, she talking ever so plaintively to three old cohorts, all seemingly off on a tour of the Black Hills. To the rugged Dakotas to get a glimpse of those cold stone faces. Monty pondering slowly that northwest passage.

Ah! I can see our man now. Rock-jawed and ripping down poop-out hill. Big stick in hand and a truckload of freedom on call. Fine subject for a granite hillside. Perhaps there lies the destination, in the great northwest. The home of the grizzly bear and the Indian.

Monty, firmly astride his charger, strolls on up to the window with his country gait, his free hand trapped in his pocket and his grin once again spreading forth. "Beg your pardon, ma'am, but I'm in need of a bus ticket."

"Yes, sir. Will you be traveling far?"

"You're dadburn right!" says Monty with a well-stifled whoop.

The clerk glances up from the window and spies Monty's chin, covered slightly with fuzz, Monty's face toward the heavens. Monty examines an old round clock with its black Roman numerals and rust frame. He glances back down at the clerk with a grin suddenly sheepish.

"I was just lookin' at that there clock yonder on the wall." Monty a bit disjointed and groping in rear pockets for his wallet.

"Son, just where do you want to go?"

"Well, I don't rightly know. I've got plenty of money here. Which direction does this here bus go to?"

"Well now, this here bus goes just about all over the place. There and back again."

Monty, casting crumpled bills beneath the cage, grins again. "I'm going as far as this here money will allow, ma'am. As far as I can. And I don't need to come back, neither."

The ticket lady, glancing up with a yellow eye, reaches forth a ticket, punched and pale, to the destitute Monty, a secretive grin there detectable to his trained eye.

Monty shuffles off past long soiled couches in a nearly empty station. The Black Hills Special meanwhile tools west in a crescendo of power, leaving a relieved Monty waving goodbye through a window, grey with the dust of the ages, at the disappearing heads of the aged. The taillights shrink round the distant corner while inside the station sit five waiting travelers. They clutch small suitcases and their heads nod, bounce, and nod again.

A short moment passes before the white lights of an incoming bus herald its arrival. Monty joins the five through the exit and climbs aboard, stowing suitcase overhead and sinking low into the plush seat.

We're off now. Like a breath of fresh wind. Leaving old Dubuque behind to wither. A warm night, quiet outside, as this massive bus pulls away from a yellow curb.

Monty reaches into a shirt pocket for the stub, nearly falls forward as the bus lurches to a halt, and the old lady, purse full of dimes, huffs and puffs on board. Off again, Monty and the six now. The grey lady shuffles down the aisle, and sits across from a short gentleman with an overly large head, and dressed in a tweed suit. Smiling sideways, she puffs: "I nearly missed the bus, being in the lavatory and all. I wonder, did they take two after all?"

The dwarf inclines his head, peering at her out of a solitary eye which revolves about a central axis like the eye of a parrot. The bus sails onward, out into the empty plains where lightning bugs bob amid corn stalks like capering stars in the dark. The lady awaits some sort of reply, dabbing at dimpled cheeks with a hanky and nodding slowly, with a smile, toward the gentleman's eye.

"I say, I don't remember seeing you about the grounds. Have you just recently moved to the home?"

The dwarf, who has a wrinkled face and two pointed ears, turns toward the window, declining to comment, and pulls a silver cloth hat with a stiff brim down low over his eyes.

Monty, sitting five seats back, sees the old lady, used so roughly but a short while before, talking and smiling and nodding to an apparently empty seat; our midget slumped low, head midway up the back and feet midway to a gum-strewn floor.

I'm damned. Here she sits talking to that there empty seat, or so it would seem. But no, now that I'm pressed, there was that short fellow with the tweeds and the hat. That grizzled-looking guy with the hat. Yes sir. But what's she doing here? Intends to floor me with the dimes still. Take me in the back while I'm dozing and leave me senseless beneath the seat.

Monty reaches into his pocket and plucks forth a half dozen small objects: a horse chestnut, a red and black bean, a tiny purple spaceman waving an ominous-looking ray-gun, two polished stones, and a red agate marble—wonderfully mottled with dark swirls and checked with moon-shaped craters.

Nothing in the world so beautiful as a marble. These chips just make it shine. Hold it to the light and a whole frozen world sparkles inside. Always there waiting, no matter what. You never want to lose your shooter. Keep it in there. In your pocket where you can pull it out and look inside like some tiny enchanted crystal ball. If you tilt it and turn it just right you'll see something there. Something you can't see out here in this odd bus, flying like the purple spaceman's ship for who knows where. Those two guys in the seat up front. Twins. Bald spot on the tops of their heads, like some grey-suited monks. Striped coats, high-water pants. May well be Tweedledee and Tweedledum, sitting so still there in those big seats. And off to the left; a desperately strange couple with a greenish tinge to their skin. Don't even want to think about that. Best duck down a bit, avoid being sighted by the old dime lady. Too late.

"Howdy, ma'am. Can't tell you how sorry I am for smacking you like that back in the station."

"Hmph," she replies, but seems to be yielding.

The dwarf, round silver hat low over the left eye, comes peeking over the back of his seat at Monty who nods civilly

and tries not to stare at the pointy ears. On impulse the grey
lady stands, smiles at the peeping dwarf, and stumbles
toward the rear, seating herself across from Monty.

"Accidents will happen, son."

"Yes, ma'am. Don't I know."

"Son?"

"Yes, ma'am?"

"Where are we going? Is this bus going toward the Black
Hills?"

"It may well be, ma'am."

"You don't know?"

"No, ma'am."

The dwarf, head showing above the back of the recliner,
fingers gripping the soft velvety fabric, pursing his lips and
wrinkling his cheeks, shakes his head in a slow negative. He
disappears.

Now what in the devil did that mean? Must go slowly
with these people. Feel them out, so to speak. No more incidents. I'm on vacation here. Permanent vacation. Time to re-
deem myself with this here lady. Fine person really, I
suppose. No use getting off, as usual, on the wrong foot.

"Excuse me, ma'am. I'll just go forward and ask the
driver. I'm sure he'll know."

"Well, yes. Perhaps you should. I'd be frightfully upset if
I were on the wrong bus."

"Yes, ma'am."

Monty, off up the aisle to speak to the driver. Bus drivers
are unusually well informed. Especially about destinations.
Barbers, bus drivers, and cowboys; they'll always know, one
way or the other.

The bus, jerking along the dark highway, across the
rolling hills of the midwest like some trackless roller-coaster
that may well go on forever. Never circle back around to that
dust-settled station; that town of sage barbers and hooting
cowboys and nothing at all but the smell of dry wind blowing along stale streets. A steep dipping hill leaves Monty
weightless in the aisle, plummeting through deep space. He
staggers forward, lunges for the back of a seat to steady him-

self and sprawls sideways, like a crab washed from its hold by the tides, into Tweedledee whose leg is thrust into the aisle.

"I say! Here now. What in the world are you doing, boy?"

"Excuse me sir. Going up to talk to the driver there. It's about where this bus is going. I'm not sure, and the lady back there might be on the wrong bus."

"You might be on the wrong bus you mean," says the green man, smirking at poor tripped-up Monty. Tweedledee and Tweedledum burst into simultaneous laughter. The dwarf tugs on the bill of his hat and turns to stare out of the window.

Oh, jeez. Got to watch that. Can't go stumbling around upsetting things like that. Always comes to no good. Must talk to the driver there, staring out through his tinted window with those yellow eyes glowing in the light of the dashboard.

"Excuse me sir, but where does this here bus go?"

"Most everywhere, boy. All over the place mostly, I suppose. Here and there."

"Yes, sir, but that lady back there is afraid she's on the wrong bus. Do we go anywhere near the Black Hills?"

"More or less," says the driver, sipping dark coffee from a stained paper cup. "More or less."

"Thank you." Monty, baffled, turns to see the grey lady, seated once more by the dwarf, pointing toward Monty and whispering terrible things. Monty tiptoes carefully past Tweedledee whose eyes have blinked shut. Asleep perhaps. A grey leg darts out into the aisle as Monty stumbles past. Raucous laughter from the man with the green skin.

Best sit down here near this lady and the dwarf. Try to make conversation. What is this thing I'm kicking about beneath the seat? A shoe, by God. An old, beaten, cast-off shoe. Like at the lake when you walk along the shore in the early morning. You find a shoe, just one, caked with sand, tongue protruding and laces gone. Who leaves those shoes there? Why don't they leave two? What do they do with the other one? Do they go home in one shoe? There's something I don't know about. Must be something. No use in trying to reason it out. Take this Greyhound bus to Mars. Grass couldn't be any less green.

Just get on and sail down the road that stretches like a dark ribbon through the waving wheat hair of the midwest. The road that narrows and narrows off into the distance to be swallowed up by the gentle curve of the horizon. From one world into the next. Like old Dad; stepping aboard that dark shadow bus one day and riding into lunacy. Dropped off at the place there, outside of town. Outside of any town I know. Stepped aboard in daylight and off again in darkness. Maybe. Maybe somewhere else. Maybe somewhere that he wouldn't want to come back from. How do I know?

"Pardon me?"

"What? Oh, yes. The driver says we might go to the Black Hills at that. It didn't seem certain though."

"What do you mean, young man. Are you having me on again? A poor old lady like me?"

Monty slouching low in the seat, trying to assure her otherwise. Perhaps best just to keep a tight lip. Don't give them anything to hold on to. Nothing to poke and jab at. There's Tweedledee and the green man, staring back. Must try to smile. Nod politely as they glance at each other and smirk. My but they're clever, those two. Like the rest of them back home. If they can't throw rocks they throw other things at you with their eyes.

"Excuse me sir," says Monty to the dwarf, always apologizing.

"Yes sir. It's a fine night out, isn't it?"

"Mmmm."

Monty snaps open his leather bag and pulls out a book, rather dog-eared and homey looking. Forget this dwarf. Plunge into the pages of this book like I plunge into the night on this bus. Forever crossing into some new land. You just have to get under way, that's all. Ride with the elves in search of the man in the moon. With the white hunter through savage Africa. Follow the trail of a grey old wizard through magic lands, far from the reaches of the cold dust wind of the plains. Take this star schooner of a bus through twirling space, bound for Mars. Just climb aboard, cut the moorings, and cast off.

The dwarf there, speaking to the grey lady in undertones. Setting her straight perhaps. He knows where we're headed and always has, by God. Anyone with pointed ears and that glittering silver hat knows something. He rides buses a lot, that one does. I bet he even knows about those lonely shoes I stumble across, now and again.

"Pardon me sir, but where are we going?"

"Eh?"

"I say, where are we bound?"

The dwarf winks. He nods toward the darkened window and points a long thin finger toward the jeweled heavens that hang so low overhead.

The bus whizzes along silently, dipping down and flying over hills that lie on the plains like grim whales on the bottom of the sea. Monty, looking out from inside a tiny flying fish, sailing amidst the black leviathan. By God! On a bus. You can go anywhere on this sucker. The bus, over a dip in the road, nosing skyward, ascending, angling straight up toward where the dwarf's finger had pointed, only a moment before. Straight up through the speckled dark as the moon and the stars seem to grow and brighten with a beckoning shimmer.

"That'd be mighty fine. Mighty fine," says Monty to no one in particular, settling back into the folds of the plush recliner, book lying open on his lap. Through the dim window the bright dots of the stars hover thick in the night sky. So thick and big that you couldn't shoot a bullet up there without hitting one of them; let alone a bus. The great circle of the red planet swings into view, misty and crisscrossed with inexplicable lines like the intricate translucent swirlings of the agate marble in Monty's pocket. The fiery eye of a winking enchantress. "By God!" breathes Monty. "Mighty fine."

The Ape-Box Affair

A good deal of controversy arose late in the last century over what has been referred to by the more livid newspapers as "The Horror in St. James Park" or "The Ape-Box Affair." Even these thirty years later, a few people remember that little intrigue, though most would change the subject rather abruptly if you broached it, and many are still unaware of the relation, or rather the lack of relation, between the actual ape-box and the spacecraft that plunked down in the Park's duck pond.

The memoirs of Professor Langdon St. Ives, however, which passed into my hands after the poor man's odd disappearance, pretty clearly implicate him in the affair. His own orang-outang, I'll swear it, and the so-called Hooded Alien are one and the same creature. There is little logical connection, however, between that creature and "the thing in the box" which has since also fallen my way, and is nothing more than a clockwork child's toy. The ape puppet in that box, I find after a handy bit of detective work, was modeled after the heralded "Moko the Educated Ape," which toured with a Bulgarian Gypsy fair and which later became the central motif of the mysterious Robert Service sonnet, "The Headliner and

the Breadliner." That the ape in the box became linked to St.
Ives's shaven orang-outang is a matter of the wildest coincidence—a coincidence that generated a chain of activities no
less strange or incredible. This then is the tale, and though the
story is embellished here and there for the sake of dramatic
realism, it is entirely factual in the main.

Professor St. Ives was a brilliant scientist, and the history
books might some day acknowledge his full worth. But for
the Chingford Tower fracas, and one or two other rather trivial affairs, he would be heralded by the Academy, instead of
considered a sort of interesting lunatic.

His first delvings into the art of space travel were those
which generated the St. James Park matter, and they occurred on, or better yet, were culminated in 1892 early in
the morning of July 2. St. Ives' spacecraft was ball-shaped
and large enough for one occupant; and because it was the
first of a series of such crafts, that occupant was to be one
Newton, a trained orang-outang who had only to push the
right series of buttons when spacebound to motivate a magnetic homing device designed to reverse the craft's direction
and set it about a homeward course. The ape's head was
shaven to allow for the snug fitting of a sort of golden conical cap which emitted a meager electrical charge, sufficient
only to induce a very mild sleep. It was of great importance
that the ape remain docile while in flight, a condition which,
as we shall see, was not maintained. The ape was also fitted
with a pair of silver, magnetic-soled boots to affix him
firmly to the deck of the ship; they would impede his movements in case he became restive, or, as is the problem with
space travel, in case the forces of gravity should diminish.

Finally, St. Ives connected a spring-driven mechanism in
a silver-colored box which puffed forth successive jets of
oxygenated gas produced by the interaction of a concentrated chlorophyll solution with compressed helium—this
combination producing the necessary atmosphere in the
closed quarters of the ship.

The great scientist, after securing the ape to his chair and winding the chlorophyll box, launched the ship from the rear yard of his residence and laboratory in Harrogate. He watched the thing career south through the starry early-morning sky. It was at that point, his craft a pinpoint of light on the horizon, that St. Ives was stricken with the awful realization that he had neglected to fill the ape's food dispenser, a fact which would not have been of consequence except that the ape was to receive half a score of greengage plums as a reward for pushing the several buttons which would affect the gyro and reverse the course of the ship. The creature's behavior once he ascertained that he had, in effect, been cheated of his greengages was unpredictable. There was nothing to be done, however, but for St. Ives to crawl wearily into bed and hope for the best.

Several weeks previous to the launching of the craft (pardon the digression here; its pertinence will soon become apparent) a Bulgarian Gypsy caravan had set up a bit of a carnival in Chelsea, where they sold the usual salves and potions and such rot, as well as providing entertainments. Now, Wilfred Keeble was a toymaker who lived on Whitehall above the Old Shades and who, though not entirely daft, was eccentric. He was also the unloved brother of Winnifred Keeble, newly monied wife of Lord Placer. To be a bit more precise, he was loved well enough by his sister, but his brother-in-law couldn't abide him. Lord Placer had little time for the antics of his wife's lowlife relative, and even less for carnivals or circuses of gypsies. His daughter Olivia, therefore, sneaked away and cajoled her Uncle Wilfred into taking her to the gypsy carnival. Keeble assented, having little use himself for Lord Placer's august stuffiness, and off they went to the carnival, which proved to be a rather pale affair, aside from the antics of Moko the Educated Ape. Actually, as far as Keeble was concerned, the ape itself was nothing much, being trained merely to sit in a great chair and puff on a cigar while seeming to pore over a copy of the *Times* which, more often than not, it held upside down or sideways or chewed at or tore up or gibbered over.

Olivia was fascinated by the creature and flew home begging her father for a pet ape, an idea which not only sent a thrill of horror and disgust up Lord Placer's spine, but also caused him to confound his brother-in-law and everything connected with him for having had such a damnable effect on his daughter. Olivia, her hopes dashed by her father's ape loathing, confided her grief to Uncle Wilfred who, although he knew that the gift of a real ape would generate conflicts best not thought about, could see no harm in fashioning a toy ape.

He set about in earnest to create such a thing and, in a matter of weeks, came up with one of those clockwork, key-crank jack-in-the-boxes. It was a silver cube painted with vivid circus depictions; when wound tightly, a comical ape got up as a mandarin and with whirling eyes would spring out and shout a snatch of verse. Wilfred Keeble was pretty thoroughly pleased with the thing, but he knew that it would be folly to go visiting his brother-in-law's house with such a wild and unlikely gift, in the light of Lord Placer's hatred of such things. There was a boy downstairs, a Jack Owlesby, who liked to earn a shilling here and there, and so Keeble called him up and, wrapping the box in paper and dashing off a quick note, sent Jack out into the early morning air two and six richer for having agreed to deliver the gift. Having sat up all night to finish the thing, Keeble crawled wearily into bed at, it seems, nearly the same hour that Langdon St. Ives did the same after launching his spacecraft.

Three people—two indigent gentlemen who seemed sea-captainish in a devastated sort of way, and a shrunken fellow with a yellow cloth cap who was somehow responsible for the chairs scattered about the green—were active in St. James Park that morning; at least those are the only three whose testimony was later officially transcribed. According to the *Times* report, these chaps, at about 7:00 AM, saw, as one of them stated, "a great fiery thing come sailing along

like a bloody flying head,"—an adequate enough description
of St. Ives's ship which, gone amok, came plunging into the
south end of the Park's duck pond.

This visitation of a silver orb from space would, in itself,
have been sufficient to send an entire park full of people
shouting into the city, but, to the three in the park, it seemed
weak tea indeed when an alien-seeming beast sailed out on
impact through the sprung hatch, a bald-headed but otherwise hairy creature with a sort of golden dunce cap, woefully
small, perched atop his head. Later, one of the panhandlers,
a gentleman named Hornby, babbled some rubbish about a
pair of flaming stilts, but the other two agreed that the thing
wore high-topped silver boots, and, to a man, they remarked
of an "infernal machine" which the thing carried daintily
between his outstretched hands like a delicate balloon as it
fled into Westminster.

There was, of course, an immediate hue and cry, responded
to by two constables and a handful of sleepy and disheveled
horse guards who raced about skeptically between the wit-
nesses while poor Newton, St. Ives's orang-outang, fuddled
and hungry, disappeared into the city. At least three journalists
appeared within half an hour's time and were soon hotfooting
it away quick as you please with the tale of the alien ship, the
star beast, and the peculiar and infernal machine.

Newton had begun to grow restless somewhere over
Yorkshire, just as the professor had supposed he would. Now
all of this is a matter of conjecture, but logic would point
with a stiffish finger toward the probability that the electronic
cap atop the ape's head either refused to function or func-
tioned incorrectly, for Newton had commenced his antics
within minutes of takeoff. There were reports, in fact, of an
erratic glowing sphere zigging through the sky above Long
Bennington that same morning, an indication that Newton,
irate, was pretty thoroughly giving the controls the once-
over. One can only suppose that the beast, anticipating a
handful of plums, began stabbing away at the crucial buttons
unaffected, as he must have been, by the cap. That it took a
bit longer for him to run thoroughly amok indicates the ex-

tent of his trust in St. Ives. The professor, in his papers, reports that the control panel itself was finally dashed to bits and the chlorophyll-atmosphere box torn cleanly from the side of the cabin. Such devastation couldn't have been undertaken before the craft was approaching Greater London; probably it occurred above South Mimms, where the ship was observed by the populace to be losing altitude. This marked the beginning of the plunge into London.

Although the creature had sorted through the controls rather handily, those first plum buttons, luckily for him, activated at least partially St. Ives's gyro homing device. Had the beast been satisfied and held off on further mayhem, he would quite possibly have found himself settling back down in Harrogate at St. Ives's laboratory. As it was, the reversing power of the craft was enough finally to promote, if not a gentle landing, at least one which, taking into account the cushion of water involved, was not fatal to poor Newton.

Jack Owlesby, meanwhile, ambled along down Whitehall, grasping the box containing Keeble's ape contraption and anticipating a meeting with Keeble's niece whom he had admired more than once. He was, apparently, a good enough lad, as we'll see, and had been, coincidentally enough, mixed in with Langdon St. Ives himself some little time ago in another of St. Ives's scientific shenanigans. Anyway, because of his sense of duty and the anticipation of actually speaking to Olivia, he popped right along for the space of five minutes before realizing that he could hardly go pounding away on Lord Placer's door at such an inhuman hour of the morning. He'd best, thought he, sort of angle up around the square and down The Mall to the park to kill a bit of time. A commotion of some nature and a shouting lot of people drew him naturally along and, as would have happened to anyone in a like case, he went craning away across the road, unconscious of a wagon of considerable size which was gathering speed some few feet off his starboard side. A horn blasted, Jack leapt forward with a shout, clutching his parcel, and a brougham, unseen behind the wagon, plowed over him like an express, the driver cursing and flailing his arms.

The long and the short of it is that Jack's box, or rather Keeble's box, set immediate sail and bounced along unhurt into a park thicket ignored by onlookers who, quite rightly, rushed to poor Jack's aid.

The boy was stunned, but soon regained his senses and, although knocked about a good bit, suffered no real damages. The mishaps of a boy, however, weren't consequential enough to hold the attention of the crowd, not even of the Lord Mayor, who was in the fateful brougham. He had been rousted out of an early morning bed by the reports of dangerous aliens and inexplicable mechanical contrivances. He rather fancied the idea of a smoke and a chat and perhaps a pint of bitter later in the day with these alien chaps and so organized a "delegation," as he called it, to ride out and welcome them.

He was far more concerned with the saddening report that the thing had taken flight to the south than with the silver sphere that bobbed in the pond. The ship had been towed to shore, but as yet no one had ventured to climb inside for fear of the unknown—an unfortunate and decisive hesitation, since a thorough examination would certainly have enabled an astute observer to determine its origin.

It was to young Jack's credit that, after he had recovered from the collision, he spent only a moment or so at the edge of the pond with the other spectators before becoming thoroughly concerned over the loss of the box. The letter from Keeble to Olivia lay yet within his coat, but the box seemed to have vanished like a magician's coin. He went so far as to stroll nonchalantly across the road again, reenacting, as they say, the scene of the crime or, in this case, the accident. He pitched imaginary boxes skyward and then clumped about through bushes and across lawns, thoroughly confounded by the disappearance. Had he known the truth, he'd have given up the search and gone about his business, or what was left of it, but he had been lying senseless when old grizzled Hornby, questioned and released by the constables, saw Jack's parcel crash down some few feet from him as he sat brooding in the bushes. In Hornby's circles one didn't look a gift horse in the fabled mouth, not for long anyway, and he had the string yanked off and the wrapper torn free in a nonce.

Now you or I would have been puzzled by the box, silvery and golden as it was and with bright pictures daubed on in paint and a mysterious crank beneath, but Hornby was positively aghast. He'd seen such a thing that morning in the hands of a creature who, he still insisted, raged along in his wizard's cap on burning stilts. He dared not fiddle with it in light of all that, and yet he couldn't just pop out of the bushes waving it about either. This was a fair catch and, no doubt, a very valuable one. Why such a box should sail out of the skies was a poser, but this was clearly a day tailor-made for such occurrences. He scuttled away under cover of the thick greenery until clear of the mobbed pond area, then took to his heels and headed down toward Westminster with the vague idea of finding a pawn broker who had heard of the alien threat and would be willing to purchase such an unlikely item.

Jack, then, searched in vain, for the box he'd been entrusted with had been spirited away. His odd behavior, however, soon drew the attention of the constabulary who, suspicious of the very trees, asked him what he was about. He explained that he'd been given a metallic looking box, and a very wonderful box at that, and had been instructed to deliver it across town. The nature of the box, he admitted, was unknown to him for he'd glimpsed it only briefly. He suspected, though, that it was a toy of some nature.

"A toy is it, that we have here!" shouted Inspector Marleybone of Scotland Yard. "And who, me lad, was it gave you this toy?"

"Mister Keeble, sir, of Whitehall," said Jack very innocently and knowing nothing of a similar box which, taken to be some hideous device, was a subject of hot controversy. Here were boxes springing up like the children of Noah, and it took no longer than a moment or two before two police wagons were rattling away, one to ferret out this mysterious Keeble, in league, like as not, with aliens, and one to inquire after Lord Placer down near the Tate Gallery. Jack, as well as

a dozen policemen, were left to continue futilely scouring
the grounds.

Somehow Newton had managed, by luck or stealth, to slip
across Victoria Street and fall in among the greengrocers and
clothing sellers along Old Pye. Either they were fairly used to
peculiar chaps in that section of town and so took no special
notice of him, or else Newton, wittily, clung to the alleys and
shadows and generally laid low, as they say. This latter possibility is most likely the case, for Newton would have been as
puzzled and frightened of London as had he actually been an
alien; orang-outangs, being naturally shy and contemplative
beasts, would, if given the choice, spurn the company of
men. The incident, however, that set the whole brouhaha going afresh was sparked by a wooden fruit cart loaded, unfortunately, with nothing other than greengage plums.
    Here was a poor woman, tired, I suppose, and at only
eight o'clock or so in the morning, with her cart of fresh
plums and two odious children. She set up along the curb,
outside a bakery. As fortune would have it, she was an altogether kindly sort, and she towed her children in to buy a
two-penny loaf, leaving her cart for the briefest of moments.
    She returned, munching a slab of warm bread, in time to
see the famished Newton, his greengages come round at last,
hoeing into handfuls of the yellowy fruit. As the *Times* has
the story, the ape was hideously covered with slime and juice,
and, although the information is suspect, he took to hallooing
in a resonant voice and to waving the box like a cudgel above
his head. The good woman responded with shouts and "a call
to Him above in this hour of dreadful things."
    As I see it, Newton reacted altogether logically. Cheated
of his greengages once, he had no stomach to be dealt with
in such a manner again. He grasped the tongue of the cart,
anchored his machine firmly in among the plums, and loped
off down Old Pye Street toward St. Ann's.
    Jack Owlesby searched as thoroughly as was sensible—
more thoroughly perhaps, for, as I said, he was prompted and

accompanied by the authorities, and as soon as the crowd in the park got wind of the possible presence of "a machine," they too savaged the bushes, surged up and down the road behind the Horse Guards, and tramped about Duck Island until the constables were forced to shout threats and finally give up their own search. The crowd thinned shortly thereafter, when a white-coated, bespectacled fellow hailing from the Museum came down and threw a tarpaulin over the floating ship.

Jack was at odds, blaming himself for the loss, but mystified and frustrated over its disappearance. There seemed to be only one option—to deliver the letter to young Olivia and then return the two and six to Mr. Keeble upon returning to the Old Shades. He set out, then, to do just that.

Inspector Marleybone was in an itch to get to the bottom of this invasion, as it were, which had so far been nothing more than the lunatic arrival of a single alien who had since fled. Wild reports of flaming engines and howling, menacing giants were becoming tiresome. But, though rumors have always been the bane of the authorities, they seem to be meat and drink to the populace, and here was no exception. Bold headlines of "Martian Invasion" and "St. James Horror" had the common man in a state, and it may as well have been a bank holiday in London by 9:00 that morning. A fresh but grossly overblown account of the plum-cart incident reached poor Marleybone at about the time he arrived back at the Yard, just as he had begun toying with the idea that there had been no starship, nor hairy alien nor dread engine, and that all had been a nightmarish product of the oysters and Spanish wine he'd enjoyed the night before. But here were fresh accounts, and the populace honing kitchen knives, and a thoroughly befuddled Wilfred Keeble without his cap, being ushered in by two very serious constables.

Keeble, who normally liked the idea of romance and grand adventure, didn't at all like the real thing, and was a bit groggy from lack of sleep in the bargain. He listened, puzzled, to Marleybone's questions, which seemed, of course, madness. There was no reference, at first, to strange metallic boxes, but only to suspected dealings with alien space invaders and to Marleybone's certainty that Keeble was responsible, almost single-handedly, for the mobs which, shouting and clanking in their curiosity, came surging up and down the road at intervals on their way to gaze at the covered ball in the pond, and to search for whatever wonderful prizes had rained on London from the heavens.

Keeble pleaded his own ignorance and innocence and insisted that he was a toy-maker who knew little of invasions, and would have nothing to do with such things had he the opportunity. Marleybone was wary but tired, and his spirits fell another notch when Lord Placer, his own eyes glazed from a night of brandy and cards at the club, stormed in in a rage.

Although it was all very well to ballyrag Keeble, it was another thing entirely with Lord Placer, and so the inspector, with an affected smile, began to explain that Keeble seemed to be mixed into the alien affair, and that a certain metallic box, thought to be a threatening device of some nature or another, had been intercepted, then lost, en route from Keeble to Lord Placer. It wasn't strictly the truth, and Marleybone kicked himself for not having taken Jack Owlesby in tow so that he'd at least have someone to point the accusatory finger at. Lord Placer, although knowing even less at this point than did his brother-in-law (who, at the mention of a silver box saw a glimmer of light at the end of the tunnel) was fairly sure he could explain the fracas away even so. Wilfred Keeble, he stated, was clearly a madman, a raving lunatic who, with his devices and fables, was attempting to drive the city mad for the sake of company. It was a clear go as far as Lord P. could determine, and although it did not lessen the horror of being dragged from a warm bed and charged as an alien invader, it was at least good to have such a simple explanation. Lunacy, Lord Placer held, was the impetus behind almost everything, especially his brother-in-law's actions, whether real or supposed.

Finally Marleybone did the sensible thing, and let the two go, wondering why in the devil he'd called them in in the first place. Although he believed for the most part Keeble's references to a jack-in-the-box, he was even more convinced of Lord Placer's hypothesis of general lunacy. He accompanied Lord Placer to his coach, apologizing profusely for the entire business. Lord P. grunted and agreed, as the horses clopped away, to contact Scotland Yard in the event that the mysterious machine should, by some twist of insane fate, show up at his door.

Lady Placer, the former Miss Keeble, met her husband as he dragged in from the coach, mumbling curses about her brother. If anyone in the family had, as the poet said, "gone round the bend," it was Winnifred, who was slow-witted as a toothpick. She was, however, tolerant of her brother, and couldn't altogether fathom her husband's dislike of him, although she set great store in old Placer's opinions, and thus often found herself in a muddle over the contrary promptings of her heart and mind. She listened, then, with great curiosity to Lord Placer's confused story of the rumored invasion, the monster in the park, and his own suspected connection with the affair, which was entirely on account of her damned brother's rumminess.

Winnifred, having heard the shouting newsboys, knew something was in the air, and was mystified to find that her own husband and brother were mixed up in it. She was thoroughly awash when her husband stumbled away to bed, but was not overly worried, for confusion was one of the humours she felt near to and was comfortable with. She did wonder, however, at the fact that Lord Placer was involved in such weird doings, and she debated whether her daughter should be sent away, perhaps to her aunt's home near Dover, until the threat was past. Then it struck her that she wasn't at all sure what the threat was, and that spaceships might land in Dover as well as London, and also that, at any rate, her husband probably wasn't in league with these aliens after all. She wandered out to her veranda to look at a magazine. It was about then, I'd calculate, that the weary Marleybone got wind of the plum business and headed streetward again, this time in the company of the Lord Mayor's delegation.

It's not to be thought that, while Scotland Yard was grilling its suspects, Newton and Jack Owlesby and, of course, old Hornby who was about town with one of the two devices, stood idle. Newton, in fact, set out in earnest to enhance his already ballooning reputation. After making off with the plum cart, he found himself unpursued, and deep into Westminster, heading, little did he know, toward Horseferry Road. It's folly for an historian in such a case to do other than conjecture, but it seems to me that, sated with plums but still ravenous, as you or I might be sated with sweets while desiring something more substantial, he sighted a melon cart wending its way toward the greengrocers along Old Pye. Newton moored his craft in an alley, his box rooted in the midst of the plums, and hastened after the melon man, who was anything but pleased with the ape's appearance. He'd as yet heard nothing of the alien threat, and so took Newton to be an uncommonly ugly and bizarrely dressed thief. Hauling a riding crop from a peg on the side of the cart, the melon man laid about him with a will, cracking away at the perplexed orang-outang with wonderful determination, and shouting the while for a constable.

Newton, aghast, and taking advantage of his natural jungle agility, attempted to clamber up a wrought-iron pole which supported a striped canvas awning. His weight, of course, required a stout tree rather than a precariously moored pole, and the entire business gave way, entangling the ape in the freed canvas. The grocer pursued his attack, the ruckus having drawn quite a crowd, many of whom recognized the ape as a space invader, and several of whom took the trailing canvas, which had become impaled on the end of Newton's conical cap, to be some sort of Arab head-gear. That, to be sure, explains the several accounts of alien-Mohammedan conspiracies which found their way into the papers. References to an assault by the invader against the melon man are unproven and, I think, utterly false.

When Newton fled, followed by the mob, he found his plum cart as he had left it—except for the box, which had disappeared.

*   *   *

Jack Owlesby hadn't walked more than a half mile, still glum as a herring over Keeble's misplaced trust, when, strictly by chance, he glanced up an alley off St. Ann's and saw a plum cart lying unattended therein. The startling thing was that, as you can guess, an odd metallic box was nestled in among the plums. Jack drew near and determined, on the strength of the improbability of any other explanation, that the box was his own, or, rather, Olivia's. He had seen the thing only briefly before it had been wrapped, so his putting the gypsy touch to it can be rationalized, and even applauded. Because he had no desire to encounter whoever stole the thing, he set out immediately, supposing himself to have patched up a ruinous morning.

Old Hornby had not been as fortunate as had Jack. His conviction that the box was extra-terrestrial was scoffed at by several pawnbrokers who, seeming vaguely interested in the prize, attempted to coerce Hornby to hand it over to them for inspection. Sly Hornby realized that these usurious merchants were in league to swindle him, and he grew ever more protective of the thing as he, too, worked his way south. His natural curiosity drew him toward a clamoring mob which pursued some unseen thing.

It seemed to Hornby as if he "sniffed aliens" in the air and, as far as it goes, he was correct. He also assumed, this time incorrectly, that some profit was still to be had from these aliens, and so, swiftly and cunningly, he left the mob on Monck Street, set off through the alleys, and popped out at about the point that Horseferry winds around the mouth of Regency Street, head-on into the racing Newton who, canvas headgear and all, was outdistancing the crowd. Hornby was heard to shout, "Hey there," or "You there," or some such, before being bowled over, the ape snatching Hornby's treasured box away as it swept past, thinking it, undoubtedly, the box that had been purloined in the alley.

Jack Owlesby, meanwhile, arrived at Lord Placer's door and was admitted through the rear entrance by the butler, an affable sort who wandered off to drum up Miss Olivia at Jack's insistence. Lord Placer, hearing from the butler that a boy stood in the hall with a box for Olivia, charged into

Jack's presence in a fit of determination. He'd played the fool for too long, or so he thought, and he intended to dig to the root of the business. He was well into the hall when he realized that he was dressed in his nightshirt and cap, a pointed cloth affair, and wore his pointy-toed silk house slippers which were, he knew, ridiculous. His rage overcame his propriety, and, of course, this was only an errand boy, not a friend from the club, so he burst along and jerked the box away from an amazed Jack Owlesby.

"Here we have it!" he shouted, examining the thing.

"Yes, sir," said Jack. "If you please, sir, this is meant for your daughter and was sent by Mr. Keeble."

"Keeble has a hand in everything, it seems," cried Lord Placer, still brandishing the box as if it were a great diamond in which he was searching for flaws. "What's this bloody crank, boy? Some hideous apparatus, I'd warrant."

"I'm sure I don't know, sir," replied Jack diplomatically, hoping that Olivia would appear and smooth things out. He was sure that Lord Placer, who seemed more or less mad, would ruin the thing.

Casting caution to the winds, Lord Placer whirled away at the crank while peering into a funnel-like tube that protruded from the end. His teeth were set and he feared nothing, not even that this was, as he had been led to believe, one of the infernal machines rampant in the city. Amid puffings and whirrings and a tiny momentary tinkling sound, a jet of bright chlorophyll-green helium gas shot from the tube, covering Lord Placer's face and hair with a fine, lime-colored mist.

A howl of outrage issued from Lord Placer's mouth, now hanging open in disbelief. It was an uncanny howl, like that of moaning elf, for the gaseous mixture, for a reason known only to those who delve into the scientific mysteries, had a dismal effect on his vocal cords, an effect not unnoticed by Lord P., who thought himself poisoned and leapt toward the rear door. Winnifred, having heard an indecipherable shriek while lounging on the veranda, was met by Olivia, fresh from a stroll in the rose garden, and the two of them were astounded to see a capering figure of lunacy, eyes awhirl in a green face, come bellowing with an elvish voice into the yard, carrying a spouting device.

Winnifred's worst fears had come to pass. Here was her husband, or so it seemed, gone amok and in a weird disguise. Lady Placer, in a gesture of utter bewilderment, clapped a hand to her mouth and slumped backward onto the lawn. Olivia was no less perplexed, to be sure, but her concern over her mother took precedence over the mystery that confronted her, and she stooped to her aid. Lady Placer was a stout-hearted soul, however, and she was up in a moment. "It's your father," she gasped in a voice that sounded as if it knew strange truths, "go to him, but beware."

Olivia was dumbfounded, but she left her mother in the care of the butler, and launched out in the company of Jack Owlesby (who was, by then, at least as confused as the rest of the company) in pursuit of her father, who was loping some two blocks ahead and still carrying the box.

It was at this point that the odd thing occurred. Newton, having lost the crowd, still swung along down Regency past stupefied onlookers. He rounded onto Bessbourough and crossed John Islip Road, when he saw coming toward him a kindred soul. Here then came Lord Placer in his own pointed cap and with his own machine, rollicking along at an impressive clip. Now apes, as you know, are more intelligent in their way than are dogs, and it's not surprising that Newton, harried through London, saw at once that Lord Placer was an ally. So, with an ape's curiosity, he sped alongside for the space of a half block down toward Vauxhal Bridge, from which Lord Placer intended to throw himself into the river in hopes of diluting the odious solution he'd been doused with. Why he felt it necessary to bathe in the Thames is a mystery until we consider what the psychologists say—that a man in such an addled state might well follow his initial whims, even though careful contemplation would instruct him otherwise.

Inspector Marleybone, the Lord Mayor, and the delegation whipped along in their brougham in the wake of the mob. As is usual in such confusion, many of those out on the chase knew little or nothing of that which they pursued.

Rumors of the alien invasion were rampant but often scoffed at, and secondary rumors concerning the march of Islam, and even that the walls of Colney Hatch had somehow burst and released a horde of loonies, were at least as prevalent. Marleybone blanched at the sight of clubs and hay forks, and the Lord Mayor, aghast that London would visit such a riot on the heads of emissaries from another planet, demanded that Marleybone put a stop to the rout; but such a thing was, of course, impossible and they gave off any effort at quelling the mob, and concentrated simply on winning through to the fore and restraining things as best they could. This necessitated, unfortunately, taking a bit of a roundabout route which promoted several dead-ends and a near collision with a milk wagon, but finally they came through, careening around the corner of Bessborough and Grosvenor and sighting the two odd companions hotly pursued by a throng that stretched from the Palace to Millbank. Here they reined in.

The Lord Mayor was unsure as to exactly what course of action to take, considering the size and activity of the crowd and the ghastly duo of cavorting box-carriers that approached. If anyone remembers Jeremy Pike, otherwise Lord Bastable, who served as Lord Mayor from '89 almost until the war, you'll recall that, as the poet said, he had a heart stout and brave, and a rather remarkable speech prepared for the most monstrous audience he was likely to encounter.

So the Lord Mayor, with Marleybone at his heels, strode into the road and held up his hands, palms forward, in that symbolic gesture which is universally taken to mean "halt." It is absurd to think that there is any significance to the fact that Newton responded correctly to the signal, despite the suggestion of two noted astronomers, because their theory— the literal universality of hand gestures—lies in Newton's other-worldliness, which, as we know, is a case of mistaken identity. Anyway, the pair of fugitives halted in flight, I believe, because it was at that point, when presented with the delegation, that Lord Placer's eyes ceased to revolve like tops and it looked as if he were "coming around." He was still very much in some nature of psychological shock, as would anyone be if thrown into a like circumstance, but he was keen-witted enough to see that here was the end of the proverbial line. As Lord Placer slowed to a stop, so did Newton, himself happy, I've little doubt, to give up the chase.

The mob caught up with the ambassadorial party in a matter of moments, and there was a great deal of tree climbing and shoulder hoisting and neck craning as the people of London pressed in along the Thames. Marleybone gazed suspiciously at Lord Placer for the space of a minute before being struck with the pop-eyed realization of the gentleman's identity.

"Ha!" shouted the Inspector, reaching into his coat for a pair of manacles. Lord Placer, sputtering, proffered his box to the delegation, but a spurt of green fume and the tick of a timing device prompted a cry of, "The devil!" from Marleybone and, "The Infernal Machine!" from a score of people on the inner perimeter of the crowd, and everyone pressed back, fearing a detonation, and threatening a panic. Another burst of green, however, seemed to indicate that the device had miscarried somehow, and a smattering of catcalls and hoots erupted from the mob.

Lord Placer, at this point, recovered fully. He tugged his cloth cap low over his eyes and winked hugely several times at Olivia as she pushed through to be by his side. Olivia took the winks to be some sort of spasm and cried out, but Jack Owlesby, good lad he, slipped Lord P. a wink of his own, and very decorously tugged Olivia aside and whispered at her. Her father made no effort to rub away the chlorophyllic mask.

The Lord Mayor stepped up, and with a ceremonious bow took the glittering aerator from Lord Placer's outstretched hands. He held the thing aloft, convinced that it was some rare gift, no doubt incomprehensible to an earthling. He trifled with the crank. As another poof of green shot forth, the crowd broke into applause and began stamping about in glee.

"Londoners!" the Lord Mayor bawled, removing his hat. "This is indeed a momentous occasion." The crowd applauded heartily at this and, like as not, prompted Newton, who stood bewildered, to offer the Lord Mayor his own curiously wrought box.

A bit perturbed at the interruption but eager, on the other hand, to parley with this hairy beast who, it was apparent, hailed from the stars, old Bastable graciously accepted the gift. It was unlike the first box, and the designs drawn upon the outside, although weird, seemed to be of curiously garbed animals: hippos with toupees and carrying Gladstone Bags, elephants riding in ridiculously small dog-carts, great toads in clam-shell trousers and Leibnitz caps, and all manner of like things. Seeing no other explanation, the Lord Mayor naturally assumed that such finery might be common on an alien star, and with a flourish of his right arm, as if he were daubing the final colours onto a canvas, he set in to give this second box a crank-up.

The crowd waited, breathless. Even those too far removed from the scene to have a view of it seemed to know from the very condition of the atmosphere that what is generally referred to as "a moment in history" was about to occur. Poor Hornby, his feet aching from a morning of activity, gaped on the inner fringe of the circle of onlookers, as Lord Placer, perhaps the only one among the multitude who dared move, edged away toward the embankment.

There was the ratchet click of a gear and spring being turned tighter and tighter until, with a snap that jarred the silence, the top of the box flew open and a tiny ape, singularly clad in a golden robe and, of all things, a night cap not at all unlike Lord Placer's, shot skyward, hung bobbing in mid-air, and, in a piping voice called out Herodotus's cryptic and immortal line: "Fear not, Athenian stranger, because of this marvel!" After uttering the final syllable the ape, as if by magic, popped down into the box, pulling the lid shut after him.

The Lord Mayor stared at Marleybone in frank disbelief, both men awestruck, when Lord Placer, his brass having given out and each new incident compounding his woe, broke for the stairs that led to the causeway below the embankment and sailed like billy-o in the direction of home. About half the mob, eager again for the chase, sallied out in pursuit. When their prey was lost momentarily from view, Jack Owlesby, in a stroke of genius, shouted, "There goes the blighter!" and led the mob around the medical college, thus allowing for Lord Placer's eventual escape. Marleybone and the Lord Mayor collared Newton, who looked likely to bolt, and were confronted by two out-of-breath constables who reported nothing less than the theft of the spacecraft by a white-coated and bearded fellow in spectacles, ostensibly from the museum, who carried official-looking papers. After towing Newton into the brougham, the delegation swept away up Mill-bank to Horseferry, lapped round behind Westminster Hospital and flew north back across Victoria without realizing that they were chasing phantoms, that they hadn't an earthly idea as to the identity or the whereabouts of the mysterious thief.

The Lord Mayor pulled his folded speech from his coat pocket and squinted at it through his pince-nez a couple of times, pretty clearly worked up over not having been able to utilize it. Marleybone was in a foul humor, having had his fill of everything that didn't gurgle when tipped upside down. Newton somehow had gotten hold of the jack-in-the-box and, to the annoyance of his companions, was popping the thing off regularly. It had to have been at the crossing of Great George and Abingdon that a dog-cart containing a tall, gaunt gentleman wearing a Tamerlane beret and with an evident false nose plunged alongside and kept pace with the brougham. To the astonishment of the delegation, Newton (a powerful beast) burst the door from its hinges, leapt out running onto the roadway, and clambered in beside Falsenose, whereupon the dog-cart howled away east toward Lambeth Bridge.

The thing was done in an instant. The alien was gone, the infernal machine was gone, the ship, likewise, had vanished, and by the time the driver of the brougham could fathom the cacophony of alarms from within his coach, turn, and pursue a course toward the river, the dog-cart was nowhere to be seen.

A thorough search of the Victoria Embankment yielded an abandoned, rented dog-cart and a putty nose, but nothing else save, perhaps, for a modicum of relief for all involved. As we all know, the papers milked the crisis for days, but the absence of any tangible evidence took the wind from their sails, and the incident of "The Ape-Box Affair" took its place alongside the other great unexplained mysteries, and was, in the course of time, forgotten.

How Langdon St. Ives (for it was he with the putty nose), his man Hasbro (who masterminded the retrieval of the floating ship), and Newton the orang-outang wended their way homeward is another, by no means slack, story. Suffice it to say that all three and their craft passed out of Lambeth Reach and down the Thames to the sea aboard a hired coal barge, from whence they made a rather amazing journey to the bay of Humber and then overland to Harrogate.

This little account, then, incomplete as it is, clears up some mysteries—mysteries that the principals of the case took some pains, finally, to ignore. But Lord Placer, poor fellow, is dead these three years, Marleybone has retired to the sea-side, and Lord Bastable . . . well, we are all aware of his amazing disappearance after the so-called "cataleptic transference," which followed his post-war sojourn in Lourdes. What became of Jack Owlesby's pursuit of Olivia I can't say, nor can I determine whether Keeble hazarded the making of yet another amazing device for his plucky niece, who was the very Gibraltar of her family in the months that followed the tumult.

So this history, I hope, will cause no one embarrassment, and may satisfy the curiosities of those who recall "The Horror in St. James Park." I apologize if, by the revelation of causes and effects, what was once marvelous and inexplicable slides down a rung or two into the realm of the commonplace; but such explication is the charge of the historian—a charge I hope to have executed with candor.

Bugs

The last customer stopped at the door to wave. Ted happily waved back. He was always happiest when customers left. This one was maybe twenty years old and wore a white T-shirt with the face of Kerouac stenciled onto it. He had bought a Beat Poets Map, studded around the perimeter with ill-drawn faces of San Francisco writers and red X's to mark the spots where those luminaries had eaten and drunk and lived the Bohemian high life. The aluminum-frame door swung shut behind him and clipped his elbow, and Ted heard just the first note of a stifled grunt.

For a moment he was cheered by the whole episode, but then he was a little ashamed. He had embarrassed the kid by asking him about the black beret that had been shoved into a back pocket of his Levi's so as to be casually displayed. And then he had made up a transparent lie about his own days in North Beach, which the kid was forced out of politeness or stupidity to swallow. It was cheap as dirt to humor a customer, but somehow Ted couldn't manage it anymore. He was out of patience all the time these days, and he hadn't any reason to be.

Today maybe he did have a reason. It was his anniversary,

and he didn't feel very anniversarylike. There was something about the expectations that went along with a gala event that was almost guaranteed to make it less gala. He had screwed up in the gift department, too. He had forgotten all about it until the last moment, then called the local florist and had a bouquet sent over along with a card that he hadn't signed. It was the sort of remembrance you'd send to a bereaved widow because you didn't want to look her in the face.

He would find a way of making it up to her. Not being a shithead for one thing. Whatever Nona had planned was going to have to be all right with him—more than all right.

Just being alone in his bookstore should have been enough to loosen him up. It was pretty nearly perfect, as bookstores went—crammed with volumes in dark wooden cabinets he had designed and built himself. There were stacks of lawyers' bookcases too, that he had very nearly stolen at an antique auction in Los Angeles years ago. Now they lined twenty feet of one wall, full of first editions and old collectable, signed books that nobody bought. His cash register numbered the day's receipts. The Beat Poets Map, at $6.50, had been sale number nine.

He picked a pink fluorite crystal out of a wooden box on the counter. Beneath it were three hand-blown marbles and a trilobite fossil. Such things were like ballast to him, or perhaps amulets. Right at the moment, though, the charms kept their own secrets. The magic had gone out of them.

He set the crystal down and stepped across to lock the door. There were forty-five minutes to go before closing, but what was he waiting for? Sale number ten? He poured himself a glass of scotch from the counter bottle and sat back in his chair. A roach ran up the wall beside him—a little brown roach of the swarming variety. It was alone, out without its friends. He slammed at it with his bare fist, missing it by six inches. The tremor in the wall jarred it loose, and it fell to the floor and scuttled under the counter. Ted waited for it to reappear, but it was too canny and stayed hidden.

He leaned back, putting up his feet, pretending to have lost interest in the roach. On the wall in front of him was a

literary map of London in Dickens's day. He had been very
proud of it twenty years ago, back when he was a student.
Around the edge were drawings of Dickens and Keats and a
dozen other nineteenth-century writers. The irony of it
nearly made him laugh, and again he regretted having poked
fun at the poor aspiring Beat. He made a silent toast to the
kid's trip north to San Francisco. He hoped the kid found
what he was looking for and that for his own sake he left the
beret at home. Then he sipped the scotch, trying to remember
the impulses that drove youth to pursue its will-o'-the wisps
and wishing that he hadn't lost most of his.

He wondered what he meant, exactly—what it was he had
lost. Impulses? Youth? Will-o'-the-wisps? He didn't much
mind losing the last two. It was a more restful world than it
had been twenty years ago. Now he was married, and he loved
his wife, to whom he'd just sent an insulting anniversary gift.
Her being big about it would make him feel that much
smaller. It was impulses that were giving him trouble. For the
last few months—he didn't like to put too fine a point on it—
he'd had trouble holding up his end of the bargain in bed.

Now Nona was making anniversary preparations. There
had been something in the wind that morning. She had even
decided against going to work. She taught music to elemen-
tary school children, shuffling from school to school with a
carton full of triangles and sticks and cymbals. She was perfect for it. She had the patience of a stone idol. He realized
that he had been simmering in slow dread ever since breakfast, anticipating Nona's anniversary surprise and thinking
about his end of the bargain.

Nona knew that he was in the dumps and had determined to
cure him. It was stress, she said. But what stress? What did he
do but lounge around? He loved books, and here were books,
lining the walls. Of course, there was the tremendous pressure
of the mob of customers, all nine of them. Maybe that was it,
fear of financial failure. He couldn't fail financially, though, because his parents had left him a private income.

The roach crept out from under the counter and made a
run for a stack of books heaped against the wall, as if it were

invisible. Ted let it go, humoring it. When it was on the wall again he'd have another try at it.

Maybe he was just being morbid. Late afternoons were a good time for it. They were also a good time for thinking about food. He had seen a cartoon once in which Little Lulu confronted death, and her entire past flashed before her eyes—a nonstop waterfall of cakes and pies and ice cream and cookies. That's how his afternoons went, remembering and anticipating food. But today he had tried to eat a cheeseburger and french fries at one. They'd been greasy and cold and he had dumped half of them into the trash.

The roach reappeared, climbing the wall not three feet behind him. He had been told that they rode in on cardboard boxes, on trains out of the east, like hoboes. They fed on glue. The creature stopped, midway up the wall, playing possum. It was a subtle animal. It had been seen, and it knew it. It lived in a violent, hateful world, what with everybody despising roaches. Ted abruptly felt sorry for the thing, sitting there at the edge of death, peering into the abyss.

On impulse, he found a box under the counter, took a glass paperweight out of it, shredded the little bit of tissue paper in the bottom, and then slid it along the wall beneath the roach, which sprinted toward the edge of the closest bookshelf. He cut off the thing's retreat, flicking it down into the box, where it crept in under the nest of shredded tissue, hiding in terror. Ted dropped a couple of scraps of leftover cheeseburger in after it, then covered the box with a piece of cardboard, which he punched full of holes. He wasn't sure what he was going to do with the roach, but he felt a certain sympathy for it, which doubled, he was surprised to find, now that he had provided the thing with a home and a meal.

He picked up his felt-tip pen and wrote *East, West, Home's Best* on the side of the box, running a little curlicue out of the tail of the last *T*. Then he wrote *Moe* underneath, which was a good enough name for a roach.

He drifted into the storeroom. Something was being suggested to him, something that he couldn't glimpse except out of the corner of his eye. His desk was a littered mess, and he had to push papers out of the way to switch on the lamp. Books lay in heaps on the floor, waiting to be priced and shelved. He couldn't bear to look at them. He found his jar of thumbtacks and emptied it onto the blotter. Then, picking up a heavy, stainless-steel letter opener and holding it like a dagger, he hacked holes into the lid of the jar.

There was a spider under the counter out front. It had been there for days, spinning its web back in the corner. Ted didn't like spiders at all, but now it occurred to him that they would be about twice as tolerable if they were set up with a house and meal, just like the roach.

He was shoveling the spider into the jar, trapping it with the lid, when someone began knocking on the door. He froze, thinking at first to stay hidden behind the counter. Carefully, he peered Indianwise around the edge of it, holding the lid on the jar. The woman at the door waved at him happily.

There was a quartz crystal as big as a baby's fist hanging on a copper chain around her neck, and her hair had been done up, apparently, with an electric fan. She wore a low-cut, ground-length muumuu, spun out of flax or chaff or something, probably in Pakistan. Twenty years ago she had been a hippy, or else hadn't been and was making up for it now. She poked the spring-hinged mailbox open and chattered through it.

Ted couldn't entirely make out what she said, but it had to do with its still being ten minutes until closing and she had driven all the way out from somewhere and. . . . He moved across to unlock the door, thinking that he didn't have a jar big enough to fit the woman into. She wedged herself into the doorway when he had pushed the door only a third open, so that she blocked his way, and he couldn't push it any farther, and she had to hunch down to shove past him, brushing against him heavily, almost intimately. She smoothed the sides of her dress as if they had got crushed coming through, and took a curious look at the spider in the jar.

She reeled backward, grimacing.

"Spider," Ted said. "His name is Clyde." He found that he was still recovering from her entrance.

"He's a *pet?*" she asked, turning so that she looked at him out of the side of her head.

"Yes, he is. Silly, isn't it? It's a form of therapy, actually—the New Age approach to phobias. Effective, too. There was a time that the very sight of such a thing would have sent me toward the door. I'm just now feeding him."

"What?" she asked. "Flies?"

"No, bits of a cheeseburger. Defeats the purpose to feed them flies. It's a sort of Garden of Eden approach to therapy. Buddhist, really. Suggested by Eastern teachings. Gandhi and that crowd." It struck him suddenly that Eastern teachings would hardly suggest feeding cows to spiders, but the woman apparently wasn't having any trouble with the notion. This is just another customer, he told himself, and probably a very nice one. Settle down.

"I'm Laurinda Bates," she said, looking intently at the jar now. The spider stood across from the food, gathering courage, as if it had tackled flies and silverfish before, but never a piece of cow. "This is fascinating. What's in here?"

"Cockroach, actually. He and I are old friends. I used to have a horror of them, like most people do, but then I read some literature written by a man who had just spent three years in Nepal, and I saw the way. It was as simple as striking up a friendship. It's sort of like the notion that a friend of so and so's is a friend of mine. Befriend one roach and suddenly you don't hold a grudge against any roach. The same goes for the spider. Change species, though, and you've got to start fresh. An attachment to a daddy longlegs doesn't transfer, say, to a black widow."

"What a beautiful notion. It's simple, really, isn't it?"

"Nothing to it, and it works, too. I'm living proof."

"I'm the same way. I owned a collie as a girl. Marvelous dog. It died when I was in high school, and I've never had another dog, but I've loved collies ever since. All of them, instantly. I've never been able to abide those little smashed up dogs, though—pugs. Always running at the nose."

"That's it exactly. Can you believe that I know a man who was terrified of butterflies?"

"Why on earth . . ."

"Well, largely because in his mind he always imagined them without wings. Take their wings off and they're pretty horrible. Nothing but long, fleshy bugs. Anyway, he couldn't bear the sight of them. But it was awful, being deprived even of that little bit of beauty. It was like finding music intolerable."

"They're miniature works of art, nature's art."

"That's it in a nut. That's just what I told him. I bought him one of those cardboard caterpillar farms and had him raise a crowd of butterflies from babyhood. He named them, kept them in his kitchen window box, in among the potted plants. Do you know when he let them loose?"

"When?" Laurinda Bates stood with her hand held gently over her mouth.

"On the morning of the Harmonic Convergence."

"No! Perfect."

"Indeed it was. It was almost artistic, wasn't it? I like to think that when those butterflies flew away, one of his most profound fears flew with them, evaporating into the morning air."

"It's poetic, really."

Ted nodded, setting Clyde on the counter. He was doing it again. The young Beat at least had been a little skeptical, but Ms. Bates was willing to buy the bridge. He should sell her a book instead and send her on her way. She didn't deserve all this tomfoolery. It was just five now, time to head home. The thought of heading home didn't much appeal to him, though. He found himself thinking about her brushing against him in the doorway.

Also, there *was* something in what he was saying. There had been an almost instantaneous change in his attitude when he had made a home for the roach. Now it wasn't a cockroach and spider living on his countertop; it was Moe and Clyde, his bug friends. There was no way on earth that he could empty them out onto the floor and step on them. It was a matter of interpersonal relationships.

It occurred to him that he was in considerably better

spirits now than he had been a half hour earlier, and that there was nothing at all to account for it except for his treatment of the bugs. Who cared that all the Harmonic Convergence and Nepal stuff was lies? He caught himself eyeing the top of her dress when she bent over to read a book spine, and he realized that he was getting stirred up. He couldn't decide, though, whether the stirrings were good news or bad. She looked up at him and smiled, and he began talking without wanting to.

"There's a cumulative effect, though. In fact, that's the theme of my thesis on the subject and the beauty of the whole process. Befriend a half dozen different sorts of spiders and all of a sudden the distinction between species starts to blur. It's a sort of therapy in which there's an almost absolute, visible threshold, if that's the word I want. There's a point where you're cured, and the only thing that will throw you is running up against some new, really outlandish bug— some South American thing, maybe. In other words, unlike other psychological therapies, this isn't just maintenance; it's nuts-and-bolts repair work."

"Thesis?" she said, blinking at him. "Have you published your findings, then?"

Ted shook his head. He smiled steadily at her, on the edge of admitting that the whole bug notion was a monstrous joke, that he hadn't read New Age philosophy except to ridicule it, and that on the morning of the Harmonic Convergence he and his friend had netted a batch of butterflies in order to drop them into killing jars and mount them.

Instead he said, "Well, writing the thesis was instructive. It was a centering exercise, really. I don't regret its not being published. To some extent publishing is vanity, isn't it? On the other hand, there's the matter of helping people. To my mind, mere publication of one's results is like sending money to a charity for other people to spend, maybe unwisely. Setting up workshops, though, therapy sessions, hands-on exercises—that's like rolling up your sleeves and wading in. It's the Calcutta approach. Mother Theresa. That's where the joy lies."

"That's where the joy lies," she repeated. "When will you have another of these ... hands-on sessions?" She smoothed her dress again and widened her eyes at him.

He shrugged, unable for the moment to speak. "Soon," he said. "I'm ... I mean to say ..." What *did* he mean to say? Right then and there? On the countertop, maybe?

"I know a number of people who would attend. I belong to a literary group, actually." She made her way farther up the aisle and stood fingering through the volumes, squinting at titles. She was just a little red-faced, as though something she had said or was thinking had embarrassed her. The still air of the shop was suddenly saturated with a sexual charge that made him both uncomfortable and agitated. He listened to the clock tick and to the press of traffic rushing past outside.

"Do you have the book by the man who was abducted by aliens?" she asked abruptly, not looking up at him.

"That would be the gentleman who was carried downstairs by space elves and taken into the woods?"

"Yes. I understand that they did the most ... awful things to him. Devices, you know. Probes. They ... Nothing was private. He found the examinations ... stimulating. Have you read it?"

"Yes," he lied. "That is, part of it. They wouldn't let him rest, apparently. I read that he had mistakenly swallowed a glass eye, in a martini glass, I think. And that night they came to him in his sleep and took him away in a ship—strapped him down to an antigravity table and ... This is actually very delicate. It's science, of course, but maybe I'm presuming too much to talk about it."

"No," said Ms. Bates. "We're adults, aren't we? I find the study of humankind utterly fascinating. There's no part of us that's taboo, is there? Really, though, a glass eye?"

Ted shrugged and moved toward the counter. For a moment he thought he'd locked the door after she had come in, and was terrified. In a pinch he could simply bolt, out the door and across the asphalt of the parking lot. "That's the claim. Anyway, they took a good look through this camera. It was referred to, not to be indelicate, as a posterior probe, and, well, what did they see but the glass eye, wedged into the intestine, apparently, *peering down into the lens.*"

"No!"

"Honor bright. So the alien doctor looks up at his patient and says, 'Don't trust us, eh?'"

It took a moment for Ms. Bates to laugh. "You're full of sunshine, aren't you?" she asked. "Full of play." She took a step toward him and favored him with a lascivious glance. It was a come-hither look if he'd ever seen one. He had thought that the joke would put the hands-on business behind them. She took another step forward, saying nothing and with a look on her face that seemed to imply that everything had been said already.

For a moment he stood just so, regarding her with a look that he hoped was noncommittal. His mind spun. What would be the consequence of *his* taking a step toward her? They would be face-to-face then. In an instant he could lock the door, dash the lights. Would such a thing cure him or kill him? She stood before him now, silently.

Responding wildly to an impulse, he checked his watch, touched his forehead in surprise, and said, "I've got to call my wife. I should have been closed up ten minutes ago. Damn it, *twenty minutes.* I'll have to tell her to try to hold up dinner. She's cooking up something nice. It's our anniversary, actually." He smiled broadly, backing toward the counter, where the telephone sat.

"Oh," Laurinda Bates said, visibly deflating. She cast him a last, appraising look, as if to say that she hadn't given up on him altogether, but would grant him a temporary reprieve. "I'd better be on my way." She wrapped her hand around her quartz crystal, sucking up its imprisoned energy. "I'll carry the memory of the butterflies with me. Every day brings new insight, every moment an unfolding flower." She nodded at him in a slow, mystical way.

He was dumbstruck for a moment. "Of course," he said weakly.

"Have you made a study of past lives?"

"Not a very intense study, no."

"I have stirrings in me that suggest we might have known each other, known each other well—in Egypt, I think, in the days of the Pharaoh. I'll see you again. I'm sure of it. Do you have a flyer for your next session?" She picked up one of his fluorite crystals and held it for a moment before laying it gingerly on the glass, as if it were evidence of something.

"Session?"

"The phobia therapy."

"Oh, that. Of course. I mean, no—no flyers or anything. What I believe in is—what is it? Spontaneity."

"So do I," she said, and let herself out the door, giving him one last gap-toothed smile.

He slumped against the counter, sliding around behind and sitting down hard in the chair. There was a finger of scotch left in his glass, so he drank it quickly and then started to pour another, but caught himself. In twenty minutes he'd be home, and would have to be on his best behavior.

He let himself out into the evening. He would come in early tomorrow to count out. It wouldn't take five minutes. Surely the woman would forget about the bug nonsense and him both. That was the way with these flighty, faddish types. They were fascinated with what was new, whether it was worth anything or not, but they lost their fascination just as easily. Today's ankh was tomorrow's junk. He drove home unsteadily, trying to make sense of the afternoon and wondering what sort of anniversary surprise poor Nona had cooked up for him.

When he got home it was just coming onto six. There was the smell of cooked chicken in the air of the living room, and of something else that he couldn't identify. He peeked into the kitchen, looking for Nona, but she wasn't there. A pan on the stove had cubes of flaccid whitish stuff in it, mixed up with bloated raisins and nuts and little round gray slices of something—mushrooms, maybe, although not apparently of any terrestrial variety. All of it was settled into a spiced broth floating with cinnamon sticks and oddly shaped seeds. There was a tofu wrapper on the sink, which explained things. Bean curd, it said. God almighty. It didn't smell bad, anyway. Nona had been incorporating Asian elements into their diet, cutting out salt and dairy products.

Next to the wrapper, propped into an upright plastic sleeve, a magazine stood open, listing recipes for an entire soup to nuts dinner. The heading at the top of the page read, "Turn Your Man Back On!" and then provided instructions not only for cooking the dinner but for serving it too—in the bathtub. There was an illustration, sketchily drawn, of a couple lounging in the tub, dinner on a tray between them, glasses of champagne in their hands. The man looked insanely happy. Nearby were smaller illustrations of ingredients, including one of a phallic-looking mushroom pushing up through what must have been a lawn—one of God's little jokes. Ted took the lid off the pot again and studied the round gray slices, wondering if he could force himself to eat them.

He heard Nona shifting around upstairs. He stepped across the room, full of determination, and there, sitting on the kitchen table, were the sad flowers he'd ordered—a fat, mixed bouquet, mostly purple. A clear plastic forklike prong jabbed up out of the middle of them and gripped a tiny card. There was something artificial and horrible about it that depressed him unspeakably, and for a moment he fought the urge to pitch the entire thing out the front door.

The smell of cooking spices almost choked him, forcing him out of the kitchen and up the stairs toward the steamy bedroom. Surely that little bit of stuff on the stove couldn't be giving off such an odor. There was soap mixed into the cinnamon, like the smell of a shop full of scented candles or bath supplies. He could hear running bathwater and soft, rainy-day piano music.

The horrible thing was that he simply wasn't in the mood for a dinnertime frolic in the tub, or a frolic of any sort. How long had it been? He fought down the compulsion to calculate it. Instead he thought about Laurinda Bates to see if he would still react to the idea of a tryst in the darkened shop. Then he stomped on the idea almost as soon as it started to work on him. He had always been fiercely monogamous, partly out of an unnameable fear. He topped the stairs and peered around the corner.

Nona jumped in surprise. She was dressed in nothing but a loose blue bathrobe and she had her hair clipped up. She smiled at him with a look that suggested he'd been a wicked boy to startle her so, but that she was ready to be a little bit playful herself, and then, oddly, she began sprinkling chopped-up shrubs into the steamy bathwater. "Rough day?" she asked, seeing something in his face.

He shrugged. "Lunatic woman came in right at closing time. Full of notions about crystal power and aliens. I had to shoo her out, but it took a while. I developed a kind of interesting notion regarding phobias, actually." He stepped into the bathroom thinking to sit down on the closed toilet, but there was already an ice bucket and bottle of white wine on it.

"You'll have to use the downstairs," she said, grinning slyly. "This one's being put to special use tonight."

"No. I only . . . I didn't want to . . ."

"Oh," she said, and then stirred the bathwater with her hand. There was no end of stuff floating in it. "Phobias?"

"Bug phobias, actually. What's all that?" he asked, trying to sound both curious and pleased. Why such a thing as leaves in the bathwater should please anyone he couldn't say, but he could see straight off that it was safest to be pleased.

"Bath herbs," she said. "They have a medicinal effect. Did you know that lemongrass and ginseng are aphrodisiacs?"

He shook his head. "No, are they? In tea, do you mean? What is this, some sort of Oriental bathtub gin?"

"After a fashion. You don't drink it though. Glass of wine?"

"Thanks," he said, relieved. She handed him an already-full glass that she'd had waiting. The bottle on ice hadn't been touched. She was planning to liquor him up, wash some of the starch out of him. He pointed at the tub. "How about those lumps?"

"Rose hips," she said. "And the flowers are lavender and shredded hibiscus. Beautiful, isn't it?"

"Very colorful." Obediently, he forced himself to think

about the tub full of floating vegetation. It ought to have been an erotic notion. Maybe the wine would help. He picked up an apple core that lay on the sink counter and dangled it over the tub, dropping it like a bomb into a cluster of lavender leaves.

"What was that?" Nona asked.

"Apple core."

"Why on earth?" It bobbed to the surface and she plucked it out, shaking it off over the sink. She opened the cupboard door and tossed it into the trash can.

"I thought it was part of the mix. Sorry."

"It was my afternoon snack. I've been working up here for two and a half hours."

This was meant to sting. She'd been slaving over a hot tub, and he wanders in off the street and starts throwing apple cores around. "Honestly," he said, looking around as if to appreciate the spent time. "I thought it went into the stew." The bathroom had been scrubbed clean. The blue tile shined in the lamplight. She'd even polished the faucets and replaced the old shower curtain with a new curtain made of transparent plastic. Nona must have exchanged the two lightbulbs for one of lower wattage, too, because the place was dim and moody.

"Give it a try," she said, in a gentle but general sort of tone that took in the whole bathroom, the whole effort.

He leaned over and kissed her. She was doing what she could; what more could he ask? Fewer herbs in the bathwater, maybe. She slipped past him and started down the stairs, then stopped and looked back in. "I'm afraid that to do this right you'll have to be all comfy in the bath, with the board set up. I'll slide in under it after serving us both. Be a dear, won't you?"

He winked at her, and as soon as she was gone, he drank off the rest of the wine in his glass. He looked around for an open bottle, but there wasn't any, nor was there any bottle opener, so he couldn't have a go yet at the bottle on ice. Just as well. He'd be staggering in an hour if he kept at it. He was already feeling a pleasant, sleepy-cheerful rush from the wine. Must be his empty stomach. That would teach him to feed his lunch to bugs. He wondered idly how Moe and Clyde were getting on as he undressed, walking out into the bedroom to toss the clothes onto the chair. Then he went back in and eased into the bathwater, ignoring the floating herbs and appreciating the heat. This was really tip-top, a hot bath was.

He heard her footsteps coming up the stairs. "Bring the corkscrew?" he asked.

"Pocket of my robe," she said, stepping into the bathroom and turning so that he could fish it out of her pocket. She held a vast tray full of stuff that he couldn't quite glimpse, and which she set on the sink counter before going back out. There was a chicken there—he knew that much from the magazine—but it was hidden under a silver dome.

He reached back and pulled the wine out of the ice bucket. She'd bought a vintage chardonnay from a suspiciously French-sounding winery in Monterey. After opening the bottle and pouring a taste into the glass, he made a show of swishing it in his mouth, of doing things right. It tasted of grapefruit and charcoal.

Leaning against the counter was a piece of enameled plywood with strips of wood tacked onto the ends to keep it from sliding off the curved rim of the tub and into the bathwater. She'd clearly been planning this extravaganza for weeks. He pulled the board across the tub, almost up against his chest, settling back against the faucet to give Nona the comfortable end.

She came back in, carrying a silver plate, which she laid on the board in front of him. Then, carefully, she set the tray full of food next to it before slipping out of her robe, grabbing up her wineglass, and climbing into the water. She looked happy, as if things were finally coming together.

"Oysters?" he asked, nodding at the silver plate. "What happened to the shells?" The oysters were heaped there, a couple of dozen of them, damned in by a wall of lemon wedges.

"I shucked them all. Less debris this way, isn't there?"

She picked up an oyster and laid it out onto her palm, giving it a good hard look. Ted did too. Somehow this whole bathtub dinner business seemed very carefully choreographed, and he was determined to play his part with the oysters and to play it heroically. The soft and flabby oyster lay there in his hand, glistening like—what?—folds of . . . He poked at it idly with his finger but then Nona raised her eyebrow at him. He smiled at her, not knowing what to say.

It struck him suddenly that oysters were reputed aphrodisiacs, too. He was literally covered with sexual stimulants. He was swimming in them, eating them, studying them. He popped the creature into his mouth and let it slither down his throat, then reached immediately for his glass, which was empty. There was a lid over one of the dishes on the tray—probably the tofu stuff. He wondered if there was one of the oddball mushrooms inside, still whole, and draped across the top of the whole mess. He wouldn't be able to bear it. "Wine?" he asked, pouring it into their glasses.

"To us," she said, holding her glass aloft. He clinked the glasses together and drank, bolting another oyster and then drinking again. Conversation dwindled. "Run a little more hot," Nona said. She sighed complacently and sank deeper into the aromatic water.

He edged forward, turning on the hot water tap. Floating herbs swirled past, forced toward Nona's end of the tub. He pushed farther forward, up against the board, partly dislodging the Fitzall-Sizes plug beneath him. There was a murmur of slowly draining water, and it occurred to him that the plumbing would quite likely suffer for their extravagant bath. He edged the plug this way and that way until the murmuring stopped, and then shut off the tap before his rear end was parboiled. He felt a certain relief, as if he had completed a nice piece of work, and done it well. The wine was giving him a sense of proportion, of satisfaction, and the steamy bath was relaxing him into a pleasant sort of pudding. "I love the taste of these," he said. "Like pier pilings."

She gave him a look.

"No, I'm serious. Like the ocean—salty and cold. It's what people ought to mean when they talk about 'natural food.' What's under the dome?"

"Herbed chicken, baked with raisins and almonds. Middle Eastern dish."

"Mmm. Sounds all right. More wine?"

"I'm okay, thanks."

He poured more for himself, realizing that very soon he would have to answer for it—not with drunkenness, but with a trip downstairs to the second bathroom. Right now it was out of the question. Nona's foot shifted, running up along the inside of his leg. She was looking at him. He looked back and wiggled his toes against her flanks, meaning to be seductive but making a poor job of it.

"We're too damned rushed all the time," she said. "That can't be healthy. It ties us up in knots."

"This is untying me," he said truthfully.

"Is it?" She brightened. "Good. It was supposed to. The idea is to manufacture a total sensory bath. Not just the tub, but the herbs, the music, the food. All the senses massaged. It's the idea of the wholeness of true relaxation."

"Wholeness." That was one of the modern words, one of the sort he couldn't stand.

"Could you save the smarmy look for some other time?" she asked.

"I wasn't looking smarmy. I meant to agree with you. I haven't been this relaxed in weeks. I just don't . . . Sometimes it spoils things to talk about them, that's all."

She would like that; he was being open and honest.

"How will we get to the bottom of things if we don't talk about them?" she asked. "Bottling them up won't help. You bottle too much up." He was silent. "I don't mean to get on your case. I'm offering this in the way of constructive criticism. No, that's the wrong word. It isn't criticism at all. But you're bottling right now, aren't you?"

"Bottling," he said. "I like that better than wholeness. It's not sanctioned jargon though, is it? It can't be. It's too good

a word. Bottling. Bottle, bottle, bottle. Sounds like the name
of a shabby moron in a Dickens novel."

After a moment he said, "Now what? I was just being
silly. It was a compliment, really." She said nothing. "Now
who's bottling?" he asked.

Her face had a distant, saddened look on it, the look of a
mother who'd just got evidence that her favorite son had
been arrested breaking into a house. He picked up the wine,
even though their glasses weren't empty. "Sorry," he said.
"I'm a little beat, that's all. Bottle?"

She smiled. "Just a little," she said.

He filled her glass then filled his own, leaving a couple of
inches of wine in the bottom of the bottle. He didn't like the
idea of empty bottles. There was something finished and sad
seeming about them, the notion, perhaps, that the party had
ended. "I'm wondering about that chicken," he said.

"What are you wondering?"

"Whether it was stewed in the same herbs we're stewing in."

She pulled the dome off, and there the thing sat, sprinkled
with sweet-smelling herbs and ground spices. Spilling out of
it were nuts and raisins. The whole thing had been cut into
pieces and then reassembled. Nona could cook; he would admit that freely.

He ran more hot water while Nona dished chicken, spooning the tofu mix onto the side of the plate. He took the whole
mess from her and instantly forked up a slice of the sugges-
tive mushroom. There was no room here for half measures.
He had to tear into the loathsome heart of the dish to get over
his antipathy to it. Who was that Watergate conspirator who
had eaten rats to overcome his fear of the creatures? He loved
politics and politicians when they carried on like that. It was
fun to imagine what sorts of things they got into when they
were alone—eating rats, dressing in their wives' clothes, plot-
ting to wreck the leaf blower in their neighbor's garage. The
rat-eating man was considered a sort of paragon now. His rat
nonsense was reminiscent of Clyde and Moe, except that
Ted's own methods tended to civilize people and bugs both;
the rat-eating approach was a reversion to savagery.

"Like the mushrooms?" Nona asked.

"Yes," he lied. "Are these the . . . you know—dick mushrooms?" He smiled at her.

She put her fork down and stared at him.

"You know, the phallic things. The picture in the magazine. Where do you buy a thing like that?"

"Ranch market. They aren't cheap, either."

"Well you've got to admit what they look like. I didn't make that up, did I?"

She rolled her eyes at him comically. What he said must have been okay—maybe because it was overtly sexual. Sexual banter was good, even if it stemmed from mushrooms. Stems, phalluses—he struggled to turn the words into something clever. He gave it up and wiggled his toes against her again, giving her what he hoped was a tantalizing look, the look of a man worked over by aphrodisiac mushrooms.

She smiled back at him and leaned forward, running her hand up his leg, and suddenly the whole idea of the bath, of Nona lounging there in the heated water, shifted and settled in, moving down out of his head and into his midsection. She paused long enough to find her wineglass on the floor, and he shifted pleasurably beneath the plywood, knocking the edge of it with his knee. A chicken leg plopped off the plate into the bathwater, an oil slick blossoming around it like a ring around the moon.

Surreptitiously he palmed it and buried it under his thigh. Nona wouldn't see it there. When she was involved with something else he would drop it over the side. He wouldn't let her know it was in the water, though; that much was certain. Not after the apple core. And there was something about oily, cooked chicken in the bathwater that would spoil the romance of the whole endeavor.

Nona bent across the plywood, shoving up against it, sliding toward him. He bent across too, to kiss her. The sight of her breasts lying heavily on the board next to the remains of the food nearly drove him wild. He breathed hard, unable to do anything with his hands above the water except to paw her shoulders. Their dinner table had lost its usefulness. He grappled it out of the way, lifting it up and across, plates and dishes and all, laying it on the bath mat. The chicken tumbled off its plate and onto the floor tiles, but it didn't matter.

The water in the tub was almost opaque—dyed a pale red-green from the herbs, many of which had gotten soggy and sunk to the bottom. As the two of them moved around in the tub, squeaking into impossible positions, flower petals rose off the bottom, swirled to the top, and sank again. Nona slid her fingers along his leg, and he sank backward, cursing the faucet under his breath when it gouged him between the shoulder blades. She looked at him almost lizardlike, from under her lashes, seeming to imply that his little libido problem had been blown to smithereens, and that it had been her doing. He could be clever if he chose. He could make jokes. But being a mere man, full of animal passions, he would fall, if only a woman knew where to push.

She stopped. Her piano-playing fingers were still.

He half-sat up, starting to speak, abruptly horrified. She shoved against his chest with her left hand, shaking her head slowly, mouth half-open, her hand tugging softly at the chicken leg. He could feel it moving under his thigh. He flexed the muscle in his leg, pinning it there. What kind of horrible joke would she think he meant by it? What kind of psychotic . . .

She gave it a good yank, nearly going over backward—not with the force of the pull but with the shock of the gristly skin having come off in her hand. She jerked it up out of the water, gaping at it and throwing it at the same moment, rising half-out of the tub like a dripping Venus. She was incapable of speech, but her face was easy enough to read. This was like the apple core in the bathtub, only a million times worse. He tried to stand up himself to reason with her. But the act was beyond reason. Any further attempts at playing the dutiful, lustful husband were useless, a filthy charade. He waved the chicken leg bone, trying to think of something funny to say, trying to smile, but realizing at the same time that a smile would cement things in the worst way. He ditched the chicken bone in the water again.

"Honestly," he said, thinking that he'd heard himself say that more than once tonight. "I didn't mean . . . It was working, damn it!"

"What was working? I don't know what you had in mind—a childish joke or something worse. But it's ruined now. The evening is ruined. Shut up for once. Don't tell me what you meant. Not now."

Then she was gone along with her bathrobe. He sat silently until the bathwater cooled down; then he got out and toweled off, trying to rub the stuck-on herbs away. He picked the chicken up off the tiles and then drained the bath until it clogged, cleaned out the mess of stuff that had jammed up the drain, and so on until the tub was empty. Then he sponged it out, piled up the dishes, ice bucket, and bottle and took the whole mess downstairs.

For fifteen minutes he lay on the couch, with dark unfocused thoughts washing through his mind in the usual pattern. First he cursed the whole notion of dinner in the bathtub, of advice out of magazines, of unnatural mushrooms, of Nona's not giving him a chance to explain himself. He'd been misunderstood. She had jumped to conclusions, which was just like her.

Soon all of that faded. It occurred to him that senseless or not, her recipe had very nearly worked. It *had* worked. And it wasn't so long out of his mind that he'd cooled off. Just thinking about it now was enough to fire him up. There must be something he could do to set things right. An apology was the first thing.

He tiptoed upstairs. She lay sleeping, completely relaxed. He stood still for a moment, letting his eyes adjust to the semidarkness. It was warm in the bedroom, and she was half out of the covers. Her breasts pushed at the thin fabric of her nightgown as she breathed, and he found himself sorting shadows from flesh, not thinking, filled with loss and desire.

She deserved more than that. She deserved more than him abandoning her and then staggering upstairs an hour later in order to paw her when what she wanted to do was sleep. He'd had his chance, and had screwed up.

He turned around and went quietly back downstairs,

drifting into the kitchen. He passed the flower arrangement on the table. The flowers were fresh and smelled wonderful. Nona had probably loved them, and him for sending them. It was the sort of thing husbands and lovers did. He hadn't given her much of a chance to say so, though.

The moon shone through the window in front of the house. He went out through the door, onto the porch, where the night was still and cool. His hand slipped and the screen door banged shut. He held his breath, listening. Crickets chirped. Two night birds called to each other from the trees across the street. He pulled his bathrobe tight, wishing he had worn his slippers. There was just the hint of a misty chill in the air, and he could smell damp concrete and vegetation.

A junebug thumped against the screen door, almost next to his ear, and he ducked away in surprise. It lay there on the ground, next to the welcome mat, kicking its spindly little legs and revolving topsy-turvy on its back. He expected it to fly off, but it didn't, and he found himself thinking up and discarding names for it and wondering what kind of a creature it was that waited for good weather in order to fling itself futilely at window screens.

He knelt next to it. The beast made a frightful buzz, trying to scare him off, maybe. He poked at it with his index finger, and it grabbed his fingertip and clung there, quieting itself, seeming to sense that it was in a safe harbor at last. He picked it up and turned his hand over, and it crawled a couple of paces up toward his knuckle, holding on. He wondered idly what he'd do with the thing.

"What's happening, Lyle?" he asked it, thinking up the name on the spot. The bug wouldn't speak to him. "Do you need a house?" he said. "Someplace to live?" He looked around for an empty flowerpot.

The porch light blinked on just then, dim and yellow. Nona stood behind the screen. She was rumpled from sleep and she looked curiously at him standing there in his bare feet, apparently talking to a bug. The silent night lay like an ocean between them, as if each of them spoke in a tongue that the other couldn't begin to understand.

Perhaps because she mistook his silence for sullenness, she turned around and walked away toward the stairs, and he was left alone, holding the junebug, for which he had found it so easy to feel compassion.

"Wait!" he shouted. He wouldn't let her get away, not this time. He flicked his finger toward the lawn, and the bug flew off dizzily into the night. He hurried across the living room to where Nona waited for him at the foot of the stairs, holding the basket of purple flowers.

Nets of Silver and Gold

My wife and I were traveling along the Normandy coast when we met John Kendal in St. Malo. It was in a hotel café—the name of the place escapes me. He sat before a tremendous plate of periwinkles, all heaped into a little seashell monument. With a long needle he poked at the things, removing the gray lump inside each and piling it neatly on the opposite side of the plate. He worked at it for the space of half an hour, and in that time I had no idea it was my old childhood friend Kendal who sat there.

So intent and delicate were his movements that he gave the impression of someone suspicious that one of the periwinkles held a tremendous pearl, which would, at any moment, come rolling out of the mouth of a dark little shell on his plate.

It wasn't until he paused for a moment to sip his wine that I looked at his face and knew who he was. People change a great deal over the years, but Kendal, somehow, hadn't. His hair was longer and wilder, and he was twenty years older than I remembered him, but that's all. His antics with the periwinkles made perfect sense.

Seeing him there laboring over the shells reminded me of

our first meeting, forty years earlier when we were both boys. On the day after I'd moved into the neighborhood I came across him lying on the street, peering down through one of the nickel-sized holes in an iron manhole cover, watching the rippling water that ran along below the street and reflected a long cylinder of sunlight that shone through the opposite hole. He told me right off that he did most of his water gazing on partly cloudy and windy days when the passing shadows would suddenly darken and obscure the water below and he could see nothing at all. He'd wait there, gazing down into utter darkness, until without any warning the clouds would pass and the diamond glint of sunlight would reappear, sparkling on the running water.

It was all a very romantic notion, and I took to practicing the art myself, although not nearly as often as did Kendal, and always vaguely fearful that I'd be run down in the road by a passing car. He had no such fears. The sunlit waters implied vague and wonderful promise to him that I sometimes felt but never fully understood.

And here he was eating periwinkles in St. Malo. He was living there. I haven't any idea how he paid his rent or bought his periwinkles and wine. It didn't seem to matter. Nor did it surprise him that we'd met by wild coincidence, twenty years and six thousand miles distant from our last meeting in California. We hadn't even communicated in the intervening years.

As we sat into the evening and talked, I was struck by the idea that he'd become eccentric. Then it occurred to me that he'd been eccentric at eight years old when he'd spent his free time peering through manhole covers. What he'd become, I can't for the life of me say. My wife, who sees things more clearly than I do, understood immediately, even as she watched him manipulate his periwinkles, that he was slightly off center. Not the sort who goes raging about the streets with an axe, but the sort who doesn't even acknowledge the street, who looks right through it, who inhabits some distant shifting world.

That isn't to say that my wife disliked him. He won her sympathies at once by carrying on about the sunsets at St.

Malo, sunsets which, for two days running, we had missed
because I hadn't had the energy to walk from the railway hotel to the old city. He could see them, he said, from his window, which overlooked the sea wall and the scores of rocky
little islands and light towers that stretched out into the ocean
along the coast there. It was spectacular, the sun sinking like
a ball of wet fire into a sea turned orange. It seemed to set
purely for the amusement of the city of St. Malo. He had the
notion that if he could find just the right sort of rowboat—
the wooden shoe of Wynken, Blynken, and Nod or the pea-
green boat of the Owl and the Pussycat—he could catch the
sun as it set and follow it into the depths of the sea.

The next afternoon my wife and I drank a beer at a café
above that same sea wall and watched the sunset ourselves.
I'll admit that Kendal was right—not a half-mile of green
sea rolled between the rocky shore and the sun when it set.
There are legends, or so we were told, that when the old gods
fished from the rocks off St. Malo, one of them cast his
golden net with such force that it encircled the sun. Thinking
that he'd ensnared a great glowing fish, he hauled it almost
into shore before realizing his error and setting it free. The
sun had been so taken with the beauty of the coastline there-
abouts that it has since followed that same path every
evening when it sails from the sky.

It's quite possible that Kendal had heard the same tale and
that his nautical pursuit of the setting sun was suggested by
it. All in all it doesn't matter much, for it's just as likely that
if he had heard the myth, he half believed it. He had the uncanny ability to make others believe such tales too, just as
he'd imbued me with a sense of the importance of watching
that sunlit water beneath the street, for reasons that I can't at
all remember, reasons that have never been defined.

So we talked that first evening over wine and food, and I
discovered that he'd never given up the business of watching,
of peering through holes. He told us that he had taken for the
summer the most amazing rooms, directly above the sea
wall. They were in the oldest part of the city, all stone and
hand-hewn timber. He'd been told by the landlady that at one

time, hundreds of years ago perhaps, his room had attached to it a stone balcony, thrusting out over the ocean beyond a heavy, studded oak door. The stones had long since broken loose and fallen into the sea, and the old door had been nailed shut against the possibility of someone stumbling through it drunk or while sleepwalking, and dropping the thirty-odd feet into the tide pools below.

There was a keyhole in the door, however, encrusted with verdigris, through which one could peer out over the sea. Kendal, it seemed, spent a good deal of time doing just that. He could as easily have watched the sunsets through either of two long, mullioned windows in the same wall, but that, he quickly insisted, wouldn't have been the same thing. There was something about keyholes—about this particular key-hole—something he couldn't quite fathom.

My wife, not knowing him as I did, insisted that he ex-plain himself, and his story, I'm afraid, went a ways toward overturning the romantic notion she'd formed of him after his eloquent description of the sunsets.

He had been in the rooms a week before he even saw the key-hole. He was engaged, he said, in certain studies. The view from the windows was such that his eyes were inevitably drawn to and through them toward the sea so that he paid lit-tle attention to the old door. One afternoon, however, he'd been sitting at his desk working at something when he no-ticed through the corner of his eye that a thin ray of sunlight slanted in through the keyhole and illuminated a little patch of carpet, evoking, he said, old memories and fresh anticipa-tion. There was nothing for him to do but peer through the keyhole.

Shimmering beyond was an expanse of pale green ocean which joined, at the abrupt line of the horizon, an almost equal expanse of blue sky. It wasn't at all an odd thing to find, quite what he'd expected, but the simple symmetry of the sea and sky with their delicate Easter egg colors kept him at the keyhole for a bit, waiting, perhaps for a gust of wind to toss the surface of the sea or for a cloud to drift into view. As it happened, a sailing ship appeared, just spars and rigging at first, then the tossing bowsprit as the ship arched up over the horizon. He hadn't any idea what sort of ship it was; he knew nothing, he told us, of ships. But it was altogether a wonderful thing as it appeared there with its billowing sails and complexity of rigging and looking for all the world as if it had sailed from another age.

He leapt up and dug about in his wardrobe for a pair of opera glasses, then returned to the window to have a closer look at the antique ship. But there was, he insisted, no ship there. It must have swung around and sailed back out to sea—curious and unlikely behavior, it seemed to him.

Out of sudden curiosity he peered once again through the keyhole, but there was only the sea and the sky lying placidly, one atop the other.

He had suspicions, he said, about the keyhole, suspicions that had been fostered years before. He half felt as if the keyhole had been waiting there for him, impossible as that sounds on the face of it, and he determined, quite literally, to keep an eye on it.

His determination faded, however, as he became once again involved in his studies. He was standing at the window late the following afternoon thinking about the sunset and toying with the idea of going down to the café for a cup of coffee. He felt a bit of a fool, he said, for his suspicions about the keyhole, and he decided that it was time to lay them to rest. So he crouched before it and peered through, seeing, to his wild surprise, not ocean and sky and sailing boats, but a study, his own study: the littered desk between cases of books, the rose-colored armchair beside a tobacco stand, the ungainly pole lamp standing like an impossible stilt-legged flamingo with a hat on. He determined to keep watch, not to look away and so lose it like he had lost the incredible ship. He'd wait, he said, until something happened, anything.

But then he began to wonder at the odds and ends heaped on the desk. They were all familiar; nothing was there that shouldn't have been. But he couldn't be sure—he couldn't swear that the millefiori paperweight, an old French globe that was the only thing of real value he owned, wasn't in the wrong spot. There it was on the left of the desk, sitting atop a copy of *Mr. Brittling Sees It Through.* Yet he was almost sure that behind him it lay next to a bowl of oranges on the right. He could picture it in his mind. It sat opposite Mr. Brittling, not atop it.

It began to irritate him, like an itch that he couldn't quite reach. He had to know about the paperweight, and yet he was sure that if he turned, even for an instant, his mysterious keyhole study would sail off in the wake of the disappearing galleon. When he finally gave up and looked away, it seemed to him that he saw, just out of the corner of his eye, the study door begin to swing open as if someone were pushing in through it. But the momentum of rising carried him off, and when he peered through again, after just the slip of an instant, there was the tranquil sea, broken just a bit by little wind waves, and the blue expanse of sky interrupted by the rag-tag end of a fleeing cloud.

He'd been right about the paperweight. He was possessed thereafter with wonder at the nature of that keyhole. You and I would have been concerned with the nature of our minds, with our sanity, but not John Kendal. Just the opposite was the case. For a week he crouched there, spending long hours, squinting until he got a headache, seeing nothing but sea and sky and, in the evening, the setting sun. He'd sneak up on it. He'd act nonchalant, as if he were bending over before it to pick up a dropped pencil or a bit of lint from the carpet. But the keyhole, he said, couldn't be fooled. He even tried whistling in a cheerful and foolish manner to add credence to his air of unconcern. At night there was nothing but darkness beyond, darkness and a little cluster of stars. Later yet a glint of moonlight shone through maddeningly, only perceptible if the room were dark and if he stood just so, somewhere near the northeast corner of the study.

Bits of fleeting doubt began to surface toward the end of the week, the suspicion, perhaps, that he'd been the victim of a particularly vivid dream brought on by an overabundance of periwinkles, which, apparently, he ate by the bushel basketful. It occurred to him that his compulsion was very much like that of a peeping tom, and that his studies were woefully neglected. Finally he simply grew tired of it. He resolved late one Saturday night that he'd had enough, that he'd made a fool of himself and that he'd quite simply put the matter to rest by having nothing more to do with it. He'd shove a wad of chewing gum into the thing if he had to, buy a key and leave it in the hole so as to block the little cylinder of sunlight that filtered in. It was the sunlight, after all, that set him off. It was all very clear to him. Psychology could explain it. He was searching for that same sunlight he'd become so familiar with as a child. Well, he'd have no more of it.

So he sat there, pretending to be reading in his chair, but thinking, of course, of the keyhole—knowing that he was thinking about it and denying it at the same time. He wondered suddenly, irrationally, if the keyhole knew he was thinking about it, and if he hadn't ought to lazy along over toward it and have one last peek—just to put the issue to rest, to dash it to bits. He could see just the faintest silver thread of watery moonbeam slanting in, vaguely illuminating that bit of carpet.

He rushed at the door, casting his book down onto the armchair, pulling his pipe out of his mouth. He'd been tormented long enough. He'd have one last look, just to satisfy himself once and for all; then he'd stuff it full of something, anything—wet paper, perhaps, or a wad of sticky tape. Through the keyhole once again was his study. His book lay on the armchair. The telltale paperweight wasn't on the desk at all. It was in the hand of a woman with whom he was utterly unfamiliar. She had the complexion of a gypsy, he said, and the most amazing black hair and dark eyes. She was watching someone, that much was certain, smiling at someone—at him?—in a pouty sort of way. It was maddening. He shouted through the keyhole at her, something which must have sounded amazing and lunatic to his neighbors. A moment later there was a shuffling outside his study door, as if someone had come to investigate and was working up the courage to knock. He looked up quickly, cursing, fearing the disturbance that didn't come. And when he returned to his keyhole a moment later, there was, of course, nothing but the dark sea and sky and a few cold stars around a gibbous moon. The study and the gypsy were gone.

He was quite convinced that they weren't in any true sense gone; that they were real couldn't be argued. He became possessed by the idea that if the contents of his study existed on both sides of that door, then the dark woman with her pouty smile did also. It was merely a matter of time, he was sure of it, before he'd turn a corner on his way to the café or the railway station and catch sight of her. It wouldn't surprise him if he bumped into her at the market. He could picture it very plainly; her packages scattering, he apologizing, scooping them up, she with a look of vague recognition on her face, wondering at him, at their chance meeting. Dinner, perhaps, would follow. Or more likely she'd go along on her way. Then, a week later, a month later, he'd board the bus for Mont St. Michelle and there she'd be, beside an empty seat. It would be fate and nothing less.

At the time of our chance meeting over periwinkles, of course, fate hadn't yet played its hand. She never reentered either of the two studies. Kendal, however, spent more time than ever at his keyhole. He had no more misgivings. And he was rewarded for his faith, mostly by the sight of an empty, book-scattered room.

Once, early one morning, he peeped through and, with a thrill of strange apprehension, saw himself at work at his desk, writing madly, scribbling things down. Papers lay on the floor. His hair was tousled. He wore his salmon-colored smoking jacket, the one with Peking dragons on the lapels, and it appeared as if he'd been up all night—assuming, of course, that the world of the keyhole operated according to the same clock time as our world. But then who could say that it wasn't our world? Kendal wondered at first what in the devil he was working on with such wild abandon. It seemed to be going very well indeed, if the thirty or forty pages on the floor weren't scrap.

He watched himself write for a time, hoping, he said, for the return of the dark woman. He was possessed by the idea that she was his lover. His manic writing paused and he sat back in his chair and tamped a bit wearily at his pipe, blowing first through the stem to clear it out. He swiveled round, bent over, closed one eye, and peered, to Kendal's sudden horror, at the keyhole. In a fit of determination he slammed his pipe into an ashtray, rose, and strode across toward the old door, bending and peering, his eye hovering not three inches from the eye of his shellfish-loving counterpart. For one strange moment, said Kendal, he didn't know absolutely who he was, or which study he occupied. He pinched himself, trite as it sounds, and convinced himself that he, at least, was no figment. "Hello!" he shouted. "There is someone here! You're not imagining things!" It felt good to reassure himself. "You're perfectly sane!" he shouted a bit louder. The eye disappeared. There was a knocking at his study door which nearly tumbled him over backward. For one sudden moment he'd been certain that the knocking had come from the door into the other study. But it hadn't. There was another knock, and when he opened the door and looked out into the hallway, there was his landlady, giving him the glad eye. She looked past him into the empty room, nodding to him, asking him some contrived question about the rent. He shook his head and was brusque with her, he said, which was unfortunate, because in truth she was a friendly sort. Her concern was justifiable. He hurried her away and bent back across to his keyhole.

The study beyond was empty. The papers on the floor had been gathered into a heap that lay beside the desk. Obviously they weren't trash. It had been a productive night, the sort that gave him a great deal of satisfaction, a sense of well-being. He watched the empty study for an hour, waiting there, and was surprised to see, suddenly, a widening patch of sunlight playing out quickly across the floor, as if someone were opening a door and a quick rush of daylight were flooding in. Just as suddenly it was cut off. It wasn't the study door that had opened in the room beyond; he could see the edge of it quite clearly off to the left of the desk. And it wasn't curtains being drawn; he hadn't any curtains. No, a door had been opened, that much was sure, and there could be no doubt which door it was.

He paused in the telling of his story and filled his glass. He'd worked himself into a state. His hand trembled. My wife raised her eyebrows at me, but Kendal didn't see it. He was lost in his tale. He ordered coffee and heaped sugar into it, begging us not to assume that he'd gone mad.

"Of course not," said my wife. "Of course not."

"What I saw," he continued, gazing into his coffee, "were little men."

My wife choked on her wine. It wasn't hard to guess why, but she made a grand effort to make it seem otherwise. Kendal held up a knowing hand and shook his head quickly, as if he were satisfied with her disbelief.

I put on a serious face. "Little men?" I said. "Midgets, do you mean?"

He shrugged.

What he had seen at first were the shadows of whoever had come through the old door. He wondered, straight off, where they had come from. After all, he had been peering through a keyhole in the door in question. There was, it seemed, a door beyond the door, and perhaps others beyond that—countless others—a veritable mirrored hallway of reflected doors with little men creeping about down the corridors, and dark women stealing out of one door and through another, and doors creaking open to reveal the wave-tossed galleon slanting in toward a rocky shore. Kendal saw endless possibility, but he hadn't enough time right then to be anything but mystified by it.

One of the little men, as he insisted on calling them, began to haul volumes out of the bookcases, tossing them around onto the floor. Another picked up the piled papers, rummaged in the desk drawer for a pair of scissors, and began cutting

paper dolls—strings and strings of them. Another wrestled
several pages away, found a pencil, and set out to doctor up
the manuscript, chewing the end of his pencil, laughing and
scribbling away. Yet another appeared, to Kendal's horror,
opening the liquor cabinet and yanking out bottles, examining labels, nodding over them with a satisfied air. Pieces of
clothing flew into sight, tossed, no doubt, from the closet by
a fifth and unseen vandal. His favorite tweed coat shot out,
folding over the shade of the pole lamp and hanging there
sadly as the liquor cabinet elf squirted at it with the soda water siphon. It was a sad state of affairs. Any possible humor
in the scene was dashed by the certain fact that it was his
rooms being ransacked, that it was his tweed jacket that lay
now in a sodden heap on the floor beside the overturned
lamp. One of the devils juggled the paperweight along with
two oranges. He was wonderfully dexterous. Kendal held his
breath. The one who had been at his clothes wandered in
with a hammer. He snatched one of the oranges from the juggler, set it atop Mr. Brittling, and smashed it to pulp. Then he
made a grab for the paperweight. Kendal was stupefied. The
juggler dropped both the weight and the orange and they
rolled out of sight behind the armchair. A struggle ensued,
one elf poking the other in the eye and yanking at his hair,
the other threatening with his hammer, fending the first off.
They collapsed onto the carpet and went scrambling out of
view. Kendal watched in futile horror the head and upper
handle of the hammer rise and fall three times above the
back of the chair. He shouted into the keyhole, screamed into
it, whacked his fist against the door. There was a general
pause within. He'd been heard. He was quite sure of it. The
elf with the soda water bottle hunched over, squinting toward
him, stepping across on tiptoe as if he were the soul of se-
crecy, and with a mad grin he aimed the siphon at the keyhole.

Kendal leapt to his feet. He wouldn't, he said, stand the
indignity of it. He felt as if he were a character in a foolish
play, as if a crowd of people were watching, laughing at his
expense. (My wife pinched me under the table.) He waited

for a moment, fully expecting soda water to splatter through the keyhole. Nothing happened. He was sure, he said, that they were hovering there, that when he looked again they'd all be waiting, laughing, would squirt him in the eye. But when he could stand it no longer, he peeked through and saw no little men, no study, no gypsy temptress—only the sea and the sky and, to his amazement, the old galleon, sails reefed, riding on the calm water a half mile off shore.

He sat most of the rest of the day in the café above the sea wall, watching the sun fall. He could see, from where he sat, the old studded door that opened into empty air, and he tried to convince himself that if he squinted sharply enough or turned his head just so, he could make out phantom shapes, figments, ghosts perhaps, fumbling around outside that door, carrying on.

He knew, he said, that he should be recording all this business about the keyhole—writing it down. In print, perhaps, the pieces would fall into order. He could look at it with an objective eye, get his bearings. The more he thought about it, the more necessary the task became, and late that evening he returned to his rooms, sat at his desk, and began to write. He scribbled feverishly, casting finished pages over his shoulder, littering the floor. He speculated and philosophized. As it grew later his ideas and the events that prompted them seemed to deepen in importance, as if the night was salting the affair with mystery. Some of it, he insisted, was shamefully maudlin—the sort of thing you write late at night and pitch into the trash in the light of day.

Early the next morning he found himself empty of ideas, seated at his desk, dressed in his smoking jacket with the Peking dragons on the lapels. It was only then that the thought struck him—the idea that he was being watched through the keyhole, that he was watching himself.

"What does all this mean?" he cried, facing the studded door. There was, of course, no response. He snatched up a clean sheet of paper and a pen. "Write a message," he wrote. "Roll it up and poke it through the keyhole." He stood before the desk holding it up so that if indeed he were watching just then he'd get a good look at it. It was a brilliant idea. He waited for a bit but nothing happened. He stepped across and peeked through the keyhole and was rewarded with the sight of the ruined study. The little men had gone and had quite apparently taken his liquor with them. He tore off excess paper from around his note and rolled what was left into a tight little tube. Then he twisted it even tighter and threaded it through the keyhole, shoving it past the far side with the end of a coat hanger. When he peered into the keyhole again the study had vanished. He was exhausted, he told us, from the ordeal. He decided at first to sleep, not so much out of the need for it, as to be on hand if the little men appeared. But then he vowed that they wouldn't hold him in thrall. He'd go about his business. Let them play their pranks! If he caught them at it he'd make it warm for them. They'd sing a sorry tune. He'd force them, he said, to take him along aboard the galleon. Just to play devil's advocate he drank two quick fingers of his best scotch—they wouldn't have all of it—and he went out onto the street, locking the door behind him, and spent the better part of the day walking, one eye out for the gypsy girl with the pouty lips.

Some time around two in the afternoon he began to grow anxious. He remembered, suddenly, the sight of the hammer rising and falling beyond the armchair, and he cursed himself for not having slipped the paperweight into his pocket. There was nothing for it but to return at once—to make sure. His wandering about town had accomplished nothing anyway. If he was fated to find the dark woman, then he'd find her, or she him. He might as well be anywhere. He hurried along, and as he drew closer to home he became more certain of what he'd find. As it turned out, he was half correct.

His study was a mess. The tweed coat was a ruin, sprayed with soda water and crushed orange. His papers were reduced to snippings and his books littered the floor. *Mr. Brittling Sees It Through* was the sorriest of the lot. The liquor cabinet was empty but for a half bottle of crème de menthe from which the cap had been removed. He was furious. He stormed back and forth, nearly stumbling over the remains of the broken paperweight that had somehow been knocked under the sleeve of his soaked coat. It lay in two neat halves, the edges of several glass canes protruding through the broken sides like little pieces of Christmas candy. The hammer from the shelf in his closet lay beside it.

Kendal raged about, trying to think, waving the hammer over his head. He strode toward the door, understanding what it was he had to do. And it was then that he saw what he hadn't expected to see: a little rolled and twisted bit of paper lying right at the edge of the carpet. He unrolled it, shaking. "Write a message," it read. "Roll it up and poke it through the keyhole."

"By God!" he shouted. "We'll see!" And he began to pry out the nails that held the door shut. It wasn't an easy thing. Not by a long sight. He had to rather beat the door up to get at them. But he was determined—he'd come to the end of his rope. One by one they squeaked loose. He paused after the fourth to peer through the keyhole, and there was the sun, the sky, a cloud. Below lay the sea, calm and glistening and dappled with sunlight, broken by a long rowboat in which sat five little men, one at the tiller and four more pulling on the oars, making away toward the setting sun and the galleon anchored offshore, heaving on the ground swell.

He wrenched at the nails. He tore at them. He knew it would do him no good to go to the windows. He couldn't get at them through the windows. He peered through the keyhole again. The rowboat was a speck on the water. Finally the last of the nails pulled loose, and, shouting, he pushed the door outward on its hinges with such a rush of relief and anticipation that he nearly pitched out into the open air. He caught himself on the old jamb and hung on, searching the horizon for the galleon. There was nothing there. At the café below him, a dozen idlers gawked up, puzzled, wondering at his antics. He couldn't be sure, he said, which world they occupied, so he searched for himself on the veranda, but didn't seem to be there. Slamming the door shut, he hurried down and asked them about the elves in the rowboat, but the lot of them denied having seen anything. They winked at each other. A fat

man with ruined shoes laughed out loud. Kendal raged at
them. He knew their kind. Did they want to see what those
filthy devils had done to his rooms? None of them did.

Kendal poked idly at his sea shells, stirring them around on
their plate. He had calmed down a bit later, he told us, regretting his folly. The people in the café would think him a
wildman, a lunatic. My wife shook her head at that. "Not at
all," she said, hoping to cheer him. He shrugged in resigna-
tion and emptied his coffee cup. From the pocket of his coat
he pulled a crystal hemisphere, his antique paperweight, and
he showed it to us very sadly, pointing out certain identifying
marks: a peculiar pink rose, a glass rod with a date in it—
1846 I believe it was. The top of the thing was spider-webbed
with cracks where it had been struck with the hammer. It
seemed to us that Kendal could hardly bear looking at it, but
that he had it with him as a bit of circumstantial evidence.

   After the shouted accusations in the café, he'd walked
about town again, searching, and had ended up at the restaurant in our hotel, eating periwinkles. It was there that we'd
found him.

   He'd been fairly buoyant, wrestling with his shellfish and
sipping wine, and, as I said, his discussion of the sunsets was
engaging. By the time he'd come to the end of his tale, however, he was as deflated as a sprung balloon. He looked very
much like a man who hadn't slept in two days. We started in
on another bottle of wine, and he toyed with the idea of eating more shellfish and spoke desultorily about his mystery,
now and then breaking into rage or rapture. He seemed particularly enthralled by the possibility that the little men had
heard him shout at them, could quite possibly have squirted
soda water into his eye through the keyhole. It seemed to hint
at connections, real connections. He had pretty well run himself down when on the sidewalk outside, in the glow of the
lamps, a little knot of people hurried past. One was an olive-
complected woman with long black hair and deep, dark,

round eyes and full lips. She looked in briefly (as did several of the others) as she walked past, disappearing quickly into the night.

Kendal sat for a moment, frozen, with a wild look in his eye. He jumped up. I wanted to protest. My wife clutched my arm, encouraging me, I suppose, to dissuade him. Enough was enough, after all. But I wasn't at all sure that he hadn't every reason to leap up as he did. He shouted his address to us as he raced out of the restaurant, forgetting entirely to pay his bill, which had amounted by then to about thirty-five francs. We settled it for him and rose to leave. There on the table, shoving out from beneath the cloth napkin, was the broken crystal paperweight with its little garden of glass flowers. I dropped it into the pocket of my coat.

I revealed to my wife, as we walked down the road toward the sea, Kendal's youthful predilection for gazing down manhole covers. There had been other habits and peculiarities— rhinestone and marble treasures that he buried roundabout in his childhood, drawing up elaborate maps, hiding them away and stumbling upon them years later with wild excitement and anticipation. I recalled that he'd once gotten hold of an old telescope and spent hours each evening gazing at the stars, not for the sake of any sort of study, mind you, but just for the beauty and the wonder of it.

My wife, of course, began to develop suspicions about poor Kendal. I produced the broken paperweight and shrugged, but she pointed out, no doubt wisely, that a broken paperweight was hardly evidence of a magical keyhole and of little men coming and going across the sea in an old galleon that no one but John Kendal could see. I put the paperweight away.

Next day we were both in agreement about one thing— that we'd look Kendal up in his rooms. My wife affected the attitude of someone whose duty it was to visit a sick friend, but I still suspect that there was more to it than that; there certainly was for me. We decided, however, to wait until evening so as to give him a chance to sleep.

We found ourselves eating supper at the café that had

figured so prominently in his story. We sat outdoors in a far corner of the terrace where we could see, quite clearly, Kendal's studded door. I admit that I could perceive no evidence of any ruined balcony—no broken corbels, no cracked stone, no rusty holes in the wall where a railing might have been secured.

We finished our meal, left the café, and followed cobbled streets up the hill. Quite truthfully, I felt a little foolish, like a Boy Scout off on a snipe hunt or a person who suspects that the man he's about to shake hands with is wearing a concealed buzzer on his palm. Part of me, however, not only believed Kendal's story, but very much wanted it to be true.

We found his rooms quite easily, but we didn't find Kendal. He wasn't in. The door was ajar about an inch, and when I knocked against it, it creaked open even farther. "Hello!" I shouted past it. There was no response. "I'll just tiptoe in to see if he's asleep," I told my wife. She said I was presuming a great deal to be sneaking into a man's rooms when he was out, but I reminded her that at one time Kendal and I had been the closest of friends. And besides, he'd quite obviously been despondent that previous evening; it would be criminal to go off without investigating. That last bit touched her. But as I say, there was no Kendal inside, asleep or otherwise. There was quite simply a mess, just as he had promised.

He'd made some effort at straightening things away. Half the books had found their way haphazardly onto the shelves; the rest were stacked on the floor. The tweed coat lay in its heap, and I'll admit that the first thing I did when I entered the room was to feel it. The top had dried in the air, but it was still wet beneath, and stiff with the juice and pulp of squashed orange. On the desk lay the copy of Wells's *Mr. Brittling Sees It Through*, covered with the remains of a second orange. His liquor cabinet sat empty but for the uncapped bottle of crème de menthe. Half of the broken paperweight lay canted over atop the desk. Clothing littered the floor about the door of the closet. All of it bore out Kendal's tale.

Protruding from the keyhole in the old door was a twisted bit of paper. My wife, as curious by then as I was, pulled the thing out and unrolled it. Written on it in block letters were the words, "I must speak to you." In what time or space they'd come to be written, I can't for the life of me say. It was impossible to know whether the message was coming or going.

My wife pushed open one of the big mullioned casement windows and I looked out at the setting sun. She called me over and pointed toward the tidepools below. There, among anemones and chitons and crabs, floated a half dozen bits of paper, some still twisted up, some relaxed and drifting like leaves. In another hour the tide would wash in and carry them away.

On impulse I bent over to have a look through that keyhole, a thrill of anticipation surging within me along with vague feelings of dread, as if I were about to tear open the lid of Pandora's box or of the merchant Abudah's chest. I certainly had no desire to have my tweed coat pulped with oranges, and yet if there were little men afoot, coming and going through magical doors . . . Well, suffice it to say that I understood Kendal's quest in quite the same ethereal and instinctive way that I understood his peering down holes in the street forty years earlier.

So I had a look. Just touching the dark sea was a vast and red sun. Silhouetted against it were the spars and masts of a wonderful ship, looping up over the horizon, driving toward shore. And rowing out toward the ship, long oars dipping rhythmically, was a tiny rowboat carrying a man with dark, wild hair. On a thwart opposite sat the olive-skinned woman. I'm certain of it. That they were hurrying to meet the galleon there can be no doubt. They were already a long way from shore.

"Do you see it?" I cried.

"Yes," said my wife, supposing that I was referring to the sunset. "Beautiful isn't it?"

"The ship!" I shouted, leaping up. "Do you see the ship?" But of course she didn't. Through the windows there was no ship to be seen. Nor was there any rowboat. "Through the keyhole!" I cried, "Quickly."

To humor me, I suppose, she had a go at it. But there was nothing in the keyhole but the tip of the sun, just a tiny arched slice now, disappearing beneath the swell. She stood up, raised her eyebrows, and gestured toward the keyhole as if inviting me to have another look for myself. Nothing but cold green sea lay beyond, tinted with dying fire. We left a note atop his desk, but either he never returned, or he hadn't the time or desire to visit us at our hotel. I suspect that the former was the case. Our train left for Cherbourg next morning.

We haven't seen him since. It's possible, of course, that we will, that his travels will lead him home again to California and that he'll look us up. He has our address. But as for myself, I rather believe that we won't, that his course is set and that his travels have led him in some other direction entirely.

The Better Boy

with Tim Powers

*K*nock knock.

Bernard Wilkins twisted the scratched restaurant butter-knife in his pudgy hand to catch the eastern sun.

There was a subtle magic in the morning. He felt it most at breakfast—the smells of bacon and coffee, the sound of birds outside, the arrangement of clouds in the deep summer sky, and the day laid out before him like a roadmap unfolded on a dashboard.

This morning he could surely allow himself to forget about the worms and the ether bunnies.

It was Saturday, and he was going to take it easy today, go home and do the crossword puzzle, maybe get the ball game on the radio late in the afternoon while he put in a couple of hours in the garage. The Angels were a half game out and were playing Oakland at two o'clock. In last night's game Downing had slammed a home run into the outfield score-board, knocking out the scoreboard's electrical system, and the crowd had gone flat-out crazy, cheering for six solid minutes, stomping and clapping and hooting until the stands were vibrating so badly that they had to stop the game to let everybody calm down.

In his living room Wilkins had been stomping right along with the rest of them, till he was nearly worn out with it.

He grinned now to think about it. Baseball—there was magic in baseball, too ... even in your living room you could imagine it, beer and hot dogs, those frozen malts, the smell of cut grass, the summer evenings.

He could remember the smell of baseball leather from his childhood, grass-stained hardballs and new gloves. Chiefly it was the dill pickles and black licorice and Cokes in paper cups that he remembered from back then, when he had played little league ball. They had sold the stuff out of a plywood shack behind the major league diamond.

It was just after eight o'clock in the morning, and Norm's coffee shop was getting crowded with people knocking back coffee and orange juice.

There was nothing like a good meal. Time stopped while you were eating. Troubles abdicated. It was like a holiday. Wilkins sopped up the last of the egg yolk with a scrap of toast, salted it, and put it into his mouth, chewing contentedly. Annie, the waitress, laid his check on the counter, winked at him, and then went off to deal with a wild-eyed woman who wore a half dozen tattered sweaters all at once and was carefully emptying the ketchup bottle onto soda crackers she'd pick out of a basket, afterward dropping them one by one into her ice water, mixing up a sort of poverty-style gazpacho.

Wilkins sighed, wiped his mouth, left a twenty percent tip, heaved himself off the stool and headed for the cash register near the door.

"A good meal," he said to himself comfortably, as if it were an occult phrase. He paid up, then rolled a toothpick out of the dispenser and poked it between his teeth. He pushed open the glass door with a lordly sweep, and strode outside onto the sidewalk.

The morning was fine and warm. He walked to the parking lot edge of the pavement, letting the sun wash over him as he hitched up his pants and tucked his thumbs through his belt loops. What he needed was a pair of suspenders. Belts weren't worth much to a fat man. He rolled the toothpick back and forth in his mouth, working it expertly with his tongue.

He was wearing his inventor's pants. That's what he had come to call them. He'd had them how many years? Fifteen, anyway. Last winter he had tried to order another pair through a catalogue company back in Wisconsin, but hadn't had any luck. They were khaki work pants with eight separate pockets and oversized, reinforced belt loops. He wore a heavy key chain on one of the loops, with a retractable ring holding a dozen assorted keys—all the more reason for the suspenders.

The cotton fabric of the trousers was web-thin in places. His wife had patched the knees six different times and had resewn the inseam twice. She wasn't happy about the idea of him wearing the pants out in public. Someday, Molly was certain of it, he would sit down on the counter stool at Norm's and the entire rear end would rip right out of them.

Well, that was something Wilkins would face when the time came. He was certain, in his heart, that there would always be a way to patch the pants one more time, which meant infinitely. A stitch in time. Everything was patchable.

"Son of a bitch!" came a shout behind him. He jumped and turned around.

It was the raggedy woman who had been mixing ketchup and crackers into her ice water. She had apparently abandoned her makeshift breakfast.

"What if I am a whore?" she demanded of some long-gone debating partner. "Did he ever give me a dollar?"

Moved somehow by the sunny morning, Wilkins impulsively tugged a dollar bill out of his trousers. "Here," he said, holding it out to her.

She flounced past him unseeing, and shouted, at no one visibly present, a word that it grieved him to hear. He waved the dollar after her halfheartedly, but she was walking purposefully toward a cluster of disadvantaged-looking people crouched around the Dumpster behind the restaurant's service door.

He wondered for a moment about everything being, in fact, patchable. But perhaps she had some friends among them. Magic after all was like the bottles on the shelves of a dubious-neighborhood liquor store—it was available in different proofs and labels, and at different prices, for anyone who cared to walk in.

And sometimes it helped them. Perhaps obscurely.

He wasn't keen on revealing any of this business about magic to anyone who wouldn't understand; but, in his own case, when he was out in the garage working, he never felt quite right wearing anything else except his inventor's pants.

Somewhere he had read that Fred Astaire had worn a favorite pair of dancing shoes for years after they had worn out, going so far as to pad the interior with newspaper in between re-solings.

Well, Bernard Wilkins had his inventor's trousers, didn't he? And by damn he didn't care what the world thought about them. He scratched at a spot of egg yolk on a pocket and sucked at his teeth, clamping the toothpick against his lip.

Wilkins is the name, he thought with self-indulgent pomposity—invention's the game.

What he was inventing now was a way to eliminate garden pests. There was a sub-sonic device already on the market to discourage gophers, sure, and another patented machine to chase off mosquitoes.

Neither of them worked worth a damn, really.

The thing that really worked on gophers was a wooden propeller nailed to a stick that was driven into the ground. The propeller whirled in the wind, sending vibrations down the stick into the dirt. He had built three of them, big ones, and as a result he had no gopher trouble.

The tomato worms were working him over hard, though, scouring the tomato vines clean of leaves and tomatoes in the night. He sometimes found the creatures in the morning, heavy and long, glowing bright green with pirated chlorophyll and wearing a face that was far too mammalian, almost human.

The sight of one of them bursting under a tramping shoe was too horrible for any sane person to want to do it twice.

Usually what he did was gingerly pick them off the stems and throw them over the fence into his neighbor's yard, but they crawled back through again in the night, further decimating the leaves of his plants. He had replanted three times this season.

What he was working on was a scientific means to get rid of the things. He thought about the nets in his garage, and the boxes of crystal-growing kits he had bought.

Behind him, a car motor revved. A dusty old Ford Torino shot toward him from the back of the parking lot, burning rubber from the rear tires in a cloud of white smoke, the windshield an opaque glare of reflected sunlight. In sudden panic Wilkins scuffed his shoes on the asphalt, trying to reverse his direction, to hop back out of the way before he was run down. The front tire nearly ran over his foot as he yelled and pounded on the hood, and right then the hooked post from the broken-off passenger-side mirror caught him by the key chain and yanked his legs out from under him.

He fell heavily to the pavement and slid.

For one instant it was a contest between his inventor's pants and the car—then the waistband gave way and the inseam ripped out, and he was watching his popped-off shoes bounce away across the parking lot and his pants disappear as the car made a fast right onto Main.

License number! He scrabbled to his feet, lunging substantially naked toward the parking lot exit. There the car went, zigging away through traffic, cutting off a pickup truck at the corner. He caught just the first letter of the license, a G, or maybe a Q. From the mirror support, flapping and dancing and billowing out at the end of the snagged key chain, his inventor's pants flailed themselves to ribbons against the street, looking for all the world as if the pantlegs were running furiously, trying to keep up with the car. In a moment the car was gone, and his pants with it.

The sight of the departing pants sent him jogging for his own car. Appallingly, the summer breeze was ruffling the hair on his bare legs, and he looked back at the restaurant in horror, wondering if he had been seen.

Sure enough, a line of faces stared at him from inside Norm's, a crowd of people leaning over the tables along the parking lot window. Nearly every recognizable human emotion seemed to play across the faces: surprise, worry, hilarity, joy, disgust, fear—everything but envy. He could hear the whoop of someone's laughter, muffled by the window glass.

One of his penny-loafers lay in the weeds of a flowerbed, and he paused long enough to grab it, then hurried on again in his stocking feet and baggy undershorts, realizing that the seat of his shorts had mostly been abraded away against the asphalt when he had gone down.

Son of a bitch, he thought, unconsciously echoing the raggedy woman's evaluation.

His car was locked, and instinctively he reached for his key chain, which of course was to hell and gone down Seventeenth Street by now. "Shit!" he said, hearing someone stepping up behind him. He angled around toward the front of the car, so as to be at least half-hidden from the crowd in Norm's.

Most of the faces were laughing now. People were pointing. He was all right. He hadn't been hurt after all. They could laugh like zoo apes and their consciences would be clear. Look at him run! A fat man in joke shorts! Look at that butt!

It was an old man who had come up behind him. He stood there now in the parking lot, shaking his head seriously.

"It was hit and run," the old man said. "I saw the whole thing. I was right there in the window, and I'm prepared to go to court. Bastard didn't even look."

He stood on the other side of the car, between Wilkins and the window full of staring people. Someone hooted from a car driving past on Sixteenth, and Wilkins flinched, dropping down to his hands and knees and groping for the hide-a-key under the front bumper. He pawed the dirty underside of the bumper frantically, but couldn't find the little magnetic box. Maybe it was on the rear bumper. He damned well wasn't going to go crawling around after it, providing an easy laugh ...

A wolf-whistle rang out from somewhere above, from an open window across Sixteenth. He stood up hurriedly.

"Did you get the license?" the old man said.

"What? No, I didn't." Wilkins took a deep breath to calm himself.

The goddam magnetic hide-a-key. It had probably dropped off down the highway somewhere. Wouldn't you know it! Betrayed by the very thing . . .

His heart still raced, but it didn't pound so hard. He concentrated on simmering down, clutching his chest with his hand. "Easy, boy," he muttered to himself, his eyes nearly shut. That was better. He could take stock now.

It was a miracle he wasn't hurt. If he was a skinny man the physical forces of the encounter would probably have torn him in half. As it was, his knee was scraped pretty good, but nothing worse than ten million such scrapes he had suffered as a kid. His palms were raw, and the skin on his rear end stung pretty well. He felt stiff, too.

He flexed his leg muscles and rotated his arms. The wolf-whistle sounded again, but he ignored it.

Miraculously, he had come through nearly unharmed. No broken bones. Nothing a bottle of Ben Gay wouldn't fix, maybe some Bactine on the scrapes.

He realized then that he still had the toothpick in his mouth. Unsteadily, he poked at his teeth with it, hoping that it would help restore the world to normalcy. It was soft and splintered, though, and no good for anything, so he threw it away into the juniper plants.

"You should have got his license. That's the first thing. But I should talk. I didn't get it either." The old man looked back toward the window, insulted on Wilkins's behalf, scowling at the crowd, which had dwindled now. "Damned bunch of assholes . . ." A few people still stood and gaped, waiting to get another look at Wilkins, hoping for a few more details to flesh out the story they would be telling everyone they met for the next six weeks. Six months, more likely. It was probably the only story they had, the morons. They'd make it last forever. "Got your car keys, didn't they?"

Wilkins nodded. Suddenly he was shaking. His hands danced against the hood of his car and he sat back heavily on the high concrete curb of a planter.

"Here now," the old man said, visibly worried. "Wait. I got a blanket in the car. What the hell am I thinking?" He hurried away to an old, beaten Chevrolet wagon, opening the cargo door and hauling out a stadium blanket in a clear plastic case. He pulled the blanket out and draped it over Wilkins's shoulders.

Wilkins sat on the curb with his head sagging forward now. For a moment there he had felt faint. His heart had started to even out, though. He wanted to lie down, but he couldn't, not there on the parking lot.

"Shock," the old man said to him. "Accompanies every injury, no matter what. You live around here?"

Wilkins nodded. "Down on French Street. Few blocks."

"I'll give you a ride. Your car won't go nowhere. Might as well leave it here. You can get another key and come back down after it. They get your wallet, too?"

His wallet gone! Of course they had got his wallet. He hadn't thought of that. He wasn't thinking clearly at all. Well, that was just fine. What was in there? At least thirty-odd dollars and his bank card and gas card and Visa—the whole megillah was gone.

The old man shook his head. "These punks," he said. "This is Babylon we're living in, stuff like this happens to a man."

Wilkins nodded and let the old man lead him to the Chevy wagon.

Wilkins climbed into the passenger seat, and the man got in and fired up the engine. He backed out terrifically slowly, straight past the window where a couple of people still gaped out at them. One of the people pointed and grinned stupidly, and the old man, winding down the window, leaned out and flipped the person off vigorously with both hands.

"Scum-sucking pig!" he shouted, then headed out down the alley toward Sixteenth, shaking his head darkly, one wheel bouncing down off the curb as he swerved out onto the street, angling up Sixteenth toward French.

"Name's Bob Dodge," the man said, reaching across to shake hands.

Wilkins felt very nearly like crying. This man redeems us all, he said to himself as he blinked at the Good Samaritan behind the wheel. "Bernard Wilkins," he said, shaking the man's hand. "I guess I'm lucky. No harm done. Could have been worse." He was feeling better. Just to be out of there helped. He had stopped shaking.

"Damn right you're lucky. If I was you I'd take it easy, though. Sometimes you throw something out of kilter, you don't even know it till later. Whiplash works that way."

Something out of kilter. Wilkins rejected the thought. "I feel . . . intact enough. Little bit sand-papered, that's all. If he'd hit me . . ." He sighed deeply; he didn't seem to be able to get enough air. "Take a right here. That's it—the blue house there with the shingles." The car pulled into the driveway, and Wilkins turned to the old man and put out his hand again. "Thanks," he said. "You want to step in for a moment, and I'll give you the blanket back. I could probably rustle up a cup of java."

"Naw. I guess I'll be on my way. I left a pal of mine back in the booth. Don't want to stiff him on the check. I'll see you down at Norm's one of these days. Just leave the blanket in the back of your car."

"I will."

Wilkins opened the car door, got out, and stood on the driveway, realizing for the first time that the blanket he was wearing had the California Angels logo on it, the big A with a halo. He watched Bob Dodge drive off. An Angels fan! He might have known it. Had he been there when Downing wrecked the big scoreboard? Wilkins hoped so.

Some destructions didn't matter, like the scoreboard, and those clear plastic backboards that the basketball players were routinely exploding a few years ago, with their energetic slam dunks. There were repairmen for those things, and the repairmen probably made more money in a week than Wilkins pulled down from Social Security in a year. He thought of his pants, beating against the street at forty miles an hour. Where were they now? Reduced to atoms? Lying in a ditch?

Hell.

He went in through the front door, and there was Molly, drinking coffee and reading the newspaper. Her pleasant look turned at once to uncomprehending alarm.

"What—?" she started to say.

"Lost the pants up at Norm's," he said as breezily as he could. He grinned at her. This was what she had prophesied. It had come to pass. "A guy drove me home. No big deal!" He hurried past her, grinning and nodding, holding tight to the blanket so that she wouldn't see where his knee was scraped. He didn't want any fuss. "I'll tell you in a bit!" he called back, overriding her anxious questions. "Later! I've got to . . . damn it—" He was sweating, and his heart was thudding furiously again in his chest. "Leave me alone! Just leave me alone for a while, will you?"

There had to be something that could be salvaged. In his second-best pair of fancy-dinners pants he plodded past the washer and dryer and down the back steps.

His backyard was deep, nearly a hundred feet from the back patio to the fence, the old boards of which were almost hidden under the branches and tendrils and green leaves of the tomato plants. Sometimes he worried about having planted them that far out. Closer to the house would have been safer. But the topsoil way out there was deep and good. Avocado leaves fell year round, rotting down into a dark, twiggy mulch. When he had spaded the ground up for the first time, he had found six inches of leafy humus on the surface, and the tomatoes that grew from that rich soil could be very nearly as big as grapefruit.

Still, it was awfully far out, way past the three big wind-milling gopher repellers. He couldn't keep an eye on things out there. As vigilant as he was, the worms seemed to take out the tomatoes, one by one. He had put out a pony-pack of Early Girls first, back in February. It had still been too cold, and the plants hadn't taken off. A worm got five of the six one night during the first week in March, and he had gone back to the nursery in order to get more Early Girls. He had ended up buying six small Beefsteak plants too, from a flat, and another six Better Boys in four-inch pots, thinking that out of eighteen plants, plus the one the worms had missed, he ought to come up with something.

What he had now, in mid June, were nine good plants. Most of the Early Girls had come to nothing, the worms having savaged them pretty badly. And the Beefsteaks were putting out fruit that was deformed, bulbous, and off-tasting.

The Better Boys were coming along, though. He knelt in the dirt, patiently untangling and staking up vines, pinching off new leaves near the flower clusters, cultivating the soil around the base of the plants and mounding it up into little dikes to hold water around the roots. Soon he would need another bundle of six-foot stakes.

There was a dark, round shadow way back in there among the Better Boys, nearly against the fence pickets; he could make out the yellow-orange flush against the white paint. For a moment he stared at it, adjusting his eyes to the tangled shadows. It must be a cluster of tomatoes.

He reached his arm through the vines, feeling around, shoving his face in among them and breathing in the bitter scent of the leaves. He found the fence picket and groped around blindly until he felt them—

No. It.

There was only one tomato, one of the Better Boys, deep in the vines.

It was enormous, and it was only half ripe. Slowly he spread his hand out, tracing with his thumb and pinky finger along the equator of the tomato.

"Leaping Jesus," he said out loud.

The damned thing must have an eight-inch diameter, ten-inch, maybe. He shoved his head farther in, squinting into the tangled depths. He could see it better now. It hung there heavily, from a stem as big around as his thumb.

Knock, knock, he thought.

Who's there?
Ether.
Ether who?
Ether bunnies.

No ball game today, he thought. No crossword puzzle.

He backed out of the vines and strode purposefully toward the garage. He hadn't planned on using the ether nets this year, but this was a thing that needed saving. He could imagine the worms eyeing the vast Better Boy from their—what, nests? Lairs?—and making plans for the evening. Tying metaphorical napkins around their necks and hauling out the silverware.

He pulled open the warped garage door and looked at the big freezer in the corner and at the draped, fine-mesh nets on the wall. The crystal might or might not be mature, but he would have to use them tonight.

He had read the works of Professor Dayton C. Miller, who had been a colleague of Edward Williams Morley, and, like Miller, Wilkins had become convinced that Einstein had been wrong—light was *not* in any sense particles, but consisted of waves traveling through a medium that the nineteenth-century physicists had called ether, the luminiferous ether.

"Luminiferous ether." He rolled the phrase across his tongue, listening to the magic in it.

Ordinary matter like planets and people and baseballs traveled through the ether without being affected by it. The ether passed through them like water through a swimming-pool net. But anything that bent light, anything like a magnifying glass, or a prism, or even a Coke bottle, participated with the ether a little, and so experienced a certain drag.

Molly had a collection of glass and crystal animals—people had offered her serious money for them, over the years—and Wilkins had noticed that in certain seasons some of them moved off of their dust-free spots on the shelf. The ones that seemed to have moved farthest were a set of comical rabbits that they had picked up in Atlantic City in—it must have been—1954. He had come to the conclusion that the effect occurred because of the angle and lengths of the rabbits' ears.

A correctly shaped crystal, he reasoned, would simply be stopped by the eternally motionless ether, and would be yanked off of the moving Earth like . . . like his pants had been ripped off of his body when the car-mirror post had hooked them.

And so he had bought a lot of crystal-growing kits at a local hobby store, and had "seeded" the Tupperware growing environments with spatially customized, rabbit-shaped forms that he'd fashioned from copper wire. It had taken him months to get the ears right.

The resulting crystalline silicon-dioxide shapes would not exhibit their ether-anchored properties while they were still in the refractive water—frozen water, at the moment—and he had not planned to put them to the test until next year.

But tonight he would need an anchor. There was the Better Boy to be saved. The year, with all of its defeats and humiliations, would not have been for nothing. He grinned to think about the Better Boy, hanging out there in the shadows, impossibly big and round. A slice of that on a hamburger . . .

Knock knock.
Who's there?
Samoa.
Samoa who?
Samoa ether bunnies.

He whistled a little tune, admiring the sunlight slanting in through the dusty window. The Early Girls and the misshapen Beefsteaks would have to be sacrificed. He would drape the nets under them. Let the worms feast on them in outer space if they had the spittle for it, as Thomas More had said.

Molly's Spanish aunt had once sent them a lacy, hand-embroidered bedspread. Apparently a whole convent-full of nuns had spent the bulk of their lifetimes putting the thing together. Frank *Sinatra* couldn't have afforded to buy the thing at the sort of retail price it deserved. Wilkins had taken great pains in laying the gorgeous cloth over their modest bed, and had luxuriated in lying under it while reading something appropriate—Shakespeare's sonnets, as he recalled.

That same night their cat had jumped onto the bed and almost instantly had vomited out a live tapeworm that must have been a yard long. The worm had convulsed on the bedspread, several times standing right up on its head, and in horror Wilkins had balled the bedspread up around the creature, thrown it onto the floor and stomped on it repeatedly, and then flung the bundle out into the yard. Eventually Wilkins and his wife had gone to sleep. That night it had rained for eight hours straight, and by morning the bedspread was something he'd been ashamed even to have visible in his trash.

When the obscuring ice melted, the rabbit-shaped crystals would be the floats, the equivalent of the glass balls that Polynesian fishermen apparently used to hold up the perimeters of their nets. The crystals would grab the fabric of the celestial ether like good tires grabbing pavement, and the lacy nets—full of tomato worms, their teeth in the flesh of the luckless Early Girls and Beefsteaks—would go flying off into space.

Let them come crawling back then, Wilkins thought gravely. He searched his mind for doubt but found none. There was nothing at all wrong with his science. It only wanted application. Tonight, he would give it that.

Still wearing his go-out-to-dinner pants, Wilkins expertly tied monkey-fist knots around the blocks of ice, then put each back into the freezer. Several times Molly had come out to the garage to plead with him to quit and come inside. He had to think about his health, she'd said. Remonstrating, he called it. "Don't remonstrate with me!" he shouted at her finally, and she went away in a huff. Caught up in his work, he simmered down almost at once, and soon he was able to take the long view. Hell, she couldn't be expected to see the sense in these nets and blocks of ice. They must seem like so much lunacy to her. He wondered whether he ought to wake her up around midnight and call her outside when the nets lifted off . . .

Luckily he had made dozens of the rabbit-forms. There would be plenty for the nets. And he would have to buy more crystal kits tomorrow.

Knock knock.
Who's there?
Consumption.
Consumption who?
Consumption be done about all these ether bunnies?
He laughed out loud.

By dinnertime he had fastened yellow and red twist ties around the edges of the nets. It would be an easy thing to attach the ether bunnies to the twist ties when the time was just right. He had spread the nets under all the tomato plants around the one that bore the prodigious Better Boy, pulling back and breaking off encumbering vines from adjacent plants. He hated to destroy the surrounding plants, but his eggs were all going into one basket here. If you were going to do a job, you did a job. Wasn't that what Casey Stengel always said? Halfway measures wouldn't stop a tomato worm. Wilkins had found that out the hard way.

Molly cooked him his favorite dinner—pork chops baked in cream of mushroom soup, with mashed potatoes and a vegetable medley on the side. There was a sprig of parsley on the plate, as a garnish, just like in a good restaurant. He picked it up and laid it on the tablecloth. Then, slathering margarine onto a slice of white bread and sopping up gravy with it, he chewed contentedly, surveying their kitchen, their domain. Outside, the world was alive with impersonal horrors. The evening news was full of them. Old Bob Dodge was right. This *was* Babylon. But with the summer breeze blowing in through the open window and the smell of dinner in the air, Wilkins didn't give a damn for Babylon.

He studied the plate-rack on the wall, remembering where he and Molly had picked up each of the souvenir plates. There was the Spokane plate, from the World's Fair in '74. And there was the Grand Canyon plate and the Mesa Verde one next to that, chipped just a little on the edge. What the hell did a chip matter? A little bit of Super-Glue if it was a bad one ...

There was a magic in all of it—the plates on the wall, the little stack of bread-slices on the saucer, the carrots and peas mixing it up with the mashed potatoes. There was something in the space around such things, like the force-field dome over a lunar city in a story. Whatever it was, this magic, it held Babylon at bay.

He remembered the cat and the Spanish bedspread suddenly, and put his fork down. But hell—the ether bunnies, the saving of the enormous tomato—tonight things would go a different way.

He picked up his fork again and stabbed a piece of carrot, careful to catch a couple of peas at the same time, dredging it all in the mushroom gravy.

He would have to remember to put the stadium blanket into the trunk. Bob Dodge ... Even the man's name had a ring to it. If God were to lean out of the sky, as the Bible said He had done in times past, and say "Find me one good man, or else I'll pull this whole damned shooting match to pieces," Wilkins would point to Bob Dodge, and then they could all relax and go back to eating pork chops.

"More mashed potatoes?" Molly asked him, breaking in on his reverie.

"Please. And gravy."

She went over to the stove and picked up the pan, spooning him out a big mound of potatoes, dropping it onto his plate, and then pushing a deep depression in the middle of the mound. She got it just right. Wilkins smiled at her, watching her pour gravy into the hole.

"Salt?"

"Doesn't need it," he said. "It's perfect."

Molly canted her head and looked at him. "A penny?"

He grinned self-consciously. "For my thoughts? They're not worth a penny—or they're worth too much to stick a number on. I was just thinking about all this. About us." He gestured around him, at the souvenir plates on the wall and the plates full of food on the table.

"Oh, I see," she said, feigning skepticism.

"We could have done worse."

She nodded as if she meant it. He nearly told her about the ether bunnies, about why he had bought the old freezer and the nets, about Einstein and Miller—but instead he found himself finally telling her about Norm's, about having nearly got run down in the parking lot. Earlier that day, when he had borrowed her keys and gone down to retrieve the car, she hadn't asked any questions. He had thought she was miffed, but now he knew that wasn't it. She'd just been giving him room to breathe.

"Sorry I shouted at you when I got home," he said when he had finished describing the ordeal. "I was pretty shook up."

"I guess you would be. I wish you would have told me, though. Someone should have called the police."

"Wouldn't have done any good. I didn't even get the guy's license number. Happened too fast."

"One of those people in Norm's must have got it."

Wilkins shrugged. Right then he didn't give a flying damn about the guy in the Torino. In a sense there had not been any guy in the Torino, just a . . . a force of nature, like gravity or cold or the way things go to hell if you don't look out. He hacked little gaps in his mashed potatoes, let in the gravy leak down the edges like molten lava out of a volcano, careful not to let it all run out. He shoveled a forkful into his mouth, and then picked up a pork chop, holding it by the bone, and nibbled off the meat that was left. "No harm done," he said. "A few bucks . . ."

"What you ought to have done after you'd got home and put on another pair of pants was drive up Seventeenth Street. Your pants are probably lying by the roadside somewhere, in a heap."

"First thing in the morning," he said, putting it off even though there was still a couple hours' worth of daylight left.

But then abruptly he knew she was right. Of course that's

what he should have done. He had been too addled. A man
didn't like to think of that sort of embarrassment, not so
soon. Now, safe in the kitchen, eating a good meal, the world
was distant enough to permit his taking a philosophical attitude. He could talk about it now, admit everything to Molly.
There was no shame in it. Hell, it *was* funny. If he had been
watching out the window at Norm's, he would have laughed
at himself, too. There was no harm done. Except that his inventor's pants were gone.

Suddenly full, he pushed his plate away and stood up.

"Sit and talk?" Molly asked.

"Not tonight. I've got a few things to do yet, before dark."

"I'll make you a cup of coffee, then, and bring it out to
the garage."

He smiled at her and winked, then bent over and kissed
her on the cheek. "Use the Melitta filter. And make it in that
big, one-quart German stein, will you? I want it to last. Nothing tastes better than coffee with milk and sugar in it an hour
after the whole thing has got cold. The milk forms a sort of
halo on the surface after a while. A concession from the
Brownian motion."

She nodded doubtfully at him, and he winked again before heading out the back door. "I'm just going down to
Builders Emporium," he said at the last moment. "Before
they close. Leave the coffee on the bench, if you don't mind."

Immediately he set out around toward the front, climbing
into his car and heading toward Seventeenth Street, five
blocks up.

He drove east slowly, ignoring the half a dozen cars angrily
changing lanes to pass him. Someone shouted something,
and Wilkins hollered, "That's right!" out the window, although he had no idea what it was the man had said.

The roadside was littered with rubbish—cans and bottles
and disposable diapers. He had never noticed it all before,
never really looked. It was a depressing sight. The search
suddenly struck him as hopeless. His pants were probably

caught on a tree limb somewhere up in the Santa Ana mountains. The police could put their best men on the search and nothing would come of it.

He bumped slowly over the railroad tracks, deliberately missing the green light just this side of the freeway underpass, so that he had to stop and wait out the long red light. Bells began to ring, and an Amtrak passenger train thundered past right behind him, shaking his car and filling the rear window with the sight of hurtling steel. Abruptly he felt cut off, dislocated, as if he had lost his moorings, and he decided to make a U-turn at the next corner and go home. This was no good, this futile searching.

But it was just then that he saw the pants, bunched up like a dead dog in the dim, concrete shadows beneath the overpass. He drove quickly forward when the light changed, the sound of the train receding into the distance, and he pulled into the next driveway and stopped in the parking lot of a tune-up shop closed for the night.

Getting out, he hitched up his dinner pants and strode back down the sidewalk as the traffic rushed past on the street, the drivers oblivious to him and his mission.

The pants were a living wreck, hopelessly flayed after having polished three blocks of asphalt. The wallet and keys were long gone.

He shook the pants out. One of the legs was hanging, pretty literally, by threads. The seat was virtually gone. What remained was streaked with dried gutter water. For a moment he was tempted to fling them away, mainly out of anger.

He didn't, though.

Would a sailor toss out a sail torn to pieces by a storm? No he wouldn't. He would wearily take out the needle and thread, is what he would do, and begin patching it up. Who cared what it looked like when it was done? If it caught the wind, and held it . . . A new broom sweeps clean, he told himself stoically, but an old broom knows every corner.

He took the pants with him back to the car. And when he got home, five minutes later, there was the cup of coffee still steaming on the bench. He put the pants on the corner of the bench top, blew across the top of the coffee, and swallowed a big slug of it, sighing out loud.

The moon was high and full. That would mean he could see, and wouldn't have to mess with unrolling the hundred-foot extension cord and hanging the trouble-light in the avocado tree. And he was fairly sure that moonlight brought out the tomato worms, too. The hypothesis wasn't scientifically sound, maybe, but that didn't mean it wasn't right. He had studied the creatures pretty thoroughly, and had come to know their habits.

He set down the foam ice chest containing the ice-encased ether bunnies, studied the nets for a moment, and then opened a little cloth-covered notebook, taking out the pencil clipped inside the spine. He had to gauge it very damned carefully. If he tied on the ice-encased bunnies too soon or too late, it would all come to nothing, an empty net ascending into the stratosphere. There was a variation in air temperature across the backyard—very slight, but significant. And down among the vines there was a photosynthetic cooling that was very nearly tempered by residual heat leaking out of the sun-warmed soil. He had worked through the calculations three times on paper and then once again with a pocket calculator.

And of course there was no way of knowing the precise moment that the worm would attempt to cross the nets. That was a variable that he could only approximate. Still, that didn't make the fine tuning any less necessary. All the steps in the process were vital.

He wondered, as he carefully wired the ether bunnies onto the nets, if maybe there wasn't energy in moonlight, too—a sort of heat echo, something even his instruments couldn't pick up. The worms could sense it, whatever it was—a subtle but irresistible force, possibly involving tidal effects. Well, fat lot of good it would do him to start worrying about that now. It clearly wasn't the sort of thing you could work out on a pocket calculator.

He struggled heavily to his feet, straightening up at last, the ice chest empty. He groaned at the familiar stiffness and shooting pains in his lower back. Molly could cook, he had to give her that. One of these days he would take off a few pounds. He wondered suddenly if maybe there weren't a couple of cold pork chops left over in the fridge, but then he decided that Molly would want to cook them up for his breakfast in the morning. That would be good—eggs and chops and sourdough toast.

She had come out to the garage only once that evening, to remonstrate with him again, but he had made it clear that he was up to his neck in what he was doing, and that he wasn't going to give himself any rest. She had looked curiously around the garage and then had gone back inside, and after several hours she had shut the light off upstairs in order to go to sleep.

So the house was dark now, except for a couple of sconces burning in the living room. He could see the front porch light, too, shining through the window beyond them.

The sky was full of stars, the Milky Way stretching like a river through trackless space. He felt a sudden sorrow for the tomato worms, who knew nothing of the ether. They went plodding along, inexorably, sniffing out tomato plants, night after night, compelled by Nature, by the fleeing moon. They were his brothers, after a fashion. It was a hard world for a tomato worm, and Wilkins was sorry that he had to kill them.

He fetched a lawn chair and sat down in it, very glad to take a load off his feet. He studied the plants. There was no wind, not even an occasional breeze. The heavy-bodied tomato worms would make the branches dip and sway as they came along, cutting through the still night. Wilkins would have to remain vigilant. There would be no sleep for him. He was certain that he could trust the ether bunnies to do their work, to trap the worms and propel them away into the depths of space, but it was a thing that he had to see, as an astronomer had to wait out a solar eclipse.

He was suddenly hungry again. That's what had come of thinking about the pork chops. He was reminded of the tomato, nearly invisible down in the depths of the vines. How many people could that Better Boy feed, Wilkins wondered, and all at once it struck him that he himself was hardly worthy to eat such a tomato as this. He would find Bob Dodge, maybe, and give it to him. "Here," he would say, surprising the old man in his booth at Norm's. "Eat it well." And he would hand Dodge the tomato, and Dodge would understand, and would take it from him.

He got up out of his chair and peered into the vines. The ice was still solid. The night air hadn't started it melting yet. But the worms hadn't come yet either. It was too soon. He found a little cluster of Early Girls, tiny things that didn't amount to anything and weren't quite ripe yet. Carefully, he pulled a few of them loose and then went back to his chair, sucking the insides out of one of the tomatoes as if it were a Concord grape. He threw the peel away, tasting the still-bitter fruit.

"Green," he said out loud, surprised at the sound of his own voice and wishing he had some salt. And then, to himself, he said, "It's nourishing, though. Vitamin C." He felt a little like a hunter, eating his kill in the depths of a forest, or a fisherman at sea, lunching off his catch.

He could hear them coming. Faintly on the still air he could hear the rustle of leaves bending against vines, even, he'd swear, the munch-munch of tiny jaws grinding vegetation into nasty green pulp in the speckled moonlight. It was a steady sussuration—there must have been hundreds of them out there. Clearly the full moon and the incredible prize had drawn the creatures out in an unprecedented way. Perhaps every tomato worm in Orange County was here tonight to sate itself.

And the ice wasn't melting fast enough. He had miscalculated.

He forced himself up out of the lawn chair and plodded across the grass to the plants. He couldn't see them—their markings were perfect camouflage, letting them blend into the shifting patches of moonlight and shadow—but he could hear them moving in among the Early Girls.

Crouched against the vines, he blew softly on the ice blocks at the outside corners of the net. If only he could hurry them along. When they warmed up just a couple of degrees, the night air would really go to work on them. They'd melt quickly once they started. Abruptly he thought of heading into the garage for a propane torch, but he couldn't leave the tomato alone with the worms now, not even for a moment. He kept blowing. Little rivulets of water were running down the edges of the ice. Cheered at the sight of this, he blew harder.

Dimly, he realized that he had fallen to his knees.

Maybe he had hyper-ventilated, or else had been bent over so long that blood had rushed to his head. He felt heavy, though, and he pulled at the collar of his shirt to loosen it across his chest. He heard them again, close to him now.

"The worms!" he said out loud, and he reached out and took hold of the nearest piece of string-bound ice in both hands to melt it. He didn't let go of it even when he overbalanced and thudded heavily to the ground on his shoulder, but the ice still wasn't melting fast enough, and his hands were getting numb and beginning to ache.

The sound of the feasting worms was a hissing in his ears that mingled with the sound of rushing blood, like two rivers of noise flowing together into one deep stream. The air seemed to have turned cold, chilling the sweat running down his forehead. His heart was pounding in his chest like a pick-axe chopping hard into dirt.

He struggled up onto his hands and knees and lunged his way toward the Better Boy.

He could see them.

One of the worms was halfway up the narrow trunk, and two more were noodling in along the vines from the side. A cramp in his chest helped him to lean in closer, although he gasped at the pain and clutched at his shirt pocket. Now he could not see anything human or even mammalian in the faces of the worms, any more than he had been able to see the driver of the hit-and-run Torino behind the sun-glare on the windshield.

He made his hand stretch out and take hold of one of the worms. It held on to the vine until he really tugged, and then after tearing loose it curled in a muscular way in his palm before he could fling it away. In his fright and revulsion he grabbed the next one too hard, and it burst in his fist—somehow, horribly, still squirming against his fingers even after its insides had jetted out and greased Wilkins's thumb.

He spared a glance toward the nearest chunk of ice, but he couldn't see it; perhaps they were melting at last.

Just a little longer, he told himself, his breath coming quick and shallow. His hands were numb, but he seized everything that might have been a worm and threw it behind him. He was panting loud enough to drown out the racket of the feasting worms, and the sweat stung in his eyes, but he didn't let himself stop.

His left arm exploded in pain when he took hold of another one of the creatures, and he half believed the thing had somehow struck back at him, and then at that moment his chest was crushed between the earth and the sky.

He tried to stand, but toppled over backward.

Against the enormous weight he managed to lift his head—and he was smiling when he let it fall back onto the grass, for he was sure he had seen the edges of the nets fluttering upward as the ether bunnies, freed at last from the ice, struggled to take hold of the fabric of space—struggled inadequately, he had to concede, against the weight of the nets and the plants and the worms and the sky, but bravely nevertheless, keeping on tugging until it was obvious that their best efforts weren't enough, and then keeping on tugging even after that.

He didn't lose consciousness. He was simply unable to move. But the chill had gone away and the warm air had taken its place, and he was content to lie on the grass and stare up at the stars and listen to his heart.

He knew that it had probably been a heart attack that had

happened to him—but he had heard of people mistaking for a heart attack what had merely been a seizure from too much caffeine. It might have been the big mug of coffee. He'd have to cut down on that stuff. Thinking of the coffee made him think of Molly asleep upstairs. He was glad that she didn't know he was down here, lying all alone on the dewy grass.

In and out with the summer night air. Breathing was the thing. He focused on it. Nothing else mattered to him. If you could still breathe you were all right, and he felt like he could do it forever.

When the top leaves of his neighbor's olive tree lit gold with the dawn sun he found that he could move. He sat up slowly, carefully, but nothing bad happened. The morning breeze was pleasantly cool, and crows were calling to each other across the rooftops.

He parted the vines and looked into the shadowy depths of the tomato plants.

The Better Boy was gone. All that was left of it was a long shred of orange skin dangling like a deflated balloon from its now foolish-looking stout stem. The ether bunnies, perhaps warped out of the effective shape by the night of strain, lay inert along the edges of the nets, which were soiled with garden dirt now and with a couple of crushed worms and a scattering of avocado leaves.

He was all alone in the yard—Molly wouldn't wake up for an hour yet—so he let himself cry as he sat there on the grass. The sobs shook him like hiccups, and tears ran down his face as the sweat had done hours earlier, and the tears made dark spots on the lap of his dinner pants.

Then he got up onto his feet and, still moving carefully because he felt so frail and weak, walked around to the front of the house.

The newspaper lay on the driveway. He nearly picked it up, thinking to take a look at the sports page. He had been so busy yesterday evening that he had missed the tail end of the ballgame. Perhaps the Angels had slugged their way into first place. They had been on a streak, and Wilkins wanted to think that their luck had held.

He turned and went into the silent house. He didn't want to make coffee, so he just walked slowly from room to room, noticing things, paying attention to trifles, from the bright morning sun shining straight in horizontally through the windows to the familiar titles of books on shelves.

He felt a remote surprise at seeing his inventor's pants on the top of the dirty clothes in the hamper in the bathroom, and he picked them up.

No wonder it had been late when Molly had finally turned out the bedroom light. She had sewn up or patched every one of the outrageous tears and lesions in the old pants, and now clearly intended to wash them. Impulsively he wanted to put them on right then and there . . . but he wouldn't. He would let Molly have her way with them, let her return the pants in her own good time. He would wear them again tomorrow, or the day after.

There was still a subtle magic in the morning.

Knock knock.

Who's there?

Samoa.

He let the pants fall back onto the pile, and then he walked slowly, carefully, into the kitchen and opened the refrigerator door. He would make breakfast for her.

The Pink of Fading Neon

There has been a good deal of dark weather here lately, although I'm not at all sure whether it is actual dark weather or simply the absence of something or other. I sometimes suspect the latter. But it is dark. Clouds overhead thick enough to be invisible. Just a dim gray and a mist of fog floating over the bay and now and then stealing ashore.

There was moss or perhaps fungus on my shoes again this morning. It appeared to be a moist gray-green fuzz but brushed away like dust. It means, I suppose, that the colors are fading—a thing I have long suspected. Away to the north beyond the tower is what appears to be, is in fact, a market. An arabesque of letters, part gone, shines in bright neon pink like a mythological flamingo that glows through the gray days, an impossible swamp bird that can stand all day on a single leg. The sign itself is inane but throws that roseate glow over the stilt legs of the tower—a water tower, they say, which sprang up in two evenings, three great legs with a cone atop, and has sat there since, for the most part, with dandelions and fuchsias sprouting about the base.

And leering beyond, half hidden behind a fence once red but now gray and dark and falling, day by day, to bits, squats an elongated metal sphere, toadlike in the weeds. Little windows hung with the tatters of curtains and neat rows of rivets in the steel skin make it appear terrestrial. But a quaint sign—a puff of wind below altogether alien lowercase letters which spell out the word "airstream" in frightful clarity—makes it appear something else altogether. The implications startled me at first—they should startle anyone—and I was curious that no passersby on the sidewalk below were similarly startled.

There was a time, in fact (not a long time to be sure; I'm a clever sort of chap), that the thing in the weeds seemed nothing but a tow-along home which, when attached to the rear of an automobile, would pursue it along the highway. But the thing appeared one evening sailing bubblelike—I glimpsed it passing across the mouth of an alley on Second Street—with nothing resembling an automobile attached to either end. I'll condescend to swear to it. A swirl of fog from the bay, wet with the smell of seaweed and tar, whirled along in its wake as if the thing itself were a leaking container of mists from some vast and lonely sea.

And speaking of weather, it occurs to me, when I recall my youth, that coupling sunshine and childhood in our minds is not, as the psychologists tell us, a symbolic confusion of objects and ideas about objects in our subconscious. It is actuality itself. The weather was more pronounced then, rain or shine, it hadn't this gray mediocrity about it.

I've heard and read, and it doesn't surprise me a bit, that the armadillos have turned back. After eons of slow northward creeping from the plains of Central America, through the jungles and swamps and deserts of Mexico while woolly mammoths and cave bears crashed through the chaparral and still, ages later, while Aztec and Toltec tribes lived in fear of loathsome toad-infested pits of skeletons in rainwater, on came the armadillos. On the march for twenty million years and culminating in unimaginable pairs of shoes and ridiculous scaled and tailed caps. All of that has reversed in an instant. Up and down the flatlands of Oklahoma, say the scientists, armadillos pause and listen and sniff the air and turn calmly about—on the march, south now, once again.

But as I say, it surprises me not at all. I read about it in a journal of scientific discovery and it fit, and fit well, like a pair of shoes. My own shoes—simulated alligator—could barely be seen this morning for the moss on them. They appeared amphibian. Anyway, I hadn't gotten beyond the first paragraph—the armadillos having barely conceived of the plan for the tremendous northern push into, over eons, civilization—when there came a knock at the door.

It was my neighbor, Monroe. His chin, it seemed, was gone. It had never amounted to much and now it was even less a chin, more a row of teeth which his lower lip couldn't quite conceal. Monroe seemed to be disappearing. He was consuming himself. His eyes had been drawn into his head in search, no doubt, for his chin. But his nose had been pulled out, like an armadillo's, and his ears hung in a sheet like those of a ring-laden African princess. And he had shrunk by several inches. The spine, they say, although made of bone, which should last as well as the rest of us, is the first to go. Monroe was becoming a dwarf. It was clear—and not unrelated, I suspect, to the shining, spheroid airstream thing in the weeds. In Monroe's weeds. A thing Monroe used to tow about behind an automobile—an incredible Hudson of ludicrous make with an insect name and with great black balloons for tires. But during the years that the automobile has gone to bits (in much the same way as its master) the little star ship of an airstream waited in the weeds and was joined, in time, by what appeared at first to be a water tower sprung up in two days on great gangling stilts, jointed at the knees.

Monroe, a dwarf through no fault of his own, in gray flannel or what seemed, superficially, gray flannel, had always tottered past, morning after morning, his eyes sucking inward with his chin, his nose and ears succumbing to the forces of gravity and stretching, beaklike and flaplike, groundward. He pattered northward up the sidewalk to the market. It was his constitutional. Along went Monroe through years of shrinking until that one morning when I, having barely begun with armadillos, heard a tapping on the door. It was sharp, yet faint, so that I listened a moment in dread. It was a skeleton's knock—hard knuckles but with no muscle left in the arm to wield them. Just a sort of clack clack clack that bamboo wind chimes might make in a breeze muffled by gray morning mists.

But the clack clack clack came again, and I gave up my armadillos and opened the door a crack, anxious, as you can easily understand, to keep the fog and the smell of seaweed and tar outside. But that, too, was futile and the mists crept in with an eye to my shoes, which I had, just that morning, wiped clean with newspaper.

There was Monroe, squinting, failing to recognize me. Failing even to recognize the very sidewalk beneath his feet. Across the road Monroe's house was enveloped in fog—fog that swirled around the sphere in the weeds, in and out of the windows, blowing the tatters of ragged curtains, fossil curtains, outward into the air. Monroe couldn't speak. Monroe couldn't see well enough to recognize me. And if he could—see, that is—he wouldn't have known me anyway. Monroe, it appeared, was lost. Lost just half a block from home and half a block from the market.

"Monroe," I said, thinking to alert him in some telling way.

"What?" He looked about him.

Monroe was lost. He was befuddled. He blinked his eyes very slowly like a chameleon—as if giving the problem a really solid bit of thought. He took pause, as they say. Then he shuffled about in a little half circle, a slow and painstaking about-face, and with my finger as an indicator tottered south toward home, the market—the whole idea of markets—abandoned.

That was some time ago, and since then there has been no Monroe. His house, it seems, remains perpetually fog enshrouded, and I'm sure that from the vantage point of Monroe's window, my own would seem the same. Monroe is still in there—dead, likely, as a doornail. And in twenty years, after the last of the armadillos has flown out of Texas, Monroe will still be dead in that gray house, a bit of dust and hair, shrunk beyond time and reason but no more dead than he is now.

The exact relation between the sphere in the weeds, the water tower, and the seaweed fog that enclosed Monroe's house, not to mention Monroe himself, is puzzling. I admit that at one time I suspected the very nature of water towers, which I thought to be storage tanks. But now, in my research, I find that they have something to do with equalizing this and that—that they are essential. Most of our mechanisms are essential. Monroe's sphere is somehow essential.

But the tower across the road is merely a silver cone atop stilts. It could house an army of aliens as easily as a hundred thousand gallons of water and no one, I fear, would care to know. It is attached to nothing at all. There are no pipes or hoses. You'll say I've read too much Wells and am frightened of Tripods. And that may be so. You can say what you like. I know what I know. I mentioned having glimpsed the airstream across the mouth of an alley off Second Street not far, in fact, from the Vance Hotel. And you will agree, by now, that it could not have been Monroe who motored it about.

But just yesterday evening, upstairs in the library, I sat reading. It was late, very late, and there was a good fog coming in off the ocean. The curtains on the windows are lace, rather sad lace I fear, gone from white to gray with the years. A pink thread of neon shone along the sill and the night outside was cold and dim and a deep resonant lowing sound muttered in from the bay—a foghorn, I hope. I nodded there in front of the electric fire, something entitled *The Story of Our Earth* open in my hand, when I heard that faint but sharp tap tap tapping. That skeletal rapping somewhere out in the night. Noises in the night tend to make one start more violently, I suppose, than the same noises would in the light of day. My book tumbled to the floor and I rose, thinking first of horrors, then of Monroe. But I recalled quickly that I was in among the shadows of bookcases on the second floor and that the tap—there it was again—was at the window. "Could Monroe . . . ?" I thought. But no; Monroe was a dwarf. Monroe was gone altogether. And I peered out into the dim night air aswirl with mist. In the pink of neon there glinted for the briefest of moments an arc of silver—the bent joint of a single stilt leg wobbling momentarily, clacking once more against the window pane, then disappearing in the fog, away toward the sea.

I squinted out at Monroe's house. The little airstream sphere glowed in the moonlight or perhaps through fog-filtered neon which had mysteriously pierced the thick mists. And the mist swirled deeper, obscuring the field of fuchsia and dandelion, fading telephone poles. The airstream shuddered and, it seemed to me then, rose from its nesting place and followed in the wake of the striding tower toward the bay.

It sounds (I know) very much like a madness. But so what? What do I care for madness? What struck me as insidious was the fact that, next morning in the dim sun of coastal autumn, both had returned and sat placid as herons among their respective weeds.

And what is true about mechanisms is that as we move from the Jurassic age of technology toward some ultimate goal, relentlessly like armadillos (and all, one day, likely to be made into preposterous hats or scaled croquet balls), all our devices become simpler and grayer and their function becomes less clear. They become primitive and bestial and even prehistoric in the most roundabout way. What must it have been like when the earth was all ocean? When there was nothing but monsters? Imagine yourself another Professor Hardwigg afloat on gray Paleozoic seas where, twenty feet beneath the surface, unbelievable whales and amphibious beasts tear at each other and then disappear into the mouths of dim primordial caves. Chambered cephalopods and trilobites and sea snails as great as Monroe's airstream creep sluggishly about dim reefs amid the rubbery stalks and bladders of seaweeds. Imagine yourself afloat on a pitching wooden raft in a prehistoric age a million years before the first armadillos would decide among themselves to wander north out of Mayan jungles toward sunlight and open spaces.

That same gray atmosphere, trust me, born again of seaweed and oceans, washes in night by night, drawn by the moon as surely as the tides. And amid fuchsias and dandelions, monsters lie humped and waiting, striding off by night in the mists. And each morning gray mold covers my shoes and sprouts from the walls along with, doubtless, the germinating seeds of tiny trilobites and nautili.

My clothing, as well as my shoes, is becoming gray felt, just as Monroe's did. All this is not madness. The armadillos have turned back, to the grand amazement of science, and so, I fear, has everything else. And the airstream, the tower, and the pink of fading neon—what are they up to? That is what is unclear. That they come and go in the night along fog-enshrouded avenues and beneath pale lunar rays is a certainty. But I'm not an impatient man. If the thing has knocked once on the windowpane, it will knock again.

The Old Curiosity Shop

The trip down from Seattle in the rattling old Mercury wagon took most of two days. Jimmerson tried to sleep for a few hours somewhere south of Mendocino along Highway 1, the Mercury parked on a turnout and Jimmerson wedged in between the spare tire, his old luggage, and some cardboard boxes full of what amounted to his possessions. None of it was worth any real money. It was just trinkets, souvenirs of his forty years married to Edna: some salt and pepper shakers from what had been their collection, dusty agates and geodes from a couple of trips to the desert back in '56, old postcards and photographs, a pair of clipper ship bookends they'd bought down in New Orleans at the Jean Lafitte Hotel, and a few books, including the Popular Science Library set that Edna had given him for Christmas a hell of a long time ago. Most of the rest of what he owned he had left in Seattle, and every mile of highway that spun away behind him made it less and less likely that he would ever return for it.

News of Edna's death had reached him yesterday in the form of a letter from the county, identifying Doyle Jimmerson as "responsible for the costs incurred by Edna Jimmerson's burial." And of course he *was* responsible—for more than just the costs. They were married, even if he hadn't seen her for nearly a year, and she had no other kin. He would have thought that Mrs. Crandle, the next-door neighbor, would have sent him the news of Edna's death sooner, but Mrs. Crandle was a terrible old shrew, and she probably hated him for how he had left, how he had stayed away. . . .

He had never felt more married to Edna than now that she was dead. His long-cherished anger and all his tired principles had fallen to dust on the instant of his reading the letter, and as he lay listening to the slow dripping of the branches and the shifting of the dark ocean beyond the car windows, he knew that he had simply been wrong—about Edna's fling with the Frenchman, Mr. des Laumes, about his own self-righteous staying-away, about his looking down on Edna from the self-satisfied height of a second-story hotel room along the waterfront in Seattle where he had lived alone these past twelve months.

There was a fog in off the ocean, and as he lay in the back of the Mercury he could hear waves sighing in the distance. The eucalyptus trees along the roadside were ghostly dark through the mists, the ocean an invisible presence below. There was the smell of dust and cardboard and old leather on the air, and water dripped onto the roof of the car from overhanging branches. Now and then a truck passed, gunning south toward San Francisco, and the Mercury swayed on its springs and the fog whirled and eddied around the misty windows.

Before dawn he was on the road again, driving south along the nearly deserted highway. Fog gave way to rain, and the rugged Pacific coast was black and emerald under a sky the color of weathered iron. It was late afternoon when he pulled into the driveway and cut the engine, which dieseled for another twenty seconds before coughing itself silent. He sat there in the quiet car, utterly unsure of himself—unsure even why he had come. He could far easier have sent a check. And

he was helpless now, worthless, no good to poor Edna, who
was already dead and buried....

Of *course* Mrs. Crandle hadn't sent him a letter. He
wasn't worth a letter. He wondered if the old woman was
watching him through the window right now, and he bent
over and looked at the front of her house. There she was, a
shadow behind the drapery, peering out at him. He could picture her face, pruned up like one of those dolls they make out
of dried fruit. He waved at her, and then, before he got out of
the car, he opened the glove compartment and looked for a
moment at the blue steel .38 that lay atop the road maps and
insurance papers and old registrations. The gun appeared to
him to be monumentally heavy, like a black hole in the heart
of the old Mercury.

He shut the glove compartment door, climbed stiffly out
of the car, and took a look at the house and yard. The di-
chondra lawn was up in dandelions and devil grass, and the
hibiscus were badly overgrown, dropping orange blossoms
onto the grass and walkway. The house needed paint. He had
been meaning to paint it when he'd left, but he hadn't. Things
had happened too fast that morning. Let the Frenchy paint it,
he had told Edna before he had walked out.

He headed up along the side of the house, where a litter of
throwaway newspapers and front-porch advertisements lay
sodden with rain, hidden in front of Edna's Dodge. Someone, probably Mrs. Crandle, had been tossing them there.
The right front tire of the Dodge was flat, and it looked like
it had been for a long time. Instantly it occurred to him that
Edna must have been sick for some time, that she hadn't been
able to get around, but he pushed it out of his mind and continued toward the back door, only then spotting the box
springs and mattress tilted against the fence by the garage.
Someone had covered it with a plastic dropcloth to save it
from the weather, but the sight of it there behind the cloudy
plastic was disorienting, and he felt as if he had been away
forever.

The house was closed up now, the curtains drawn, and he
had to jiggle his key in the lock to turn the bolt. The door

creaked open slowly, and he stepped in onto the linoleum
floor after wiping his feet carefully on the mat. At once he
felt the emptiness of the house, as if it were hollow, rever-
berating with his footsteps. He walked as silently as he could
through the service porch and into the kitchen, where the tile
counter was empty of anything but a glass tumbler still
partly full of water. He reached for it in order to pour it into
the sink, but then let it alone and went out into the dining
room, straightening a chair that was out of place at the table.
The old oriental carpet was nearly threadbare outside the
bedroom door (Edna had always wanted him to step past it,
so as not to wear it out before its time) and seeing it now, that
footworn patch of rug, he felt the sorrow in the house like a
weight.

He listened at the bedroom door and allowed himself to
imagine that even now she sat inside, reading in the chair by
the window, that he could push the door open and simply tell
her he was sorry, straighten things out once and for all. If
only he had a chance to *explain* himself! He reached for the
doorknob, hesitated, dizzy for a moment with the uncanny
certainty that all the emptiness in the house was drifting out
from within that single room, wafting under the door, settling
on the furniture, on the carpets, on the lampshades and
books like soot in a train yard.

Setting his teeth, he turned the knob and pushed open the
door, peering carefully inside. Very nearly everything was as
he remembered: the chairs by the window, the long bookcase
on the wall, their bird's-eye maple chests, the cedar trunk at
the foot of the bed. He walked in, crossing the floor to the
bedside table. On top of it lay a glass paperweight, a silver
spoon, and a faded postcard with a picture of a boardwalk on
it—Atlantic City? Jimmerson almost recognized it. He had
been there before, he and Edna had. He picked up the paperweight and looked into its translucent glass, clouded by
milky swirls. He could almost see a face in the swirls, but
when it occurred to him that it was Edna's face, he set it
down again and turned to the bottom shelf of the table. A
liqueur glass sat there. There was a greenish residue in the

bottom, an oily smear, which smelled vaguely of camphor and juniper and weeds. He set the glass down and forced himself to look at the bed.

It was a single bed now, and although it wasn't a hospital bed, there were cloth and Velcro restraints affixed to the frame—wrist and ankle restraints both.

He rang Mrs. Crandle's doorbell, then stood back a couple of steps so as not to push her. She opened the door wide—no peering through the crack—and the look on her face held loathing and indifference both. "So you've come back," she said flatly. Her white hair hung over her forehead in a wisp, and her house smelled of cabbage and ironing.

"I've come back."

"Now that Edna's dead you've come back to take her things." She nodded when she said this, as if it stood to reason.

"*Our* things, Mrs. Crandle," he said unwisely.

"You have *no* claim," she said, cutting him off. "You walked out on that poor woman and left her to that . . . parlor rat. You might as well have killed her yourself. You *did* kill her. As sure as you're standing here now, Doyle Jimmerson, you took the breath of life right out of that poor woman." She stared at him, and for a moment he thought she was going to slam the door in his face.

"I didn't kill her, Mrs. Crandle. After forty years of marriage she chose another man, and I . . ."

"She chose nothing," Mrs. Crandle said. "She met a man who was a conversationalist, unlike some men I could name, a man of culture and breeding, and you flew off the handle. What did she want for herself but some of the finer things in life?—a nice dinner now and then at the French Café instead of once a month at the Steer Inn. You're beer and skittles, Doyle Jimmerson, but a little bit of Edna wanted a glass of champagne. That's all she wanted, Mr. Jimmerson, if you're capable of taking my meaning. And when she stood up for herself, you walked out, as if she was having some kind of affair."

"A conversationalist? *That's* what he was? I can think of a couple of other terms that aren't half as polite. Even you called him a parlor rat. Him and his stinking chin whiskers, his damned champagne. I couldn't stand it. I told her what I'd do before I'd stand it." But even when he said it he knew it was false. Anyone can stand anger. He could simply have thrown his anger out with the bath water. Loneliness and betrayal were another matter, not so easy to throw out. What had Edna suffered? The question silenced him.

"Yes, I did call him a rat," Mrs. Crandle said evenly. "And I'll just remind you that you abandoned your wife to that creature, even though you knew what he was. You couldn't take him, so you left Edna to take him. And *she* found out too late, didn't she? All of us did. Now she's dead and you've come down here to gloat. You won the war. To the victor go the spoils, eh?"

"I'm not the victor, Mrs. Crandle. I didn't win."

"No, you didn't, Mr. Jimmerson. You lost something more than you know."

He nodded his agreement. He couldn't argue with that. "What do you mean she found out 'too late'? Did the Frenchman have anything to do with . . ."

"Nothing and everything, I guess you could say. No more nor less than you had."

"Help me out here, Mrs. Crandle. Edna . . . she wouldn't tell me much."

"Well I'll tell you a thing or two. You went inside that house just now, that house where you yourself should have been living this last long year. And so maybe you've seen the room where she died. I was with her there in the last couple of weeks. I stayed by her."

"I thank you for that."

She looked at him in silence for a moment, as if she were tired of him. "You saw the bed?"

"I saw the bed, Mrs. Crandle. I saw the restraints."

"There was almost nothing left of her there at the end. That's all I can tell you. And I mean *nothing*. She was empty, Mr. Jimmerson, like something made out of sea foam. Any gust of wind might have blown her into the sky. At night, when the moon was overhead, she . . . she would start drifting away, poor thing."

"The moon . . ." he said, not quite comprehending. The word "lunacy" crept into his mind. He pictured that lonely bed again, Mrs. Crandle sitting in Edna's seat by the window, knitting and knitting while Edna drifted away, strapped to the bed frame, their old double bed out in the driveway going to bits in the weather. "She . . . When she called the last couple of times she sounded a little confused. Like she had lost track of things, you know. She even forgot who I was, who she had called. I guess I just didn't grasp that."

"That's a crying shame."

"Worse than that. I was pretty sure of myself, Mrs. Crandle—sure that I was in the right. What I mean is that I was so damned self-righteous that I put top spin on everything she said. Heaven help me I even twisted what she didn't say. She can tell me all about the Frenchman, was what I thought at the time, but she doesn't know her own damned husband of forty years. Hell," he said, and he rubbed his face tiredly, conscious now that rain was starting to fall again, pattering against the porch roof. "I guess I thought she was trying to get my goat."

"And so you got mad again. You hung up the phone."

"I did. I got mad. I was a damned fool, Mrs. Crandle, but there's not a thing that I can do about it now."

"Well, you're right about that, anyway, if it's any consolation to you."

"Tell me about it, then. Was it Alzheimer's?"

"I'm sure I don't know. I'm not certain it was in the medical books at all. It was a wasting disease. That's all I can tell you. Sorrow did it. Sorrow and abandonment. Gravity weighed too heavily upon her, Mr. Jimmerson, and when it looked like it would crush her, she did what she had to do. *She made herself light.* That's the only truth you'll find down here. I can't tell you anything more than that." Mrs. Crandle swung the door nearly shut now, and he shoved his foot against the jamb to block it.

"Where is she, Mrs. Crandle? You can tell me that much."

"Over at Angel's Flight," she said through the nearly closed door. "They buried her last week. No service of course, except for the Father from up at the Holy Childhood. He said a few words alongside the grave, but it was just me and a couple of the others from the old bridge club. I suppose you can get over there tonight and make your peace if you want to. Or leastwise you can *try* to make your peace. I hope you can find the words." She shut the door firmly now, against his shoe, and then opened it long enough for him to jerk his foot out before slamming it shut again.

He hadn't gotten anything out of her except bitterness, which was as much as he deserved. He headed down the porch steps, realizing that he hadn't really wanted to know about the bed restraints. What he wanted to know was what had gone through her mind while he was sitting full of self-pity up in Seattle. What she had thought about *him*, about the long years that they were married, what her loneliness *felt* like. He had lost her for a year, and he wanted that year back, along with all the rest that he hadn't paid any attention to. No matter that it was bound to be a Pandora's box, full of sorrow and demons, and perhaps without Hope at the bottom, either.

Evening had fallen, with big clouds scudding across the sky in a wild race, the rain falling steadily now. He headed up Lemon Street through the downpour. The street lamps were on, haloed by the misty rain, and the gutters already ran with water. Living rooms and front porches were lighted, and he saw a man and a woman looking out through a big picture window at the front of one of the houses, watching the rain the way people sit and watch a fire in a fireplace. He thought of where he would sleep tonight and knew that it wouldn't be among the dusty ghosts in the house; the back of the Mercury would be good enough for him, parked in the driveway, despite what Mrs. Crandle would think and what it would do to his back.

Where Lemon dead-ended into Marigold, he turned up

through the big wrought iron gates of the cemetery, and drove slowly toward the stone building nearly hidden in the shade of a cluster of vast trees. Vines climbed the walls of the three-story granite mausoleum, and light shone out from within a deep lamp-lit portico in the tower that served as an entry. There was a second high tower at the rear of the building, lit by lamps hidden on the mausoleum roof. This second tower was clearly a columbarium, the hundreds of wall niches set with tiny doors. A stone stairway spiraled upward around it, and rainwater washed down the stairs now as if it were a mountain cataract. Beyond the tower lay a hundred feet of lawn strewn with headstones, and beyond that a walnut grove stretched away into the darkness, the big white-trunked walnut trees mostly empty of leaves. Above the shadowy grove the moon shone past the edge of a cloud. Jimmerson angled the Mercury into a parking stall, cut the engine, and sat watching for another moment as an owl flew out of the grove and disappeared beneath the eaves of the tower. He got out of the car, slammed the door, and hunched through the rain, ducking in under the portico roof where he rang the bell.

He heard footsteps inside, and the arched door opened slowly to reveal a high-ceilinged room with stone floors and dark wood paneling. The man in the doorway was tall and thin, with a stretched, Lincolnesque face and a rumpled black suit. Jimmerson stepped into the room, which smelled of gardenias, and the man swung the door shut against the rain.

"It's a hellish night," he said, and he nodded at Jimmerson. "I'm George Gladstone."

"Doyle Jimmerson, Mr. Gladstone. I'm glad to meet you."

"I see. You must be Edna Jimmerson's . . . ?"

"Husband." He felt like a fraud. "I was in Seattle when I heard. On business. I drove straight down."

"I'm certain you got here as quickly as you could, Mr. Jimmerson, and welcome to Angel's Flight." A long sideboard stood against the far wall of the room, and on top of the sideboard was a bowl of floating gardenia blossoms and an iron clock. The sound of the ticking clock filled the mausoleum. A gilt-framed painting hung above the sideboard depicting a man and a woman dressed in robes, ascending into heaven in defiance of gravity. An arched door stood open in the clouds, and the Earth lay far below. Here and there above it more people were ascending, tiny wingless angels rising into the sky against the blue of the ocean.

"Very nice picture," Jimmerson said. And he peered more closely at the door in the clouds, at the light that shone from beyond it. There was something in the spiral brush strokes that looked like eyes, hundreds of them, staring out from heaven at the world of the living.

"We like to think of ourselves as a celestial depot, Mr. Jimmerson."

"That's a comforting thought." He turned his back on the painting. "I wonder if I could see . . . Edna's grave. My wife. I realize it's late, and the weather and all . . ."

"Yes, of course you can."

"You don't have to take any trouble. If you'll just show me the way . . ."

"No trouble at all, Mr. Jimmerson. Give me a moment and I'll see to the equipage." Jimmerson followed him into an adjacent room, where a display of coffins was laid out, the coffins set into niches along a stone wall, all of them tilted up at the head end to better show them off. Light shone down on them from candle-flame bulbs in iron chandeliers high above in the ceiling, but the light was dim and the room full of shadows cast by the coffins and by the complex framework of iron that supported them. Jimmerson looked them over, vaguely and shamefully wondering which sort Edna had been buried in—nothing expensive, probably.

They were apparently arranged in order of extravagance. A simple coffin-shaped pine box lay nearest the door, the two-piece lid nailed tight on the bottom and hinged open at the top to reveal a quilted satin lining within. There was a fancier box next to it, some sort of exotic veneer with chrome hardware, and next to that a white-lacquered box with gold handles and a round glass viewing window. Jimmerson stepped across to it and looked in through the porthole, then gasped and trod back when he saw that there was someone inside—a man, pale and thin and with his coat collar too high on his neck.

He forced himself to take another look, and he saw this time that it was a display dummy, its hair very neatly combed and its cheeks rouged. A fly had gotten inside somehow and died, and it lay now on the white satin pillow alongside the dummy's head. It occurred to him that he ought to point the fly out to Gladstone, just for the sake of friendliness, but Gladstone had utterly disappeared, and the mausoleum was silent but for the ticking of the entryway clock. Jimmerson ran his hand over the polished ebony of the next casket, and then walked along past a half dozen more—gold-leafed, inlaid, and carved and with handles and hasps and doodads of silver and ivory. There was an Egyptian sarcophagus, the lid thrown back and supported by a heavy-linked chain. The raised image on the lid was of a pharaoh-looking robed man with a conical beard, his arms crossed, his head turned to the side. In his hands he held a richly painted ankh and a striped serpent, and within the casket, tilted against a brass easel, lay an explanatory placard suggesting that instead of a pharaoh, the image of your loved one might be fashioned on the lid, holding anything at all in his hands—a favorite tie, a fountain pen, a golf club. The casket was extra wide, the paneled sides fit with slots that contained a pair of decorative flasks and a cut crystal tumbler. There were other slots left empty, book-size cubbyholes and a sliding glass panel suitable for a framed photograph.

"All the comforts of home," Gladstone said, coming into the room. "Room at the foot end for a companion as well. Mr. Hemming, the car dealer from Santa Ana, was interred with his dog."

"They killed the dog?" Jimmerson asked, horrified.

"Oh heavens no. The dog died of grief. It's not at all uncommon. Dogs are particularly sensitive that way." He stared at Jimmerson for a moment, as if he intended the comment to make some sort of point, a not very obscure point, and then he said, "Perhaps you'd like to see a little something."

Jimmerson followed him out of the room, back toward the rear of the mausoleum where their footsteps echoed down a long corridor lit with flickering wall sconces. There were heavy wooden doors in the stone walls on either side. Gladstone stopped at one of the doors, removed a skeleton key from his pocket, and unlocked the bolt, swinging it open on its hinges to reveal a room containing half a dozen steel tables. A cord emerged from a slot at the bottom of one of the tables, and floating like a helium balloon some few feet from the ceiling, tethered by its foot to the cord, was what appeared to be a shroud-draped human corpse, its face and bare feet exposed to the dim light of the room.

Jimmerson at first took it for another dummy, and he glanced at the ceiling, expecting to see wires. There were none. He stared at it, uncomprehending, but then with a growing certainty that the thing's pale flesh and stringy hair was in fact the flesh and hair of a dead man. Gladstone stepped across and tugged on the cord, which wound down into the table. The corpse descended a couple of feet and then floated slowly upward again when he let go of the cord, its feet swinging around in a clockwise direction, then back again. "He'll come down on his own fairly soon," Gladstone said, seeing the look on Jimmerson's face. "These cases always do. It takes about twelve hours for the spirit to flee the body after death, and then the remains are earthbound once again. Often there's nothing left but a paper shell, easily inflatable if the family wants an open casket funeral."

"What . . . what on earth did he die of?"

"A broken heart, Mr. Jimmerson. I'll tell you that plainly. Medical science calls it 'voluntary dwindling' when they call it anything at all. Which they don't, for the most part. It's utterly beyond the grasp of medicine. These are matters of the spirit, by and large. And it's rare, I can assure you, that we get two such advanced cases in a single week." He stared at Jimmerson again, who suddenly remembered the restraints on Edna's deathbed. What had Mrs. Crandle said about Edna's "drifting away"? Had she been speaking literally . . . ?

"Was Edna . . . ?"

Gladstone nodded slowly, and Jimmerson leaned against the plaster wall to steady himself.

"She's out of harm's way now," Gladstone said, patting Jimmerson's arm. "Let's have a look at her grave, shall we?"

He led the way down the corridor again, Jimmerson stumbling along after him, until they came out into a sort of stone gardener's shed with a lean-to roof. Mud-caked spades and shovels stood tilted against the wall, and a steel backhoe scoop lay on the floor alongside the iron debris of a dismantled engine, greasy pistons and bolts and hoses dumped haphazardly on the ground. Two yellow rain slickers hung from hooks by the door, and Gladstone stepped over the engine parts and took them down, handing one to Jimmerson. It had an attached hat with a wide brim, and the coat itself hung to Jimmerson's knees. Gladstone passed him a black umbrella, then opened the door and stepped out into the rain, which was falling more lightly now.

Jimmerson followed him along a narrow stone path, hoisting his umbrella against the mist and turning it into the wind, which gusted through the trees, sweeping down a litter of dead oak leaves that whirled away across the grounds. The night smelled of wet leaves and clay, and the moon shone between the clouds, the headstones casting long shadows on the grass. The path wound in a wide circle toward the walnut grove, past a lily-choked fish pond and a cluster of mossy concrete benches. Gladstone finally stopped at the edge of a small, gently sloping hill where a rectangle of new turf covered a tiny grave. They stood silently for a moment.

"It's awfully small," Jimmerson whispered at last.

Gladstone nodded. "It's not uncommon," he said, "that a dwindler can fit into a casket the size of shoe box, once the spirit has flown. And it's not without its advantages, I suppose, when all is said and done. Very conservative burial, spatially speaking."

"Will there be a headstone?" Jimmerson asked. "I guess it's up to me to order one."

"One should arrive from the stonecutters late next week,

.actually. It was paid for by a Mr. des Laumes, I believe the name was. French gentleman. You must have known him." Gladstone gave him a sidewise glance, then looked quickly away.

"Cancel the order," Jimmerson told him.

"It's too late for that," Mr. Jimmerson. "The work's underway. Very elaborate, too."

"I don't want elaborate. I want simple. This Frenchman's got no right to order a headstone. Who gave him permission to shove his oar in?"

"Permission, Mr. Jimmerson? In the absence of any other offering . . ." He shrugged helplessly. "Of course, now that you've returned . . ."

"That's right. Now that I've come home Mr. des Laumes's headstone can go to hell. If the work's already started, then I'll pay for it. Mr. des Laumes can have it back with interest, too—on top of his head."

"As you wish, sir," Gladstone said. "It only has to snow once before I get the drift." He nodded and winked, shook Jimmerson's hand, and then moved off down the path again, heading back toward the mausoleum. Jimmerson stayed by the graveside, forcing himself to simmer down. By God, he wouldn't let this Frenchman give him another moment of grief, not one more moment—especially not here at Edna's grave.

It struck him suddenly that he ought to have brought flowers, something . . . a keepsake of some sort. His boxes of stuff were still in the Mercury, and he looked out across the hundred yards of rainy night toward the shadowy station wagon, picturing the clusters of quartz crystals they'd brought home from Death Valley and the pair of conical ceramic tornadoes from Edna's family reunion back in Kansas.

But what would he do with them?—scatter salt and pepper shakers across the grave like amulets? He knelt in the grass and ran his hand over the wet squares of turf fitted over the grave, and he felt the freshening rain patter against his slicker. He didn't bother with the umbrella now, but pulled the hat brim down over his forehead, closed his eyes, and tried to pray.

Prayer didn't come easily. He tried again, trying to concentrate, to focus, but almost at once he doubted his own sincerity, and the prayer fell to pieces. His father had told him years ago that a man couldn't pray when he was drunk, and although Jimmerson wasn't a drinking man, he had enough experience to take his meaning. Now it seemed to him that a guilty man had an even more precarious time praying than a drunken man, and for a long time his mind went round and round with partly formed apologetic phrases, half of them addressed to Edna, half addressed to the sky, until finally he shoved the hat back off his head and knelt in the rain with his forehead in his hands, utterly defeated.

He looked up finally to find the moon high in the sky, free of the walnut grove now. Down by the fish pond there was the shadow of Gladstone waiting patiently in his yellow slicker on one of the concrete benches. Jimmerson rose to his feet, his knees creaking beneath him, and walked carefully downhill to the path, where he looked back at Edna's grave.

She wouldn't speak to him. She couldn't. She had gone on.

Jimmerson stood once again in the room with the clock and the flowers, where he had just signed the work order for Edna's headstone—her true headstone, a simple granite slab: loving wife of Doyle Jimmerson, marriage date as well as birth and death. Jimmerson had contracted for the plot adjacent to hers, too, and paid for a twin headstone for himself.

"I'm afraid I still don't entirely understand Edna's death," he said, standing finally in the open doorway.

"No less than I do, perhaps," Gladstone told him. "These deaths are always a mystery—the secret of the deceased, you know. I'm familiar with the physical manifestations at the end, of course, but the progress of the disease itself is not in my province."

Jimmerson nodded. "So it's not a virus? It's not something she caught?"

"Caught?" He shook his head. "No more than you'd say that a fish catches a baited hook. Rather the other way around."

"Hook? What do you mean?"

"Let's just say that voluntary dwindling isn't entirely voluntary, Mr. Jimmerson. It's voluntary in the main, of course. As I understand it, no one dwindles unless he chooses to dwindle. But the process can be . . . *facilitated*, perhaps. Suggested."

"Facilitated how?" The Frenchman's face leaped into his mind again, complete with the fact of Mrs. Crandle's apparently despising the man. He had been right!—the man was a cad; although the knowledge of having been right looked like damnation to him. Had he left Edna to some sort of murderer?

"I'm rather at a loss," Gladstone said. "It's my policy to know nothing more than it pays me to know. I might be able to help you, though, although the word 'help' . . ." He shook his head.

"I'd appreciate that, Mr. Gladstone. Anything you can do for me."

Gladstone stared at him again, narrowing his eyes. "You recall the man in the embalming room, tethered to the cord . . . ?"

"Yes, of course."

"He told me much the same thing once, not so very long ago. Death of an old friend, in his case. They'd had some kind of sad falling out and hadn't spoken in years. So I'll caution you to be particularly careful of what you learn, Mr. Jimmerson. And I'll tell you that Mr. des Laumes has purchased more than one headstone in his day."

With the help of Gladstone's map, Jimmerson found the curiosity shop downtown. It was near the Plaza, and from the sidewalk the shop was apparently empty. The linoleum floor was cracked and buckled, scattered with yellowed newsprint and empty White Rock and Nehi soft drink bottles that hadn't been sold in grocery stores for years. The windows were hung with cobwebs, and the broad sills were covered with a heavy layer of dust and dead bugs and a litter of old business cards. Jimmerson and Edna had often remarked on the shop when they'd walked downtown. Leases near the

Plaza were at a premium, yet the shop had gone untenanted since either of them could remember.

As he stood outside, looking in at the window, it seemed to him that the place had a curious perspective to it. He couldn't quite tell how deep it was. The walls were hung with mirrors, dim with dust, and the hazy reflections, depending upon where he stood, made the store appear sometimes to be prodigiously deep, sometimes to be a space so narrow that it might have been one-dimensional, cleverly painted on the window glass. The front door, weathered and paint-scaled, was nailed shut, and a number of envelopes had been dumped through the brass mail slot over the years, many of them with long-out-of-date postage stamps.

Gladstone's map led him around the corner, past a Middle Eastern deli and a shop selling Italian antiques. The day was windy, the sky full of tearing clouds, and Jimmerson pulled his coat tightly around him, turning another corner and heading north now, searching for the mouth of the alley that Gladstone had assured him lay at the back of the old buildings. There was the smell of Turkish coffee in the air, and of wet sidewalks and open Dumpsters, and he walked straight past the alley before he knew it. It wasn't really an alley as such, but was a circular doorway in the brick façade of the buildings, and it opened into a sort of courtyard, a patch of gray sky showing far overhead. Jimmerson peered into the dimly lit recess before stepping over the high curb and into the sheltered twilight. The courtyard was utterly silent, the walls blocking even the traffic noise on the street. He walked hesitantly along the wall, trailing his right hand, and watching to see if there was anyone about. He felt as if he were trespassing, and he was ready to apologize and get the hell out if he were challenged at all. But the courtyard was empty, the brick pavers up in weeds as if no one had walked there for an age.

A row of high, shuttered windows with an iron balcony looked down from the second story; the lower story was nothing but weathered brick, uninterrupted except for a single deeply set door with a heavy brass knocker and a tiny peephole. Jimmerson stood looking for a moment at the door. Gladstone had described it to him, and, seeing it now, he felt as if he were at the edge of something, as if something were pending, as if opening it would change things irreversibly and forever.

A gust of wind blew into the courtyard, kicking up a little wind devil of leaves and trash and dust, and Jimmerson ducked into the doorway recess, out of the turmoil. He put his hand on the door knocker, but the door was apparently unlatched, and it immediately slammed open, propelled by the wind. Jimmerson slipped inside, pressing the door shut behind him, and stood for a moment in the quiet darkness, letting his eyes adjust. He heard sounds now, the shuffling of paper and a noise that sounded like the muted cawing of a crow, and he stepped carefully along down the hallway toward what was clearly the back door of a shop that fronted on the Plaza, the door's wavy glass window dimly lighted from the other side. Hesitantly, he rapped on the glass, ready to convince himself that there was nobody there, that Gladstone was a lunatic. The floating corpse might as easily have been a clever balloon. And Mrs. Crandle was so stupefyingly obscure that . . .

He heard a voice from beyond the door, and he knocked again, harder this time.

"Come in," someone said, and Jimmerson turned the knob and pushed the door open, looking past it at the interior of a cluttered curiosity shop. He nearly tripped over an elephant's-foot umbrella stand that held a dozen dusty umbrellas, some of them so old and shopworn that their fabric was like dusty lace. There were thousands of books stacked on open shelves, tilting against the walls, piled in glass-fronted cases alongside crystal wineglasses and flasks and decanters. There was a tarnished silver ice bucket with *S.S. Titanic* inscribed on the front, and fishbowls full of marbles, and no end of salt and pepper shakers—grinning moon men and comical dogs and ceramic renditions of characters out of ancient comic strips. The skeleton of a bird hung from the ceiling, and beneath it stood propped-open trunks full of doilies and tablecloths and old manuscripts. A painting of an ape and another of a clipper ship reclined against a long wooden counter scattered with boxes of old silverware and candlesticks and hinges and dismantled chandeliers. The silver seemed to shimmer where it lay, and there appeared above it a brief crackling of flame, like a witch fire, that died out again with a whoosh of exhalation.

He noticed a crow on a high perch, staring down at him, its head tilted sideways. The crow hopped along the perch, clicking its beak, and then said, "Come in," three times in succession. Beyond the crow's perch, back past the clutter of collectibles and curiosities, lay more rooms full of stuff. He could make out toasters and fans and other pieces of electrical gadgetry, old clothes and musical instruments and coffee mugs and articles of wooden furniture, most of it apparently thrift store junk. Back in the shadows something rose slowly into the air and then descended again, and there was the brief sound of moaning from somewhere deep in the shop, and another gleam of witch fire that ran along the tops of the books leaving a ghostly trail behind it that drifted lazily to the ceiling.

There was a movement behind the counter, and Jimmerson saw that a man sat back there on a tall stool. He was a small man with compressed features, possibly a dwarf, and he read a heavy book, his brow furrowed with concentration, as if he were unaware that Jimmerson had come into the shop.

A sign on the counter read, "Merchandise taken in pawn. Any items left over thirty days sold for expenses." Another sign read, "All items a penny. No refunds." Jimmerson looked around again, this time in growing astonishment. The shop was packed with collectibles, some of them clearly valuable antiques. A suit of armor in the corner appeared to be ancient—a museum piece—and there was a glass case of jewelry that sparkled like fireflies even in the dim shop light. The all-items-a-penny sign must be some sort of obscure, lowball joke.

"Selling or buying?" the dwarf asked him suddenly, and Jimmerson realized that he had put the book down and leaned forward on his stool. There was a lamp on the counter, a great brass fish that illuminated half his face. The other half remained in shadow, giving him a slightly sinister appearance. "Lucius Pillbody," the dwarf said, extending his hand.

"Doyle Jimmerson," Jimmerson told him. "I guess I'm really just . . . curious."

"People who are just curious can't find me," Pillbody said. "So don't be coy. Either you've got something to sell to me or else you're looking to buy."

"I'd simply like to ask you a couple of questions, if I could. My wife died recently. Her name was Edna Jimmerson."

"*That* Jimmerson! Of course. Wonderful woman. Very good customer."

"She bought a good deal, then?" He could easily imagine Edna buying almost any of this stuff, taking it home by the bagful—although he hadn't seen any evidence of it in the house aside from the odds and ends on the bedside table.

"I can't recall that she bought anything," Pillbody said. "But then that's hardly surprising. Why would she?"

"Well . . . A penny? Why wouldn't she?"

"Because, Mr. Jimmerson, like most of our customers she was interested in lightening ship, throwing the ballast overboard, you know, unencumbering herself."

"I guess I don't know. I've been away."

"I mean to say that she pawned a goodly number of her own possessions." He waved his hand, gesturing at the lumber of stuff in the shop. "Heaven knows how much of this was hers. I don't keep books, Mr. Jimmerson. I used to separate things out a bit—Mr. Jones on the east wall and Mr. Smith on the west wall, figuratively speaking, which worked well enough if Smith and Jones were willing to let go of a great deal of merchandise. But what about Mr. so-and-so, who came in with a single item and never returned?"

Jimmerson shook his head helplessly.

"Well, I could tag it, of course, and arrange it on a shelf, alphabetically, say. But there were a hundred Mr. so-and-sos and I was always losing track. Tags would fall off. I'd have a

busy week and have to find a second shelf to handle the over-
stock. In thirty days, of course, the merchandise would come
off that shelf and find its way onto yet another shelf. And nobody *ever* claims their pawn, Mr. Jimmerson. In all my years
in the business only a couple of resolute customers have
changed their mind and asked for their merchandise back.
Possessions, Mr. Jimmerson, are a great weight to most
people, and I'm afraid that your wife was no exception, if
you'll pardon my saying so."

Jimmerson nodded blankly. Apparently he knew far less
about Edna than he thought he did. He had never really paid
attention, never tried to see the world the way she saw it. He
had always been too caught up in his own point of view, in
his own way of seeing things. Even with this damned
Frenchman. Edna obviously found something in the man that
she couldn't find in Doyle Jimmerson. What was it? Jimmerson had never asked, never even thought about it.

"Anyway, now there's no order to things," Pillbody said.
"Smith and Jones are scattered far and wide. I made some effort—when was it? midcentury, I guess—to order things according to *type*, but to tell you the truth, that didn't work out
very well either. A certain amount of the merchandise is—
what do you call it? Off color, perhaps. Obscene is nearer the
mark. I'm talking about the product, let's say, of a particularly disturbed mind, of the human id at its darker levels:
your murderer, your pervert. You'd be astonished at what
you'd find in here, Mr. Jimmerson. Objective tokens of murder and rape. Illicit sex. The sort of trash that you or I would
repress, you know, hide away from the light. Does that aston-
ish you?"

"I don't know," Jimmerson said. "I guess I *am* astonished."

"All of it went into the room back in the southeast corner,
what I used to call the parlor room. Full to overflowing, I can
assure you. Now and then a customer would come in, feigning interest in books or jewelry or what have you, but by and
by he'd disappear into the parlor room, and I knew what sort
of thing he was *really* after, groping around back there in the
dark. There was one man, a Mr. Ricketts, who frequented the

parlor room. One of my best customers, if you want to define the word purely in terms of copper coins, which none of us do. Mint?"

"Pardon me?" Jimmerson asked. He was utterly baffled now. Murder? Perversion in the parlor room? No *wonder* this place was hidden away.

The man held out a small bowl of white mints. Jimmerson shook his head, and the man shrugged. "Looks just like Depression glass, doesn't it?"

He tilted the bowl, allowing Jimmerson to get a better look at it. It was pink, and had a sort of repeating pineapple pattern on it. There was something not quite symmetrical about the bowl, though, as if it had gotten hot and partly collapsed of its own weight, and it had a heavy seam down the center of it, as if it had broken and been welded back together. In each of the pineapples there was a depiction of the same human face, vaguely angry, its eyes half shut.

The face looked remarkably familiar to Jimmerson. The bowl too, for that matter, although he couldn't for the life of him place it. The dwarf set it down carefully.

"What finally happened," Pillbody said, "was that the parlor room began to stink. Even now you've noticed a certain smell on the air." He squinted seriously, as if Jimmerson might dispute this somehow, but Jimmerson nodded in agreement. He had gotten a whiff of it now and then, an undefinable smell of rot. "It was almost poetic. Artistic, you might say. The smell would draw this man Ricketts the way rotten meat draws flies, not to put too fine a point on it. Well, I simply couldn't stand it any longer. I have to work here. If I had my way, I'd throw all of it out, straight into the bin. But then of course I don't have my way, do I? Which of us does? So finally I fell upon the idea of scattering the stuff throughout the store, an item here, another item there, and when they weren't any longer in close proximity, they stank a good deal less, although it took years for them to really settle down. Meanwhile I moved—how shall I put it?—a more pleasant selection of merchandise into the parlor room. Much of what we receive here is not altogether unpleasant, after all, at least to you or I. The problem was essentially solved, aside from the telltale remnants surfacing here and there. Too much order, I said to myself, and you start to breed problems. Things start to stink. Unfortunately, one can still detect the odor back there in the parlor room, especially on a rainy day, when the air is heavy. It's like spilled perfume that's soaked into the floorboards. And of course I still get the same sort of customer nosing his way back there, although Mr. Ricketts has been dead these twenty years. Killed by his own filthy habits, I might add."

Jimmerson nodded blankly, then picked up the candy dish again and looked hard at the pattern in the glass, at the unpleasant repeated face. . . .

It was his own face.

He was suddenly certain of it, and the realization nearly throttled him. He looked in surprise at Pillbody, who merely shrugged.

"As you've no doubt realized, that was one of your wife's items, Mr. Jimmerson."

"Can I buy it?" He hardly knew what he meant by asking. If it had belonged to Edna, though, he wanted it, no matter what it cost. No matter how strange and inexplicable.

"I'm afraid that raises a fairly delicate question, Mr. Jimmerson."

"What question? If I know the answer . . ." He gestured helplessly.

"Has Mrs. Jimmerson . . . passed on?"

"Last week."

"Then the bowl's for sale. Let me find something else to put the mints in." He rummaged around under the counter, finally drawing out what looked like a tin basin. "I got this from a barber's wife," he said. "Take a look." He held the basin up so that Jimmerson looked into the bottom side, which was highly polished, almost a mirror. Instead of his own reflection Jimmerson saw a man with a beard looking back out at him, his throat cut from ear to ear, blood running down into the white cloth tied around his neck. He recoiled from the sight of it, and Pillbody set it down on the counter.

"Doesn't affect the flavor of the mints at all," he said, and he dumped the candy out of Edna's bowl and into the basin. "That'll be a penny." He held out his hand.

"Just a penny?"

"Just one. Everything's a penny. But I'll warn you. If you try to return it, you'll pay considerably more to get rid of it than you paid to possess it. Could be entirely impossible, out of the question, unthinkable."

"I don't want to return it," Jimmerson said, and he dug in his pocket for a penny. The dwarf took the coin from him and set it on the counter. Jimmerson looked around then, suddenly certain that he could find more of Edna's things, and straightaway he saw a familiar pair of salt and pepper shakers—ceramic tornadoes, one of them grinning and the other looking like the day of judgment.

"Were these . . . ?" Jimmerson started to ask.

"Those too. Only two weeks ago."

This was uncanny. Jimmerson had the same shakers in his box in the back of the Merc. Except his were smaller, he was sure of it now, and the faces not so clearly defined. One of these had the unmistakable appearance of Edna's dead Aunt Betsy, and the ceramic platform that they stood on was divided by a piece of picket fence that recalled the rickety fence around the Kansas farm where Edna had grown up. His own salt and peppers had no such fence.

"You're certain these were hers?" Jimmerson asked.

"Absolutely."

"I don't recall that she owned any such thing. We bought a similar pair years ago, in the Midwest, but they're different from these. They're in my car, in fact, parked out front." He waved his hand, but realized that he no longer had any idea where "out front" was. His shoulders ached terribly, and he felt as if he had been carrying a heavy pack on his back for hours. His ears were plugged, too, and he wiggled his jaw to clear them.

"These were *very* recent acquisitions," Pillbody said. "Mrs. Jimmerson brought them to me along with the candy bowl. It's not surprising that you were unaware of them."

Jimmerson fished out another penny. "All right, then. I'll take these, too," he said.

Pillbody shook his head. "I'm afraid not, Mr. Jimmerson."

"I don't understand."

"One thing at a time, sir. You'll overload your circuitry otherwise. You'd need heavy gauge wiring. Good clean copper. The best insulation."

"*Circuitry?* Insu*lation?* By God then I guess I'll take the whole shebang," Jimmerson said, suddenly getting angry. What a lot of tomfoolery! He gestured at the counter, at the books in the wall behind it, taking it all in with a wave of his hand. He pulled his wallet out of his back pocket and found a twenty-dollar bill. "Start with the jewelry," he said, slapping the money down, "and then we'll move on to this collection of salt shakers. We'll need boxes, because I've got more money where this came from. I'll clean this place out, Mr. Pillbody, if that's what it takes to get Edna's merchandise back, and if my money's no good here, then we'll take it up with the Chamber of Commerce and the Better Business Bureau this very afternoon."

Pillbody stared at him. "Let me show you a little something," he said quietly, echoing Gladstone's words, and he reached down and pulled aside a curtain in the front of the counter. Inside, on a preposterously heavy iron stand, sat what appeared to be a garden elf or a manlike gargoyle, perhaps carved out of stone. Its face had a desperate, constricted look to it, and it squatted on its hams, its head on its knees and its hands pressed against the platform it sat on. "Go ahead and pick it up," Pillbody said. "That's right. Get a grip on it."

Baffled, Jimmerson bent over, put his hands on the statue, and tried to lift it, but the thing was immovable, apparently epoxied to the platform on which it sat. Seen up close, its face was stunningly lifelike, although its features were pinched and distorted as if by some vast gravity of emotion. Jimmerson stepped away from it, appalled. "What the hell is it?" he asked. "What's going on here?"

"It's mighty heavy, isn't it?"

"This is some kind of trick," Jimmerson said.

"Oh, it's no trick," Pillbody said. "It's a dead man. He's so shatteringly compressed that I guarantee you that a floor jack wouldn't lift him. A crane might do the trick, if you could get one in through the door."

"I don't understand," Jimmerson said, all the anger gone now. He was sure somehow that Pillbody wasn't lying, any more than Gladstone had been lying about the floating corpse. "Does this have something to do with Edna, with the dwindling that Mr. Gladstone mentioned?"

"The dwindling?" Pillbody said. "After a fashion I suppose it does. This was a gentleman who quite simply spent too much money. I don't have any idea what he *thought* he was buying, but he endeavored, much like yourself, to purchase several hundred dollars' worth of merchandise all at once. He was, how shall I put it? A parlor room client, perhaps. In my own defense, I'll say that I had never had any experience along those lines, and I quite innocently agreed to sell it to him. This was the result." He gestured at the garden elf.

"How?" Jimmerson said. "I don't . . ."

Pillbody shrugged theatrically. "I didn't either. The man was simply crushed beneath the weight of it, piled on top of him suddenly like that. Surely you can feel it, Mr. Jimmerson, the terrible pressure in this shop?"

"Yes," Jimmerson said. His very bones seemed to grind together within him now, and he looked around for some place to sit down. He thought he heard the floorboards groaning, the very foundation creaking, and there was the sound of things settling roundabout him: the crinkle of old paper, the sigh of what sounded like air brakes, a grainy sound like sand shoveled into a sack, the witch fires leaping and dying . . .

"It's like the sea bottom," Pillbody whispered. "The desperate pressures of the human soul, as heavy and as poisonous as mercury when they're decocted. Our gentleman was simply crushed." He shook his head sadly. "I can't tell you how much work it was to get him up onto the iron plinth here. We had to reinforce the floor. Here, let me get you a chair, Mr. Jimmerson."

He dragged a rickety folding chair from behind the counter now and levered it open, then drew the drape across the front of the thing in the counter cubbyhole. Jimmerson sat down gratefully, but immediately there was the sound of wooden joints snapping, and the seat of the chair broke loose from the legs and back, and Jimmerson slammed down onto the wooden floor where he sat in a heap among the broken chair parts, trying to catch his breath.

"My advice is simply to take the candy dish, Mr. Jimmerson. Tomorrow's another day. Tomorrow's always another day."

Jimmerson climbed heavily to his feet, steadying himself against the counter. He took the dish and nodded his thanks, and Pillbody picked his penny up off the counter and dropped it into a slot cut into the back of the fish lamp. Jimmerson plodded heavily toward the door. He had the curious feeling that he was falling, that he was so monstrously heavy he was plummeting straight through the center of the Earth and would shoot feet first out the far side. He reached unsteadily for the doorknob, yanked the door open, and stepped into the dim hallway, where, as if from a tremendous distance, he heard the dull metallic clang of the penny finally hitting the bottom of the brass fish. There was the sound of an avalanche of tumbling coins, and then silence when the door banged shut behind him.

He felt the wind in his face now, the corridor stretching away in front of him like an asphalt highway, straight as an arrow, its vanishing point visible in the murky distance. Moss-hung trees rushed along on either side of him, and he knew he was on the road again, recognized the southern Louisiana landscape, the road south of New Orleans where he and Edna had found a farmhouse bed and breakfast. The memory flooded in upon him, and he gripped the candy dish, pressing it against his chest as the old Pontiac bounced along the rutted road, past chickens and low-lying swampland, weathered hovels and weedy truck patches. Edna sat silently beside him, gazing out the window. Neither of them had spoken for a half an hour.

She had bought the candy dish from an antique store along the highway—late yesterday afternoon? It seemed like a lifetime ago. It seemed as if everything he could remember had happened to him late yesterday afternoon, his entire past rolling up behind the Pontiac like a snail shell. The memory of their argument—his argument—was abruptly clear in his mind. He heard his own voice, remembered how clever it had been when he had called her a junkaholic, and talked about how she shouldn't spend so much of their money on worthless trash. He saw the two of them in that little wooden room with the sloped ceiling, the four-poster bed: how after giving her a piece of his mind, he had knocked the candy dish onto the floor and broken it in two. She had accused him of knocking it off on purpose, which of course he said he hadn't, and he had gotten sore, and told her to haul the rest of the junk she'd bought out of its bags and boxes—the ceramics and glassware, the thimbles and postcards and knickknacks—and he'd cheerfully fling the whole pile of it into the duck pond.

He shut his eyes, listening to the tires hum on the highway. Had he knocked the dish onto the floor on purpose? Certainly he hadn't meant to break it, to hurt Edna. It was just that . . . Damn it, he couldn't remember what it was. All justification had vanished. His years-old anger looked nutty to him now. What damned difference did it make that Edna wanted a pink glass candy dish? He wished to God he had bought her a truckload of them. His cherished anger had been a bottomless well, but now that she was gone, now that the whole issue of candy dishes was a thing of the irretrievable past, he couldn't summon any anger at all. It was simply empty, that well.

He glanced out the car window at a half dozen white egrets that stood stilt-legged in a marsh, and he reached across the seat and tried to pat her leg, but he couldn't reach her. She sat too far away from him now. He accelerated, pushing the car over a low rise, the sun glaring so brightly on

the highway ahead that he turned his face away. He held the
dish out to her, but she ignored him, watching the landscape
through the window, and the sorrow that hovered in the air
around her like a shade was confused in his mind with the
upholstery smell of their old pink and gray Pontiac. The car
had burned oil—a quart every few days—but they had
driven it through forty-two states, put a lot of highway behind them, a lot of miles.

"Take it," he whispered.

But even as he spoke it seemed to him that she was fading, slipping away from him. There was the smell of hot oil
burning on the exhaust manifold, and the sun was far too
bright through the windshield, and the tires hummed like a
swarm of bees, and the candy dish slipped out of his hand
and fell into two pieces on the gray fabric of the car seat.

When he came to himself he was outside again, standing
in the wind, the door that led to the curiosity shop closed behind him. He searched the paving stones for the broken
candy dish, but it was simply gone, vanished. He tried the
door, but it was locked now. He banged the door knocker,
hammering away, and the sound of the blows rang through
the courtyard, echoing from the high brick walls.

The Café de Laumes lay two blocks west of the Plaza, near
the old train station. It shared a wall with Tubbs Cordage
Company, and across the street lay a vacant lot strewn with
broken concrete from a long-ago demolished building. In the
rainy evening gloom the café looked tawdry and cheerless
despite the lights glowing inside. There was no sign hanging
outside, just an address in brass numbers and a menu taped
into the window. He watched the café door from the Mercury,
not quite knowing what he wanted, what he was going to do.
He opened the glove box and looked again at the .38 that lay
inside, and then he gazed for a moment through the windshield, his mind adrift, the rain falling softly on the lamplit
street. He shut the glove box and climbed tiredly out of the

car, walking across the street and around the side of the
building, its windows nearly hidden by overgrown bushes.

He was alone on the sidewalk, the cordage company
closed up, the nearest headlights three blocks away on the
boulevard. He ducked in among the bushes, high-stepping
through a tangle of ivy and parting the branches of an elephant ear so that he could see past the edge of the window.
The café was nearly empty—just an old man tiredly eating a
cutlet at a corner table and two girls with bobbed hair hud-
dled deep in conversation over a tureen of mussels. Jimmerson saw then that there was a third table occupied, a private
booth near the kitchen door. It was des Laumes himself, his
curled hair brushed back, a bottle of wine on the table in front
of him. His plate was heaped high with immense snails, and
he probed in one of them with a long-tined fork, dragging out
a piece of yellow snail meat and thrusting it into his mouth,
wiping dripped sauce away with a napkin. His chin whiskers
worked back and forth as he chewed, and the sight of it made
Jimmerson instantly furious. He thought of going back out to
the car, fetching the .38 out of the glove box, and giving the
sorry bastard a taste of a different sort of slug. . . .

But then he recalled the broken candy dish, and somehow
the anger vanished like a penny down a storm drain, and
when he searched his mind for it, he couldn't find it. To hell
with des Laumes. He hunched out of the bushes again and
walked up the sidewalk to where an alley led along behind
the café. The building was deeper than it had appeared to be,
a warren of rooms that ran back behind the cordage company. It was an old building, too—hard to say how old, turn
of the century, probably, perhaps an old wooden flophouse
that had been converted to a café. There were a couple of
windows aglow some distance along the wall, and beyond
them a door with a little piece of roof over it. Jimmerson
tried the door, but it was locked, bolted from the inside. He
spotted a pile of wooden pallets farther up the alley, and he
hurried toward them, pulling one of the pallets off the pile
and dragging it along the asphalt until he stood beneath the

window. He tilted it gingerly against the wall and climbed up
the rungs until he could see in over the sill.

A high-ceilinged room lay beyond the window, a table in
the corner, a row of beds along one long wall, a big iron safe
near the door, some packing crates and excelsior piled in a
heap on the floor. The beds rose one atop the other like bunks
in an opium den. Each of the beds had a small shelf built at
the foot end, with a tiny wine glass hanging upside down in
a slot, and a small decanter of greenish liquid, possibly wine,
standing on the shelf. Three of the beds were hidden by curtains, and Jimmerson wondered if there were sleepers behind them, like dope fiends on the nod. He heard a rhythmic
sighing on the air of the alley around him—what sounded
like heavy, regular breathing, a somnolent, lonely sound that
reminded him somehow of Edna's deathbed. A man entered
the room now, the old cutlet eater from inside the café. He
moved haltingly, as if he were half asleep, and without a
pause to so much as take off his shoes, he climbed into one
of the bunks and pulled the curtain closed.

Another of the curtains moved, pushing out away from
the bed hidden behind it, and as Jimmerson watched, a man
in a wrinkled suit and stubble beard rolled out from beneath
the curtain and balanced precariously on the side rail of the
bunk, apparently still asleep. Jimmerson braced himself, expecting him to tumble off onto the floor, but instead he tilted
slowly back and forth, as if buoyed up by whatever strange
currents circulated in the room. He muttered something in-
audible, and the muttering dissolved into a muffled sob. And
then he tilted forward again so that he seemed to cling to the
bed with a knee and an elbow. There was the sudden crash of
something hitting the wooden floorboards directly beneath
him, and at that instant he lofted toward the ceiling like Gladstone's dead man. But there was a tether tied to his ankle, the
other end of the tether affixed to an iron ring bolted to the bed
frame, and the man leveled off and floated peacefully just below the ceiling.

The object on the floor was clearly a teddy bear, or at least the replica of a teddy bear, and from where Jimmerson stood it appeared to have been contrived with uncanny verisimilitude—apparently out of rusty cast iron. It looked worn from years of handling, its nose pushed aside, one of its eyes missing, a clump of stuffing like steel wool shoving out of a tear in its leg.

Along the wall opposite stood an open cabinet divided into junk-filled cubbyholes, much of it reminiscent of the stuff in Pillbody's shop—bric-a-brac mostly, travel souvenirs and keepsakes. Jimmerson made out what appeared to be an old letterman's sweater, a smoking pipe, a carved seashell, a tiny abacus, a copper Jell-o mold in the shape of a child's face, an exquisitely detailed statue of a nude woman, her face downcast, her hands crossed demurely in front of her. He saw then that there were name placards on each of the cubbyholes, hung on cup hooks as if for easy removal.

He stepped backward off his makeshift ladder, his hands trembling, and started back down the alley toward the street, although he knew straightaway that he wasn't going anywhere. Gladstone had warned him about this, so it wasn't any vast surprise. He had largely come to understand it, too— what Pillbody's curiosities amounted to, what it was that Edna had sold, why she had grown more and more vacant as the months had slipped past. He thought about the odds and ends on her bedside table, the medicinal-smelling bottle with the green stain, the liqueur glass, and he wondered if one of these narrow beds had been hers, a sort of home away from home.

Retracing his steps to the pallet, he climbed back up to the lighted window and forced himself to read the names one by one, spotting Edna's right away, the third cubbyhole from the left. He could see that there was something inside, pushed back into the shadows where it was nearly hidden from view, something that caught the light. He strained to make it out— a perfume bottle? A glass figurine? He searched his memory, but couldn't find such an object anywhere.

The door opened at the far end of the room now, and an old woman walked in, followed by des Laumes. Her hair was a corona of white around her head, and she was wrinkled enough to be a hundred years old. The floating man had descended halfway to the floor, as if he were slowly losing buoyancy, and the old woman grabbed his shoe and a handful of his coat and steered him toward his bed again, pushing him past his curtain so that he was once again hidden from view. She bent over to pick up the thing on the floor, but des Laumes had to help her with it, as if it were incredibly heavy. Together they shoved it into a cubbyhole marked "Peterson." She turned and left then, without a word.

Des Laumes remained behind, looking around himself as if suspicious that something was out of order. He appeared to be sniffing the air, and he held a hand up, extending his first finger as if gauging the direction of the wind. Jimmerson moved to the corner of the window, hiding himself from view. A moment later he peered carefully past the window casing again.

The Frenchman held the statue of the woman in his hand now, scrutinizing it carefully. Then he peeked inside one of the cubbyholes and retrieved a glass paperweight that appeared to Jimmerson to be packed with hundreds of tiny glass flowers. Des Laumes held it to the light, nodded heavily, and walked across to the safe, spinning the dial. He swung the door open, placed the statue and the paperweight inside, and shut the door.

Jimmerson climbed down again and set off up the alley. His thinking had narrowed to a tiny focus, and his hands had steadied. Within a few seconds he had the .38 out of the glove compartment. He slipped the gun into his trousers pocket, then walked straight across the street, up the flagstone path to the café. The door opened and the two girls with the bobbed hair came out, arguing heatedly now, neither one of them looking happy. Jimmerson slipped past them through the open door, face to face with des Laumes himself, who stood there playing the host now. The Frenchman reached for a menu, gestured, and moved off toward a table before realizing who Jimmerson was. He turned around halfway across the empty café, a look of theatrical surprise on his face. "What a pleasure," he said.

"Can I have a word with you somewhere private?" Jimmerson spoke to him in the tone of an old and indebted friend.

"It's very private here," the man said to him. "How can I help you?" His face was bloated and veined, as if corrupted from years of unnameable abuse, and he reeked of cologne, which only half hid a ghastly odor reminiscent of the stink in Pillbody's "parlor room."

"*Help* me?" Jimmerson asked, hauling the gun out of his pocket and pointing it at the Frenchman's chest. "Better to help yourself. I'll follow you into the back." He gestured with the gun.

"I've been shot before," des Laumes told him, shrugging with indifference, and Jimmerson pulled the trigger, aiming high, blowing the hell out of a brass wall sconce with a glass shade. The sound of the gun was crashingly loud, and startled horror passed across des Laumes's face as he threw his hands up.

Someone peered out of the kitchen—the chef apparently—and Jimmerson waved the pistol at him. "Get the hell out of here," he shouted, and the man ducked back into the kitchen. There was the sound of a woman's voice then, and running feet. A door slammed, and the kitchen was silent. "Let's go," Jimmerson said, aiming the gun with both hands at the Frenchman's stomach now. The man turned and headed back through the café, past the kitchen door, down a hallway and into the room with the beds. Keeping the pistol aimed at des Laumes, Jimmerson reached into Edna's cubbyhole and pulled out the trinket inside—a glass replica of what appeared to be the old Pontiac.

He hesitated for a moment before slipping it into his pocket, steeling himself for the disorienting shift into the past, into the realm of Edna's memory. Probably he would lose des Laumes in the process. The Frenchman would simply take the pistol away from him, maybe shoot him right then and there.

But nothing happened. He might as well have dropped his car keys into his pocket. "The safe," Jimmerson said.

Des Laumes shrugged again. "What is it that you want?" he asked, turning his palms up. "Surely . . ."

"What I want is to shoot you to pieces," Jimmerson told him. "I don't know what you are—some kind of damn vampire I guess. But I don't have one damn thing to lose by blowing the living hell out of you right now. You should know that, you . . . stinking overblown bearded twit." He stepped forward, closing in with the pistol as if he would shove it up the Frenchman's nose. The man fell back a step, putting up his hands again and shaking his head. "Now open the safe," Jimmerson told him.

The Frenchman spun the dial and opened the safe door, then stepped aside and waved at it as if he were introducing a circus act. "Clean it out," Jimmerson told him. "Put everything into the boxes." He picked up a packing crate and set it on the floor in front of the safe, and des Laumes took objects out one by one and laid them in, packing the excelsior around them.

"This is common theft," the Frenchman said, shaking his head sadly.

"That's right," Jimmerson told him. "And it'll be a common hole in the head for the good Pierre if he doesn't hurry the hell up. That's it, monsieur, the statue, too. Now the stuff in the cabinet. Fill those boxes." He thought about the chef, the rest of them that had fled through the back door. Would they go to the police? He made up his mind right there on the spot: if he heard sirens, if the door flew open and des Laumes was saved, Jimmerson would shoot the man dead before he handed over the gun.

Des Laumes filled a second packing crate and then a third, until every last piece of bric-a-brac lay in the crates. Except for the glass automobile, Jimmerson hadn't recognized any of it as Edna's. And even if des Laumes knew the source of the things in the safe, he wouldn't tell Jimmerson the truth about them. The man was an end-to-end lie, with nothing at all to recommend him but his idiotic beard like a runover tar brush. Jimmerson was heartily sick of the sight of it, and with the .38 he motioned des Laumes against the wall, away from the sleeping people on the beds. He easily pictured killing the man, shooting the hell out of him, leaving him dead and bloody on the ground.

But somehow the taste of it was like dust in his mouth. How would there be any satisfaction in it? He could as easily picture Gladstone shaking his head sadly, and the idea filled him with shame. More trouble, more pain—anger like a drug, like alcohol, like lunacy, having its way with him again.

There were no sirens yet, no need to hurry.

"Sit down," he said, and des Laumes, his face white now, slumped obediently against the wall. Holding the gun on him, Jimmerson removed one of the liqueur-filled decanters from its niche in the shelf above an empty bed. "Drink it like a good boy," he said, handing it to him, and he held the pistol against the man's ear. Des Laumes stared at him, as if he were making up his mind. He shook his head feebly and started to speak. And then, as if suddenly changing his mind, he heaved a long sigh, shrugged, and drank off the contents of the decanter.

"That's it," Jimmerson said. "Down the hatch." He fetched out another decanter, and forced him to drink that one, too, and then a third and a fourth. All in all there must have been two quarts of the stuff, and the room reeked with the camphor and weeds smell of it.

Des Laumes's face had rapidly taken on a green pallor, and he looked around himself now, a growing bewilderment and horror in his eyes. He clutched his expanding stomach and slowly began to rock forward and backward, his head bouncing with increasing force off the wall behind, his eyes jerking upward in their sockets, a green scum at the corners of his mouth. Jimmerson backed away in case the man got sick, watching as the rocking intensified and des Laumes began to jackknife at the waist like a mad contortionist, his forehead driving impossibly against the floorboards, a piglike grunting issuing from somewhere deep inside him.

Jimmerson awakened the four sleepers, two women and two men—the old cutlet eater and poor Peterson. The women, both of whom still clutched their handbags, were surprisingly young and bedraggled, and they looked out from their beds, blinking their eyes, growing slowly aware of des Laumes's thrashing on the floor. One by one Jimmerson helped them down, untethering them from the beds, unbolting the back door and letting them out into the alley. Mr. Peterson walked like a man on the moon, high-stepping through the puddle, and it occurred to Jimmerson to offer him back his cast-iron teddy bear for ballast, but he saw that it wouldn't be a kindness to him. Soon enough he'd be heavy again.

When the four of them had reached the street, Jimmerson hauled the packing crates out into the night and then headed around the café to where the Mercury was parked. He climbed inside, fired it up, and swung around the corner into the alley, letting the engine idle while he loaded the crates into the rear of the car along with his own boxes of junk.

There was a noise from inside the café like rocks hitting the walls, and Jimmerson looked in through the door, which was partly blocked by des Laumes himself. The Frenchman had levitated a couple of feet off the floor, and his body spasmed in midair like a pupating insect in a cocoon. The room roundabout him was strewn with unidentifiable junk—rusty iron and dirty glass and earthy ceramic objects, misshapen and stinking. Jimmerson pulled the door shut and climbed into the Mercury, slamming the car door against the sounds of knocking and grunting and moaning, and backed away down the alley, swinging out into the street and accelerating toward home as the rain began to fall again. He reached into his pocket and took out the glass Pontiac, which he set carefully on the top of the dashboard so that it caught the rainy glow of passing headlights, and it was then that it dawned on him that he should have left des Laumes a penny.

*   *   *

He had needed every cubic inch of the big rental truck in order to clean out Pillbody's shop. The dwarf had made him sign a release, and had talked obscurely about Jimmerson's "aim being true." "On the up and up," he had said. "*Solid* copper wiring. *No* imperfections." But he had taken the thousands of pennies happily enough, although he had refused to drop them into the brass fish until Jimmerson had packed up what he wanted and driven away. Jimmerson had wanted it all, and Pillbody had worked alongside him, running wheelbarrows full of curiosities out the back and across the courtyard to where Jimmerson had backed the truck up to the circular brick doorway of the courtyard.

The truck crept east along Maple Street now, the engine laboring, the overload springs jammed flat, the tires mashed against the rims, the truck bed heaving ominously from side to side. Jimmerson sat hunched in the driver's seat, which sagged beneath his weight, and he fought to see the road in front of him as bits and pieces of arcane and exotic imagery stuttered through his mind like subliminal messages, almost too rapidly to comprehend. His skin twitched and jerked with competing emotions: dark fears rising into euphoric happiness, dropping away again into canyons of sadness, soaring to heights of lunatic glee. Somewhere in the depths of his mind he heard the clatter of pennies cascading and was dimly aware of the howling of the truck engine and the smell of hot oil and burning rubber. There was the sound of a hose bursting, and a wild cloud of steam poured out from under the hood, and in the swirling vapors a startling array of faces appeared and disappeared. Edna's face came and went, and he recognized the face of the bearded man with the bloody neck, and felt a stab of vicious and shameless satisfaction for the duration of a blink of an eye, and then one face was replaced by another and another and another, a dozen at a time, a hundred—a tide of shifting visages soaking away into the sands of his ponderous and overloaded memory.

Now and then he came to himself, heard the truck creaking

and groaning, saw that he had made his way some few feet
farther up the road, felt the seat springs burrowing against
his thighs, the cramping of muscles, the pressure on his
bones and his teeth. His breath rasped in and out of his lungs
and his head pounded and the truck engine steamed and
roared. Edna's face appeared before him time and again now,
and he was swept with her memories—the memory of a fire
in a hearth on a rainy night, the two of them in easy chairs,
an atmosphere of utter contentment that he squirreled away
in his mind, holding fast to it, and yet at the same time crip-
pled by the thought that she had given this memory away too,
that joy might have become as great a burden to her as sorrow. . . .

He saw that he was nearly at Oak Street, nearly home, and
he cranked the steering wheel around to the right, felt the
weight of the load shift ponderously, the truck tilting up onto
two wheels. For a moment he thought he was going over, and
in that impossibly long moment the pennies continued to fall
into Pillbody's brass fish, and the faces whirled in the steam
in wild profusion, and Jimmerson felt himself crushed like a
lump of coal by a vast, earth-heavy pressure.

He opened his eyes when he felt the sun on his face next
morning. He lay slumped on the seat in the cab of the truck,
and he moved his arms and legs gingerly, testing for breaks
and strains. His jaws ached, and his joints felt stiff and sore,
as if he were recovering from a flu. He sat up and looked out
the window. Somehow he had made it home, alive, although
he had only the vaguest recollection of arriving—the truck
shutting down with a metal-breaking clank, hard rain beating
on the roof off and on through the night.

He opened the door and stepped down onto the street, seeing that he had driven the passenger side of the truck right
up over the curb, and the wheels were sunk now in the wet
lawn. Most of the paint was gone from the truck body, apparently shivered off, and the tires were flayed to pieces. The

truck bed was nearly emptied, scattered with just a few odds and ends of bric-a-brac. Late yesterday evening Pillbody had finally given up counting pennies and purchases, but even so they must have come awfully close to square in the transaction if this was all that had been left unpaid for. Jimmerson climbed heavily up onto the bed and filled a crate with the leftovers, then climbed down again and hauled it into the garage where he had taken des Laumes's three crates yesterday morning. He set about methodically smashing each object to fragments with a sledgehammer, making sure that none of them could ever be sold, not even for a penny. Peterson's iron bear took the most work, but finally it too crumbled into a hundred chunky little fragments that Jimmerson dumped into a pickle jar and capped off. And now, with Pillbody's stuff either consumed or broken, and des Laumes's café cleaned out, the whole lot of it was once again a memory, a thing of the past.

He went inside where he showered and shaved and changed into fresh clothes, and then he hauled the single bed outside and threw it onto the back of the truck, replacing it in the bedroom once again with the double bed from out by the garage. Edna's remembrances—the paperweight, the postcard, the silver spoon, and the glass Pontiac—he put into the curio cabinet in the living room. He would never know what they meant, and their presence in the house would remind him of that. He opened the windows finally, to let the air in, and then went out through the front door, climbed into the Mercury, and drove downtown.

The curiosity shop was emptied out, no longer a mystery. The old storefront, with its dusty litter, its confusing mirrors, and its nailed-shut door had been swept clean, and he could see through the window into the rear of the shop now, clear back into Pillbody's parlor room where workmen were rolling fresh paint onto the walls. He got back into the Mercury and headed west. The Café des Laumes had collapsed on itself, the windows shattered, the walls fallen in, the roof settled over the wreck like a tilted hat. Jimmerson wondered if des Laumes himself was in there, under the rubble, whether the man had simply imploded in the end. To hell with him. It didn't matter anymore.

He swung a U-turn, rested his arm along the top of the seat, and drove back south toward the cemetery, where he would try once again to pray.

Doughnuts

In the west, a couple of stars still shone, but the eastern sky
was full of color. Some people went their whole lives and
never saw that—the color of the day when it was new. And it
smelled like morning, too. That was the best thing about being up early, the way the day smelled when it was fresh, before the sun cooked it.

Walt let the car idle while he watched the sleeping neighborhood through the windshield. Sometimes the world was
an end to end marvel to him, and the quiet activities of his
own street seemed exotic and wonderful. Last night, late,
there had been an immense possum on the lawn, and this
morning, he noticed now, the wisteria blossoms in the vines
over the porch were just opening up in an airy waterfall of
pale purple flowers.

Amanda, his wife, loved a blooming wisteria, and she
knew how to prune them in the winter so that the flower buds
were left on the bare vines. One year Walt had done the job,
going after the vines with a hedge clippers, and there were no
blooms at all that spring.

He bent down to shove a couple of empty doughnut bags
under the seat, then dusted the sugar crumbs off the floorboard

carpet. Then, in no hurry at all, he pulled away from the curb and headed north. Amanda wouldn't be up for an hour yet. Plenty of time to make his morning run up to Lew's Doughnuts for a couple of sinkers. Lew's coffee was terrible, but he was the king of doughnuts. He had made some concessions to modern notions about health—cut out the tropical oils and introduced a whole wheat and honey doughnut that was actually pretty good—but he still sold the pure product.

Amanda couldn't see doughnuts in the noonday sun, whole wheat or no whole wheat, which was largely why Walt made his run early, while she was still asleep. He hadn't eaten a doughnut in three days, although he had dreamed about eating them last night, and he found that he was full of anticipation now. Amanda had been controlling his diet over the weekend, chipping away at his cholesterol level, which to his mind sure as hell wasn't high enough for him to give up doughnuts. They were pretty much the only vice he had left.

His daily trip up to Lew's while Amanda slept had become a pleasant, solitary ritual over the past few months, spoiled only by the shadow of a vague and ill-defined guilt over being forced to hide it from her. But whose fault was that? He didn't want to hide it from her. And it had lately occurred to him that he was solidly comfortable only when he was within easy driving distance of a doughnut shop—something that would only alarm Amanda, so he kept the notion to himself.

He pulled into the parking lot, which was empty of cars aside from one lone junker sitting in front of the Chief Auto Parts store. Along with the doughnut shop, the parts store was open all night. Automobile breakdowns and doughnut habits—neither one of those kept regular hours.

Then he noticed that Lew's old Packard wasn't parked at the edge of the lot like it ought to be. That was no good. What it meant, probably, was that Lew was taking the morning off and the hired help was working the counter. Walt had wanted to *talk* doughnuts, not just eat them, but the hired help, whoever it was this month, wouldn't know anything about the subject. Next month they'd quit and go to work for a plumber or at a bookstore, and they wouldn't know anything about that either.

He cut the engine and coasted into a parking stall, the car rolling under the shadow of the sign on the boulevard, a big tire-sized glazed doughnut that read "Lew's All-Niter" in illuminated letters—except that right now the sign was dark despite the early hour. Lew probably had it hooked up to some kind of photoelectric timer in order to save energy.

Sunlight on the shop window obscured the racks of doughnuts inside, but Walt didn't need to see through the window to know which rack was which. The cake doughnuts would be lined up on the left, the raised doughnuts on the right. Crullers were segregated off to the side on a big baking tray. Lew was a little ashamed to sell the crullers at all, since they were pseudo-doughnuts at best, but they appealed to an effete crowd whose money was hard to turn down. They were a dime a throw more than any of the other doughnuts, too, even though they were mostly air and sugar. In all other doughnut matters it was art before business. Lew hadn't given in to bran muffins and croissants like the chain shops had.

Walt climbed out of the car, lost now in the usual mental debate over the virtues of crumb doughnuts over apple fritters. Lew's fritters weren't big—which was all right; you didn't want a pound of soggy dough—but they were cooked crisp around the edge and had plenty of apple and cinnamon. Walt had a passion for crumb doughnuts, though, and also for a good glazed. A plain glazed doughnut, Lew had told him once, was the true quill.

He pushed against the aluminum bar on the glass door, and then walked straight into it when the door didn't swing open. The place was locked up. He cupped his hands against the window and peered through at the glass cases full of racks. There was a sparse display of oddball doughnuts lying in disarray, obviously day-olds. Without thinking he tapped on the window, but there was no sign of movement inside despite the light being on in the back room where the deep-fat fryers were.

"Hell," he said out loud, and looked at the street with a

sinking heart. It was empty of traffic. The car that had been parked in front of the auto parts store was gone, and for one quick moment Walt felt utterly alone in the world. Where would he get a doughnut? He hurried past his car, down the walkway to the auto parts store. Thank heaven there was someone behind the counter. It wasn't the end of humanity after all.

"What happened to Lew?" Walt asked, pushing in through the door and nodding to the auto parts man.

He looked up from a magazine and shrugged. "What he told me is that there wasn't any money in being open all night anymore. Nothing but bums and drunks coming in. He got fed up. Spur of the moment. Changed his hours day before yesterday, just like that." He snapped his fingers decisively.

Walt nodded as if he understood, although bums or no bums, Lew's decision to shut down at night was hard to justify. He had been open all night for twenty years. A man didn't just pack it in after that long. "What time does he open now?" Walt asked, checking his watch. It was barely six.

"Eight."

"Eight?" The word stunned him. What was the point of opening up at all? Eight was the middle of the morning.

"There's that new French bakery up near the Safeway. They open at six. All kinds of pastries."

"Pastries?" Walt said, too loud and with a hollow ring to his voice that must have made him sound desperate. He realized suddenly that he had picked up a cardboard container of windshield wipers and was gesturing with them. He put them down, and the auto parts man looked vaguely relieved. He was just trying to be helpful with the French pastry suggestion. There was no point in Walt's flying off the handle.

"Not many all-night doughnut places around anymore," the man said. "Not in this part of town. Dying breed."

"Yeah," Walt said. "I guess so. It's like the blue laws or something." He went back out into the sunlight, which seemed abnormally bright now. There was more traffic on the street. The morning was starting up, and it filled him with a directionless urgency. He still had a little time, so after looking in at the doughnuts in the window again, he walked around to the alley behind the stores, half hoping to see Lew's Packard back there. There was nothing but a couple of overflowing Dumpsters and an old beat-up couch sitting in scattered trash. Three painted metal doors let out onto the alley from the rear of the shops.

Walt walked slowly toward the Dumpsters, squinting at the stenciled-on signs on the doors. The first one was Lew's, adjacent to a Dumpster full of greasy cardboard cylinders covered with old doughnut and coffee grounds. He found himself thinking that some of the doughnuts didn't look half bad, but immediately recoiled from the thought.

He rapped on the door with his knuckles, and then, when there was no response, he knocked harder, jiggling the knob. If it was unlocked, then someone was there. He could get their attention and buy a few of those day-olds on the rack just to tide him over.

There was the sound of a door opening, thirty feet down the alley, and the man from the auto parts store looked out, started to say something, then apparently recognized him. "You still looking for Lew?" he asked. "I told you he ain't there."

Walt felt like a criminal. Thank God he'd got his hand off the doorknob. "I thought if there was anybody working I'd try to buy some day-olds. My wife sent me down after doughnuts, and I've got to come home with something. You know how women are." He laughed weakly.

The man nodded very slowly. "Well, I told you his place don't open till eight," he said. "Why don't you run along out of here?"

"Sure," Walt said, trying to smile. His face was trembling, though, out of embarrassment. He turned around hurriedly and headed for the street again. Chased out of an alley by a shopkeeper! That hadn't happened to him in thirty-odd years, not since he was a kid. He climbed into his car and backed out of the space, anxious to get out of there. In the rearview mirror he could see the auto parts man taking down his license number on a sheet of paper, and he flushed with shame.

Amanda was apparently still asleep when he got home, and the house was quiet. He found himself pacing, entirely at loose ends. He was supposed to work on Amanda's greenhouse today. That's why he'd gotten up so early, that and the sinkers. That's what his father had called them—sinkers. The two of them had always stopped on Saturday mornings for coffee and glazed doughnuts on their way to fish off the pier. How long ago had that been? He didn't like to think about it.

He was being compulsive, of course. He knew that, and he knew that it should have scared him a little bit. Except that, damn it, a man ought to be able to eat a doughnut now and then without being beat up by guilt. The problem, clearly, wasn't that he wanted a doughnut—half the population of the world probably wanted a doughnut—it was that Lew had decided to break with tradition and take up banker's hours.

It was nearly seven. Usually Amanda was up by seven, but she'd been out late playing Bunko last night. With a little luck she'd really sleep in, and he'd still be able to pull something off, late as it was. On impulse, he went into the kitchen and ransacked the cookbooks, looking for a doughnut recipe. He found nothing but a lengthy account of the intricacies of deep fat frying. Maybe he could make up his own recipe—a couple of cups of flour, some sugar. Yeast? He realized that he hadn't a clue.

Irritable now, he looked out the back window at the half-framed greenhouse in the corner of the yard. He had bought a couple dozen old wooden windows at various garage sales, and the idea was to frame the things up into some sort of edifice. Amanda wanted him to keep it simple, and he was agreeable up to a point. He had come up with a couple of bright ideas, though, including a device for rolling and unrolling a shade net, depending on the position of the sun. Thinking about Lew's unlit sign had started him up. The automatic shade device could run off a slow-speed electric drill hooked up to a photoelectric eye. There was no reason you couldn't rig it to open and close ventilation windows in the ceiling, too, if you put your mind to it.

He began to work a plan out in his head—cotton rope and pulleys and a scissors jack—and in a moment he was fired up with the idea of work. To hell with the doughnuts. He had gone without them for three days; he could easily stretch it to four. His embarrassment in the alley today would be a lesson to him. He flipped to a calorie chart in the back of a cook-book and calculated how many calories he would save this week alone if he laid off doughnuts altogether.

Amanda had a point there. He wasn't a fat man by any means, but then he couldn't eat like he used to either. For twenty-five years he had bought pants with a thirty-four inch waist, and he had made a bargain with himself that he would go to his grave wearing the same size pants. But unless he died soon he was going to have to work at it a little bit. He walked out into the living room toward the front door, multi-plying a week's worth of saved calories times fifty-two, but then subtracted two weeks for doughnut holidays. The idea amused him. You didn't have to swear off forever. He would take it one day at a time, starting now. Temperance was the key. And it was a perfect morning to start, what with Lew be-traying him like that.

He popped the trunk of Amanda's Toyota, looking for her scissors jack in order to rig up a prototype of the greenhouse device. Lying in the otherwise clean trunk was a big shop-ping bag with two shoe boxes inside. He stood for a moment looking in at them, the idea of finding the jack abolished from his mind. More shoes. Amanda needed more shoes like an octopus needed more arms.

He pulled out one of the boxes and looked inside. A cash register receipt lay across a pair of cobalt blue shoes with red stitching and tiny heels that were good for nothing beyond punching dents in the hardwood floor. The other box held an identical pair—same size, same price: sixty bucks a pair. A hundred and twenty bucks! He couldn't remember the last time he had spent that much on anything.

Carrying the bag, he headed back into the house and up the stairs. Amanda was awake, sitting up in bed and reading a book. As always, he was struck with how pretty she was when she had her reading glasses on. Looking at her, he very nearly forgot about the shoes, except that on the floor, near the window seat, there were three more pair, the result of last week's spree.

"Hi," she said cheerfully. "Coffee?"

"Didn't make any," he said.

She saw what he was carrying then, and he knew by her hesitation that she was defensive about it. Probably she had been intending to sneak the shoes in later in the day, while he was out back working his tail off.

"Thanks," she said, nodding at the bag. "I picked those up at the mall yesterday. They were on sale. Half price."

"Not bad," Walt said, pretending to be astonished. "Two hundred-forty bucks worth of shoes for a measly hundred-twenty. That's money in the bank."

Seconds ago he had meant to be reasonable, but he realized now that he was peeved and that he hadn't kept the ironic edge out of his voice. But damn it, women and shoes . . .

"What's got into you?" Amanda asked, taking off her glasses.

"Me?" Walt said incredulously. "Nothing's got into *me*. I'm just hauling in the shoes that you hid in the car, that's all. Don't read anything more into it than that."

"*Hid* in the car? That's asinine, of course. Although if it was true it wouldn't surprise anyone, seeing you carry on like this. One glance at a couple of pairs of shoes and you're so mad you can barely speak."

"A *couple* of pairs?" Walt said, turning around and pulling open her closet door. The interior of the closet was a cornucopia of shoes, shoes of every color and shape, maybe sixty or eighty pairs in boxes, the lids torn off the top boxes to reveal the toe-to-heel shoes inside, each pair lying in a little bed of tissue paper. He gestured at them. "Tell me this isn't compulsive behavior."

"Your behavior or mine?" she said flatly.

"Blue with red stitching? The problem," he said, just getting warmed up, "is that there are something like four million color combinations in the known universe. You *can't* put together a shoe arsenal big enough to have them all covered, especially if you intend to cover them twice. You've got to stop somewhere this side of the poorhouse."

"Don't be condescending with your idiot arithmetic," she said. "And as far as the poorhouse goes, it's Aunt Janet's money, you'll remember, that's keeping us out of it. It's why I'm sleeping in and you're out tinkering with the greenhouse. It's why *both* of us are taking an extended holiday instead of working like everyone else. *My* Aunt Janet."

He glared at her but couldn't think of anything to say. She had him there.

"In fact," she said, lightening up a little now that he was at least partly silenced, "I bought the blue and red shoes to wear with the dress *you* bought me for my birthday. We're going out Saturday night. Remember?"

"Of course I remember. My memory isn't the issue here. But two pairs of the *same* shoe?"

"What can I say? I like them. They were perfect. They aren't going out of style. They were a bargain."

"A bargain! What happened to the days when you could get a good pair of shoes for thirty bucks?"

"Gone," she said.

He shook his head. You couldn't reason with her. The shoes were a monkey on her back.

"And what shoes are *you* going to wear Saturday night?" she asked him, dragging in a red herring.

It threw him farther off, but then he saw the toes of his good leather shoes sticking out from under the bed, and he reached down and pulled them out. "These," he said. "The shoes I *always* wear. A rag, a little bit of Kiwi polish . . . These shoes have five year's wear on them. Ninety-dollar shoes. I bought them for thirty-four-fifty."

"Then you should have two pairs," Amanda said. "I think the warranty's about shot on this one." Her voice was icy, as if she had tried to throw a little oil on water, but he wouldn't quit stirring it up. She put her glasses back on, the argument just about over. "Look at the soles."

He turned them upside down, exposing a half-dollar size hole in the bottom of one of the shoes. "What?" he said "we're going to be praying next Saturday night? You think I'm going to be crawling around on my hands and knees? What I'm going to do, by the way, is take these down to the shoe repair. For ten bucks Le Wing tacks on a new sole. Bingo, they've got another five year's wear in them. I might *never* buy a new pair."

"What you don't know," she said, letting up on him suddenly, "is how handsome you look when you're all dressed up. You look just like Fred Astaire. I mean it. If you'd pay some attention to yourself sometimes you'd notice the kind of looks you get from women when you put on the dog just a little."

"You know what I think?" he said. "I think that's just vanity, and I for one am going to do without it."

"You know what I think?" she asked evenly.

"What?"

"I think those shoes make you look like a bum. They're an embarrassment."

"I embarrass you, eh? Is that it? I'm an embarrassment?"

"We're talking about your shoes."

"We were talking about your shoes, actually. Although you're right—somehow I'm the one who ended up being insulted. Why is that? How come I turn out to be the injured party?"

"*Are* you the injured party?

"Forget it," he said. "Just forget it. I wake up on what's probably the nicest day in the year and by eight o'clock it's wrecked."

Amanda said nothing. She had picked up her book and was reading it, or pretending to. He knew it was over. Somehow they'd had a fight over the shoes, and like all such fights it came down to nothing but hard feelings. "I'm going down to the hardware store," he said, looking at the floor. "Be back in half an hour."

She was silent. He realized that she was really ticked off. It was true that the blue shoes, now that he thought about it, would go pretty nicely with the dress he'd bought her. The vanity comment had been insulting, too. There had been no call for that. "I'll start the coffee," he said.

She had turned a page in her book, still saying nothing. She wouldn't cut him any kind of slack. He was very nearly apologizing by offering to make coffee, but she wouldn't go for it. As usual, she'd let him stew for a while. Then he could apologize again, more explicitly, beg her forgiveness, and she could be magnanimous and give in.

Fuming again, he went back downstairs and out the front door, neglecting the coffee pot. He climbed into the car and started the engine, racing the motor to warm it up. He caught his reflection in the rearview mirror and smoothed down his hair, turning his face so that his cheekbones were accentuated by shadow, trying to find Fred Astaire in there someplace. He gave up. To hell with counting calories. No one would appreciate it anyway except those mythical women who goggled at him when he wore the right pair of shoes. A husband was a solitary creature in the end, and he was a fool to think he could please anyone but himself.

He drove off, rolling the stop sign at the end of the street, and in a couple of minutes he was at the doughnut shop. There were a number of cars in the parking lot now, and people standing on the sidewalk, waiting for Lew to unlock the door. Walt climbed out of the car and hurried across the lot to join them.

The selection, he decided, just wasn't up to par. There were no strawberry doughnuts at all. Not that he was a strawberry doughnut man more than once a month, but he hated to see a diminished selection like that. There were no maple-frosted cake doughnuts, either, just maple bars, which tended to be too much of a good thing. Half-size bars would be a hell of an innovation. He ought to mention all this to Lew, but he knew he wouldn't. His desire to talk doughnuts had fled. He'd buy a couple of glazed and get out of there.

The guy in front of him, it turned out, was buying a cartload of doughnuts to take to work—twelve dozen in all. Lew offered to throw in another dozen free, and the man took him up on it. Before he was done he had wiped out the glazed doughnuts entirely, every damned last one. Walt nearly hit him.

For a moment he considered flat out asking him to leave a couple, but then he decided that maybe Lew had a rack of them cooling in the back room. Glazed doughnuts were big movers; there was always another rack waiting. Better to take a chance on that than to start begging. It hadn't come to *that* yet. And he could always shift to crumb doughnuts, too, and go with glazed tomorrow morning. And the morning after that.

He drove home with a box of glazed after all—not fresh, but day-olds, what he'd seen on the rack early in the morning. Lew had given him a break on the price, sold him a full dozen for a dollar and threw in a couple of jellies to boot. You couldn't beat that—less than eight cents apiece. What was that ad where you could feed a kid for a month on thirty bucks? Hell, they could eat doughnuts till the cows came home for half that.

When he got home he took the doughnuts into the garage. There was no use starting any trouble. Amanda wasn't in the mood for it. He put the box on the bench. The two crumb doughnuts he'd eaten in the car hadn't quite been enough, so he polished off two of the glazed while he fiddled around, hauling odds and ends from the big barrel of junk parts, letting his mind run on the prototype.

There was nothing at all wrong, he decided, with day-old glazed. All in all there were two classes of glazed doughnut—the big, airy kind popularized in Asian-owned doughnut shops, and the traditional flattened glazed that was almost crispy and was heavy with sugar. There were plenty of people who would argue with him, but he didn't go much for the airy kind. There was something faddish about them, something pretentious. Lew had pretty much the same notion, and the slightly stale quality of the day-olds in the box, Walt was pleased to find, actually accentuated what it was about a glazed that made it, as Lew had so eloquently put it, the true quill.

He ate half of a third doughnut, but then suddenly felt sick, and he threw the remaining half into the trash. Eleven doughnuts left. He wondered if he could freeze them with any success at all in order to have a source when times were tough, like this morning. Amanda would find them though. Better to leave them in the garage.

He went out into the backyard and started hammering away at the greenhouse, and in about a half hour Amanda came out with a cup of coffee for him.

"You can be such a yo-yo," she said, smiling at him. He felt like a creep.

"Fred Astaire," he said, rolling his eyes.

"I meant that."

"You wouldn't believe the device I've figured out to shade the greenhouse," he said, happier now. "All automatic. We can put in a switch and work it from inside the house. Let me show you what I've got in mind." Together they walked toward the garage. Then Walt remembered the box of doughnuts lying in plain sight on the bench. "Tell you what," he said, stopping abruptly. "Let me put it together for you—a prototype. It wouldn't mean anything now anyway." He smiled at her and she shrugged.

"Whatever you say," she said. "I'm going to run down to the nursery for potting soil and bedding plants. Want to go along?"

"Naw." He waved the idea away. "I'm wasting daylight. You go ahead and buy mulch, or whatever it is. I'll stay here."

He worked for hours, as if work were a curtain he could draw across the morning's mistakes. Amanda came and went, visiting nurseries, hauling flats of plants in from the trunk of her car. Walt wondered idly, more than once, if she was stopping at the mall when she was out, if shoe stores drew her as irresistibly as doughnut shops drew him. Shoes! He was damned if he was going to worry about something as insignificant as a shoe sole. Life was too full of authentic horrors.

Now and then he fetched tools out of the garage, but he avoided looking at the box on the bench. It made him uneasy, like a cocked gun, and at one point he considered just facing up to it, going in there and slamming it to pieces with a two-by-four and pitching it into the trash. That was crazy, though. It was just doughnuts. He put the thought out of his mind and went to work, cutting up redwood boards for window jambs.

But he found himself daydreaming about the box, picturing it there in the dark garage among the wood shavings and used slips of sandpaper. Suddenly he had a vision of himself dead, the long, unnumbered years passing away. Dust settled over the workbench and floor of the garage, covering the tools and scraps of wood in a gray layer as the dying sun turned in a red sky. The mummified doughnuts lay there stiff and dry in their cardboard sarcophagus, painted with the fading doughnut logo from Lew's All-Niter.

He felt suddenly weak. He realized that his hands were shaking so badly that he could hardly hold the hammer, and his head ached to beat the band. He turned on the garden hose and drank as much water as he could hold, and felt temporarily better. Going without lunch was what did it. You couldn't eat sugar for breakfast and then try to get by on coffee for the rest of the day. Sooner or later you came down hard from that load of sugar. What in the hell had he been thinking about? He had very nearly had the D.T.'s there for a minute.

What he needed, he decided suddenly, was a hair of the dog. The idea was highly amusing. If nothing else, it would stop these abominable shakes. And anyway, eleven doughnuts lay there in a box on the bench, and there was no excuse for that if he didn't eat them—or at least one or two. It was largely a matter of economics. The day-olds had been a damned good buy, or would be if he ate them. If he let them petrify, though, they were money down a rat hole. He was reminded instantly of Amanda and her half-price shoes. The difference was that he was going to *eat* the doughnuts, whereas Amanda would wear the shoes maybe once or twice and then lose them in the salad of shoes cluttering the closet floor.

And he had already binged that morning anyway; there was no use forming resolutions now. Tomorrow morning he

would pack it in, give it up for good. In fact, he would an-
nounce it to Amanda, and that would cement it. That was a
hell of a serious step, that kind of self-revelation in front of
your wife. You couldn't back away after that.

The few hours that the doughnuts had sat there hadn't hurt
them much. The sugar on the outside had melted, but all in
all they had held up as well as anyone could expect. The jelly
doughnuts seemed a little excessive right then, so Walt ate
two of the glazed, and then went back out and drank more
water out of the hose. His hands had steadied out, his head
had quit throbbing, and he felt almost like working again. For
a moment he wondered whether he shouldn't fiddle with
the photoelectric gadgetry like he'd promised Amanda, but
clearly it was too late in the afternoon to start something that
complicated.

Then it came to him that Amanda was driving around
town without a jack in the trunk. It would be his luck entirely
if she blew a tire and found herself stranded. Walking around
to the garage, he looked out toward the front of the house.
The Toyota was parked at the curb. He grabbed the jack off
the benchtop with the idea of putting it away, and then
headed down the driveway.

There was a woman's voice just then, and he turned to
find his neighbor out watering the lawn. "Hi, Sue," he said,
waving the jack cheerfully. "Water my lawn while you're at
it, will you?"

She waved back with the hand that was holding the hose,
spraying water in his direction.

"Hey!" he said, jumping aside.

She laughed. "You asked." She walked toward him, sprinkling the lawn on either side. "Is Amanda getting dressed up
for the progressive dinner Saturday night?"

"Yeah," Walt said, standing by the trunk. "Her birthday
dress."

"You wearing your birthday suit too?"

"You know I don't go in for dirty talk," he said to her.

"Seriously," she said. "What kind of birthday dress?
Nice? Evening wear?"

"Yeah, I guess," Walt said. "Sort of." He unlocked the trunk, and the lid popped open. "Some kind of dress. You know, all one piece."

"A one-piece," she said, nodding her head as if he were an idiot. "I'll ask her myself."

A shopping bag lay in the trunk. Walt looked away for a moment and then looked back at it, unbelieving. There was a shoe box in it. What did this mean, that she had been out hitting shoe stores all afternoon? He dropped the jack into the trunk and pulled the box out of its bag.

"Shoes!" Sue said, looking over his shoulder.

"Yeah."

"Let me see."

He pulled the lid off and held the box out. Inside was a pair of plain leather shoes, nothing fancy, but somehow, in some way that he couldn't quite identify, they looked expensive as hell. There was no receipt this time. He looked into the bag, but there was nothing in there either.

He realized that his neighbor's eyes were as wide as half dollars. "Ferragamo," she said.

"Is that it?"

She nodded, looking at the interior of the box as if it held a diamond tiara.

"Nice, eh? Good shoe?"

"Man!" she said, and nodded again. "How much did you have to give for them?"

"What?" Walt said, not quite taking it in.

"I'm not being nosy, I just . . . Tell me how much? Bob is such a damned skinflint! I'm going to hold this over his head for years. Jeeze, I can't believe a man would buy a pair of Ferragamos for his wife. Especially not her husband, if you know what I mean."

"How much do you think?" Walt asked, alarmed now. Amanda had clearly lost her mind. "Take a guess." He realized he was talking through clenched teeth and made an effort to relax.

"A thousand?"

"A thousand! Good God!" He reeled back against the car and sat down hard on the bumper.

"More?" she asked. "Or did you get them on sale? What's wrong?"

"Yeah," Walt said. "Nothing." He felt faint. "I got them on sale." He looked at the bag in the trunk. "At Neiman Marcus."

"Still, they must have been plenty. I guess I don't need to know exactly. They're normally a four-figure buy, though. I know that much. Bob might buy them if they were half price."

Walt shook his head as if it beat all, Bob's being a tight-wad. Bob was going to kill him, of course, spoiling Amanda like that. Maybe Walt would just come clean with him, admit that Amanda had a thing for shoes, and that it had gotten a little out of hand. He couldn't, though. You didn't rat on your wife. He would just have to brass it out if Bob said anything to him. Some men were tight-fisted, some weren't. It wasn't his fault if he had a generous spirit.

He put the shoes back in the box and shut the trunk. He sure as hell wasn't going to wave them in Amanda's face like he had that morning. It hadn't done a nickel's worth of good anyway. More likely it had led to this latest atrocity. He wondered if there was any hope for her after all. There was that TV ad from where was it?—Mt. Sinai Hospital—having to do with addictions therapy. What the hell had the number been? He couldn't remember. Of course there was some little chance that she would be feeling guilty about now, wrangling with the ghost of Aunt Janet. Maybe she'd come clean if he just left her alone.

He found himself in the garage again. A thousand bucks! That was sheer insanity. You could buy two cows for that kind of money, one for each foot, and get change back, too. He opened the doughnut box and pulled out another glazed. It tasted like cardboard to him, but he ate it anyway, to prove a point, and then ate another. He closed the box back up and pushed it away. Feeling a little queasy, he plastered on a smile and went in through the kitchen door. Amanda was chopping up vegetables at the counter, putting together a salad.

"Build the prototype?" she asked.

"No. No time for it. I pounded nails all afternoon. How about you?" She looked nice, fixed up as if to make an evening out of it. There were a couple of steaks marinating in a pan and a bottle of champagne in the ice bucket. But Walt couldn't see anything but the shoes, looming in his mind like the ghost at the feast.

There was no question of him eating. He realized he was nauseated. Automatically he thought about the doughnuts, about how many he had eaten that day. What?—Six? Eight? More like ten.

"Something wrong?" Amanda asked. "You don't look too good."

He nearly blurted it out right there. Clearly she was setting in to butter him up with the steaks and champagne and all. And what after that? An intimate evening in front of the fire? He half wished he hadn't found the shoes at all. Or eaten those last two doughnuts, which were playing nine ball in his stomach.

"I'm . . . not feeling too well," he said. "Touch of the flu, I think." A wave of nausea struck him, worse this time. "I'll head upstairs. Lie down for a minute."

"Should I put the steaks away?"

"What? I don't care," he said angrily. "Turn them into a pair of shoes." He bolted for the stairs, barely making it to the bathroom in time. He was sweating and shaking again when he sat down on the edge of the bed, but after a few minutes of resting he felt better. He could hear kitchen sounds down below. Amanda had switched on the stereo, some kind of lazy-man's jazz.

"You coming down?" Her voice sounded from the bottom of the stairs.

He got up slowly, anticipating a bad stomach. He was all right, though. Too damned many doughnuts; that was the long and short of it. Well, that was it. That was the end. He was taking the pledge. Cold turkey. On the wagon. Tick-a-lock, doors and windows. He went back downstairs, full of determination.

Amanda was dancing in the kitchen, tossing the salad with a flourish of the wooden utensils. She was obviously high on shoes. She had gone on a bender herself, but shoes, unlike doughnuts, didn't make you sick with nausea and regret. He watched her until she saw his face and stopped.

"What?" she said.

"You know damned well what."

"Suppose you tell me anyway."

"Suppose you tell me."

"Let's see . . ." She waved the salad spoon in the air and squinted, as if she could see a thought balloon forming over her head. "I give."

"The shoes."

"What shoes?"

"You know damned *well* what shoes!" he shouted, flying into a rage. "Don't *bait* me. You've got a problem. A big one. How much, a thousand?"

"Guess."

"Guess! I don't have to guess. Sue told me. A thousand dollars! No human being on earth needs a thousand-dollar pair of shoes. It's obscene. I don't care whose Aunt Janet corked off and left you money. You'd better rein it in." He nodded his head at her.

"Or what? What if I don't 'rein it in'?"

Speechless, he looked around the kitchen for something to vent his fury on, something to smash up, maybe. Something to crush. He grabbed the champagne bottle by the neck, tore off the foil, untwisted the wire, and yanked the cork out. Then, his hand trembling, he poured his glass full, the bubbles rushing down over the side. Upending the glass, he downed the champagne at a gulp.

"You're really ticked off," Amanda said to him, smiling. Apparently she thought it was funny.

He stood there breathing.

"They're Sue's shoes."

"What?"

"The shoes in the trunk," Amanda said. "They belong to *Sue,* dummy. Bob bought them for her, believe it or not. She brought them over to show me today, and as a sort of joke we put them in the trunk."

"As a sort of *joke?*" He stared at her. It was unbelievable. His own wife, telling him this. The rottenest sort of betrayal. He poured another glass of champagne, then shoved the bottle back into the ice bucket.

"I was wondering if you'd go searching through my car again," she said, "looking for evidence."

He blinked at her. "I *didn't* go searching through your car."

"This morning you didn't?"

"This morning I was looking for a scissors jack, to build my . . . my prototype."

"Your prototype." She nodded. "And this afternoon? The prototype again?"

"I was putting it *back.*" Without another word he set his glass down and walked away, out of the kitchen and up the stairs. He wasn't hungry anyway. Methodically he got undressed and put on his pajamas, then found his book and climbed into bed, flopping back down onto his pillow in order to stare at the ceiling. There was the sound of paper crackling under his head, and he jerked back up again, scrabbled around, and looked into his pillow case.

Puzzled at what he saw, he dumped it out, over the edge of the bed. About a hundred white paper bags fell out, each one with the logo from Lew's All-Niter on the front. "What the hell?" he wondered, getting up. Then he knew what it was, the stash from under the front seat of his car, the bags he had been stuffing under there for months.

He closed his eyes for a moment. It had come to this, had it?—open season on him. He picked up the pile of bags and went quietly back downstairs. Amanda was sitting at the kitchen table sipping champagne, her book open in front of her. She glanced up at him and smiled, apparently still thinking it was all a grand joke, that they could laugh at it together.

"I was looking for my prototype," she said, seeing what it was he was carrying.

Silently, he dumped the bags on the table, dusted sugar crumbs off his hands, and walked away again, up the stairs.

*　　*　　*

He lay there alone all evening, trying to read. He wasn't going to budge. By God if there was an apology due, it wasn't
due from him. He had been set up, ridiculed. Amanda had
thrown the doughnut business into his face, kicked him when
he was already down. And his conversation with Sue, out at
the curb, him carrying on like some kind of damned Pinoc-
chio . . . it didn't bear thinking about.

He was suddenly hungry. He smelled the steaks searing
now, on the Farberware grill. Well, Amanda could eat his, for
all he cared. To hell with food. The thought of her eating
without even inviting him down, though . . .

He heard Sue come in shortly after that, the two of them
whispering down there, no doubt discussing him. There was
the sound of laughter. For a moment he thought about storming downstairs and setting them straight. He actually got out
of bed. But then he caught sight of himself in the mirror and
saw that his pajamas made him look like a fool. He didn't
have the energy to get dressed.

At ten he began to wonder whether she meant to sleep on
the downstairs couch. Maybe she was already asleep, or had
gone out. There was no sound at all below. He turned the
light off and lay there thinking, listening to his stomach
growl, unable to sleep. He wondered if it was the end of his
marriage, and toyed with the idea of calling a lawyer in the
morning, rig it so that Amanda would overhear the call. He
wasn't serious about the lawyer, but a prank like that would
serve her right after her trick with the shoes.

He began to think about the prototype, assembling it
piece by piece in his head so that he could picture the web of
ropes and pulleys and counterweights and springs, all of it
tugging and spinning, windows opening and closing like the
workings of his brain, which right then was an overactive
mess. It seemed unlikely that he would ever sleep normally
again. He was monumentally hungry, too, but he was damned
if he was going downstairs after a snack. Amanda would just
have to live with the idea of him alone and starving upstairs.

He got up finally and put on his robe and slippers. Nothing made him madder than being unable to sleep.

As quietly as he could he tip-toed downstairs. She was probably asleep in the den, but he decided against looking in. If she were awake she would think he had come down to make amends, and that wouldn't do. This time *she* would be the one to apologize.

It was a warm night outside, the sky clear and full of stars. He wondered if the possum were somewhere around as he eased open the garage door and flipped on the light. He felt a certain affinity to it, to its solitary nocturnal habits. The garage was a comforting place to be late at night like this. It was as if he were getting away with something by being out there, as if he were hoodwinking time.

He opened the doughnut box and sorted through the few that remained. The glazed didn't appeal to him, maybe because he'd got sick after eating the last two. They were leathery-stiff, too, like old road kill. There was a good chance the jelly doughnuts would have held up, though, with the jelly inside to keep them moist. He pulled one out, leaned his elbows on the bench, and took a bite, chewing moodily while his eyes traced the avenues of holes in the pegboard on the wall.

Idly, he fished out one of the glazed, laid it on the benchtop, and mashed it flat with a piece of wood. He mashed the three other glazed the same way, remembering the day his father had broken up all his smoking pipes on his anvil, all the time smoking one last pipeful of tobacco.

He had come out with some vague notion of assembling the prototype, putting in a couple of hours out there. But the bits of rope and the wooden pulleys scattered on the bench didn't speak to him. They were so much sad junk now. And of course the scissors jack was lying in the trunk of the Toyota again.

He picked out the last jelly doughnut. One for the road. That was absolutely it. He had been riding the doughnut train, but now it was the end of the line. He could see the terminal, rushing at him out of the night. He bit deeply into the thing, hitting the pocket of jelly just as a knock sounded at the nearly closed door. Jumping in surprise, he smeared the doughnut up his face, a glop of jelly filling one of his nostrils. He spun around, trying to hide the doughnut.

Amanda stood at the half open door, still dressed, but in her bedroom slippers. He could feel the jelly dripping down his upper lip, and he tried to clean it off with his tongue. She had started to speak, but apparently couldn't get the words out, and her eyes shifted away from his jelly-smeared face to the bench top where the weirdly flattened doughnuts lay amid the refuse of the prototype.

She looked at his face again, without, he thought, any humor in her eyes at all. "Why don't you come to bed?" she asked. "I'm sorry about the shoes and the doughnut bags and all. I didn't know you were that . . . serious."

Even then he wanted to protest. Serious how? No sense of humor? A serious doughnut habit? He started to point to the flattened doughnuts, to show her just how serious he really was, but then abruptly he saw the futility in it, and he flipped off the light and followed her into the house.

They took Walt's car next morning, but Amanda drove. Walt felt foggy and subdued. He couldn't argue with her suggestion that they find him a new pair of shoes before Saturday night. Apparently, there was a firestorm of sales raging at the mall. And as a concession to him they were stopping at Le Wing's Shoe Repair on the way. Amanda had no problem with his putting new soles on the old shoes, which were lying now on the backseat. You could patch nearly anything, no matter how shabby and worn out it had become.

He realized suddenly that she was turning north up the boulevard, past Lew's All-Niter. He sat on his hands and stared out the windshield, conscious of her glancing at him. What did she expect, the shakes? Doughnut withdrawal?

Cut it out, he told himself. It had been his decision to go on the wagon. He hadn't said anything about it to her. She had caught him with the jelly doughnuts at midnight, hiding in the garage, but even so it had been her that had apologized—for the shoe trick and for the bags in the pillow. Walt had felt like a four-year-old. This morning there had been no mention of any of it, only the new shoes suggestion, the visit to the mall.

Without warning she turned into the lot, past Lew's Packard, and pulled into a space. "I wouldn't mind a couple of crullers," she said.

He blinked at her. "Crullers? You're kidding?"

"Why would I be kidding? I never said I hated doughnuts. *You're* the one who said that. Let's get a couple to go."

"It's not . . . It's not that. It's just that crullers aren't . . ." He realized that he was jabbering, that he had no real idea what he wanted to say, what he wanted.

"Aren't what? What on earth are you talking about?"

"Never mind," he said, getting out of the car. "Chocolate, strawberry, or . . . white?"

"Chocolate, thanks."

Except for Walt, Lew's was empty of customers. There were plenty of doughnuts left, including a rack of glazed, just out of the back room.

"What'll it be?" Lew asked, swabbing down the top of the counter with a rag.

"Two crullers," Walt said. "Chocolate."

Lew squinted at him, cocking his head to the side as if his hearing had abruptly gone bad.

"For the wife," Walt said, gesturing toward the parking lot.

Lew nodded, satisfied with that, and put the crullers in a bag. "What else?" he asked. "Couple of sinkers for you?"

Walt hesitated for a second, lost in thought, looking over the doughnuts—the glazed twists, the jellies, the chocolate and maple bars, the apple fritters. . . . Somehow the assortment of multicolored frosteds reminded him of the shoes on the bottom of Amanda's closet.

"Two glazed," he said, making up his mind. "A crumb, too. And cut that crumb doughnut in half, right down the center." Walt paid him and went out through the aluminum door, back into the morning sunshine, carrying his and Amanda's doughnuts in a paper bag.

On Going Home Again

For the couple of years that I was a graduate student, and for a few years when I was out of college, I earned a living as a construction laborer working for a company called Kent's Construction Services. It was at that stage in my life that I learned most of what I know about doughnuts and about knocking things to pieces. Kent's Construction Services would tear down and clean up anything. We demolished old garages out in Eagle Rock, mucked out goat pens in Anaheim, excavated collapsed sewer pipes in Cypress, shoveled and swept mud-flooded streets in Huntington Beach. On one cheerful summer morning we found ourselves yanking clapboards off the side of a house in Long Beach when an astonished old woman, carrying her half-empty coffee cup, came out through the kitchen door and informed us that the house we wanted to tear down was in fact the abandoned house next door. It struck us even then that we were damned lucky she had been at home that morning, and not down at Albertson's buying the week's groceries. You can picture her getting off the bus on the distant corner, already hearing the thud of the sledgehammer beating her chimney apart, the whine of the chain saw hacking through her eaves . . .

The only consistent theme to any of these odd jobs were morning doughnuts. We did a lot of freeway flying in those days, in an old Ford truck that had somewhere over three hundred thousand miles on it. We fired that truck up early, pre-breakfast, and although we sometimes hit a liquor store for Hostess Cupcakes and Cokes, the food of choice in the morning was doughnuts. In the story you're holding in your hands, when Walt shoves the doughnut bag under the front seat of his car along with all the rest of the empties, what I was thinking about was the seat of that old Ford. Every once in a while, when we pulled in at the dump out in Brea or Capistrano or Whittier, we'd sweep the paper trash and smashed cups and aluminum cans out through the open door, but on any given day there was a startling amount of trash crammed under there, mostly doughnut bags, always white, printed with a wide array of doughnut shop logos. It wasn't until later that it dawned on me that I might have made a serious collection of those bags, like people do with matchbooks or menus or theater ticket stubs.

There was a place out in Huntington Beach that had so-so doughnuts, and yet was elevated, so to speak, because it served them so delicately—nestled in wax paper in those pastel-colored plastic baskets. There was a tremendously old Winchell's out in Anaheim that was rumored to be a haven for dope dealers who worked the counter and would listen for obscure and telltale doughnut-and-dope orders—"carry out" instead of "to go" for instance, or "bag, no box." We hit the place regularly because of its so-called Kona coffee. This was in the days when Yuban was pretty much the best coffee money could buy, and the very idea of exotic coffee was worth the trip across town. It would be years yet before I'd drink pure Kona coffee in Hawaii and eat what is arguably the best doughnut in the world, the Hawaiian malasada, a globe-shaped glazed doughnut that is quite possibly superior even to the astonishing New Orleans beignet.

Sadly, what happened over the years, at least in southern California, is that most of the independent doughnut shops disappeared, one by one, or were bought up by Winchell's or Donut Star and the other super chains. Nostalgia aside, I'm not sure that a mom and pop doughnut was really any better than a chain doughnut, but I miss a few of those long-departed shops, and I find that these twenty years later I have a surprisingly good recollection of the doughnuts of my youth. The king (or queen) of southern California doughnut shops was Mrs. Chapman's out on 7th Street and Pacific Coast Highway in Long Beach. Mrs. Chapman's had one of those once-ubiquitous doughnut signs that were six times the size of a truck tire and could be seen hovering like a halo in the early morning smog from six or eight blocks away. The shop itself had a long counter as well as about twenty booths, and in front of every revolving counter stool, and at the window edge of every booth, there was a miniature juke-

box—songs ten cents a throw or three for a quarter. You
never actually heard the songs you punched in, because the
machinery was already loaded with dimes and quarters, but
there was some satisfaction in the idea that other customers,
half an hour or an hour hence, would have to listen to your
favorite songs instead of their own. Mrs. Chapman's doughnuts were mostly pretty good, but their glazed doughnut was
perfection—very puffy, crisp with sugar—probably the only
doughnut that could climb shamelessly into the ring with a
malasada or a beignet, to cripple a metaphor from Hemingway. It was worth a five-mile detour, even on a busy morning,
and the sad decline of Mrs. Chapman's was one of the great
doughnut tragedies of the second half of the twentieth
century.

A few years back, just for the hell of it, Lew Shiner and I
drove out there on our way to the beach one morning. We
talked doughnuts in the car, and I remember that I was going
on about crumb doughnuts, and Lew was listening and nodding, letting me get it out of my system. When I'd played myself out, he told me, quite simply and earnestly, that the plain
glazed doughnut was "the true quill," and I'm humble enough
to say that his words were evidently and profoundly right.

We pulled into Mrs. Chapman's, and as I'd feared, the
place had gone the way of all flesh. New management and
renovation had wrecked it. An era had passed away and the
jukeboxes with it, all of it hauled away to the dump in the
back of an old truck. The doughnut shop was still there on
7th Street, and with the same name, but the ghost of Mrs.
Chapman had long since fled. We bought half a dozen
sinkers to go—passable doughnuts at best—and once again I
learned the sad lesson that you can't go home again.

We headed on down to Huntington Beach, where it turned
out that unlike the problem with doughnut whims, the ocean
was happily indifferent to the "things of man," to borrow a
phrase from Hopkins. There were fairly good waves breaking
at the end of Magnolia Street that morning—as there will be
long after we've all eaten our last doughnuts in the shadow of

the gravestone. In November, God willing, I'll be in Honolulu again on Thanksgiving day: Diamond Head, off the lighthouse if it's not blown out in the early morning; Kewalo Basin if it is; and on the way home, malasadas, Leonard's Bakery, Kapahulu Street.

Jim Blaylock
Orange, California

Two Views of a Cave Painting

I'm opposed to giving advice and making weighty state-
ments on general principle; we're wrong as often as not,
and look like fools. But it's safe to say this: ruination, utter
ruination, might be as close to us now as is the proverbial
snake, and but for the grace of the Deity and the cleverness
of friends, we might at any moment find that by a slip of
memory we've brought about the collapse of worlds.

I wouldn't have thought it so. I've believed that there was
room in our lives for casual error, that we could shrug and
grin and suffer mild regret and the world would wag along
for better or worse. Well, no more; recent events have proven
me wrong. The slightest slip of the hand, the forgetting of
the most trivial business, the uttering of an unremarkable bit
of foolishness might plunge us, as Mr. Poe would have it,
into the maelstrom. It fell out like this:

We'd been out on the Salisbury Plain — Professor Langdon St. Ives; his man Hasbro; and myself, Jack Owlesby—
digging for relics. I haven't got much taste for relics, but the
company was good, and there is an inn that goes by the name
of The Quarter Pygmy in Andover where I've eaten Cornish
pasty that was alone worth the trip down from London.

St. Ives discovered, quite by accident one hot, desolate, fly-ridden afternoon, a cave beneath an isolated hillside, covered in shrub and lost to the world thousands of years ago. If you've been to Salisbury and ridden across the plain as a tourist in a coach-and-four, then you know how such a thing could be; there's nothing there, for the most part, to attract anyone but an archeologist, and most of them are chasing down Druids. St. Ives was after fossils.

And he found them too; by the bushel-basketful. They littered the cave floor, dusty and dry, the femurs of megatheria, the tusks of wooly mammoths, the jawbones of heaven-knows-what sorts of sauria. St. Ives rather suspected they'd be there. He intended, he said, to make use of them.

The cave had been occupied in a distant age. Neanderthal man had lived there, or at least had come and gone. There was a cave painting, is what I'm trying to say, on the wall. I know nothing of the art of painting on cave walls, but I can tell you that this one was very nice indeed. It was the painting of a man, bearded and hairy-headed like an unkempt lion and barely decent with a loose covering of pelts. His countenance was bent into a thoughtful frown—a pensive cave man, if such a thing were possible. The painting was a self-portrait, and, said St. Ives, in quality it rivaled the famous bison painting from the cave of Altamira, Spain, or the reindeer drawings from the cavern of Aurignac. The artist had caught his own soul in berry-tinted oil, as well as his beetling brow and shaggy head.

This strikes you, I'm certain, as a weighty discovery. But you'd look in vain in the scientific journals for word of it. Our enterprises there fell out rather ill, as you might have judged from the tone of the first page of this account, and it's only recently that I've been able to take up the pen and reveal the grim truth of it. In the months since our return from that cave on the Salisbury Plain I've invented reasons, any number of them, to cast a shadow over our enterprise. St. Ives and Hasbro, the two men who might have given me away, are gentlemen through and through, and have kept quiet on the score. But you might have read in the *Times* a week past news of an explosion—an "upheaval of the earth," I believe they called it, in their uncomprehending, euphemistic way—which collapsed a section of countryside a bit north and west of Andover on the Salisbury Plain. They heard the explosion, no doubt, at the Pygmy. In fact, I know they did; I was there, and I heard it myself.

"An act of God!" cried the Royal Academy, and so unwittingly they paid the highest compliment, albeit it a trifling exaggeration, that they've paid yet to my mentor and friend, Langdon St. Ives. The business had his mark on it, to be sure, although I'll insist that I myself had no hand in it. With the collapse of the bit of countryside, however, was buried forever the only known evidence of my abominable folly, and buried along with it were months of worry and guilt, which St. Ives no doubt grew weary and sorrowful for at long last.

I wish to heaven such were the end of it, but I can't, of course, be entirely sure. I'm taking it on faith here. In matters involving the curiosities of traveling in time, and the complexities of meddling with the very structure of the universe itself, one must expect the odd surprise: the Neanderthal man in a hair piece, the Azilian mummy with a Van Dyke beard. One never knows, does one? It fell out like this:

When the volcano business was over with and St. Ives's great nemesis, Dr. Ignacio Narbondo, had been swallowed by a frozen lake in Scandinavia, the professor had, for the first time in decades, the leisure time to pursue a study he'd gotten on to some ten years earlier. Time travel isn't news anymore. Mr. H. G. Wells has put it to good use in a book which the casual reader would doubtless regard as a fiction. And perhaps it was. I, certainly, haven't seen the wonderful machine, although I have met the so-called Time Traveler, or someone masquerading as the man, broken and teary-eyed at Lady Beech-Smythe's summer house in Tadcaster. He was weeping into his ale glass—a man who had seen more than was good for him.

I have too, which is what I'm writing about here. Though to be more accurate, it wasn't so much what I *saw* that has stayed my pen these past months as what I *did*. This, then, is a confessional as much as anything else, and if it's wrath such a thing provokes, I'm your man to suffer it.

St. Ives, in a word, had cast upon a way to travel through time, quite independent of the methods of Wells's hero. The professor had been studying iridium traces in fossil bone, and had developed theories about the decline of the prehistoric monsters. But it wasn't entirely the scientific data that put him in the way of a method to leap through time, it was something *other* than that. I won't say *more* than that, for there is no room here to drag in questions of a spiritual or mythologic nature.

Let it suffice that there is something *in* a fossil—in the stony little trilobite which, five hundred million years ago, crept along Devonian sea bottoms; or, say the femur of a great toothed whale that shared Focene seas with fish lizards and plesiosaurs. St. Ives possessed, I remember, the complete skeletal remains of a pterodactyl, which reposed in mid-flight twelve feet above the floor of his vast library in Harrogate, as if the books and busts and scattered furniture of the room below were the inhabitants of a Cretaceous jungle clearing, and the thunder of the train rattling past toward Stoke Newington were the ebb and flow of prehistoric tides on a trackless beach.

There is enchantment in a fossil, is what I mean to say. St. Ives saw that straightaway. It might well be enchantment that scientists of the graph-and-caliper variety would wave into nonexistence if they had a chance at it. But Haitian islanders, in their ignorance of modern science, can dissolve a man's nose by splashing chicken blood into the face of a doll. I've seen it done. Hand the chicken blood and the doll—made of sticks and rags—to the president of the Royal Academy, and ask *him* to have a go at it. Your man's nose will be safe as a baby.

There are forces at work, you see, that haven't yet been quantified. They hover roundabout us in the air, like wraiths, and you and I are blind to them. But a man like St. Ives—that man carries with him a pair of spectacles, which, in a fit of sudden inspiration, he claps over his eyes. He frowns and squints. And there, winging it across the misty, cloud-drift sky, is—what? In this case it was a device which would enable him to travel through time. I don't mean to say that the device *itself* could be seen winging it through the clouds. I was speaking figuratively there. I'm afraid, now that I'm pressed, that my discussion of his device must remain in that vague and nebulous level, for I'm no scientist, and I hadn't a foggy notion on that morning when I stepped into the device and clutched the copper grips, whither the day's adventure might take me. It was enough, entirely enough, that I had St. Ives's word on the matter.

It wasn't electricity, despite the copper, nor was it explosives that hurtled us backward through time. There was a shudder and a gust of faint wind that smelled like the first fall of rain on paving stones. The little collection of fossils that were heaped on a copper plate on the floor between us shook and seemed for the moment to levitate. I had the frightening sensation of falling a great distance, of tumbling head over heels through a black void. At the same time it seemed as if I were watching myself fall, as if somehow I were having one of those out-of-body experiences that the spiritualists rely upon. In short, I was both falling and hovering above my falling self at one and the same time. Then, after an immeasurable passage through the darkness, an orange and murky light began to dawn, and without so much as a sigh, the fossils settled and the falling rush abated. I was whole once more, and together we stepped out into the interior of that cavern on Salisbury Plain.

I'd seen the cavern before, of course, any number of times in a distant age, and so I was understandably surprised that the painting of the cave man was missing. On the wall were sketches of Paleolithic animals, freshly drawn, the oily paint still soft. I remembered them as a sort of background for the more intricately drawn human in the foreground. St. Ives immediately pointed out what I should have understood—that the artist had only begun his work, and that he would doubtless finish it in the days that followed.

If we had arrived an hour earlier or later, we might well

have caught him at it. St. Ives was relieved that such a thing hadn't happened. The cave artist mustn't see us, said the Professor. And so adamant was he on the issue that he hinted, to my immense surprise, that if he *had* been there, laboring over the tail of an elephant, turning around in wonder to see us appear out of the mists of time, we mightn't have any choice but to kill the man then and there—and not with the pistol in St. Ives's bag, but we must crush his head with a stone and, God help us, finish his cave painting ourselves. St. Ives produced a sketch of it, accurate to the last hair of the man's unkempt beard.

Traveling in time, it was to turn out, was a vastly more complicated business than I could have guessed. The curious talk of beaning the cave man with a stone was only the beginning of it. St. Ives had unearthed his fossils in that very grotto, and, in the years that followed, he had stumbled across two immeasurably sensible ideas: first, that the use of fossil forces as a means of time travel would impel one not just *anywhere* in prehistory, but to that time in prehistory from whence came the fossil. Second, one had to make very sure, when he disappeared from one age and appeared abruptly in another, that he didn't, say, spring into reexistence in the middle of a tree or a hillside or, heaven help him, in the space occupied by some poor cave painter bent over his work. This last we had had to take our chances on.

St. Ives determined that by launching from the interior of the cave itself, utilizing fossils discovered at that precise spot—perhaps the gnawed bones of a Cro-Magnon feast— we would be guaranteed a landing, so to speak, in the very same cave thirty-five thousand years past, and not in an adjacent tree-thick forest. The reasoning was sound. It would have been much more convenient, of course, to have launched from the laboratory in Harrogate, and so have dispensed with the arduous task of secretly transporting the device and the fossils nearly three hundred kilometers across central England. But that wouldn't have done at all. St. Ives assures me that a very grand and destructive explosion might have been the result, and the three of us reduced to atoms.

So there we were, three men from 1902, carrying Gladstone bags, scrutinizing a cave painting on which a real live Neanderthal man had been daubing paint a half hour earlier, utterly unaware that hurtling toward him through the depths of time was a machine full of spectacled men from the future. It would almost have been worth it to see his face when we winked into existence behind him. Well, not entirely worth it, I suppose; not if we'd had to beat him with a stone.

The morning was fast declining, and although we had, as I said, Ruhmkorff lamps, and had brought along food in our bags, and so could have passed a comfortable enough night there on the plain, St. Ives was in a hurry to finish his research and be off. The lamps were an emergency precaution, he said. If all went according to plan, we'd while away the afternoon and launch at dusk. We mustn't be seen, he reminded us again. We had accomplished a third of our mission by having arrived at all—the half-completed painting was proof enough that we'd effectively disposed of several hundred centuries. We would accomplish another third when we found ourselves safe at home at last, or at least once again in our own century, where we could spend the night on the plain if we chose to. The final third was simple enough, it seemed to me: we'd observe, is what we'd do. A "field study" St. Ives called it, although it seemed to *him* to be the most ticklish business of the lot. We would lounge about, keeping ourselves hidden behind a tumble of rock a hundred meters above the cave, and every now and again we'd pop up and snap a photograph of a wandering bison or cave bear, and haul the evidence back to London, where the Royal Academy would be toppled onto their collective ear.

I hefted my bag and slung a tripod over my shoulder and made as if to set out. St. Ives nearly throttled himself stopping me. "Your footprints!" he said, pointing to the soft silt of the cave floor. And there, sure enough, were the prints of a pair of boots bought in Bond Street, London, either three weeks or thirty-five centuries earlier, I couldn't have said for certain at the time. St. Ives yanked a feather duster out of his bag and went to work on the prints. He was a man possessed.

There mustn't be a trace, he said, of our coming and going. It took us the better part of an hour, sneaking and skulking and breaking our backs with the hurry of it, to transport the machine, which, thank heaven, was remarkably light and could be partially dismantled, up to our aerie in the rocks. Then we were at it for another hour in the gloom of evening, dusting away tracks, replacing pebbles kicked aside in haste, grafting the snapped limb of a scrub plant back onto itself—taking frightful care, in other words, that no sentient being could remark our passing, and all the time Hasbro keeping watch above, whistling us into hiding at the approach of so much as a rodent.

We daren't, said St. Ives, meddle with anything. The slightest alteration in the natural state of the landscape might have ungovernable consequences in ages to come. The universe, it seems, is but a tenuous, delicate composition, rather like the reflected jumble of tinted jewels in a kaleidoscope. If one holds still while gazing into the end of the thing, the jewels sit there perfectly at ease, as if the reflected pattern isn't a clever ruse after all, but is a church window fixed into a wall of cut stone. But the slightest jiggling—the blink of an eye or the tremor of a sudden chill—casts the jewels into disarray, and no earthly amount of twisting and shaking and wishing will fetch them back again in the lost order. And so goes the universe.

What if a bug, said St. Ives, were crushed inadvertently underfoot, and that bug weren't as a result, eaten, say, by the toad which, historically, would have eaten that bug had the bug not been crushed by a bootheel that had no business being there in the first place. That toad might die—mightn't he?—for lack of a bug to eat, or from having eaten another bug out of desperation that he hadn't ought to have eaten. And the wild dog that would have eaten the toad, he'd go hungry, you see, and attempt the conquest of a toad which the universe had earmarked for an utterly different dog, who, everything being built upon everything else, like the crystals, as I said, in a kaleidoscope, would have to turn out and eat a rabbit. And that rabbit, which otherwise would have lived into a satisfying old age and bore six dozen rabbits very much like it, would be dead—wouldn't it?—and no end of prehistoric beasts would be denied the pleasure of dining on those six dozen rabbits.

You see how it goes. When St. Ives laid it out for me I was transfixed. I could tell straightaway that our puny comings and goings through the veil of time were as nothing in the eyes of the universe, compared to the brief few hours we intended to spend among the stones of the hillside. A bug and a toad and six dozen rabbits and pretty soon the entire local crowd is in an uproar. The universe they thought they could depend on has gone to smash. A megatherium looks for roots to nibble one morning and the roots are gone, because a half score wild dogs have moved to the coast where the rabbit population is more dependable, and the rabbits, finding travel a safer thing than it was last week, reproduce tenfold and make up, as they say, for lost time. Their offspring eat the roots that the megatherium thought he could count on and so he eats someone else's roots and so on and so on, magnified over countless centuries.

The crowning result is that the people of London aren't the people of London anymore at all. The Romans never arrived, for reasons that can be traced, if one had the right instruments, to the crushed bug. The Greeks, say, got in before them, and lived in the countryside in huts, spinning philosophies, and made peace with their Celtic neighbors and the Middle Ages crept past without so much as a mention of feudal states. I can tell you that it boggled my mind, to use the popular phrase, when St. Ives told me about it. That crushed bug, depend on it, would send the jewels tumbling, and where they'd fall, no one on Earth could puzzle out, try as he might and given a notebook and pen to calculate with.

We were dusty and hot before we were done that evening. A mammoth had come past, as if looking for something he'd lost, and St. Ives snapped a dozen photographs of the beast before it ambled away. Then a rhinoceros of some vintage appeared, and out came the camera again. I was a frightful mass of dirt and stinging insects and, indelicate as it sounds, perspiration, and was surprised to find a pool of clear water in the rocks, the product of a slowly running spring. I spent a cool half hour scrubbing up, and was happy enough to have brought along the requisite toiletries.

One is tempted—or at least I am—to dispense with the niceties when traveling rough. What purpose is there in trimming one's mustache, you ask, when one is tenting in the Hebrides? We can take a lesson from Robinson Crusoe, who maintained a degree of gentility even when lost forever, he supposed, on a desert island. Which one of us wouldn't have run naked with the savages before the month was gone? Not Crusoe. And so with me. I tread on the temptation to run with the savages, and although in truth I neglected to bring a pair of mustache scissors (we were to be away, at most, for half a day) I carried with me a comb and brush and a bottle of rose oil, and, as I say, I wielded those tools to good effect while St. Ives, caught up in the fever of his picture-taking, let me go about my business.

And I was careful. There were tiny fish, in fact, down in that shallow pool, fish that had no need for a dose of rose oil. I skimmed three broken hairs from the placid surface— which surface I had used as a mirror—and I put the hairs in my pocket and carried them back with me.

I had finished up and felt entirely restored when the sun, with a rapidity which never fails to amaze me, sank beyond the primeval horizon. Night descended like a lead curtain, and almost at once there sounded roundabout us such a shrieking and mewling and growling as I hope never to hear again. The night was alive with prowling beasts, and us with neither shelter nor fire. We were at it again, hustling the machine back into the cave. Our cave painter hadn't yet returned. With a cloth thrown over a lamp, once again we scoured out our footprints, watching with wary nervousness the pairs of eyes that shined at us out of the darkness. We launched an hour after sunset, and I heartily believed, along with St. Ives and Hasbro, that we left behind us not a trace of our having been there—nothing which might in the least joggle the delicate mechanism of the temporal and spatial universe.

We arrived in the twentieth century, in the familiar cave on the Salisbury Plain. All of us, since St. Ives's remonstrances, were leery of what we'd find. Stonehenge, we feared, would be whisked away and replaced by a picket fence enclosing a pumpkin patch. The wagon load of tourists bound for Wiltshire would have their hats on backward or would wear spectacles the size and shape of starfish. When one thought about it, it seemed almost a miracle that no such incongruity confronted us when we peered out of the door of that cave. There was the plain, dusty and hot, Marlborough to the north, Andover to the east, London, for aught we could determine, bustling along the shores of the Thames some few miles away, beyond the horizon.

I, for one, breathed a hearty sigh of relief. The last third of our mission had been ticked off the list, and another chapter in the great book of the adventures of Langdon St. Ives had come to a happy close. His camera was full of photographs. His time machine was faultless. There lay our cart and tarpaulin. We had only to load the device and the gear and away. The Royal Academy was a plum for the plucking.

I hefted my bag, grinning. For the moment. Something, however, seemed to be tugging at the corners of my mouth, effacing the grin. What was it? I gave St. Ives a look, and he could see quite clearly, from the puzzlement on my face, that something was amiss. I felt, abruptly, like a caveman smitten across the noggin with a stone.

My toiletries kit— I'd left it by the spring! There wasn't a thing in it, beyond a comb and brush, a bar of soap and a bottle of rose oil for the hair. I tore open my bag, hoping, in spite of my certain knowledge to the contrary, that I was wrong. But such wasn't the case. The kit was gone, lost in the trackless centuries of the past.

Our first thought was to retrieve it. But that wouldn't do. As fine as St. Ives's calculations were, we might as easily arrive a week early or a week late. We might appear, as I've said, while the cave painter was at work, and have to knock him

senseless in order to squelch the news of our scissoring at the
fabric of time. The universe mustn't get onto us, although, as
I pointed out to St. Ives, it already had, due to my incalculable
stupidity. St. Ives pondered for a moment. Returning would,
quite likely, compound the problem. And there was our
wagon, wasn't there? The universe hadn't gone so far afoul as
to have eradicated our wagon. Surely the Romans had arrived
after all. Surely the megatherium had nosed a sufficient quan-
tity of roots out of the dirt to satisfy itself and the universe
both. The toad had eaten his bug and all was well. The panic
had been for nothing.

We turned, intending to dismantle the ship, to hoist it onto
the wagon preparatory to returning to Harrogate via London.
There on the wall before us was the cave painting—the like-
ness of the artist himself, the scattered beasts beyond. We
stood gaping at it, unbelieving. I blinked and stepped forward, running my hand across the time-dried paint. Was this
some monstrous hoax? Had some grinning devil had a go at
the painting at our expense while we dawdled in pre-history?

The painting was wonderfully detailed—his broad nose,
his overhung brow, his squinty little pig eyes. But instead of
that troubled frown, his face was arched with a faint half
smile that da Vinci would have paid to study. His hair, in another lifetime shaggy and wild, was parted down the center
and combed neatly over his ears. The artist had been clever
enough to capture the sheen of rose oil on it, and the passing
centuries hadn't diminished it. His beard, still monumental
by current standards, was combed out and oiled into a cylinder like the beard of a pharoah. My comb was thrust into it
by way of ornament. He held my brush in one hand; in the
other, gripped at the neck and drawn with reverential care,
was the bottle of hair oil, tinted pink and orange in the dying
sunlight.

I fear that after the shock of it had drained the color from my
face, I pitched over onto that same article and had to be
hauled away bodily in the cart. The rest you know. The cave on

the Salisbury plain is no more, and, happily, the tenuous and brittle fabrication of the universe isn't quite so tenuous and brittle after all. Or so I tell myself. With the cave went the great mass of St. Ives's evidence. His photographs were cried down as frauds—waxwork dummies covered in horsehair. He's planning another journey, though. He's found the fore-leg of a dinosaur in a sandpit in the forest near Heidelberg, and he intends to compel it to spirit us back to the Age of Reptiles.

Whether I accompany him or stay in Harrogate to look after the tropical fish is a matter I debate with myself daily. You can understand what an unsettling thing it must be to teeter on the brink of bringing down the universe in a heap, and then to be snatched away at the last moment by the timely hand of Providence. And besides, I'm thinking of writing a monograph on the Crusoe matter—a little business regard-ing the civilizing influences of a good tortoiseshell comb. Desperate as it was, the incident of the toiletries bag, has rather revived my interest in the issue. The truth of it, if I'm any judge, has been borne out quite nicely.

The Idol's Eye

I won't say that this was the final adventure of Professor Langdon St. Ives and his man Hasbro—Colonel Hasbro since the war—but it was certainly the strangest and the least likely of the lot. Consider this: I know the Professor to be a man of complete and utter veracity. If he told me that he had determined, on the strength of scientific discovery, that gravity would reverse itself at four o'clock this afternoon, and that we'd find ourselves, as Stevenson put it, scaling the stars, I'd pack my bag and phone my solicitor and, at 3:59, I'd stroll out into the center of Jermyn Street so as not to crack my head on the ceiling when I floated away. And yet even *I* would have hesitated, looked askance, perhaps covertly checked the level of the bottles in the Professor's cabinet if he had simply recounted to me the details of the strange occurrence at the Explorers Club on that third Thursday in April. I admit it— the story is impossible on the face of it.

But I was there. And, as I say, what transpired was far and away more peculiar and exotic than the activities that, some twenty years earlier, had set the machinery of fate and mystery into creaking and irreversible motion.

It was a wild and rainy Thursday, then, that day at the club. March hadn't gone out like any lamb; it had roared right along, storming and blowing into April. We—that is to say, the Professor, Colonel Hasbro, Tubby Frobisher, John Priestly (the African explorer and adventurer, not the novelist), and myself, Jack Owlesby—were sitting about after a long dinner at the Explorers Club, opposite the Planetarium. Wind howled outside the casements, and rain angled past in a driving rush, now letting off, now redoubling, *whooshing* in great sheets of grey mist. It wasn't the sort of weather to be out in, you can count on that, and none of us, of course, had any business to see to anyway. I was looking forward to pipes and cigars and a glass of this or that, maybe a bit of a snooze in the lounge and then a really first-rate supper—a veal cutlet, perhaps, or a steak and mushroom pie and a bottle of Burgundy. The afternoon and evening, in other words, held astonishing promise.

So we sipped port, poked at the bowls of our pipes, watched the fragrant smoke rise in little lazy wisps and drift off, and muttered in a satisfied way about the weather. Under those conditions, you'll agree, it couldn't rain hard enough. I recall even that Frobisher, who, to be fair, had been coarsened by years in the bush, called the lot of us over to the window in order to have a laugh at the expense of some poor shambling madman who hunched in the rain below, holding over his head the ruins of an umbrella that might have been serviceable twenty or thirty years earlier but had seen hard use since, and which, in its fallen state, had come to resemble a ribby-looking inverted bird with about half a dozen pipe-stem legs. As far as I could see, there was no cloth on the thing at all. He had the mannerisms correct, that much I'll give him. *He* seemed convinced that the fossil umbrella was doing the work. Frobisher roared and shook and said that the man should be on the stage. Then he said he had half a mind to go down and give the fellow a half crown, except that it was raining and he would get soaked. "That's well and good in the bush," he said, "but in the city, in civilization, well . . ." He shook his head. "When in Rome," he said. And he forgot about the poor bogger in the road. All of us did, for a bit.

"I've seen rain that makes this look like small beer," Frobisher boasted, shaking his head. "That's nothing but fizzwater to me. Drizzle. Heavy fog."

"It reminds me of the time we faced down that mob in Banju Wangi," said Priestly, nodding at St. Ives, "after you two"—referring to the Professor and Hasbro—"routed the pig men. What an adventure."

It's moderately likely that Priestly, who kept pretty much to himself, had little desire to tell the story of our adventures in Java, incredible though they were, which had transpired some twenty years earlier. You may have read about them, actually, for my own account was published in *The Strand* some six months after the story of the Chingford Tower fracas and the alien threat. But as I say, Priestly himself didn't want to, as the Yanks say, spin any stretchers; he just wanted to shut Frobisher up. We'd heard nothing but "the bush" all afternoon. Frobisher had clearly been "out" in it—Australia, Brazil, India, Canton Province. There was bush enough in the world; that much was certain. We'd had enough of Frobisher's bush, but of course none of us could say so. This was the club, after all, and Tubby, although coarsened a bit, as I say, was one of the lads.

So I leapt in on top of Priestly when I saw Frobisher point his pipe stem at St. Ives. Frobisher's pipe stem, somehow, always gave rise to fresh accounts of the ubiquitous bush. "Banju Wangi!" I half shouted. "By golly!" I admit it was weak, but I needed a moment to think. And I said it loud enough to put Frobisher right off the scent.

"Banju Wangi," I said to Priestly. "Remember that pack of cannibals? Inky lot of blokes, what?" Priestly nodded, but didn't offer to carry on. He was satisfied with simply recalling the rain. And there *had* been a spectacular rain in those Javanese days, if you can call it a rain. Which you can't, really, no more than you would call a waterfall a faucet or the sun a gas lamp. A monsoon was what it was.

Roundabout twenty years back, then, it fell out that

Priestly and I and poor Bill Kraken had, on the strength of Dr.
Birdlip's manuscript, taken ship to Java where we met, not
unexpectedly, Professor St. Ives and Hasbro, themselves returning from a spate of very dangerous and mysterious space
travel. The alien threat, as I said before, had been crushed,
and the five of us had found ourselves deep in cannibal-
infested jungles, beating our way through toward the Bali
Straits in order to cross over to Penginuman where there lay,
we fervently prayed, a Dutch freighter bound for home. The
rain was sluicing down. It was mid-January, smack in the
middle of the northwest monsoons, and we were slogging
through jungles, trailed by orangutans and asps, hacking at
creepers, and slowly metamorphosing into biped sponges.

On the banks of the Wangi River we stumbled upon a
tribe of tiny Peewatin natives and traded them boxes of
kitchen matches for a pair of long piroques. Bill Kraken gave
his pocket watch to the local shaman in return for an odd
bamboo umbrella with a shrunken head dangling from the
handle by a brass chain. Kraken was, of course, round the
bend in those days, but his purchase of the curious umbrella
wasn't an act of madness. He stayed far drier than the rest of
us in the days that followed.

We set off, finally, down the Wangi beneath grey skies and
a canopy of unbelievable green. The river was swollen with
rain and littered with tangles of fallen tree trunks and vegetation that crumbled continually from either shore. Canoeing
in a monsoon struck me as a trifle *outré*, as the Frenchman
would say, but St. Ives and Priestly agreed that the very wild-
ness of the river would serve to discourage the vast and
lumbering crocodiles which, during a more placid season,
splashed through the shallows in frightful abundance. And
the rain itself, pouring from the sky without pause, had a
month before driven most of the cannibal tribes into higher
elevations.

So we paddled and bailed and bailed and paddled, St. Ives
managing, through a singular and mysterious invention of
his own, to keep his pipe alight in the downpour, and I anticipating, monsoon or no, the prick of a dart on the back of my

neck or the sight of a toothy, arch-eyed crocodile, intent upon dinner.

Our third night on the river, very near the coast, we found what amounted to a little sandy inlet scooped into the riverside. The bank above it had been worn away, and a cavern, overhung with vines and shaded by flowering acacias and a pair of incredible teaks, opened up for some few yards. By the end of the week it would be underwater, but at present it was high and dry, and we required shelter only for the night. We pushed the piroques up onto the sand, tied them to tree trunks, and hunched into the little cavern, lighting a welcome and jolly fire.

That night was full of the cries of wild beasts, the screams of panthers and the shrill peep of winging bats. More than once great clacking-jawed crocodiles crept up out of the river and gave us the glad eye before slipping away again. Pygmy hippopotami stumbled up, to the vast surprise of the Professor, and watched us for a bit, blinking and yawning and making off again up the bank and into the undergrowth. St. Ives insisted that such beasts were indigenous only to the continent of Africa, and his observation encouraged Priestly to tell a very strange and sad tale—the story of Doctor Ignacio Narbondo. This Doctor Narbondo, it seems, practiced in London in the eighteenth century. He claimed to have developed any number of strange serums, including one which, ostensibly, would allow the breeding of unlike beasts: pigs with fishes and birds with hedgehogs. He was harried out of England as a vivisectionist, although he swore to his own innocence and to the efficacy of his serum. Three years later, after suffering the same fate in Venice, he set sail from Mombasa with a herd of pygmy hippos, determined to haul them across the Indian Ocean to the Malay Archipelago and breed them with the great hairy orangutans that flourished in the Borneo rain forests.

He was possessed, said Priestly, with the idea of one day docking at Marseilles or London and striding ashore flanked by an army of the unlikely offspring of two of the most ludicrous beasts imaginable, throwing the same fear into the civilized world that Hannibal must have produced when, with ten score of elephants, he popped in from beyond the Alps. Narbondo, however, was never seen again. He docked in Surabaja, disappeared into the jungles with his beasts, and, as they say of Captain England in Mauritius, went native. Whether Narbondo became, in the years that followed, the fabled Wildman of Borneo is speculation. Some say he did, some say he died of typhus in Bombay. His hippopotami, however, riddled with Narbondo's serum, multiplied within a small area of Eastern Java.

The explanation of the existence of the hippos seemed to whet St. Ives's curiosity. He questioned Priestly for an hour, in fact, about this mysterious Doctor Narbondo, but Priestly had merely read about the mad doctor in Ashbless's *Account of London Madmen* (a grossly unfair appellation, at least in regard to Doctor Narbondo) and he could remember little else.

St. Ives, Hasbro, and I, of course, already knew of the existence of this Narbondo, and of his secret identity, for he was not, as Frosbinder alleged, Ignacio Narbondo, who lies frozen in a Scandanavian Tarn. He was (and still is) Ignacio Narbondo's long-lost twin brother Ivan, who had stolen his brother's name and traded on his reputation before the name and reputation fell into disrepute. His flight from England had less to do with vivisection than with the sworn enmity of the enraged Ignacio, an enmity that is now long cooled, if you'll allow me a moment of levity.

Half a dozen times that night I awakened to the sounds of something crashing in the forest above, and twice, blinking awake, I saw wide, hairy faces, upside down, eyes aglow, peering at us from overhead—jungle beasts, hanging from the vine-covered ledge above to watch us as we slept. Visions of the supposed Narbondo's hippo-apes flitted through my dreams, and when daylight wandered through the following morning, I was convinced that many of the past night's visitations had not been made merely by the creatures of dreams, but had actually been the offspring, so to speak, of the misanthropic Doctor Narbondo.

We had a brief respite from the rain that morning, and, determined to make the most of it, we loaded our gear aboard the piroques and prepared to clamber in. The sun broke through the clouds about then, and golden rays slanted through the forest ceiling, stippling the jungle floor and setting off an opera of bird cries and monkey whistling. We stood and stared at the steamy radiance of the forest, beautiful beyond accounting, then turned toward the canoes. A shout from Hasbro, however, brought us up short. He'd seen something, that much was certain, in the jungle beyond the riverside cavern.

"What ho, man?" said St. Ives, anxious to be off yet overwhelmed with scientific curiosity.

"A temple of sorts, sir," said Hasbro, pointing away into the forest. "I believe I see some sort of stone monolith or altar, sir. Perhaps a shrine to some heathen god."

And sure enough, bathed now in sunlight was a little clearing in the trees. In it, scattered in a circle, were half a dozen stone rectangles, one almost as large as an automobile, all crumbling and half-covered with creepers and moss.

Bill Kraken, still suffering from the poulp madness that had so befuddled him in the past months, gave out a little cry and dashed past Hasbro up the bank and into the forest. The rest of us followed at a run, fearing that Bill would come to harm. If we had known what lay ahead, we would have been a bit quicker about it even yet.

What we found in the clearing was that circle of stone monoliths, crumbling, as I've said, with age. Dozens of bright green asps rested in the sunshine atop the stones, watching us through lazy eyes. Four wild pigs, rooting for insects, crashed off into the vegetation, setting off the flight of a score of apes which had, hitherto, been hidden away overhead in the treetops. In the midst of the circle of stones sat a peculiar and indescribably eerie statue, carved, it seemed, entirely of ivory. It was old, though clearly not so old as the monoliths surrounding it, and it was minutely carved; its mouth looked as if it were ready to speak, and its jaw was square and determined and revealed just a hint of sadness.

On closer inspection it clearly wasn't ivory that it had been carved from, for the stone, whatever it was, was veined with thin blue lines.

It was uncanny. Professor St. Ives speculated at first that it was some sort of rare Malaysian marble. And very fine marble at that—marble that Michelangelo would have blathered over. More astonishing than the marble, though, were its eyes—two great rubies, faceted so minutely that they threw the rays of the tropical sun in a thousand directions. And it was those ruby eyes that not only cut short our examination of the ruined ring of altars and the peculiar idol, but which were the end of poor old Bill Kraken, a fine scientist in his own right before falling into the hands of the aliens after Birdlip's demise.

It was the flash of sunlight from those rubies that had instigated Kraken's charge up the slope and into the clearing. While the rest of us had gathered about commenting on the strange veined stone, Bill had stood gaping, clutching his umbrella, hypnotized by the ruby lights which, as the forest foliage swayed in the breezes overhead, now shading the jungle floor, now opening and allowing sunlight to flood in upon us, played over his face like the glints of light thrown from one of those spinning mirrored globes that dangle from the ceiling of a ballroom.

Suddenly and in an instant, as if propelled from a catapult, he sprang past St. Ives, hurled Priestly aside, and jabbed the tip of his umbrella in under one of the ruby eyes—the left eye, it was; I remember it vividly. He pried furiously on the thing as St. Ives and Hasbro attempted to haul him away. But he had the strength of a madman. The eye popped loose, rolling into the grasses, and Mad Bill shook off his two friends, wild in his ruby lust. He cast down his umbrella and dived for the gem, convinced, I suppose, that St. Ives and Hasbro and, no doubt, Priestly and myself were going to wrestle him for it. What brought him up short and froze the rest of us to the marrow there in that steamy jungle sun was a long, weary, ululating howl—a cry of awful pain, of indefinable grief—that soared out of the jungle around us, carried on the wind, part of the very atmosphere.

Our first thought after that long frozen instant was, of course, of cannibals. Bill snatched up the stone and leapt down the path toward the piroques with the rest of us, once again, at his heels.

Before night fell we had paddled out into the Bali Straits, never having caught a glimpse of those supposed cannibals nor seen the hint of a flying spear. There lay the Dutch freighter the *Peter Van Teeslink*. A week later Bill Kraken died of a fever in Singapore, shouting before he went of wild jungle beasts and of creatures that lay waiting for him in the depths of the sea and of a grinning sun that blinded him and set him mad.

We buried him there in Singapore on a sad day. St. Ives was determined to bury the ruby with him—to let him keep the plunder which had, it seemed certain, brought about his ruination. But Priestly wouldn't consider it. The ruby alone, he said, would pay for the entire journey with some to spare. To bury it with Kraken would be to submit, as it were, to the lusts of a madman. And Kraken, only six months previously, had been as sane as any of us. Keep the ruby, said Priestly. If nothing else it would provide for Kraken's son, himself almost as mad as his father. Hasbro agreed with Priestly as did, after consideration, St. Ives. The Professor, I believe, had an uncommon and inexplicable (in the light of his scientific training) fear of the jewel. But that's just conjecture. In the forty-five years I've known him he's demonstrated no fears whatsoever. He's too full of curiosity. And the ruby, finally, was a curiosity. It was certainly that.

Such were the details of our journey down the Wangi River as I related them that day at the Explorers Club. Everyone present at the table except Tubby Frobisher had, of course, been along on that little adventure, and I rather suspected that Tubby would just as soon I'd kept the story to myself, he being full of his own wanderings in the bush and having no acquaintance whatsoever with eastern Java or Bill Kraken. It was the ruby, in the end, that fetched his attention.

For some moments he'd been hunched forward in his chair, squinting at me, puffing so on his cigar that it burned like a torch. He slumped back as I ended the tale and plucked the cigar from his mouth. He paused for a moment before standing up and stepping slowly across to the window to look for his stranger on the street. But the man had apparently moved along.

There was a crashing downstairs about then—a slamming of doors, high voices, the clattering of failing cutlery. "Close that off!" shouted Frobisher down the stairwell. There was an answering shout, indecipherable, from below. "Shut yer gob!" Frobisher shouted, tapping ashes onto the rug.

One of the club members, Isaacs, I believe, from the Himalayan business, advised Frobisher to shut his. Under other circumstances, I'm sure, Tubby would have flown at the man, but he was too full of our Javanese ruby, and he barely heard the man's retort. It was quiet again downstairs. "By God," said Frobisher, "I'd give my pension to have a look at that damned ruby!"

"Impossible," I said, relighting my pipe, which I'd let grow cold during my narrative. "The ruby hasn't been seen in five years. Not since Giles Connover stole it from the museum. It was the ruby that brought about his end; that's what I believe— just as surely as it brought about the death of Bill Kraken."

I expected St. Ives to disagree with me, point out that I was possessed by superstition, that logic didn't and couldn't support me. But he kept silent, having once been possessed, I suppose, by the same unfounded fears—fears that had been a product of the weird, moaning cry that had assailed us there in the jungle some twenty years before.

"It certainly has had a curious history," said St. Ives with just the trace of a smile on his face. "A very curious history."

"Has it?" said Frobisher, stabbing his cigar out into the ashtray. "You didn't manage to sell it, then?"

"Oh, we sold it," St. Ives said. "Almost at once. Within the week of our return, if I'm not mistaken."

"Four days, sir, to be precise," put in Hasbro, who had an irritating habit of exactitude, one that had been polished and tightened over his eighty-odd years. "We docked on a Tuesday, sir, and sold the ruby to a jeweler in Knightsbridge on the following Saturday afternoon."

"Quite," said St. Ives, nodding toward him.

A waiter wandered past about then with a tea towel over his arm. Simultaneously there was another crash downstairs, a chair being upset it sounded like, and an accompanying shout. "What the devil is that row?" demanded Frobisher of the waiter. "This is a club, man, not a bowling green!"

"Quite right, sir," the waiter said. "We've had a bit of a time with an unwanted guest. Insists on coming in to have a look around. He's very persistent."

"Throw the blighter into the rubbish can," said Frobisher. "And bring us a decanter of whisky, if you will. Laphroaig. And some fresh glasses."

"Ice?" the waiter asked.

Frobisher gave him a wilting look and chewed on his cigar. "Just the filthy whisky. And tell that navvy downstairs that Tubby Frobisher will horsewhip him on the club steps at three o'clock if he's still about." Frobisher checked his watch. "That's about six and a half minutes from now."

"I'll tell him, sir, just as you say. But the man is deaf as a stone, as far as I can make out, and he wears smoked glasses, so he's quite possibly blind too. Threats haven't done much to dissuade him."

"Haven't they, by God!" shouted Frobisher. "Dissuade him, is it! I'll dissuade the man. I'll dissuade him from here to Chelsea. But let's have that whisky first. Did I say we needed glasses too?"

"Yes, sir," said the waiter. And off he went toward the bar.

"So this ruby," Frobisher said, settling back in his seat and plucking another cigar from inside his coat. "How much did it fetch?"

"A little above twenty-five thousand pounds," said St. Ives, nodding to Hasbro for affirmation.

"Twenty-five thousand six hundred fifty, sir," the colonel said.

Frobisher let out a low whistle.

"And it brought almost twice that at an auction at Sotheby's two weeks after," I put in. "Since then it's been bought and sold a dozen times, I imagine. The truth is, no one wants to keep it. It was owned, in time, by Isador Persano, and we all know what came of that, and later by Lady Braithewaite-Long, whose husband, of course, was involved in that series of ghastly murders near Waterloo Station."

"Don't overlook Preston Waters, the jeweler," said Priestly with an apparent shudder—a recollection, no doubt, of the grisly horror that had befallen the very Knightsbridge jeweler who had given us the twenty-five thousand pounds.

"The thing's cursed, if you ask me," I said, clearing debris from the table to make room for our newly arrived decanter of Scots whisky. Frobisher, sighing heartily, poured a neat bit into four glasses.

"None for me, thanks," Priestly said when Frobisher approached the fifth glass with the upturned decanter. "I'll just nip at this port for a bit. Whisky eats me up. Tears my throat bones to shreds. I'd be on milk and bread for a week."

Frobisher nodded, pleased, no doubt, to consume Priestly's share himself. He tilted his glass back and sucked a bit in, rolling it about in his mouth, relishing it. "That's the stuff, what?" he said, relaxing. "If there were one thing that would drag me back in out of the bush, it wouldn't be gold or women, I can tell you. No, sir. Not gold or women."

I assumed that it was whisky, finally, that would drag Tubby Frobisher out of the bush, though he never got around to saying so. I got in ahead of him. "Where do you suppose that ruby lies today, Professor?" I asked, having a taste of the Scotch myself. "Did the museum ever get it back?"

"They didn't want it, actually," said St. Ives. "They were offered the thing free, and they turned it down."

"The fools," Frobisher said. "They didn't go for all that hocus-pocus about a curse, I don't suppose. Not the bloody museum."

St. Ives shrugged. "There's no denying that it cost them a tremendous amount of trouble—robbery and murder and the like. And it's possible that they thought the man who offered it to them was a prankster. No one, of course, with any sense would give the thing away. I rather believe that they never considered the offer serious."

"I'd bet they were afraid of it," said Priestly, who had come to fear the jewel himself in the years since our return. "I wish now that we'd buried the bloody thing with Kraken. Do you remember that ghastly cry in the jungle? That wasn't made by any cannibals."

Hasbro raised an eyebrow. "Who do you suggest cried out, sir?" he asked in his cultivated butler's tone—a tone that alerted you to the sad fact that you were about to say something worthless and foolish.

Priestly gazed into his port and shrugged.

"I like to believe," said St. Ives, always the philosopher, "that the jungle itself cried out. That we had stolen a bit of her very heart, broken off a piece of her soul. I was possessed with the same certainty that we'd committed a terrible crime that possesses me when I see a fine old building razed or a great tree cut down—a tree, perhaps, that had seen the passing of two score generations of kings and, being a part of those ages, has been imbued with their history, with their glory. Do you follow me?"

Hasbro nodded. I could see he took the long view. Priestly appeared to be lost in the depths of his port, but I knew that he felt pretty much the same way; he just couldn't have stated it so prettily. Leave it to the Professor to get to the nub.

"Trash!" said Frobisher. "Gouge 'em both out, that's what I would have done. Imagine a pair of such rubies. A matched pair!" He shook his head. "Yes, sir," he finished, "I'd give my pension just to get a glimpse of one. Just a glimpse."

St. Ives, smiling just a bit, wistfully perhaps, reached into the inside pocket of his coat, pulled out his tobacco pouch and unfolded it, plucking out a ball of tissue twice the size of a walnut. Inside it was the idol's eye—the very one.

Frobisher leapt with a shout to his feet, his chair slamming over backward on the carpet. Isaacs, dozing in a chair by the fire, awoke with a start and shouted at Frobisher to leave off. But Tubby, taken so by surprise at St. Ives's coolness and by the size of the faceted gem that lay before him, red as thin blood and glowing in the firelight, failed to hear Isaacs's complaint. He stood and gaped at the ruby, his pension secure.

"How . . ." I began, at least as surprised as Frobisher. Priestly acted as if the thing were a snake; his pipe clacked in his teeth.

There was a wild shout from downstairs. Running footsteps echoed up toward us. A *whump* and crash followed as if something had been hurled into the wall. Then, weirdly, a blast of air sailed up the stairwell and blew past us, as if a door had been left open and the winds were finding their way in.

But the peculiar thing, the thing that made all of us, in that one instant, abandon the jewel and turn, waiting, watching the shadow that rose slowly along the wall of the stairwell, was the nature of that wind, the smell of that wind.

It wasn't the wet, cold breeze blowing down Baker Street. It wasn't a London breeze at all. It was a wind that blew down a jungle river—a warm and humid wind saturated with the smell of orchid blooms and rotting vegetation, that seemed to suggest the slow splash of crocodiles sliding off a muddy bank and the rippling silent passage of a tiger glimpsed through distant trees. The shadow rose on the stairs, frightfully slowly, as if whatever cast it had legs of stone and was creeping inexorably along—clump, clump, clump—toward some fated destination. And within the footsteps, surrounding them, part of them, were the far-off cries of wild birds and the chattering of treetop monkeys and the shrill cry of a panther, all of it borne on that wind and on that ascending shadow for one long, teeming, silent moment.

And what we saw first when the walker on the stairs clumped into view was the bent tip of an umbrella—the sprung umbrella hoisted by Frobisher's stroller. Ruined as the umbrella was, I could see that the shaft was a length of deteriorated bamboo, crushed and black with age and travel. And there, at the base, dangling by a green brass chain below the grip that was clutched in a wide, pale hand, was what had once been a tiny, preserved head, nothing but a skull now, yellow and broken and with one leathery strip of dried flesh still clinging in the depression below the eye socket.

We all shouted. Priestly smashed back into his chair. St. Ives bent forward in eager anticipation. We knew, wild and impossible

as it seemed, what it was that approached us up the stairs on that
rainy April day. It wore, as the waiter had promised, a pair of
glasses with smoked lenses, and was otherwise clad in cast-off,
misshapen clothing that had once been worn, quite clearly, by
people in widely different parts of the world: Arab bloused
trousers, a Mandalay pontoon shirt, wooden shoes, a Leibnitz
cap. His marbled jaw was set with fierce determination and his
mouth opened and shut rhythmically like the mouth of a conger
eel, his breath *whooshing* in and out. He reached up with his free
hand and tore the smoked glasses away, pitching them in one
sweeping motion against the wall where they shattered, spraying poor, dumbfounded Isaacs with glass shards.

   In his right eye shone a tremendous faceted ruby, identical
to the one that lay before St. Ives. Light blazed from it as if it
were alive. His left eye was a hollow, dark socket, smooth and
black and empty as night. He stood at the top of the stairs,
chest heaving, creaking with exertion. He looked, so to speak,
from one to the other of us, fixing his stare on the ruby glowing atop the table. His arm twitched. He let go of Bill
Kraken's umbrella, and the thing dropped like a shot to the
floor, the jawbone and half a dozen yellow teeth breaking
loose and spinning off across the oak planks. His entire de-
meanor seemed to lighten, as if he were drinking in the sight
of the ruby like an elixir, and he took two shuffling steps
toward it, swinging his arm ponderously out in front of him,
pointing with a trembling finger toward the prize on the table.
There could be no doubt what he was after, no doubt at all.

   And for me, I was all for letting him have it. Under the circumstances it seemed odd to deny him. St. Ives was of a like
mind. He went so far as to nod at the gem, as if inviting the
idol (we can't mince words here, that's what he was) to scoop
it up. Frobisher, however, was inclined to disagree. And I
can't blame him, really. He hadn't been in Java with us
twenty years past, hadn't seen the idol in the ring of stones,
couldn't know that the sad umbrella lying on the floor had
belonged to Bill Kraken and had been abandoned, as if in
trade, for the priceless, ruinous gem among the asps and or-
chids of that jungle glade.

He stepped forward then, foolishly, and said something equally foolish about horsewhipping on the steps of the club and about his having been in the bush. A great, marbled arm swept out, *whump*ing the air out of foolish old Frobisher and knocking him spinning over a library table as if he had been made of *papier-mâché*. Frobisher lay there senseless.

St. Ives at that point played his trump card: "Doctor Narbondo!" he said, and then waited, anticipating, watching the idol as it paused, contemplating, stricken by a rush of ancient, thin memory. Priestly hunched forward, mouth agape, tugging at his great white beard. I heard him whisper, "Narbondo!" as if in echo to St. Ives's revelation.

The idol stared at the Professor, its mouth working, moaning, trying to speak, to cry out. "Nnnn . . ." it groaned. "Nnnar, Nnarbondo!" it finally shouted, screwing up its face awfully, positively creaking under the strain.

Doctor Narbondo! It seemed impossible, lunatic. But there it was. He lurched forward, pawing the air, stumbling toward the ruby, the idol's eye. One pale hand fell on the edge of the table. The glasses danced briefly. Priestly's port tumbled over, pouring out over the polished wood in a red pool. The rain and the wind howled outside, making the fire in the great hearth dance up the chimney. Firelight shone through the ruby, casting red embers of reflected light onto Narbondo's face, bathing the cut-crystal decanter, three-quarters full of amber liquid, in a rosy, beckoning glow.

Narbondo's hand crept toward the jewel, but his eye was on that decanter. He paused, fumbled at the jewel, dropped it, his fingers clutching, a sad, mewing sound coming from his throat. Then, with the relieved look of a man who'd finally crested some steep and difficult hill, as if he'd scaled a monumental precipice and been rewarded with a vision of El Dorado, of Shangri-la, of paradise itself, he grasped the decanter of Laphroaig and, shaking, a wide smile struggling into existence on his face, lifted it toward his mouth, thumbing the stopper off onto the tabletop.

Hasbro responded with instinctive horror to Narbondo's obvious intent. He plucked up Priestly's unused glass, said,

"Allow me, sir," and rescued the decanter, pouring out a good inch and proffering the glass to the gaping Narbondo. I fully expected that Hasbro would sail across and join Frobisher's heaped form unconscious on the floor. But that wasn't the case. Narbondo hesitated, recollecting, bits and pieces of European culture and civilized instinct filtering up from unfathomable depths. He nodded to Hasbro, took the proffered glass, and, swirling the whisky around in a tight, quick circle, passed it once under his nose and tossed it off.

A long and heartfelt sigh escaped him. He stood there just so, his head back, his mouth working slowly, savoring the peaty, smoky essence that lingered along his tongue. And Hasbro, himself imbued with the instincts of the archetypal gentleman's gentleman, poured another generous dollop into the glass, replaced the stopper, and set the decanter in the center of the table. Then he uprighted Frobisher's fallen chair and motioned toward it. Narbondo nodded again heavily, and, looking from one to the other of us, slumped into the chair with the air of a man who'd come a long, long way home.

Thus ends the story of, as I threatened in the early pages, perhaps the strangest of all the adventures that befell Langdon St. Ives, his man Hasbro, and myself. We ate that cutlet for supper, just as I'd planned, and we drained that decanter of whisky before the evening was through. St. Ives, his scientific fires blazing, told of his study over the years of the history of the mysterious Doctor Narbondo, of his slow realization that the curiously veined marble of the idol in the forest hadn't been marble at all, had, indeed, been the petrified body of Narbondo himself, preserved by jungle shaman and witch doctors using Narbondo's own serums. His eyes, being mere jellies, were removed and replaced with jewels, the optical qualities of the oddly wrought gems allowing him some vague semblance of strange vision. And there he had stood for close upon two hundred years, tended by priests from the tribes of Peewatin natives until that fateful day when Bill Kraken had gouged out his eye. Narbondo's weird reanimation and slow journey west over the long years would, in itself, be a tale long in the telling, as would that of St. Ives's quest for the lost ruby, a search that led him, finally, to a curiosity shop near the Tate Gallery where he purchased the gem for two pound six, the owner sure that it was simply a piece of cleverly cut glass.

At first I thought it was wild coincidence that Narbondo should arrive at the Explorers Club on the very day that St. Ives appeared with the ruby. But now I'm sure that there was no coincidence involved. Narbondo was bound to find his eye, and if St. Ives hadn't retrieved it from the curiosity shop, then Narbondo would have.

The doctor, I can tell you, is safe and sound and has done us all a service by renewing Langdon St. Ives's interests in the medical arts. Together, take my word for it, they work at perfecting the curious serums. Where they work will, I'm afraid, have to remain utterly secret. You can understand that. Curiosity seekers, doubting Thomases, and modern-day Ponce de Leons would flock forth gaping and demanding if his whereabouts were generally known.

And so it was that Doctor Narbondo returned. He had no army of supporters, no mutant beasts from the Borneo jungles, no hippos and apes with which to send a thrill of terror across the continent, no last laugh. Cold reality, I fear, can't measure up to the curious turnings of a madman's dreams. But if it was a grand and startling homecoming he wanted when he set sail for distant jungle shores two hundred years ago, he did quite moderately well for himself; I think you'll agree.

Paper Dragons

Strange things are said to have happened in this world—some are said to be happening still—but half of them, if I'm any judge, are lies. There's no way to tell sometimes. The sky above the north coast has been flat gray for weeks—clouds thick overhead like carded wool not fifty feet above the ground, impaled on the treetops, on redwoods and alders and hemlocks. The air is heavy with mist that lies out over the harbor and the open ocean, drifting across the tip of the pier and breakwater now and again, both of them vanishing into the gray so that there's not a nickel's worth of difference between the sky and the sea. And when the tide drops, and the reefs running out toward the point appear through the fog, covered in the brown bladders and rubber leaves of kelp, the pink lace of algae, and the slippery sheets of sea lettuce and eel grass, it's a simple thing to imagine the dark bulk of the fish that lie in deepwater gardens and angle up toward the pale green of shallows to feed at dawn.

There's the possibility, of course, that winged things, their counterparts if you will, inhabit dens in the clouds, that in the valleys and caverns of the heavy, low skies live unguessed beasts. It occurs to me sometimes that if without warning a man could draw back that veil of cloud that obscures the heavens, snatch it back in an instant, he'd startle a world of oddities aloft in the skies: balloon things with hovering little wings like the fins of pufferfish, and spiny, leathery creatures, nothing but bones and teeth and with beaks half again as long as their ribby bodies.

There have been nights when I was certain I heard them, when the clouds hung in the treetops and foghorns moaned off the point and water dripped from the needles of hemlocks beyond the window onto the tin roof of Filby's garage. There were muffled shrieks and the airy flapping of distant wings. On one such night when I was out walking along the bluffs, the clouds parted for an instant and a spray of stars like a reeling carnival shone beyond, until, like a curtain slowly drawing shut, the clouds drifted up against each other and parted no more. I'm certain I glimpsed something—a shadow, the promise of a shadow—dimming the stars. It was the next morning that the business with the crabs began.

I awoke, late in the day, to the sound of Filby hammering at something in his garage—talons, I think it was, copper talons. Not that it makes much difference. It woke me up. I don't sleep until an hour or so before dawn. There's a certain bird, Lord knows what sort, that sings through the last hour of the night and shuts right up when the sun rises. Don't ask me why. Anyway, there was Filby smashing away some time before noon. I opened my left eye, and there atop the pillow was a blood-red hermit crab with eyes on stalks, giving me a look as if he were proud of himself, waving pincers like that. I leaped up. There was another, creeping into my shoe, and two more making away with my pocket watch, dragging it along on its fob toward the bedroom door.

The window was open and the screen was torn. The beasts were clambering up onto the woodpile and hoisting themselves in through the open window to rummage through my personal effects while I slept. I pitched them out, but that evening there were more—dozens of them, bent beneath the weight of seashells, dragging toward the house with an eye to my pocket watch. It was a migration. Once every hundred

years, Dr. Jensen tells me, every hermit crab in creation gets
the wanderlust and hurries ashore. Jensen camped on the
beach in the cove to study the things. They were all heading
south like migratory birds. By the end of the week there was
a tiresome lot of them afoot—millions of them to hear
Jensen carry on—but they left my house alone. They dwindled as the next week wore out, and seemed to be straggling
in from deeper water and were bigger and bigger: The size of
a man's fist at first, then of his head, and then a giant, vast as
a pig, chased Jensen into the lower branches of an oak. On
Friday there were only two crabs, both of them bigger than
cars. Jensen went home gibbering and drank himself into a
stupor. He was there on Saturday, though; you've got to give
him credit for that. But nothing appeared. He speculates that
somewhere off the coast, in a deep-water chasm a hundred
fathoms below the last faded colors, is a monumental beast,
blind and gnarled from spectacular pressures and wearing a
seashell overcoat, feeling his way toward shore.

At night sometimes I hear the random echoes of far-off
clacking, just the misty and muted suggestion of it, and I
brace myself and stare into the pages of an open book, firelight glinting off the cut crystal of my glass, countless noises
out in the foggy night among which is the occasional clack
clack clack of what might be Jensen's impossible crab,
creeping up to cast a shadow in the front-porch lamplight, to
demand my pocket watch. It was the night after the sighting
of the pig-sized crabs that one got into Filby's garage—
forced the door apparently—and made a hash out of his
dragon. I know what you're thinking. I thought it was a lie
too. But things have since fallen out that make me suppose
otherwise. He did, apparently, know Augustus Silver. Filby
was an acolyte; Silver was his master. But the dragon business, they tell me, isn't merely a matter of mechanics. It's a
matter of perspective. That was Filby's downfall.

There was a gypsy who came round in a cart last year. He
couldn't speak, apparently. For a dollar he'd do the most
amazing feats. He tore out his tongue, when he first arrived,
and tossed it onto the road. Then he danced on it and shoved

it back into his mouth, good as new. Then he pulled out his entrails—yards and yards of them like sausage out of a machine—then jammed them all back in and nipped shut the hole he'd torn in his abdomen. It made half the town sick, mind you, but they paid to see it. That's pretty much how I've always felt about dragons. I don't half believe in them, but I'd give a bit to see one fly, even if it were no more than a clever illusion.

But Filby's dragon, the one he was keeping for Silver, was a ruin. The crab—I suppose it was a crab—had shredded it, knocked the wadding out of it. It reminded me of one of those stuffed alligators that turns up in curiosity shops, all eaten to bits by bugs and looking sad and tired, with its tail bent sidewise and a clump of cotton stuffing shoved through a tear in its neck.

Filby was beside himself. It's not good for a grown man to carry on so. He picked up the shredded remnant of a dissected wing and flagellated himself with it. He scourged himself, called himself names. I didn't know him well at the time, and so watched the whole weird scene from my kitchen window: his garage door banging open and shut in the wind, Filby weeping and howling through the open door, storming back and forth, starting and stopping theatrically, the door slamming shut and slicing off the whole embarrassing business for thirty seconds or so and then sweeping open to betray a wailing Filby scrabbling among the debris on the garage floor—the remnants of what had once been a flesh-and-blood dragon, as it were, built by the ubiquitous Augustus Silver years before. Of course I had no idea at the time. Augustus Silver, after all. It almost justifies Filby's carrying on. And I've done a bit of carrying on myself since, although as I said, most of what prompted the whole business has begun to seem suspiciously like lies, and the whispers in the foggy night, the clacking and whirring and rush of wings, has begun to sound like thinly disguised laughter, growing fainter by the months and emanating from nowhere, from the clouds, from the wind and fog. Even the occasional letters from Silver himself have become suspect.

Filby is an eccentric. I could see that straightaway. How he finances his endeavors is beyond me. Little odd jobs, I don't doubt—repairs and such. He has the hands of an archetypal mechanic: spatulate fingers, grime under the nails, nicks and cuts and scrapes that he can't identify. He has only to touch a heap of parts, wave his hands over them, and the faint rhythmic stirrings of order and pattern seem to shudder through the crossmembers of his workbench. And here an enormous crab had gotten in, and in a single night had clipped apart a masterpiece, a wonder, a thing that couldn't be tacked back together. Even Silver would have pitched it out. The cat wouldn't want it.

Filby was morose for days, but I knew he'd come out of it. He'd be mooning around the house in a slump, poking at yesterday's newspapers, and a glint of light off a copper wire would catch his eye. The wire would suggest something. That's how it works. He not only has the irritating ability to coexist with mechanical refuse; it speaks to him, too, whispers possibilities.

He'd be hammering away some morning soon—damn all crabs—piecing together the ten thousand silver scales of a wing, assembling the jeweled bits of a faceted eye, peering through a glass at a spray of fine wire spun into a braid that would run up along the spinal column of a creature which, when released some misty night, might disappear within moments into the clouds and be gone. Or so Filby dreamed. And I'll admit it: I had complete faith in him, in the dragon that he dreamed of building.

In the early spring, such as it is, some few weeks after the hermit crab business, I was hoeing along out in the garden. Another frost was unlikely. My tomatoes had been in for a week, and an enormous green worm with spines had eaten the leaves off the plants. There was nothing left but stems, and they were smeared up with a sort of slime. Once when I was a child I was digging in the dirt a few days after a rain, and I unearthed a finger-sized worm with the face of a human being. I buried it. But this tomato worm had no such face. He was pleasant, in fact, with little piggy eyes and a smashed-in sort of nose, as worm noses go. So I pitched him over the fence into Filby's yard. He'd climb back over—there was no doubting it. But he'd creep back from anywhere, from the moon. And since that was the case—if it was inevitable—then there seemed to be no reason to put him too far out of his way, if you follow me. But the plants were a wreck. I yanked them out by the roots and threw them into Filby's yard, too, which is up in weeds anyway, but Filby himself had wandered up to the fence like a grinning gargoyle, and the clump of a half-dozen gnawed vines flew into his face like a squid. That's not the sort of thing to bother Filby, though. He didn't mind. He had a letter from Silver mailed a month before from points south.

I was barely acquainted with the man's reputation then. I'd heard of him—who hasn't? And I could barely remember seeing photographs of a big, bearded man with wild hair and a look of passion in his eye, taken when Silver was involved in the mechano-vivisectionist's league in the days when they first learned the truth about the mutability of matter. He and three others at the university were responsible for the brief spate of unicorns, some few of which are said to roam the hills hereabouts, interesting mutants, certainly, but not the sort of wonder that would satisfy Augustus Silver. He appeared in the photograph to be the sort who would leap headlong into a cold pool at dawn and eat bulgur wheat and honey with a spoon.

And here was Filby, ridding himself of the remains of ravaged tomato plants, holding a letter in his hand, transported. A letter from the master! He'd been years in the tropics and had seen a thing or two. In the hills of the eastern jungles he'd sighted a dragon with what was quite apparently a bamboo ribcage. It flew with the xylophone clacking of windchimes, and had the head of an enormous lizard, the pronged tail of a devil-fish, and clockwork wings built of silver and string and the skins of carp. It had given him certain ideas. The best dragons, he was sure, would come from the sea. He was setting sail for San Francisco. Things could be purchased in Chinatown—certain "necessaries," as he put it in his letter to Filby. There was mention of perpetual motion, of the building of an immortal creature knitted together from parts of a dozen beasts.

I was still waiting for the issuance of that last crab, and so was Jensen. He wrote a monograph, a paper of grave scientific accuracy in which he postulated the correlation between the dwindling number of the creatures and the enormity of their size. He camped on the cliffs above the sea with his son, Bumby, squinting through the fog, his eye screwed to the lens of a special telescope—one that saw things, as he put it, particularly clearly—and waiting for the first quivering claw of the behemoth to thrust up out of the gray swells, cascading water, draped with weeds, and the bearded face of the crab to follow, drawn along south by a sort of migratory magnet toward heaven alone knows what. Either the crab passed away down the coast hidden by mists, or Jensen was wrong—there hasn't been any last crab.

The letter from Augustus Silver gave Filby wings, as they say, and he flew into the construction of his dragon, sending off a letter east in which he enclosed forty dollars, his unpaid dues in the Dragon Society. The tomato worm, itself a wingless dragon, crept back into the garden four days later and had a go at a half-dozen fresh plants, nibbling lacy arabesques across the leaves. Flinging it back into Filby's yard would accomplish nothing. It was a worm of monumental determination. I put him into a jar—a big, gallon pickle jar, empty of pickles, of course—and I screwed onto it a lid with holes punched in. He lived happily in a little garden of leaves and dirt and sticks and polished stones, nibbling on the occasional tomato leaf.

I spent more and more time with Filby, watching, in those days after the arrival of the first letter, the mechanical bones and joints and organs of the dragon drawing together. Unlike his mentor, Filby had almost no knowledge of vivisection. He had an aversion to it, I believe, and as a consequence his creations were almost wholly mechanical—and almost wholly unlikely. But he had such an aura of certainty about him, such utter and uncompromising conviction that even the most unlikely project seemed inexplicably credible.

I remember one Saturday afternoon with particular clarity. The sun had shone for the first time in weeks. The grass hadn't been alive with slugs and snails the previous night—a sign, I supposed, that the weather was changing for the drier. But I was only half right. Saturday dawned clear. The sky was invisibly blue, dotted with the dark specks of what might have been sparrows or crows flying just above the treetops, or just as easily something else, something more vast— dragons, let's say, or the peculiar denizens of some very distant cloud world. Sunlight poured through the diamond panes of my bedroom window, and I swear I could hear the tomato plants and onions and snow peas in my garden unfurling, hastening skyward. But around noon great dark clouds roiled in over the Coast Range, their shadows creeping across the meadows and redwoods, picket fences, and chaparral. A spray of rain sailed on the freshening offshore breeze, and the sweet smell of ozone rose from the pavement of Filby's driveway, carrying on its first thin ghost an unidentifiable sort of promise and regret: the promise of wonders pending, regret for the bits and pieces of lost time that go trooping away like migratory hermit crabs, inexorably, irretrievably into the mists.

So it was a Saturday afternoon of rainbows and umbrellas, and Filby, still animated at the thought of Silver's approach, showed me some of his things. Filby's house was a marvel, given over entirely to his collections. Carven heads whittled of soapstone and ivory and ironwood populated the rooms, the strange souvenirs of distant travel. Aquaria bubbled away, thick with water plants and odd, mottled creatures: spotted eels and leaf fish, gobies buried to their noses in sand, flatfish with both eyes on the same side of their heads, and darting anableps that had the wonderful capacity to see above and below the surface of the water simultaneously and so, unlike the mundane fish that swam beneath, were inclined toward philosophy. I suggested as much to Filby, but I'm not certain he understood. Books and pipes and curios filled a half dozen cases, and star charts hung on the walls. There were working drawings of some of Silver's earliest accomplishments, intricate swirling sketches covered over with what were to me utterly meaningless calculations and commentary.

On Monday another letter arrived from Silver. He'd gone along east on the promise of something very rare in the serpent line—an elephant trunk snake, he said, the lungs of which ran the length of its body. But he was coming to the west coast, that much was sure, to San Francisco. He'd be here in a week, a month, he couldn't be entirely sure. A message would come. Who could say when? We agreed that I would drive the five hours south on the coast road into the city to pick him up: I owned a car.

Filby was in a sweat to have his creature built before Silver's arrival. He wanted so badly to hear the master's approval, to see in Silver's eyes the brief electricity of surprise and excitement. And I wouldn't doubt for a moment that there was an element of envy involved. Filby, after all, had languished for years at the university in Silver's shadow, and now he was on the ragged edge of becoming a master himself.

So there in Filby's garage, tilted against a wall of roughcut fir studs and redwood shiplap, the shoulders, neck, and right wing of the beast sat in silent repose, its head a mass of faceted pastel crystals, piano wire, and bone clutched in the soft rubber grip of a bench vise. It was on Friday, the morning of the third letter, that Filby touched the bare ends of two microscopically thin copper rods, and the eyes of the dragon rotated on their axes, very slowly, blinking twice, surveying the cramped and dimly lit garage with an ancient, knowing look before the rods parted and life flickered out.

Filby was triumphant. He danced around the garage, shouting for joy, cutting little capers. But my suggestion that we take the afternoon off, perhaps drive up to Fort Bragg for lunch and a beer, was met with stolid refusal. Silver, it seemed, was on the horizon. I was to leave in the morning. I might, quite conceivably, have to spend a few nights waiting. One couldn't press Augustus Silver, of course. Filby himself would work on the dragon. It would be a night and day business, to be sure. I determined to take the tomato worm along for company, as it were, but the beast had dug himself into the dirt for a nap.

This business of my being an emissary of Filby struck me as dubious when I awoke on Saturday morning. I was a neighbor who had been ensnared in a web of peculiar enthusiasm. Here I was pulling on heavy socks and stumbling around the kitchen, tendrils of fog creeping in over the sill, the hemlocks ghostly beyond dripping panes, while Augustus Silver tossed on the dark Pacific swell somewhere off the Golden Gate, his hold full of dragon bones. What was I to say to him beyond, "Filby sent me." Or something more cryptic: "Greetings from Filby." Perhaps in these circles one merely winked or made a sign or wore a peculiar sort of cap with a foot-long visor and a pyramid-encased eye embroidered across the front. I felt like a fool, but I had promised Filby. His garage was alight at dawn, and I had been awakened once in the night by a shrill screech, cut off sharply and followed by Filby's cackling laughter and a short snatch of song.

I was to speak to an old Chinese named Wun Lo in a restaurant off Washington. Filby referred to him as "the connection." I was to introduce myself as a friend of Captain Augustus Silver and wait for orders. Orders—what in the devil sort of talk was that? In the dim glow of lamplight the preceding midnight such secret talk seemed sensible, even satisfactory; in the chilly dawn it was risible.

It was close to six hours into the city, winding along the tortuous road, bits and pieces of it having fallen into the sea on the back of winter rains. The fog rose out of rocky coves and clung to the hillsides, throwing a gray veil over dew-fed wildflowers and shore grasses. Silver fence pickets loomed out of the murk with here and there the skull of a cow or a goat impaled atop, and then the quick passing of a half-score of mailboxes on posts, rusted and canted over toward the cliffs along with twisted cypresses that seemed on the verge of flinging themselves into the sea.

Now and again, without the least notice, the fog would disappear in a twinkling, and a clear mile of highway would appear, weirdly sharp and crystalline in contrast to its previous muted state. Or an avenue into the sky would suddenly appear, the remote end of which was dipped in opalescent blue and which seemed as distant and unattainable as the end of a rainbow. Across one such avenue, springing into clarity for perhaps three seconds, flapped the ungainly bulk of what might have been a great bird, laboring as if against a stiff, tumultuous wind just above the low-lying fog. It might as easily have been something else, much higher. A dragon? One of Silver's creations that nested in the dense emerald fog forests of the Coast Range? It was impossible to tell, but it seemed, as I said, to be struggling—perhaps it was old—and a bit of something, a fragment of a wing, fell clear of it and spun dizzily into the sea. Maybe what fell was just a stick being carried back to the nest of an ambitious heron. In an instant the fog closed, or rather the car sped out of the momentary clearing, and any opportunity to identify the beast, really to study it, was gone. For a moment I considered turning around, going back, but it was doubtful that I'd find that same bit of clarity, or that if I did, the creature would still be visible. So I drove on, rounding bends between redwood-covered hills that might have been clever paintings draped along the ghostly edge of Highway One, the hooks that secured them hidden just out of view in the mists above. Then almost without warning the damp asphalt issued out onto a broad highway and shortly thereafter onto the humming expanse of the Golden Gate Bridge.

Some few silent boats struggled against the tide below. Was one of them the ship of Augustus Silver, slanting in toward the Embarcadero? Probably not. They were fishing boats from the look of them, full of shrimp and squid and bug-eyed rock cod. I drove to the outskirts of Chinatown and parked, leaving the car and plunging into the crowd that swarmed down Grant and Jackson and into Portsmouth Square.

It was Chinese New Year. The streets were heavy with the smell of almond cookies and fog, barbecued duck and gunpowder, garlic and seaweed. Rockets burst overhead in showers of barely visible sparks, and one, teetering over onto the street as the fuse burned, sailed straightaway up Washington, whirling and glowing and fizzing into the wall of a curio shop, then dropping lifeless onto the sidewalk as if embarrassed at its own antics. The smoke and pop of firecrackers, the milling throng, and the nagging senselessness of my mission drove me along down Washington until I stumbled into the smoky open door of a narrow, three-story restaurant. Sam Wo it was called.

An assortment of white-garmented chefs chopped away at vegetables. Woks hissed. Preposterous bowls of white rice steamed on the counter. A fish head the size of a melon blinked at me out of a pan. And there, at a small table made of chromed steel and rubbed formica, sat my contact. It had to be him. Filby had been wonderfully accurate in his description. The man had a gray beard that wagged on the tabletop and a suit of similar color that was several sizes too large, and he spooned up clear broth in such a mechanical, purposeful manner that his eating was almost ceremonial. I approached him. There was nothing to do but brass it out. "I'm a friend of Captain Silver," I said, smiling and holding out a hand. He bowed, touched my hand with one limp finger, and rose. I followed him into the back of the restaurant.

It took only a scattering of moments for me to see quite clearly that my trip had been entirely in vain. Who could say where Augustus Silver was? Singapore? Ceylon? Bombay? He'd had certain herbs mailed east just two days earlier. I was struck at once with the foolishness of my position. What in the world was I doing in San Francisco? I had the uneasy feeling that the five chefs just outside the door were having a laugh at my expense, and that old Wun Lo, gazing out toward the street, was about to ask for money—a fiver, just until payday. I was a friend of Augustus Silver, wasn't I?

My worries were temporarily arrested by an old photograph that hung above a tile-faced hearth. It depicted a sort of weird shantytown somewhere on the north coast. There was a thin fog, just enough to veil the surrounding countryside, and the photograph had clearly been taken at dusk, for the long, deep shadows thrown by strange hovels slanted away landward into the trees. The tip of a lighthouse was just visible on the edge of the dark Pacific, and a scattering of small boats lay at anchor beneath. It was puzzling, to be sure—doubly so, because the lighthouse, the spit of land that swerved round toward it, the green bay amid cypress and eucalyptus was, I was certain, Point Reyes. But the shantytown, I was equally certain, didn't exist, couldn't exist.

The collection of hovels tumbled down to the edge of the bay, a long row of them that descended the hillside like a strange gothic stairway, and all of them, I swear it, were built in part of the ruins of dragons, of enormous winged reptiles—tin and copper, leather and bone. Some were stacked on end, tilted against each other like card houses. Some were perched atop oil drums or upended wooden pallets. Here was nothing but a broken wing throwing a sliver of shade; there was what appeared to be a tolerably complete creature, lacking, I suppose, whatever essential parts had once served to animate it. And standing alongside a cooking pot with a man who could quite possibly have been Wun Lo himself was Augustus Silver.

His beard was immense—the beard of a hill wanderer, of a prospector lately returned from years in unmapped goldfields, and that beard and broad-brimmed felt hat, his oriental coat and the sharp glint of arcane knowledge that shone from his eyes, the odd harpoon he held loosely in his right hand, the breadth of his shoulders—all those bits and pieces seemed almost to deify him, as if he were an incarnation of Neptune just out of the bay, or a wandering Odin who had stopped to drink flower-petal tea in a queer shantytown along the coast. The very look of him abolished my indecision. I left Wun Lo nodding in a chair, apparently having forgotten my presence.

Smoke hung in the air of the street. Thousands of sounds—a cacophony of voices, explosions, whirring pinwheels, oriental music—mingled into a strange sort of harmonious silence. Somewhere to the northwest lay a village built of the skins of dragons. If nothing else—if I discovered nothing of the arrival of Augustus Silver—I would at least have a look at the shantytown in the photograph. I pushed through the crowd down Washington, oblivious to the sparks and explosions. Then almost magically, like the Red Sea, the throng parted and a broad avenue of asphalt opened before me. Along either side of the suddenly clear street were grinning faces, frozen in anticipation. A vast cheering arose, a shouting, a banging on Chinese cymbals and tooting on reedy little horns. Rounding the corner and rushing along with the maniacal speed of an express train, careered the leering head of a paper dragon, lolling back and forth, a wild rainbow mane streaming behind it. The body of the thing was half a block long, and seemed to be built of a thousand layers of the thinnest sort of pastel-colored rice paper, sheets and sheets of it threatening to fly loose and dissolve in the fog. A dozen people crouched within, racing along the pavement, the whole lot of them yowling and chanting as the crowd closed behind and, in a wave, pressed along east toward Kearny, the tumult and color muting once again into silence.

The rest of the afternoon had an air of unreality to it, which, strangely, deepened my faith in Augustus Silver and his creations, even though all rational evidence seemed to point squarely in the opposite direction. I drove north out of the city, cutting off at San Rafael toward the coast, toward Point Reyes and Inverness, winding through the green hillsides as the sun traveled down the afternoon sky toward the sea. It was shortly before dark that I stopped for gasoline.

The swerve of shoreline before me was a close cousin of that in the photograph, and the collected bungalows on the hillside could have been the ghosts of the dragon shanties, if one squinted tightly enough to confuse the image through a foliage of eyelashes. Perhaps I've gotten that backward; I can't at all say anymore which of the two worlds had substance and which was the phantom.

A bank of fog had drifted shoreward. But for that, perhaps I could have made out the top of the lighthouse and completed the picture. As it was I could see only the gray veil of mist wisping in on a faint onshore breeze. At the gas station I inquired after a map. Surely, I thought, somewhere close by, perhaps within eyesight if it weren't for the fog, lay my village.

The attendant, a tobacco-chewing lump of engine oil and blue paper towels, hadn't heard of it—the dragon village, that is. He glanced sideways at me. A map hung in the window. It cost nothing to look. So I wandered into a steel and glass cubicle, cold with rust and sea air, and studied the map. It told me little. It had been hung recently; the tape holding its corners hadn't yellowed or begun to peel. Through an open doorway to my right was the dim garage where a Chinese mechanic tinkered with the undercarriage of a car on a hoist.

I turned to leave just as the hovering fog swallowed the sun, casting the station into shadow. Over the dark Pacific swell the mists whirled in the seawind, a trailing wisp arching skyward in a rush, like surge-washed tidepool grasses or the waving tail of an enormous misty dragon, and for a scattering of seconds the last faint rays of the evening sun shone out of the tattered fog, illuminating the old gas pumps, the interior of the weathered office, the dark, tool-strewn garage.

The map in the window seemed to curl at the corners, the tape suddenly brown and dry. The white background tinted into shades of antique ivory and pale ocher, and what had been creases in the paper appeared, briefly, to be hitherto unseen roads winding out of the redwoods toward the sea.

It was the strange combination, I'm sure, of the evening, the sun, and the rising fog that for a moment made me unsure whether the mechanic was crouched in his overalls beneath some vast and finny automobile spawned of the peculiar architecture of the early sixties, or instead worked beneath the chrome and iron shell of a tilted dragon, frozen in flight above the greasy concrete floor, and framed by tiers of heater hoses and old dusty tires.

Then the sun was gone. Darkness fell within moments, and all was as it had been. I drove slowly north through the village. There was, of course, no shantytown built of castaway dragons. There were nothing but warehouses and weedy vacant lots and the weathered concrete and tin of an occasional industrial building. A tangle of small streets comprised of odd, tumbledown shacks, some few of them on stilts as if awaiting a flood of apocalyptic proportions.

But the shacks were built of clapboard and asphalt shingles—there wasn't a hint of a dragon anywhere, not even the tip of a rusted wing in the jimsonweed and mustard.

I determined not to spend the night in a motel, although I was tempted to, on the off chance that the fog would dissipate and the watery coastal moonbeams would wash the coastline clean of whatever it was—a trick of sunlight or a trick of fog—that had confused me for an instant at the gas station. But as I say, the day had, for the most part, been unprofitable, and the thought of being twenty dollars out of pocket for a motel room was intolerable.

It was late—almost midnight—when I arrived home, exhausted. My tomato worm slept in his den. The light still burned in Filby's garage, so I wandered out and peeked through the door. Filby sat on a stool, his chin in his hands, staring at the dismantled head of his beast. I suddenly regretted having looked in; he'd demand news of Silver, and I'd have nothing to tell him. The news—or rather the lack of news—seemed to drain the lees of energy from him. He hadn't slept in two days. Jensen had been round hours earlier babbling about an amazingly high tide and of his suspicion that the last of the crabs might yet put in an appearance. Did Filby want to watch on the beach that night? No, Filby didn't. Filby wanted only to assemble his dragon. But there was something not quite right—some wire or another that had gotten crossed, or a gem that had been miscut—and the creature wouldn't respond. It was so much junk.

I commiserated with him. Lock the door against Jensen's crab, I said, and wait until dawn. It sounded overmuch like a platitude, but Filby, I think, was ready to grasp at any reason, no matter how shallow, to leave off his tinkering.

The two of us sat up until the sun rose, drifting in and out of maudlin reminiscences and debating the merits of a stroll down to the bluffs to see how Jensen was faring. The high tide, apparently, was accompanied by a monumental surf, for in the spaces of meditative silence I could just hear the rush and thunder of long breakers collapsing on the beach. It seemed unlikely to me that there would be giant crabs afoot.

   The days that followed saw no break in the weather. It
continued dripping and dismal. No new letters arrived from
Augustus Silver. Filby's dragon seemed to be in a state of
perpetual decline. The trouble that plagued it receded deeper
into it with the passing days, as if it were mocking Filby, who
groped along in its wake, clutching at it, certain in the morning that he had the problem securely by the tail, morose that
same afternoon that it had once again slipped away. The creature was a perfect wonder of separated parts. I'd had no notion of its complexity. Hundreds of those parts, by week's
end, were laid out neatly on the garage floor, one after another in the order they'd been dismantled. Concentric circles
of them expanded like ripples on a pond, and by Tuesday of
the following week masses of them had been swept into coffee cans that sat here and there on the bench and floor. Filby
was declining, I could see that. That week he spent less time
in the garage than he had been spending there in a single day
during the previous weeks, and he slept instead long hours in
the afternoon.

   I still held out hope for a letter from Silver. He was, after
all, out there somewhere. But I was plagued with the suspicion that such a letter might easily contribute to certain of
Filby's illusions—or to my own—and so prolong what with
each passing day promised to be the final deflation of those
same illusions. Better no hope, I thought, than impossible
hope, than ruined anticipation.

   But late in the afternoon, when from my attic window I
could see Jensen picking his way along the bluffs, carrying
with him a wood and brass telescope, while the orange glow
of a diffused sun radiated through the thinned fog over the
sea, I wondered where Silver was, what strange seas he
sailed, what rumored wonders were drawing him along jungle paths that very evening.

   One day he'd come, I was sure of it. There would be
patchy fog illuminated by ivory moonlight. The sound of
Eastern music, of Chinese banjos and copper gongs would
echo over the darkness of the open ocean. The fog would

swirl and part, revealing a universe of stars and planets and the aurora borealis dancing in transparent color like the thin rainbow light of paper lanterns hung in the windswept sky. Then the fog would close, and out of the phantom mists, heaving on the ground swell, his ship would sail into the mouth of the harbor, slowly, cutting the water like a ghost, strange sea creatures visible in the phosphorescent wake, one by one dropping away and returning to sea as if having accompanied the craft across ten thousand miles of shrouded ocean. We'd drink a beer, the three of us, in Filby's garage. We'd summon Jensen from his vigil.

But as I say, no letter came, and all anticipation was so much air. Filby's beast was reduced to parts—a plate of broken meats, as it were. The idea of it reminded me overmuch of the sad bony remains of a Thanksgiving turkey. There was nothing to be done. Filby wouldn't be placated. But the fog, finally, had lifted. The black oak in the yard was leafing out and the tomato plants were knee-high and luxuriant. My worm was still asleep, but I had hopes that the spring weather would revive him. It wasn't, however, doing a thing for Filby. He stared long hours at the salad of debris, and when in one ill-inspired moment I jokingly suggested he send to Detroit for a carburetor, he cast me such a savage look that I slipped out again and left him alone.

On Sunday afternoon a wind blew, slamming Filby's garage door until the noise grew tiresome. I peeked in, aghast. There was nothing in the heaped bits of scrap that suggested a dragon, save one dismantled wing, the silk and silver of which was covered with greasy hand prints. Two cats wandered out. I looked for some sign of Jensen's crab, hoping, in fact, that some such rational and concrete explanation could be summoned to explain the ruin. But Filby, alas, had quite simply gone to bits along with his dragon. He'd lost whatever strange inspiration it was that propelled him. His creation lay scattered, not two pieces connected. Wires and fuses were heaped amid unidentifiable crystals, and one twisted bit of elaborate machinery had quite clearly been danced upon and lay now cold and dead, half hidden beneath the bench. Delicate thises and thats sat mired in a puddle of oil that scummed half the floor.

Filby wandered out, adrift, his hair frazzled. He'd received a last letter. There were hints in it of extensive travel, perhaps danger. Silver's visit to the west coast had been delayed again. Filby ran his hand backward through his hair, oblivious to the harrowed result the action effected. He had the look of a nineteenth-century Bedlam lunatic. He muttered something about having a sister in McKinleyville, and seemed almost illuminated when he added, apropos of nothing, that in his sister's town, deeper into the heart of the north coast, stood the tallest totem pole in the world. Two days later he was gone. I locked his garage door for him and made a vow to collect his mail with an eye toward a telling exotic postmark. But nothing so far has appeared. I've gotten into the habit of spending the evening on the beach with Jensen and his son, Bumby, both of whom still hold out hope for the issuance of the last crab. The spring sunsets are unimaginable. Bumby is as fond of them as I am, and can see comparable whorls of color and pattern in the spiral curve of a seashell or in the peculiar green depths of a tidepool.

In fact, when my tomato worm lurched up out of his burrow and unfurled an enormous gauzy pair of mottled brown wings, I took him along to the seaside so that Bumby could watch him set sail, as it were.

The afternoon was cloudless and the ocean sighed on the beach. Perhaps the calm, insisted Jensen, would appeal to the crab. But Bumby by then was indifferent to the fabled crab. He stared into the pickle jar at the half-dozen circles of bright orange dotting the abdomen of the giant sphinx moth that had once crept among my tomato plants in a clever disguise. It was both wonderful and terrible, and held a weird fascination for Bumby, who tapped at the jar, making up and discarding names.

When I unscrewed the lid, the moth fluttered skyward some few feet and looped around in a crazy oval, Bumby charging along in its wake, then racing away in pursuit as the monster hastened south. The picture of it is as clear to me now as rainwater: Bumby running and jumping, kicking up glinting sprays of sand, outlined against the sheer rise of mossy cliffs, and the wonderful moth just out of reach overhead, luring Bumby along the afternoon beach. At last it was impossible to say just what the diminishing speck in the china-blue sky might be—a tiny, winged creature silhouetted briefly on the false horizon of our little cove, or some vast flying reptile swooping over the distant ocean where it fell away into the void, off the edge of the flat earth.

We Traverse Afar

with Tim Powers

Harrison sat in the dim living room and listened to the train. All the sounds were clear—the shrill steam whistle over the bass chug of the engine, and even, faintly, the clatter of the wheels on the track.

It never rained anymore on Christmas Eve. The plastic rain gauge was probably still out on the shed roof; he used to lean over the balcony railing outside the master bedroom to check the level of the water in the thing. There had been something reassuring about the idea of rainwater rising in the gauge—nature measurably doing its work, the seasons going around, the drought held at bay. . . .

But he couldn't recall any rain since last winter. He hadn't checked, because the master bedroom was closed up now. And anyway the widow next door, Mrs. Kemp, had hung some strings of Christmas lights over her back porch, and even if he *did* get through to the balcony, he wouldn't be able to help seeing the blinking colors, and probably even something like a Christmas wreath on her back door.

Too many cooks spoil the broth, he thought, a good wine needs no bush, a friend in need is one friend too many, leave me alone.

She'd even knocked on his door today, the widow had; with a paper plate of Christmas cookies! The plate was covered in red and green foil and the whole bundle was wrapped in a Santa Claus napkin. He had taken the plate, out of politeness; but the whole kit and caboodle, cookies and all, had gone straight into the Dumpster.

To hell with rain anyway. He was sitting in the old leather chair by the cold fireplace, watching snow. In the glass globe in his hand a little painted man and woman sat in a sleigh that was being pulled by a little frozen horse.

He took a sip of vodka and turned the globe upside down and back again, and a contained flurry of snow swirled around the figures. He and his wife had bought the thing a long time ago. The couple in the sleigh had been on their cold ride for decades now. Better to travel than to arrive, he thought, peering through the glass at their tiny blue-eyed faces; they didn't look a day older than when they'd started out. And still together, too, after all these years.

The sound of the train engine changed, was more echoing and booming now—maybe it had gone into a tunnel.

He put the globe down on the magazine stand and had another sip of vodka. With his nose stuffed full of Vick's Vapo-Rub, as it was tonight, his taste buds wouldn't have known the difference if he'd been drinking V.S.O.P. brandy or paint thinner, but he could feel the warm glow in his stomach.

It was an old LP record on the turntable, one from the days when the real hi-fi enthusiasts cared more about sound quality than any kind of actual music. This one was two whole sides of locomotive racket, booming out through his monaural Klipshorn speaker. He also had old disks that were of downtown traffic, ocean waves, birds shouting in tropical forests....

Better a train. Booming across those nighttime miles.

He was just getting well relaxed when he began to hear faint music behind the barreling train. It was a Christmas song, and before he could stop himself he recognized it— Bing Crosby singing "We Three Kings," one of her favorites.

He'd been ready for it. He pulled two balls of cotton out of the plastic bag beside the vodka bottle and twisted them into his ears. That made it better—all he could hear now was a distant hiss that might have been rain against the windows.

Ghost rain, he thought. I should have put out a ghost gauge.

As if in response to his thought, the next sip of vodka had a taste—the full-orchestra, peaches-and-bourbon chord of Southern Comfort. He tilted his head forward and let the liquor run out of his mouth back into the glass, and then he stood up and crossed to the phonograph, lifted the arm off the record and laid it in its rest, off to the side.

When he pulled the cotton out of his ears, the house was silent. There was no creaking of floorboards, no sound of breathing or rustling. He was staring at the empty fireplace, pretty sure that if he looked around he would see that flickering rainbow glow from the dining room; the glow of lights, and the star on the top of the tree, and those weird little glass columns with bubbles wobbling up through the liquid inside. Somehow the stuff never boiled away. Some kind of perpetual motion, like those glass birds with the top hats, that bobbed back and forth, dipping their beaks into a glass of water, forever. At least with the Vick's he wouldn't smell pinesap.

The pages of the wall calendar had been rearranged sometime last night. He'd noticed it right away this morning when he'd come out of what used to be the guest bedroom, where he slept now on the single bed. The pink cloud of tuberous begonias above the thirty-one empty days of March was gone, replaced by the blooming poinsettia of the December page. Had he done it himself, shifted the calendar while walking in his sleep? He wasn't normally a sleepwalker. And sometime during the night, around midnight probably, he'd thought he heard a stirring in the closed-up bedroom across the hall, the door whispering open, what sounded like bedroom slippers shuffling on the living room carpet.

Before even making coffee he had folded the calendar back to March. She'd died on St. Patrick's Day evening, and in fact the green dress she'd laid out on the queen-size bed still lay there, gathering whatever kind of dust inhabited a closed-up room. Around the dress, on the bedspread, were still scattered the green felt shamrocks she had intended to sew onto it. She'd never even had a chance to iron the dress, and, after the paramedics had taken her away on that long-ago evening, he'd had to unplug the iron himself, at the same time that he unplugged the bedside clock.

The following day, after moving out most of his clothes, he had shut the bedroom door for the last time. This business with the calendar made him wonder if maybe the clock was plugged in again, too, but he was not going to venture in there to find out.

Through the back door, from across the yard, he heard the familiar scrape of the widow's screen door opening, and then the sound of it slapping shut. Quickly he reached up and flipped off the lamp, then sat still in the darkened living room. Maybe she wasn't paying him another visit, but he wasn't taking any chances.

In a couple of minutes there came the clumping of her shoes on the front steps, and he hunkered down in the chair, glad that he'd turned off the train noise.

He watched her shadow in the porch light. He shouldn't leave it on all the time. It probably looked like an invitation, especially at this time of year. She knocked at the door, waited a moment and then knocked again. She couldn't take a hint if it stepped out of the bushes and bit her on the leg.

Abruptly he felt sheepish, hiding out like this, like a kid. But he was a married man, for God's sake. He'd taken a vow. And a vow wasn't worth taking if it wasn't binding. She will do him good and not evil all the days of her life, said Proverbs 31 about a good wife; her lamp does not go out at night.

Does not go out.

His thoughts trailed off into nothing when he realized that the woman outside was leaving, shuffling back down the steps. He caught himself wondering if she'd brought him something else to eat, maybe left a casserole outside the door. Once she'd brought around half a corned beef and a mess of potatoes and cabbage, and like the Christmas cookies, all of it had gone straight into the garbage. But the canned chili he'd microwaved earlier this evening wasn't sitting too well with him, and the thought of corned beef . . .

He could definitely hear something now from the closed-up bedroom—a low whirring noise like bees in a hive—the sewing machine? He couldn't recall if he had unplugged it too, that night. Still, it had no excuse. . . .

He grabbed the cotton balls, twisting them up tight and jamming them into his ears again. Had the bedroom door moved? He groped wildly for the lamp, switched it on, and with one last backward glance he went out the front door, nearly slamming it behind him in his haste.

Shakily, he sat down in one of the white plastic chairs on the porch and buttoned up his cardigan sweater. If the widow returned, she'd find him, and there was damn-all he could do about it. He looked around in case she might have left him something, but apparently she hadn't. The chilly night air calmed him down a little bit, and he listened for a moment to the sound of crickets, wondering what he would do now. Sooner or later he'd have to go back inside. He hadn't even brought out the vodka bottle.

Tomorrow, Christmas day, would be worse.

What would he say to her if the bedroom door should *open*, and she were to step out? If he were actually to *confront* her . . . A good marriage was made in heaven, as the scriptures said, and you didn't let a thing like that go. No matter what. Hang on with chains.

After a while he became aware that someone up the street was yelling about something, and he stood up in relief, grateful for an excuse to get off the porch, away from the house. He shuffled down the two concrete steps, breathing the cold air that was scented with jasmine even in December.

Some distance up the block, half a dozen people in robes were walking down the sidewalk toward his house, carrying one of those real estate signs that looked like a miniature hangman's gallows. No, only one of them was carrying it, and at the bottom end of it was a metal wheel that was skirling along the dry pavement.

Then he saw that it wasn't a real estate sign, but a cross.

The guy carrying it was apparently supposed to be Jesus, and two of the men behind him wore slatted skirts like Roman soldiers, and they had rope whips that they were snapping in the chilly air.

"Get along, King of the Jews!" one of the soldiers called, obviously not for the first time, and not very angrily. Behind the soldiers three women in togas trotted along, shaking their heads and waving their hands. Harrison supposed they must be Mary or somebody. The wheel at the bottom of the cross definitely needed a squirt of oil.

Harrison took a deep breath, and then forced jocularity into his voice as he called, "You guys missed the Golgotha off-ramp. Only thing south of here is the YMCA."

A black couple was pushing a shopping cart up the sidewalk from the opposite direction, their shadows stark under the streetlight. They were slowing down to watch Jesus. All kinds of unoiled wheels were turning tonight.

The biblical procession stopped in front of his house, and Harrison walked down the path to the sidewalk. Jesus grinned at him, clearly glad for the chance to pause amid his travail and catch his breath.

One of the women handed Harrison a folded flier. "I'm Mary Magdalene," she told him. "This is about a meeting we're having at our church next week. We're on Seventeenth, just past the 5 Freeway."

The shopping cart had stopped too, and Harrison carried the flier over to the black man and woman. "Here," he said, holding out the piece of paper. "Mary Magdalene wants you to check out her church. Take a right at the light, it's just past the freeway."

The black man had a bushy beard but didn't seem to be older than thirty, and the woman was fairly fat, wearing a sweatsuit. The shopping cart was full of empty bottles and cans sitting on top of a trash bag half full of clothes.

The black man grinned. "We're homeless, and we'd sure like to get the dollar-ninety-nine breakfast at Norm's. Could you help us out? We only need a little more."

"Ask Jesus," said Harrison nervously, waving at the robed

people. "Hey Jesus, here's a chance to do some actual *thing* tonight, not just march around the streets. This here is a genuine homeless couple, give 'em a couple of bucks."

Jesus patted his robes with the hand that wasn't holding the cross. "I don't have anything on me," he said apologetically.

Harrison turned to the Roman soldiers. "You guys got any money?"

"Just change would do," put in the black man.

"Nah," said one of the soldiers, "I left my money in my pants."

"Girls?" said Harrison.

Mary Magdalene glanced at her companions, then turned back to Harrison and shook her head.

"Really?" said Harrison. "Out in this kind of neighborhood at night, and you don't even have quarters for phone calls?"

"We weren't going to go far," explained Jesus.

"Weren't going to go far." Harrison nodded, then looked back to Mary Magdalene. "Can your church help these people out? Food, shelter, that kind of thing?"

The black woman had walked over to Jesus and was admiring his cross. She liked the wheel.

"They'd have to be married," Mary Magdalene told Harrison. "In the church. If they're just . . . living together, we can't do anything for them."

That's great, thought Harrison, coming from Mary Magdalene. "So that's it, I guess, huh?"

Apparently it was. "Drop by the church!" said Jesus cheerfully, resuming his burden and starting forward again.

"Get along, King of the Jews!" called one of the soldiers, snapping his length of rope in the air. The procession moved on down the sidewalk, the wheel at the bottom of the cross squeaking.

The black man looked at Harrison. "Sir, could we borrow a couple of bucks? You live here? We'll pay you back."

Harrison was staring after the robed procession. "Oh," he said absently, "sure. Here." He dug a wad of bills out of his pants pocket and peeled two ones away from the five and held them out.

The man took the bills. "God bless you. Could we have the five too? It's Christmas Eve."

Harrison found that he was insulted by the God bless you. The implication was that these two were devout Christians, and would assuredly spend the money on wholesome food, or medicine, and not go buy dope or wine.

"No," he said sharply. "And I don't care what you buy with the two bucks." Once I've given it away, he thought, it shouldn't be my business. Gone is gone.

The black man scowled at him and muttered something obviously offensive under his breath as the two of them turned away, not toward Norm's and the dollar-ninety-nine breakfast, but down a side street toward the mini-mart.

Obscurely defeated, Harrison trudged back up to his porch and collapsed back into the chair.

He wished the train record was still playing inside—but even if it had been, it would still be a train that, realistically, had probably stopped rolling a long time ago. Listening to it over and over again wouldn't make it move again.

He opened the door and walked back into the dim living room. Just as he closed the door he heard thunder boom across the night sky, and then he heard the hiss of sudden rain on the pavement outside. In a moment it was tapping at the windows.

He wondered if the rain gauge was still on the roof, maybe measuring what was happening to Jesus and the black couple out there. And he was glad that he had had the roof re-done a year ago. He was okay in here—no wet carpets in store for him.

The vodka bottle was still on the table, but he could see tiny reflected flickers of light in the glassy depths of it—red and green and yellow and blue; and, though he knew that the arm of the phonograph was lifted and in its holder, he heard again, clearly now, Bing Crosby singing "We Three Kings."

To hell with the vodka. He sat down in the leather chair and picked up the snow globe with trembling fingers. "What," he said softly, "too far? Too long? I thought it was supposed to be forever."

But rainy gusts boomed at the windows, and he realized that he had stood up. He pried at the base of the snow globe, and managed to free the plug.

Water and white plastic flecks bubbled and trickled out of it, onto the floor. In only a minute the globe had emptied out, and the two figures in the sleigh were exposed to the air of tonight, stopped. Without the refraction of the surrounding water the man and the woman looked smaller, and lifeless.

"Field and fountain, moor and mountain," he whispered. "Journey's done—finally. Sorry."

He was alone in the dark living room. No lights gleamed in the vodka bottle, and there was no sound but his own breath and heartbeat.

Tomorrow he would open the door to anyone who might knock.

The Shadow on the Doorstep

It was several months after I had dismantled my aquaria that I heard a rustling in the darkness, a scraping of what sounded like footsteps on the front porch of my house. It startled me out of a literary lethargy built partly of three hours of Jules Verne, partly of a nodding acquaintance with a bottle of single malt scotch. In the yellow glow of the porch lamp, through the tiny, distorting panes of the mullioned upper half of the oaken door, I saw only a shadow, a face perhaps, half turned away. The dark outline of it was lost in the shaded confusion of an unpruned hibiscus.

The porch itself was a rectangular island of hooded light, cut with drooping shadows of potted plants and the rectilinear darkness of a pair of weather-stained mission chairs. Encircling it was a tumult of shrubbery. Beyond lay the street and the feeble glow of globed lamps, all of it washed in pale moonlight that served only to darken that wall of shrubbery, so that the porch with its yellow bug light and foliage seemed a self-contained world of dwindling enchantment.

I couldn't say with any confidence, as I sat staring in sudden, unexplained horror at the start this late visitor had given me, that the leafy appendages thrusting away on either side of him weren't arms or some strange mélange of limbs and fins. With the weak light at his back he was a fishy shadow suffused in the amber aura of porchlight, something which had crawled dripping out of a late Devonian sea.

In the interests of objectivity, I'll say again that I had been reading Jules Verne. And it's altogether reasonable that a mixture of the book, the shadows, the embers aglow in the fireplace, the late hour, and a morbid suspicion that nothing but trouble travels in the suburbs after dark combined to enchant into existence this troublesome shade that was nothing, in fact, but the scraping of a branch of hibiscus against the windowpane. But you can understand that I wasn't anxious to open the door.

I put the book down silently, the afterimage of the interior of the Nautilus slanting across my consciousness and then submerging, and I remember wondering at the appropriateness of the scene in the novel: the crystal panels bound in copper beyond which floated transparent sheets of water illuminated by sunlight; the lazy undulations of eels and fishes, of lampreys and Japanese salamanders and blue and silver clouds of schooling mackerel. Slipping into the shadows beyond the couch, I pressed myself against the wall and crept into the darkened study where a window would afford me a view of most of the porch.

My aquaria, as I've said, were dismantled some months earlier, six, I believe—the water siphoned out a window and into a flower bed, the waterweeds collapsed in a soggy heap, the fish astonished to find themselves imprisoned in a three-gallon bucket. These last I gave to a nearby tropical fish store; the empty aquaria with its gravel and lumps of petrified stone I stored beneath a bench in the shed under my avocado tree. It was a sad undertaking, all in all, like bundling up pieces of my boyhood and packing them away in a crate. I sometimes have the notion that opening the crate would restore them wholesale, that the re-creation of years gone by could be effected by dragging in a hose and filling the tanks with clear water, by banking the gravel around rocks heaped to form dark caverns, the entrances of which are shadowed by the reaching tendrils of waterweeds through which glow watery rays of reflected light. But the visitor on the porch that night dissuaded me.

Three aquarium shops sit neatly in my memory by day and are confused and shuffled by night, giddily trading fishes and façades, all of them alive with the hum and bubble of pumps and filters and the damp, musty smell of fishtanks drip dripping tropical water onto concrete floors. One I discovered by bicycle when I was thirteen. It was a clapboard house on a frontage road along a freeway, the exhaust of countless roaring trucks and automobiles having dusted the peeling white paint with black grime. Inside sat dozens of ten-gallon tanks, poorly lit, the water within them half evaporated. There wasn't much to recommend it, even to a thirteen-year-old, aside from a door in the back—what used to be a kitchen door, I suppose—that led along a gravel path to what had been a garage. These thirty years later I can recall the very day I discovered it, the gravel path that is, easily a year after my first bicycle journey to the shop. I'd wandered around inside, shaking my head at the condition of the aquaria, despising the guppies and goldfish and tetras that swam sluggishly past their scattered dead companions. My father waited in a Studebaker at the curb outside, drumming his fingers along the top of the passenger seat. A sign in pencil scrawl attracted my eye, advertising another room of fish "outside." And so out I stepped along that gravel path, shoving into the darkened back half of the garage, which was unlit save for the incandescent bulbs in aquarium reflectors. I shut the door behind me for no other reason than to keep out sunlight. Banks of aquaria lined three walls, all of them a deep greenish-black, the water within lit against a backdrop of elodea and Amazon swordplant and the waving, lacy branches of ambulia and sagitarius. There was the faint bursting of fine bubbles that danced toward the surface from aerators trapped beneath mossy stones. On the sandy floor of one aquarium lay a half dozen mottled freshwater rays from the Amazon, their poisonous tails almost indistinguishable from the gravel they rested on. A half score of buffalo-head cichlids hovered in the shelter of an arched heap of waterfall rock, under which was coiled the long, finny, serpent's tail of a reedfish.

The aquarium seemed to me to be prodigiously deep, a trick, perhaps, of reflection and light and the clever arrangement of rocks and water plants. But it suggested, just for a moment, that the shadowed water within was somehow as vast as the sea bottom or was a sort of antechamber to the driftwood and pebble floor of a tropical river. Other aquaria flanked it. Gobies peered up at me from out of burrows in the sand. An enormous compressiceps, flat as a plate, blinked out from behind a tangle of cryptocoryne grasses. Leaf fish floated amid the lacy brown of decaying vegetation, and a hovering pair of golf ball-sized puffers, red eyes blinking, tiny pectoral fins whirring like submarine propellers, peered suspiciously from beneath a ledge of dark stone. There was something utterly alien about that room full of fishes, existing in manufactured amber light, a thousand miles removed from the dusty gravel of the yard outside, from the roaring freeway traffic not sixty feet distant. I stood staring, oblivious to the time, until the door swung open in a flood of sunlight and my father peeked in. In the sudden illumination the odd atmosphere of the room seemed to decay, to disperse, and it reminds me now of what must happen to a forest glade when the sun rises and dispels the damp enchanted pall summoned each night by moonlight from the roots and mulch and earth of the forest floor.

One dimmed tank was lit briefly by the sunlight, and in it, crouched behind a tumble of dark stone, was an almost hidden creature with an enormous head and eyes, the eyes of a squid or a spaniel, eyes that were lidded, that blinked slowly and sadly past the curious scattered decorations of its tank: a half dozen agate marbles, a platoon of painted lead soldiers, a brass sheriff's star, and a little tin shovel angling from a bucket half full of tilted sand and painted in tints of azure and yellow, a scene of children playing along a sunset beach.

I was old enough and imaginative enough to be struck by the incongruity of the contents of that aquarium. I wasn't, though, well enough schooled in ichthyology to remark on the lidded eyes of the creature in the tank—which is just as well. I was given over to nightmares as it was. A year passed before I had occasion to visit the shop beside the freeway again, and I can recall bicycling along wet streets through intermittent showers, hunched over in a yellow, hooded slicker, my pantlegs soaked from the knees down, rewarded finally with the sight of no shop at all, but of a vacant lot, already up in weeds, the concrete foundation of the clapboard house and garage brown with rainwater and mud.

Here it was nearly midnight, thirty years later, and something was stirring on my front porch. Wind out of the west shuffled the foliage, and I could hear the sighing of fronds in the queen palms along the curb. I stood in shadow, wafered against a tilted bookcase, peering past the edge of the casement at nothing. There was a rustling of bushes and swaying shadow. Something—what was it?—was skulking out there. I was certain. Hairs prickled along the back of my neck. A low, mournful boom of distant thunder followed a windy clatter of raindrops. The wet, ozone smell of rain on concrete washed through the room, and I realized with a start that a window had blown open behind me. I turned and pushed it shut, crouching below the sill so as not to be seen, thinking without meaning to of wandering in the rain across the ruins of the tropical fish shop, searching in the weeds for nothing I could name and finding only shards of broken glass and a ceramic fishbowl castle the color of an Easter egg. I slipped tight the bolt on the window and crept across to my bookcase, peering once again out into the seemingly empty night where the branches of hibiscus with their drooping pink flowers danced in the wind and rain.

In San Francisco, in Chinatown, in an alley off Washington, lies the second of the three aquarium shops. I was a student at the time. I'd eaten a remarkable dinner at a restaurant called Sam Wo and was wandering along the foggy evening street, looking for a set of those compressed origami flowers that bloom when dropped into water, when I saw a sign depicting Chinese ideographs and a lacy-looking tri-colored

koi. I slouched down a narrow alley between canted buildings, the misty air smelling of garlic and fog, barbecued
duck and spilled garbage. Through a slender doorway veiled
with the smell of musty sand sounded the familiar hum of
aquaria.

The shop itself was vast and dark beneath low ceilings.
Dim rooms, lost in shadow, stretched away beneath the street,
scattered aquarium lights glowing like misty distant stars.
Flat breeding tanks were stacked five deep on rusted steel
stands below a row of darkened transom windows that
fronted the alley. Exotic goldfish labored to stay afloat, staring through bubble eyes, their caudal fins so enormously
overgrown that they seemed to drag the creatures backward.
One of the fish, I remember, was the size and shape of a
grapefruit, a stupendous freak bred for the sake of nothing
more than curiosity. Illogically, perhaps because of my having stumbled years earlier upon that shed full of odd fish
along the freeway, it occurred to me that the more distant
rooms would contain even more curious fish, so I hesitantly
wandered deeper, under Washington, I suppose, only to discover that yet farther rooms existed, that rooms seemed to
open onto others through arched doors, the ancient plaster of
which was so discolored and mossy from the constant hu-
midity that it appeared as if the openings were chipped out of
stone. Vast aquaria full of trailing waterweeds sat bank upon
bank, and in them swam creatures that had, weeks earlier,
lurked in driftwood grottoes in the Amazon and Orinoco.

There was something about the place that brought to mind
the shovel and bucket, the promise of pending mystery, perhaps horror. Each aquarium with its shadowy corners and
heaped stone and lacy plants seemed a tiny enclosed world,
as did the shop itself, utterly adrift from the noisy Chinatown
alleyways and streets above, which crisscrossed in a foggy
tapestry of a world alien to the hilly sprawl of San Francisco,
each successive layer full of wonder and threat. There was
something in my reaction to it akin to the attraction Professor Aronnax felt to the interior of the Nautilus with its library of black-violet ebony and brass, its twelve thousand

books, its luminous ceilings and pipe organ and jars of mol-
lusks and sea stars and black pearls larger than pigeons' eggs
and its glass walls through which, as if from within an aquarium, one had a night and day view of the depths of the sea.

I was confronted on the edge of the second chamber by a
tiny Oriental man, his face lost in shadow. I hadn't heard him
approach. He held in his hand a dripping net, large enough to
snare a sea bass, and he wore rubber boots as if he were in the
habit of clambering into aquaria to pursue fish. His sudden
appearance startled me out of a peculiar frame of mind that
accounted for, I'm certain, the curious idea that in the faint,
pearl-like luminosity of aquarium light, the arm and hand
that held the net were scaled. I found my way to the street. He
hadn't said anything, but the slow shaking of his head had
seemed to indicate that I wasn't entirely welcome there, that it
was a hatchery, perhaps, a wholesale house in which casual
strollers would find nothing that would interest them.

And it was nothing, years later, that I found on the front
porch. The wind blew rain under the eaves and against the
panes of the window. Water ran along them in rivulets, distorting even further the waving foliage on the porch, making
it impossible to determine whether the dark places were
mere shadow or were more than that. I returned to my couch
and book and fireplace, piling split cedar logs atop burned
down fragments, and blowing on the embers until the wood
popped and crackled and firelight danced on the walls of the
living room. It must have been two o'clock in the morning by
then, a morbid hour, it seems to me, but somehow I was dis-
inclined toward bed, and so I sat browsing in my book, idly
sipping at my glass, and half listening to the shuffle and
scrape of things in the night and the occasional rumble of
faraway thunder.

I couldn't, somehow, keep my eyes off the door, although I
pretended to continue to read. The result was that I focused on
nothing at all, but must have fallen asleep, for I lurched awake
at the sound of a clay flower pot crashing to bits on the porch
outside, the victim, possibly, of a rainy gust of wind. I sat up,
tumbling Jules Verne to the rug, a half-formed dream of tilted

pier pilings and dark, stone pools of placid water dissolving into mist in my mind. A shadow loomed beyond the door. I snatched at the little pull-chain of the wall sconce overhead and pitched the room into darkness, thinking to hide my own movements as well as to illuminate those of the thing on the porch.

But almost as soon as the light evaporated, leaving only the orange glow of the settled fire, I switched the light back on. It was futile to think of hiding myself, and as for whatever it was that lurked on the threshold, I hadn't any monumental desire to confront it. So I sat trembling. The shadow remained, as if it watched and listened, satisfied to know that I knew it was there.

There had been another tropical fish store, in San Pedro in a dockside street of thrift stores and bars and boarded-up windows. The harbor side of the street was built largely upon pilings, and below the slumping wooden buildings were shadowy broken remnants of abandoned wharfs and the shifting, gray Pacific tide. The windows of the shop were obscured by heavy dust that had lain on the cracked panes for years, and there were only dim, scattered lights shining beyond to indicate that the building wasn't deserted. A painted sign on the door read "Tropical Rarities—Fish and Amphibia," and below it, taped to the inside of the door and barely visible through the dust, was a yellowed price list, advertising, I recall, Colombian horned frogs and tiger salamanders, at prices twenty years out of date.

The door was locked. But from within, I was certain of it, came the humming of aquaria and the swish-splash of aerated water against a background of murmuring voices. Had I been ten years younger, I would have rapped on the glass, perhaps shouted. But my interest in aquaria had waned, and I had come to the neighborhood, actually, to purchase tickets for a boat ride to Catalina Island. So I turned to leave, only vaguely curious, noting for the first time a wooden stairway angling steeply away toward the docks, its stile gate left carelessly ajar. I hesitated before it, peering down along the warped bannister, and saw hanging from the wooden siding of the building a simple, wordless sign depicting ideographs and a tri-colored koi. It was the shock of curious recognition as much as anything that impelled me down those stairs, grinning foolishly, rehearsing what it was I'd say to whomever I'd meet at the bottom.

But I met no one—only the lapping of dark water against the stones and a scattering of red crabs that scuttled away into the shadows of mossy rock. Overhanging buildings formed a sort of open-air cellar, dark and cool and smelling of mussels and barnacles and mud flats. At first the darkness within was impenetrable, but as I shaded my eyes and stepped into the shadows I made out a half dozen dim rings of mottled stone—amphibian pools I imagined, their sides draped with trailing water plants.

"Hello," I called, timorously, I suppose, and was met with silence except for a brief splashing in one of the pools. I stepped forward hesitantly. I had no business being there, but I was struck with the idea that I must see what it was that dwelt within those circular pools.

The first appeared to be empty of life aside from great tendrils of tangled elodea and a floating carpet of broad-leaf duckweed. I knelt on the wet stone and swept the duckweed aside with my hands, squinting into the depths. Some few bits of clouded daylight filtered in from above, but the feeble illumination was hardly enough to lighten the pool. Something, though, glistened for a moment below, as if beckoning, signifying, and I found myself glancing around me guiltily even as I rolled up my shirtsleeve. In for a penny ... I thought to myself, plunging my arm in up to the shoulder.

There was a movement then beneath the water, as if the pool were deeper than I'd thought and I'd disturbed the solitude of some submerged creature. I groped among plants and gravel, nearly dipping my ear into the water. There it was, lying on its side. My fingers closed over the half hoop of its handle just as a slow scuffling sounded from the far end of the twilit room.

I stood up, prepared for heaven knew what, holding in my hand, impossibly, a familiar tin pail, its side dented in now, its blue ocean bent over and half submerging the children still at play, these many years later, along its sandy beach. Before me crouched a small Oriental man, staring oddly, as if he half recognized my face and amazed to find me, it seemed, in the act of purloining that bent, toy pail. I dropped it into the pool, began to speak, then turned and hurried away. The man who had confronted me wore no rubber boots, and he carried no enormous fishnet in his hand. In the dim halflight of that strange ocean side grotto his skin, at a hasty glance, was nothing more than skin. I could insist for the sake of cheap adventure that he was scaled, gilled, perhaps, with webbed hands and an ear-to-ear mouth. And he easily might have been. I left without a backward glance, focusing on the alligatored blue paint of the ramshackle stairway, on the shingled roof that rose into view on the opposite side of the street as I climbed, step by creaking step. I drove home, I recall, punching randomly on the buttons of my car radio, turning it on and off, aware of the incongruity, the superfluousness of the music and the newscasts and the foolish and alien radio chatter.

The incident rather took the wind out of the sails of my tropical fish collecting—sails that were half furled anyway. And certain odd, otherwise innocent, pictures began to haunt my dreams—random images of pale, angular faces, of painted lead soldiers scattered in a weedy lot, of the furtive movement of fish in weed-shadowed aquaria, of a wooden signboard swinging and swinging in wind-driven rain.

Beyond the locked front door lies nothing more than the shadow of evening foliage, stirring in the rainy wind. Common sense would have it so, would say, in a smug and tiresome voice, that I've been confused by a dangerous combination of coincidence and happenstance. It would be an invitation to madness not to heed such a voice.

But it's not a night for heeding voices. The wind and rain lash at the dark shubbery, the shadows waver and dance. Through the window glass nothing at all can be seen beyond the pallid light of the porch lamp. Two hours from now the sun will rise, and with it will come a manufactured disregard for the suggestion of connections, of odd patterns behind the seemingly random. The front porch—rainwater drying in patches, the mission chairs sitting solid and substantial, the oranges and pinks of hibiscus bloom grinning at the day—will be inhabited only by a hurrying, square-jawed milkman in a white cap and by the solid clink of bottles in a galvanized metal basket.

Myron Chester and the Toads

All this happened some months ago. Not that it makes any real difference. It might have mattered hugely if the aliens hadn't left, if things had gone a bit differently and people weren't so pig-stupid. But like my neighbor Mrs. Krantz, they mostly can't see past their noses without getting their eyes crossed.

On April twenty-third a dry goods salesman from Tampa was whisked off through space aboard an alien starship. That's what he said on the news. He was on television eighteen times on Tuesday, once on Wednesday, and not at all since. I'd like to think that the aliens took him away again, that he inhabits a bubble home in some distant galaxy and has learned to manipulate the controls of a magnetic air car shaped like a fish. But that's not the case. I can see him right now, in fact, in the moonlight glowing along the shore on the pond behind my house. It's two in the morning and he's scouring the country-side for toads. His name, you might recall, is Myron Chester.

He's still a dry goods salesman in Tampa, but his business isn't worth a fig. Almost everyone saw him on television or heard him on the radio, chattering like an ape about creatures in a glowing ship, about gilled, amphibious, eye-goggling star dwellers, the enormous offspring of toads and alligators that shunted him up and down the thoroughfares of the Milky Way—for some reason, for a lark probably. He wasn't sure. He'd thought at first that they meant to harm him; they'd take his brain out and hook it up to some sort of device. He'd be a piece of machinery. But that didn't happen. They just drove him around. They shook his hand. They communicated telepathically, hardly moved their lips.

Nobody wanted any more of his dry goods after that. That's what I think. You don't buy tea towels and string from a madman. When I was in Tampa I found his warehouse out on the road to the airport. The salt air off the Gulf had corroded the tin roof over the years, and now he didn't make enough money to repair it. When storms blow in it rains all over his dry goods. I stopped in there and shook his hand. But that was a month after his incredible ride aboard the starship, and the television interview had soured him. He never should have opened his mouth, he said. Now his business wasn't worth a fig. Not a fig. And it was going from bad to worse. They wouldn't leave him alone, he said.

Who? I asked, just to make sure. I thought I knew who he meant. *What* he meant, rather. A tremendous toad croaked outside the window off and on as we talked, and twice in the twenty minutes I was there he went out searching for it, making little clicking and smacking noises as if trying to attract a cat. Funny behavior, really, in light of the supposed nature of that toad.

But I was happy about one thing—that he knew that *I* knew that he wasn't just idly chasing toads. That didn't serve to pep him up much, though. My testimonial, lord knows, wouldn't help him sell dry goods.

I'll tell you how I stumbled upon the aliens. I have some astonishing collections, books mostly—books and kaleidoscopes, about forty kaleidoscopes. Almost no one collects them, even though everyone, at one time or another, has gazed through the lens of a kaleidoscope and has understood, at least for an instant, that the jeweled symmetry glowing in the sunlight at the end of that dark corridor is possessed of the ancient and magical enchantment of an Aladdin's lamp or of a glowing, carnival spaceship in the dark of the starry heavens. There can't be any mistaking it.

I read not long ago about an Eastern European magician with the unlikely, probably assumed, name of Wegius. It sounded like the name of a cartoon duck. This Wegius, one way or another, managed through astounding coincidence, while turning a pair of matched kaleidoscopes—one before either eye and with a single, geared crank—to cause the jewels within each to fall into like patterns simultaneously. His acolyte, working amid bubbling chemical apparatus in an adjoining room, heard a wild shriek and, rushing in, found his master catatonic in a chair. The two kaleidoscopes on the table before him sat frozen in twin symmetry. The acolyte gazed first into one and then into the other, and understood the curious coincidence that had befallen the magician. His master, he conjectured, had been drawn in through the meshing of those faceted reflections, had fallen into a land from which he hadn't any hope—or any desire, likely—of returning.

The magician lived on in his suspended state, taking neither food nor drink, for nearly twenty-five years. The acolyte found himself growing daily more tempted to peer into both mysteriously frozen kaleidoscopes at once, but he was too cautious; he feared for his soul. He cast the kaleidoscopes, crank and all, into a fire and left them there to melt in an alchemical stew along with other reputedly magical debris.

That story might have been fabricated, but it's given me a certain amount of hope. I've built any number of the things since, filling them with combinations of gems and mounting them like binoculars so as to be able to involve both eyes at once. The task is almost hopeless. The possible combinations of identical jewels as they sweep about and fall away and hide behind each other and creep up the sides of their chambers seems infinite. It probably *is* infinite; I don't know. If it is, don't tell me.

Late on the night of the twenty-third I sat in my study overlooking the pond and the little section of glades that runs along toward the back of my house. It was humid, I remember. The window was open. Frogs croaked in the weeds around the pond. It must have been past midnight. It was my idea to gaze through the twin kaleidoscopes toward the light of the full moon. Romantic notion, you'll say; it's not as romantic as it sounds. The moon's light is ample on a bright night, and if the corridor of the kaleidoscope is long enough and the circumference small enough, the circle of the moon entirely covers the glass, and the patterns appear to be reflected against the moon's very surface. I'm sure that the process gives me an edge against that infinitude of changing patterns.

So I was squinting into the twin lenses of the kaleidoscopes, moonlight bouncing off the triple mirrors in the corridors. The jewels, their color faded, were falling and shifting into angular glass flowers. My thumb and forefinger moved desperately slowly the knob that turns the cylinders, pausing each time the little heaps of gems overbalanced and a jewel or two tumbled free and changed the pattern as irreversibly as a creeping glacier crumbles and alters the face of a mountainside. My eyes, almost involuntarily, flitted the 240,000-odd miles across space—first focusing on the revolving jewels, then on nothing, then on the moon.

I saw by chance the descent of the starship, glowing, falling through the night sky, silhouetted for one crystal moment against the pale yellow lamp of the full moon.

At first I thought it was just a random combination of tumbling jewels in the kaleidoscope, but that could hardly have been the case: I'd seen the strange, falling ship with both eyes, through both kaleidoscopes at once.

I leaped up and extinguished the two candles that burned in the room. All was silent. The night air was tense, waiting, watching. The toads and crickets didn't make a peep. I went outside and climbed onto the roof of the house. My shadow in the moonlight stretched away over the rooftop and lost itself in the shifting darkness of the great pepper tree that shades half the roof. One by one the toads and frogs began to croak and the air roundabout slackened. Off in the swamps there was a glowing—far too bright to have been a swarm of fireflies, although it was the same sort of greenish phosphorescent shimmer. The glow faded and was gone. I slid down and went back to my kaleidoscope, and it was then that I was stricken with a wild thought.

It was possible, in the light of what I'd seen, that an alien starship had tumbled out of the heavens and across the lenses of my scope. It was also possible—and I began to think that it might, indeed, have happened—that an identical combination of gems had, miraculously, fallen within each of the twin corridors. If the latter were the case, I thought wildly, then I'd accomplished my goal and had entered that land into which the magician Wegius had wandered five hundred years ago. My excitement dwindled, though, when I realized that the magical land was in no way different from the mundane universe I'd just vacated.

In fact, my neighbor, Mrs. Krantz, came out about then and shouted at her dog. What if Wegius, I thought, what if *I*, for that matter, had willfully become a catatonic in one world in order to occupy a magical land in which Mrs. Krantz shouted perpetually at her dog? And no sooner had the thought struck me than Mrs. Krantz burst out again: "Shut up! *Shut* up! *Will* you shut up!" Her dog barked, an hysterical, high-pitched yelp. It dashed around with its tail between its legs. It howled. It slammed into a tree. Mrs. Krantz howled after it. "Shurrup! Shurr*up!*" I'd been condemned to a lunatic's hell. Wegius had made a grim, unfathomable mistake. But how had Mrs. Krantz gotten there? She had no kaleidoscopes. Impossibly, it had to have been a starship that I'd seen, and not a peculiar and coincidental assortment of jewels.

Early next morning, who was on the television but the dry goods salesman from Tampa. I watched all that day. Eighteen times he was on, like I said. Newscasters made light of his story. One, around midday, couldn't contain himself and kept leering and winking into the camera. Aliens were thick as sand fleas, he said, snorting a little as he laughed. It was very funny. He pretended to misunderstand, to apprehend that Myron Chester was referring to Colombians. Was he sure it wasn't a downed plane, flying in illicit narcotics? Were they using telepathy or just talking Spanish? They go so fast, you know. It's almost hypnotizing. Sounds like gibberish, really.

He winked away at the camera, and each wink, I suppose, drove another nail into the coffin that held the dry goods company. Tea towel orders fell off. Balls of string stacked up in the warehouse. Baling wire rusted. The corrugated roof was eaten by salt air off the gulf. Rain blew in and mold sprouted and night winds scattered dry goods across the lonely countryside. Things fell to bits. Mrs. Krantz's dog went spectacularly mad. I waited for some further sign.

On the day following, Myron Chester was on the television only once. Madmen aren't much fun in the long run. They wear out. That same morning, a monstrous turtle, an alligator snapper, appeared on Mrs. Krantz's driveway. It was impossibly large—as big as the hood of a car. That's not hyperbole; it's the truth, and it was a startling sight. Mrs. Krantz was at it with a broom. She danced around it, pounded on its shell, poked at it, shouted insanely. The turtle sat there perplexed, its head darting in and out. It bit off the tip of the broom handle. Mrs. Krantz was wild with broom madness. She dashed into the house and returned with a great long butcher knife in one hand and—I swear it—a cast iron skillet in the other. Did she want to eat the creature? I can't say. I watched all this from the window.

The turtle had scuttled away toward the pond. She saw it splash into the shallows and disappear. Her dog went berserk, capering around and around the yard, smashing into fences, caroming off trees, twirling, somersaulting, yowling. "*Will* you shut up!" shouted Mrs. Krantz, chasing after it, waving the skillet.

Two alligators appeared on the pond later that afternoon. There was nothing remarkable about them. One of my neighbors said that they'd tramped in from the glades, another that there was an underground outlet to the pond, a subterranean river, an amphibious highroad traveled by turtles and alligators and unbelievable toads. "You watch," he said, and I told him I would. I did, too. But what I learned, I learned by purest chance, wildest coincidence.

It was late afternoon, evening actually. The television had given up on the alien threat, and the moon was up over the trees; I could sit in my study window and watch it rise. But it was a pale moon yet, with watery rays that wouldn't have any substance until nightfall, an hour or so away. So I gazed through the twin kaleidoscopes, carefully manipulating the controls out of habit. There was no use watching the moon, so I pointed the scopes at the late sun's reflection on the pond. The jewels fell and fell. Colored snowflakes metamorphosed, collapsed, expanded. Sapphires and rubies crossed paths and resulted in dozens of momentary amethysts. My mind was on the mysterious turtle that had come up out of the pond—the impossible turtle. Such creatures didn't exist outside of dreams. I idly turned the iron crank, thinking of unlikely beasts. My eyes ceased to focus on the crystals, drifting out, in a manner of speaking, through the corridors of the kaleidoscope toward the pond, with its subterranean rivers—rivers that ran into the swamps, into the sea, into the center of the Earth.

For twenty minutes I sat thus. It's possible that I repeated Wegius's fluke any number of times and didn't see it. My mind wrestled with aliens. Peculiarities in the movement of the jewels, finally, made me attend to my business. I blinked and squinted. I thought that the shimmer of my eyelashes was muddling the clarity of the lenses. There were lines that had nothing to do with the gems—refractions of light, I thought at first, rays of the sun angling up off the surface of the pool and reflected from one to the other of the mirrors. They had the appearance of the crinkles in very old glass or of the vertices of clear crystal. But as I watched them, wondering at the phenomenon, puzzling over it, I began to see certain patterns, to suspect certain truths. The glassy threads and the swirls of faint color had little to do with the rainbow gems of the kaleidoscope. And this, as I say, I discovered through mere, uncanny coincidence.

I watched the faint, slow movement of the shimmering lines. I peered at them, tried to focus through the lenses. The lines receded and disappeared. My eyes chased them along the dark corridors, in among the tumbling stones. The apparitions hovered there, like a distant star that flickers in the corner of your eye but disappears entirely when you try to catch it. I thought of the falling ship that drifted across the ivory face of the moon, and I let my eyes once again wander out past the jewels and into the dimming evening toward the shadow-encircled pond. Finally, focusing on nothing, I saw them.

It was as if they were made of very clear ice or of striated glass, and they seemed to capture the late, cold rays of the sun and the first feeble rays of the rising moon and reflect a universe of colors. They appeared to me then not so much as creatures from the stars, but as the stars themselves.

The sun set, the moon rose, and the rainbow colors dancing on the pond faded in the moonlight, into blues and deep purples—the colors of a sky at dawn. They waited there, outside my window. In time I became aware that my legs were cramped. I was on my way to becoming a frozen Wegius. It was impossible to look away, but in the end I did. I stood and stretched and half expected Mrs. Krantz to smash out raging and waving broomsticks and kitchen devices as a sort of counterpoint to my aliens. But that wasn't the case.

What I saw out on the pond, through the common, undistorting window glass in the casement, were the two alligators sitting together, soaking in the rays of the moon. A black circle floated nearby. When it raised its head, I recognized it: the giant snapper that had had the misfortune to stray up onto Mrs. Krantz's driveway. And atop it, I swear, perched like Solomon on his throne, was a stupendous toad—the toad of creation, the toad to end all toads. I thought of my conversation with the neighbor, of the subterranean river, of the "unbelievable toads." "You watch," he had said, and I'd thought him a lunatic. I admit it.

It was a clever idea, I suppose, disguising themselves as amphibians. Or it would have been had they given it more study—shrunk the turtles, kept the toads out of the water. That subterranean river, I know now, is a river into the stars, figuratively speaking. My neighbor was closer to the truth than he knew.

About a week ago I saw Myron Chester clambering along the shore of the pond at midnight. He stumbled not so much because of the darkness as because of frantic haste. There was a good moon, and the pond was marbled with shadow and silver light. He was searching for them; that much was clear. He stooped; he peered into the dark water; he swatted at an insect. He hunched along, watching the ground. I saw him wave frantically, but I couldn't see the object of his attention—something that floated, on the pond. Nothing came of it. He stooped again, scrabbling in a heap of stones up on the bank. When he straightened he held a toad in his hands. He seemed to be speaking to it. He gesticulated wildly with his free hand, debating, insisting, pleading. The toad sat mute. It might have croaked once or twice—I was too far away to hear—but that's about all. It was quite simply the wrong toad, with no access to spaceships of any sort. And, to its great good luck, it quite apparently didn't care about such things; it felt no kinship to the aliens and was indifferent to Myron Chester and to starships and to the promise of pending enchantment. Just to make absolutely sure, I watched his search through the kaleidoscopes. There was no doubt; the dancing colors had vanished long since. The aliens were gone. I'd seen them go.

Two months ago, again on a moonlit night, Mrs. Krantz's dog ran amok. Its howling was astonishing. I had been asleep, but it carried on in such a dismal way that I hurried upstairs and lit my candle. The beast, when I saw him through the window, lay on his back like a bug. The pond was still and empty. The alligators had disappeared. Off in the west a fading green radiance lit the glades as if a convention of glowworms and fireflies was just then breaking up and the creatures were blinking out and wandering off.

The alien ship, beaded with lights, sailed up into the heavens, arcing again across the grinning face of the moon—a finned, silver vessel bound for a distant shore. In a moment it was just another star.

The dog ceased to howl and hasn't suffered any fits in the months since. Myron Chester, as I said, frequents the pond now at night, searching out toads, pursuing axolotls, questioning turtles, hoping to stumble across that curious pair of alligators. Sometimes I regret not having given the man a glimpse of the aliens through the kaleidoscopes. It's quite possible that the sight would have satisfied him.

But I don't think so. It may have driven him wild like Mrs. Krantz's dog, which, I suspect, also knew of the existence of the aliens. Who can say? Now I'm not so sure what he meant when he revealed, there at the crumbling warehouse, that *they* wouldn't leave him alone. Was he plagued by amphibia that he suspected to be star beasts, or by the promise he'd seen within that glowing ship? It seems likely to me now that he searches for El Dorado along the shores of that little pond at night, for an avenue to the stars.

As for me, I'm still at my vigil. I have renewed faith in the enchantment of moonlight washing across the tumbling, re-flected jewels in the kaleidoscopes, but I don't depend on aliens or search along the banks of an empty pond at mid-night. It's unlikely that they'll return. They didn't find much here to attract them. It's a pity, as I said, that they didn't study us a bit more before choosing to appear as amphibia. They were bound to be whacked with broomsticks and threatened with knives and skillets. I wish Myron Chester could have set them straight. But he, of course, didn't know they wore dis-guises.

I suppose I suffer the same fate as the dry goods man, even though I've seen things a bit more clearly. As far as I know, I haven't yet replicated Wegius's coincidence. I'm watching the jewels fall, off and on, as I write this, and as I do I can hear Myron Chester splashing along out in the night, talking with toads. It would be very funny if, about now, the jewels would fall in Wegius's twin showers, and I'd let out a shriek and tumble in among them, never to return.

You'd find me, perhaps months from now, after the news-papers piled up on the porch and the trumpet flower vines covered and obscured the house. I'd be in a cold stupor, and this would be one of those unfinished narratives that were popular in the pulps. It would end with a cry of startled sur-prise and a last wavy, trailing stain of ink; then silence.

Unidentified Objects

In 1956 the downtown square mile of the city of Orange was a collection of old houses: craftsman bungalows and tile-roofed Spanish, and here and there an old Queen Anne or a gingerbread Victorian with geminate windows and steep gables, and sometimes a carriage house alongside, too small by half to house the lumbering automobiles that the second fifty years of the century had produced. There were Studebakers at the curbs and Hudsons and Buicks with balloon tires like the illustrations of moon-aimed rockets on the covers of the pulp magazines.

Times were changing. Science was still a professor with wild hair and a lab coat and with bubbling apparatus in a cellar; but in a few short years he would walk on the moon— one last ivory and silver hurrah—and then, as if in an instant, he would grow faceless and featureless and unpronounceable. There would come the sudden knowledge that Moon Valley wasn't so very far away after all, and neither was extinction; that the nation that controlled magnetism, as Diet Smith would have it, controlled almost nothing at all; and that a score of throbbing bulldozers could reduce the jungled wilds around Opar and El Dorado to desert sand in a few short, sad years. The modern automobile suddenly was slick and strange, stretched out and low and with enormous fins that swept back at the rear above banks of superfluous taillights. They seemed otherworldly at the time and were alien reminders, it seems to me now, of how provincial we had been, balanced on the back edge of an age.

The pace of things seemed to be accelerating, and already I could too easily anticipate stepping out onto my tilted front porch some signifying morning, the wind out of the east, and seeing stretched out before me not a shaded avenue of overarching trees and root-cracked sidewalks but the sleek, desert-like technology of a new age, a new suburbia, with robots in vinyl trousers sweeping fallen leaves into their own open mouths.

There is a plaza in the center of town, with a fountain, and in the autumn—the season when all of this came to my attention—red-brown leaves from flowering pear trees drift down onto the sluggish, gurgling water and float there like a centerpiece for a Thanksgiving table. On a starry evening, one November late in the seventies, I was out walking in the plaza, thinking, I remember, that it had already become an artifact, with its quaint benches and granite curbs and rose garden. Then, shattering the mood of late-night nostalgia, there shone in the sky an immense shooting star, followed by the appearance of a glowing object, which hovered and darted, sailing earthward until I could make out its shadow against the edge of the moon and then disappearing in a blink. I shouted and pointed, mostly out of surprise. Strange lights in the sky were nothing particularly novel; I had been seeing them for almost twenty years. But nothing that happens at night among the stars can ever become commonplace. At that late hour, though, there was almost certainly no one around to hear me; or so I thought.

So when she stood up, dropping papers and pencils and a wooden drawing board onto the concrete walk, I nearly shouted again. She had been sitting in the dim lamplight, hidden

to me beyond the fountain. Dark hair fell across her shoulders in
a rush of curl and hid her right eye, and with a practiced sweep
of her hand she pulled it back in a shock and tucked it behind
her ear, where it stayed obediently for about three quarters of a
second and then fell seductively into her face again. Now, years
later, for reasons I can't at all define, the sight of a dark-haired
woman brushing wayward hair out of her eyes recalls without
fail that warm autumn night by the fountain.

She had that natural, arty, blue-jeans-and-floppy-sweater
look of a college girl majoring in fine arts: embroidered
handbag, rhinestone-emerald costume brooch, and translucent
plastic shoes the color of root beer. I remember thinking right
off that she had languorous eyes, and the sight of them re-
flecting the soft lamplight of the fountain jolted me. But the
startled look on her face implied that she hadn't admired my
shouting like that, not at eleven o'clock at night in the otherwise deserted plaza.

There was the dark, pouting beauty in her eyes and lips of
a woman in a Pre-Raphaelite painting, a painting that I had
stumbled into in my clodlike way, grinning, I thought, like a
half-wit. I too hastily explained the shooting star to her, gesturing too widely at the sky and mumbling that it hadn't been
an ordinary shooting star. But there was nothing in the sky
now besides the low-hanging moon and a ragtag cloud, and
she said offhandedly, not taking any notice of my discom-
fort, just what I had been thinking, that there was never anything ordinary about a shooting star.

I learned that her name was Jane and that she had
sketched that fountain a dozen times during the day, with the
blooming flowers behind it and the changing backdrop of
people and cars and weather. I almost asked her whether she
hadn't ever been able to get it quite right, but then, I could
see that that wasn't the point.

Now she had been sketching it at night, its blue and green
and pink lights illuminating the umbrella of falling water
against night-shaded rosebushes and camphor trees and box-
wood hedges.

It was perfect—straight out of a romantic old film. The

hero stumbles out of the rain into an almost deserted library, and at the desk, with her hair up and spectacles on her nose, is the librarian who doesn't know that if she'd just take the glasses off for a moment . . .

I scrabbled around to pick up fallen pencils while she protested that she could just as easily do it herself. It was surely only the magic of that shooting star that prevented her from gathering up her papers and going home. As it was, she stayed for a moment to talk, assuming, although she never said so, that there was something safe and maybe interesting in a fancier of shooting stars. I felt the same about her and her drawings and her root beer shoes.

She was distracted, never really looking at me. Maybe the image of the fountain was still sketched across the back of her eyes and she couldn't see me clearly. It was just a little irritating, and I would discover later that it was a habit of hers, being distracted was, but on that night there was something in the air and it didn't matter. Any number of things don't matter at first. We talked, conversation dying and starting and with my mind mostly on going somewhere—my place, her place—for a drink, for what? There was something, an atmosphere that surrounded her, a musky sort of sweater and lilacs scent. But she was distant; her work had been interrupted and she was still half lost in the dream of it. She dragged her hand in the water of the fountain, her face half in shadow. She was tired out, she said. She didn't need to be walked home. She could find her way alone.

But I've got ahead of myself. It's important that I keep it all straight—all the details; without the details it amounts to nothing. I grew up on Olive Street, southwest of the plaza, and when I was six and wearing my Davy Crockett hat and Red Ryder shirt, and it was nearly dusk in late October, I heard the ding-a-linging of an ice cream truck from some distant reach of the neighborhood. The grass was covered with leaves, I remember, that had been rained on and were limp and heavy. I was digging for earthworms and dropping

them one by one into a corral built of upright sticks and
twigs that was the wall of the native village on Kong Island.
The sky was cloudy, the street empty. There was smoke from
a chimney across the way and the cloud-muted hum of a distant airplane lost to view. Light through the living room window shone out across the dusky lawn.

The jangling of the ice cream bell drew near, and the
truck rounded the distant corner, the bell cutting off and the
truck accelerating as if the driver, anticipating dinner, had
given up for the day and was steering a course for home. It
slowed, though, when he saw me, and angled in toward the
curb where I stood holding a handful of gutter-washed earthworms. Clearly he thought I'd signaled him. There were pictures of frozen concoctions painted on the gloss-white sides of
the panel truck: coconut-covered Neapolitan bars and grape
Popsicles, nut and chocolate drumsticks, and strawberry-
swirled vanilla in paper cups with flat paper lids. He labori-
ously climbed out of the cab, came around the street side to
the back, and confronted me there on the curb. He smiled and
winked and wore a silver foil hat with an astonishing bill,
and when he yanked open the hinged, chrome door there was
such a whirling of steam off the dry ice inside that he utterly
vanished behind it, and I caught a quick glimpse of cardboard bins farther back in the cold fog, stacked one on top of
another and dusted with ice crystals.

I didn't have a dime and wouldn't be allowed to eat ice
cream so close to dinnertime anyway, and I said so, apologizing for having made him stop for nothing. He studied my
earthworms and said that out in space there were planets
where earthworms spoke and wore silk shirts, and that I
could fly to those planets in the right sort of ship.

Then he bent into the freezer and after a lot of scraping
and peering into boxes found a paper-wrapped ice cream
bar—a flying saucer bar, the wrapper said. It was as big
around as a coffee cup saucer and was domed on top and fat
with vanilla ice cream coated in chocolate. He tipped his hat,
slammed his door, and drove off. I ate the thing guiltily while
sitting beneath camellia bushes at the side of the house and

lobbing sodden pink blooms out onto the front yard, laying siege to the earthworm fortress and watching the lamps blink on one by one along the street.

There are those incidents from our past that years later seem to us to be the stuff of dreams: the wash of shooting stars seen through the rear window of the family car at night in the Utah desert; the mottled, multilegged sun star, as big as a cartwheel, inching across the sand in the shallows of a northern California bay; the whale's eyeball floating in alcohol and encased in a glass fishing float in a junk store near the waterfront; the remembered but unrecoverable hollow sensation of new love. The stars vanish in an instant; the starfish slips away into deep water and is gone; the shop with its fishing float is a misty dream, torn down in some unnumbered year to make room for a hotel built of steel and smoked glass. Love evaporates into the passing years like dry ice; you don't know where it's gone. The mistake is to think that the details don't signify—the flying saucer bars and camellia blooms, rainy autumn streets and lamplight through evening windows and colored lights playing across the waters of a fountain on a warm November evening.

All the collected pieces of our imagistic memory seem sometimes to be trivial knickknacks when seen against the roaring of passing time. But without those little water-paint sketches, awash in remembered color and detail, none of us, despite our airy dreams, amount to more than an impatient ghost wandering through the revolving years and into an increasingly strange and alien future.

I came to know the driver of the ice cream truck. We became acquaintances. He no longer sold ice cream; there was no living to be made at it. He had got a penny a Popsicle, he said, and he produced a slip of paper covered with numbers—elaborate calculations of the millions of Popsicles he'd have to sell over the years just to stay solvent. Taken altogether

like that it was impossible. He had been new to the area then
and hadn't got established yet. All talk of money aside, he
had grown tired of it, of the very idea of driving an ice
cream truck—something that wouldn't have seemed possible
to me on the rainy evening of the flying saucer bar, but which
I understand well enough now.

He had appeared on our front porch, I remember, when
I was ten or eleven, selling wonderful tin toys door-to-door.
My mother bought a rocket propelled by compressed air. It
was painted with bright circus colors, complete with flames
swirling around the cylindrical base of the thing. Looking
competent and serious and very much like my ice cream man
was a helmeted pilot painted into a bubblelike vehicle on the
top of the rocket, which would pop off, like a second stage,
when the rocket attained the stupendous height of thirty or
forty feet. I immediately lost the bubble craft with its painted
astronaut. It shot off, just like it was supposed to, and never
came down. I have to suppose that it's rusting in the branches
of a tree somewhere, but I have a hazy memory of it simply
shooting into the air and disappearing in a blink, hurtling up
through the thin atmosphere toward deep space. Wasted
money, my mother said.

Our third meeting was at the Palm Street Market, where I
went to buy penny candy that was a nickel by then. I was thirteen, I suppose, or something near it, which would have made
it early in the sixties. The clerk being busy, I had strayed over
to the magazine shelves and found a copy of *Fate*, which I
read for the saucer stories, and which, on that afternoon, was
the excuse for my being close enough to the "men's" magazines to thumb through a couple while the clerk had his back
turned. I had the *Fate* open to the account of Captain Hooton's
discovery of an airship near Texarkana, and a copy of something called *Slick* or *Trick* or *Flick* propped open on the rack
behind. I read the saucer article out of apologetic shame in between thumbing through the pages of photographs, as if my
reading it would balance out the rest, but remembering nothing of what I read until, with a shock of horror that I can still
recall as clearly as anything else in my life, I became aware

that the ice cream man, the tin toy salesman, was standing behind me, reading over my shoulder.

What I read, very slowly and carefully as three fourths of
my blood rose into my head, was Captain Hooton's contempt
for airship design: "There was no bell or bell rope about the
ship that I could discover, like I should think every well-
regulated air locomotive should have." At the precise moment of my reading that sentence, the clerk's voice whacked
out of the silence: "Hey, kid!" was what he said. I'd heard it
before. It was a weirdly effective phrase and had such a freezing effect on me that Captain Hooton's bit of mechanical
outrage has come along through the years with me uninvited,
pegged into my memory by the manufactured shame of that
single moment.

Both of us bought a copy of *Fate*. I *had* to, of course, although it cost me forty cents that I couldn't afford. I remember
the ice cream man winking broadly at me there on the sidewalk, and me being deadly certain that I had become as transparent as a ghost fish. Everyone on Earth had been on to my
little game with the magazine. I couldn't set foot in that market
without a disguise for a solid five years. And then, blessedly, he
was gone, off down the street, and me in the opposite direction.
I stayed clear of the market for a couple of months and then
discovered, passing on the sidewalk, that the witnessing clerk
was gone, and that went a long way toward putting things right,
although Captain Hooton, as I said, has stayed with me. In fact,
I began from that day to think of the ice cream man as Captain
Hooton, since I had no idea what his name was, and years later
the name would prove strangely appropriate.

It was in the autumn, then, that I first met Jane on that November night in the plaza, and weeks later when I introduced
her to him, to Captain Hooton. She said in her artistic way
that he had a "good face," although she didn't mean to make
any sort of moral judgment, and truthfully his face was almost inhumanly long and angular. She said this after the
three of us had chatted for a moment and he had gone on his

way. It was as if there were nothing much more she could say about him that made any difference at all, as if she were distracted.

I remember that it irritated me, although why it should have I don't know, except that he had already begun to mean something, to signify, as if our chance meetings over the years, if I could pluck them out of time and arrange them just so, would make a pattern.

"He dresses pretty awful, doesn't he?" That's what she said after he'd gone along and she could think of nothing more to say about his face.

I hadn't noticed, and I said so, being friendly about it.

"He's smelly. What was that, do you think?"

"Tobacco, I guess. I don't know. Pipe tobacco." She wasn't keen on tobacco, or liquor either. So I didn't put too fine a point on it because I didn't want to set her off, to have to defend his smoking a pipe. It was true that his coat could have used a cleaning, but that hadn't occurred to me, actually, until she mentioned it, wrinkling up her nose in that rabbit way of hers.

"I keep thinking that he's got a fish in his pocket."

I smiled at her, suddenly feeling as if I were betraying a friend.

"Well . . ." I said, trying to affect a dropping-the-subject tone.

She shuddered. "People get like that, especially old people. They forget to take baths and wash their hair."

I shrugged, pretending to think that she was merely trying to be amusing.

"He's not that old," I said. But she immediately agreed. That was the problem, wasn't it? You wouldn't think . . . She looked at my own hair very briefly and then set out down the sidewalk with me following and studying my shadow in the afternoon sun and keeping my hands away from my hair. It looked neat enough there in the shadow on the sidewalk, but I knew that shadows couldn't be trusted, and I was another five minutes worrying about it before something else happened, it doesn't matter what, and I forgot about my hair and my vanity.

Her own hair had a sort of flyaway look to it, but perfect, if you understand me, and it shone as if she'd given it the standard hundred strokes that morning. A dark-red ribbon held a random clutch of it behind her ear, and there was something in the ribbon and in the way she put her hand on my arm to call my attention to some house or other that made me think of anything but houses. She had a way of touching you, almost as if accidentally, like a cat sliding past your leg, rubbing against you, and arching just a little and then continuing on, having abandoned any interest in you. She stood too close, maybe, for comfort—although *comfort* is the wrong word because the sensation was almost ultimately comfortable—and all the while that we were standing there talking about the lines of the roof, I was conscious only of the static charge of her presence, her shoulder just grazing my arm, her hip brushing against my thigh, the heavy presence of her sex suddenly washing away whatever was on the surface of my mind and settling there musky and soft. There hasn't been another man in history more indifferent to the lines of a roof.

In the downtown circular plaza each Christmas, there was an enormous Santa Claus built from wire and twisted paper, lit from within by a spiral of pin lights, and at Halloween, beneath overcast skies and pending rain, there were parades of schoolchildren dressed as witches and clowns and bed-sheet ghosts. Then in spring there was a May festival, with city dignitaries riding in convertible Edsels and waving to people sitting in lawn chairs along the boulevard. One year the parade was led by a tame ape followed by fezzed Shriners in Mr. Toad cars.

Twice during the two years that Jane studied art, while the town shrank for her and grew cramped, we watched the parade from a sidewalk table in front of Felix's Café, laughing at the ape and smiling at the solemn drumming of the marching bands. The second year one of the little cars caught fire and the parade fizzled out and waited while a half-dozen capering Shriners beat the fire out with their jackets. It was easy to laugh then, at the ape and the Edsels and the tiny cars, except that even then I suspected that her laughter was half cynical. Mine wasn't, and this difference between us troubled me.

In the summer there was a street fair, and the smoky aroma of sausages and beer and the sticky-sweet smell of cotton candy. We pushed through the milling crowds and sat for hours under an ancient tree in the plaza, watching the world revolve around us.

It seems now that I was always wary then that the world in its spinning might tumble me off, and there was something about the exposed roots of that tree that made you want to touch them, to sit among them just to see how immovable they were. But the world couldn't spin half fast enough for her. You'd have thought that if she could get a dozen paintings out of that fountain, then there would be enough, even in a provincial little town like this one, to amuse her forever.

Captain Hooton always seemed to be turning up. One year he put on a Santa costume and wandered through the shops startling children. The following year at Halloween he appeared out of the doorway of a disused shop, wearing a fright wig and carrying an enormous flashlight like a lighthouse beacon, on the lens of which was glued a witch cut out of black construction paper. He climbed into a sycamore tree in front of Watson's Drugs and shined the witch for a half hour onto the white stone façade of the bank, and then, refusing to come down unless he was made to, was finally led away by the police. Jane ought to have admired the trick with the flashlight, but she had by then developed a permanent dislike for him because, I think, he didn't seem to take her seriously, her or her paintings, and she took both of those things very seriously indeed, while pretending to care for almost nothing at all.

He ate pretty regularly for a time at Rudy's counter, at the drugstore. It was a place where milk shakes were still served in enormous metal cylinders and where shopkeepers sat on red Naugahyde and ate hot turkey sandwiches and mashed potatoes and talked platitudes and weather and sports, squinting and nodding. Captain Hooton wasn't much on conversation. He sat alone usually, smoking and wearing one of those caps that sports car enthusiasts wear, looking as if he were pondering something, breaking into silent laughter now and then as he watched the autumn rain fall and the red-brown sycamore leaves scattering along the street in the gusting breeze.

There was something awful about his skin—an odd color, perhaps, too pink and blue and never any hint of a beard, even in the afternoon.

A balding man from Fergy's television repair referred to him jokingly as Doctor Loomis, apparently the name of an alien visitor in a cheap, old science-fiction thriller. I chatted with him three or four times when Jane wasn't along, coming to think of him finally as a product of "the old school," which, as Dickens said, is no school that ever existed on Earth.

There were more sightings of things in the sky—almost always at night, and almost always they were described in slightly ludicrous terms by astonished citizens, as if each of them had mugged up those old issues of *Fate*. The things were egg-shaped, wingless, smooth silver; they beamed people up through spiraling doors and motored them around the galaxy and then dropped them off again, in a vacant lot or behind an apartment complex or bowling alley and with an inexplicable lapse of memory. The *City News* was full of it.

Once, at the height of the sightings, men in uniforms came from the East and the sightings mysteriously stopped. Something landed in the upper reaches of my avocado tree one night and glowed there. Next morning I found a cardboard milk carton smelling of chemicals, the inside stained the green of a sunlit ocean, lying in the leaves and humus below. It had little wings fastened with silver duct tape. The bottom of it had been cut out and replaced with a carved square of pumice, a bored-out carburetor jet glued into the center of it.

It happened that Captain Hooton lived on Pine Street by that time, and so did I. I rented half of a little bungalow and took walks in the evening when I wasn't with Jane. His house was deceptively large. From the street it seemed to be a narrow, gabled Victorian with a three-story turret in the right front corner, and with maybe a living room, parlor, and kitchen downstairs. Upstairs there might have been room for a pair of large bedrooms and a library midway up in the turret. There was a lot of split clinker brick mortared onto the front in an attempt to make the house look indefinably European, and shutters with shooting stars cut into them that had been added along the way. Old newspapers piled up regularly on the front porch and walk as if he were letting them ripen, and the brush-choked flower beds were so overgrown that none of the downstairs windows could have admitted any sunlight.

Jane seemed to see it as being a shame—the mess of weeds and brush, the cobbled-together house, the yellowing papers. Somehow I held out hope that it would strike her as—what?—original. Eccentric, maybe. At first I thought that they were too much alike in their eccentricities. I considered her root beer shoes and her costume jewelry and her very fashionable and practiced disregard for fashion and her perfectly disarranged hair, and it occurred to me that she was art, so to speak—artifice, theater. And although she talked about spontaneity, she was a marvel of regimentation and control, and never more so than when she was being spontaneous. The two of them couldn't have been more unalike.

He was vaguely alarming, though. You couldn't tell what he was thinking; his past and his future were misty and dim, giving you the sort of feeling you get on cheap haunted-house thrill rides at carnivals, where you're never quite sure what colorful, grimacing thing will leap out at you from behind a plywood partition.

I could see the rear of his house from my backyard, and from there it appeared far larger. It ran back across the deep lot and was a wonder of dormers, gables, and lean-to closets, all of it overshadowed by walnut trees and trumpet flower vines on sagging trellises and arbors. Underneath was a sprawling basement, which at night glowed with lamplight through above-ground transom windows. The muted ring of small hammers and the hum of lathes sounded from the cellar at unwholesomely late hours.

The double doors of his garage were fastened with a rusted iron lock as big as a man's hand, and he must have had a means by which to enter and leave the garage—and perhaps the house itself—without using any of the visible doors. I rarely saw him out and about. When I did, he sometimes seemed hardly to know me, as if distracted, his mind on mysteries.

Once, while I was out walking, I came across him spading up a strip of earth beneath his kitchen window, breaking the clods apart and pulling iron filings out of them with an enormous magnet. I recalled our distant meeting behind the ice cream truck, but by now he seemed to remember it only vaguely. I took him to be the sort of eccentric genius too caught up in his own meanderings to pay any attention to the mundane world.

He'd started a winter garden there along the side of his house, and a dozen loose heads of red-leaf lettuce grew in the half-shade of the eaves. We chatted amiably enough, about the weather, about gardens. He gave me a sidewise squint and asked if I'd seen any of the alleged "saucers" reported in the newspaper, and I said that I had, or at least that I had seen some saucer or another months ago. He nodded and frowned as if he'd rather hoped I hadn't, as if the two of us might have sneered at the notion of it together.

A spotted butterfly hovered over the lettuce, alighting now and then and finally settling in "to eat the lettuce alive," as he put it. He wouldn't stand for it, he said, and very quietly he plucked up a wire-mesh flyswatter that hung from a nail on the side porch, and he flailed away at the butterfly until the head of lettuce it had rested on was shredded. He seemed to think it was funny, particularly so because the butterfly itself had got entirely away, had fluttered off at the first sign of trouble. It was a joke, an irony, a metaphor of something that I didn't quite catch.

He gave me a paper sack full of black-eyed peas and disappeared into the house, asking after the "young lady" but not waiting for an answer, and then shoving back out through the door to tell me to return the sack when I was through with it, and then laughing and winking and closing the door, and winking again through the kitchen window so that it was impossible to say what, entirely, he meant by the display.

There wasn't much I could have told him about the "young lady." Much of what I might have said would already be a reminiscence. The thing that mattered, I suppose, was that she made me weak in the knees, but I couldn't say so. And she was entirely without that clinging, dependent nature that feeds a man's vanity at first but soon grows tiresome. Jane always talked as if she had places to go to, people to meet. There was something in the tone of her voice that made such talk sound like a warning, as if I weren't invited along, or weren't up to it, or were a momentary amusement, like the May parade, perhaps, and would have to suffice while she was stuck there in that little far-flung corner of the globe.

She wanted to travel to the Orient, to Paris. I wanted to travel, too. It turned out that her plans didn't exclude me. I would go along—quit work and go, just like that, spontaneously, wearing a beret and a knapsack. And that's just what I did, finally, although without the beret; I'm not the sort of a man who can wear a hat. I'm too likely to affect the carefree attitude and then regret the hat, or whatever it is I'm wearing, and then whatever it is I'm not wearing but should have. It's a world of regrets, isn't it? Jane didn't think so. She hadn't any regrets, and said so, and for a while I was foolish enough to admire her saying so. I don't believe that Captain Hooton would have understood her saying such a thing, let alone have admired it.

I brought around his paper sack, right enough, two days later, and he took it from me solemnly, nodding and frowning. At once he blew it up like a balloon—inflated it until it was almost spherical—and then, waving a finger in order to show me, I suppose, that I hadn't seen anything yet, he pulled a slip of silver ribbon out of his vest pocket, looped it around the bunched paper at the bottom, and tied it off. He lit a kitchen match with his fingernail and held it to the tails of the ribbon. Immediately the inflated sack began to glow and rocketed away through the curb trees like a blowfish, the ribbons trailing streams of blue sparks. It angled skyward in a rush and vanished.

I must have looked astonished, thinking of the milk carton beneath my tree. He pretended to smoke his pipe with his ear. Then he sighted along the stem as if it were a periscope, and made whirring and clicking sorts of submarine noises with his tongue. Then waggling his shoulders as if generally loosening his joints, he blew softly across the reeking pipe bowl, dispersing the smoke and making a sound uncannily like Peruvian pan-pipes. He was full of tricks. He suddenly looked very old—certainly above seventy. His hair, which must have been a transplant, grew in patterns like hedgerows, and in the sunlight that shone between the racing clouds, his skin was almost translucent, as if he were a laminated see-through illustration in a modern encyclopedia.

And so one evening late I knocked on the cellar window next to his kitchen door, then stood back on the dewy lawn and waited for him. He was working down there, tinkering with something; I could see his head wagging over the bench.

In a moment he opened the door, having come upstairs. He didn't seem at all surprised to see me skulking in the yard like that but waved me in impatiently as if he had been waiting for my arrival, maybe for years, and now I'd finally come and there was no time to waste.

The cellar was impossibly vast, stretching away room after room, a sort of labyrinth of low-ceilinged, concrete-floored rooms. I couldn't be certain of my bearings any longer, but it seemed that the rooms must have been dug beneath the driveway alongside his house as well as under the house itself—maybe under the house next door; and once I allowed for such a thing, it occurred to me that his cellars might as easily stretch beneath my own house. I remembered nights when I had been awakened by noises, by strange creaks and clanks and rattles of the sort that startle you

awake, and you listen, your heart going like sixty, while you
tell yourself that it's the house "settling," but you don't believe it. And all this time it might have been him, muffled beneath the floor and perhaps a few feet of earth, tapping away
at a workbench like a dwarf in his mine.

All of this filled my head when I stood on the edge of his
stairs, breathing the musty cellar air. It was late, after all, and a
couple of closets with lights casting the shadows of doorways
and shelves might have accounted for the illusion of vast size.
We wandered away through the clutter, with me in my astonishment only half-listening to him, and despite all the magical
debris, what I remember most, like an inessential but vivid element in a dream, was his head ducking and ducking under
low, rough-sawn ceiling joists that were almost black with age.

I have a confused recollection of partly built contrivances,
some of them moving due to hidden, clockwork mechanisms,
some of them sighing and gurgling, hooked up to water pipes
curling out of the walls or to steam pipes running in copper ar-
teries toward a boiler that I can't remember seeing but could
hear sighing and wheezing somewhere nearby. There were pen-
dulums and delicate hydraulic gizmos, and on the corner of
one bench a gyroscope spun in a little depression, motivated,
apparently, by nothing at all. The walls were strewn with charts
and drawings and shelves of books, and once, when we bent
through a doorway and into a room inhabited by the hovering,
slowly rotating hologram of a space vehicle, we surprised a
family of mice at work on the remains of a stale sandwich.
What did they make, I wonder, of the ghost of the spacecraft?
Had they tried to inhabit it, to build a nest in it? Would it have
mattered to them that they were inhabiting a dream?

What did I make of it? *Here's Captain Hooton's airship,*
I remember thinking. *Where's the bell rope?* But it wasn't his
airship, not exactly; the ship itself was in an adjacent room.

The whole thing was a certainty in an instant—the lights
in the sky, the odd debris beneath the avocado tree, even the
weird pallor of his see-through skin. It had all been his doing
all these years. That's no surprise, I suppose, when it's taken

altogether like this. When all the details are compressed, the patterns are clear.

He had come from somewhere and was going back again. With the lumber of mechanical trash spread interminably across bench tops, and the cluttered walls and the mice, and him with his pipe and hat, he seemed so settled in, so permanent. And yet the continual tinkering and the lights on at all hours made it clear that he was on the edge of leaving—maybe in a week, maybe in the morning, maybe right now; that's what I thought as I stood there looking at the ship.

It was nearly spherical, with four curved appendages that were a hybrid of wings and legs and that held the craft up off the concrete floor. Circular hatches ringed the ship, each covered with lapped plates that looked as if they'd spiral open to expose a door or a glassed-over window. The metal of the thing was polished to the silver shine of a perfect mirror that stretched our reflections like taffy as I stood listening to him tell me how we were directly under the backyard, and how he would detonate a charge, and one foggy night the ship would sail up out of the ground in a rush of smoke and dirt and be gone, affording the city newspapers their last legitimate saucer story.

I didn't tell Jane about it. There were a lot of things I couldn't or wouldn't tell her. I wanted some little world of my own, which was removed from the world we had together, but which, of course, could be implied now and then for effect, but never revealed lest it seem to her to be amusing. One day soon the papers would be full of it anyway—the noise in the night, the scattered sightings of the heaven-bound craft, the backyard crater. There would be something then in being the only one who knew.

And he no doubt wasn't anxious that the spaceship became general knowledge. There was no law against it, strictly speaking, but if they'd jailed him for the trick with the flashlight and the paper witch, or rather for refusing to come down out of a tree, then who could say what they might do if they got wind of a flying saucer buried in a cellar?

Then there was the chance that I might be aboard. He was willing to take me along. We talked about it all that night, about the places I'd see and the people I'd meet—a completely different sort of crowd than Jane and I would run into in our European travels.

It was then, about two years after I'd met Jane, that I gave up the house on Pine Street and moved in with her. She was free of school at last and was in an expansive, generous mood, which I'll admit I took advantage of shamelessly, and when, in early July, she received money from home and bought a one-way ticket to Rome, I bought one, too, only mine was a round-trip ticket with a negotiable return date. That should have bothered her, my having doubts, but it didn't. She didn't remark on it at all. From the start it had been my business—another aspect of her modern attitude toward things, an attitude I could neither share nor condemn out loud.

The rest is inevitable. I returned and she didn't. Captain Hooton was gone, and there was a crater with scorched grass around the perimeter of it in the backyard of his empty house. I might have gone along with him. But I didn't, and what I get to keep is the memory of it all—the hologram, so to speak, of the ship and of faded desire, having given up the one for the already fading dream of the other.

There's the image in my mind of a card house built of picture postcards pulled from a rusting wire rack of memories—the sort of thing that even a mouse wouldn't live in, preferring something more permanent and substantial. But then, nothing is quite as solid as we'd like it to be, and the map of our lives, sketched out across our memory, is of a provincial little neighborhood, crisscrossed with regret and circumscribed by a couple of impassable roads and by splashes of bright color that have begun to fade even before we have them fixed in our memory.

Individual Story Copyrights